PRAISE FOR MAUREEN LANG

Bees in the Butterfly Garden

"This character-driven historical . . . represents Lang at her best. Though her many fans will surely enjoy it, consider giving this title also to patrons who like Amanda Harte and Tamera Alexander."

LIBRARY JOURNAL

"Lang's talent shines through in this first of the Gilded Legacy series. The grandeur of the era is evident in the story, the charming characters, [and] the beautifully descriptive prose!"

ROMANTIC TIMES

"The premise of this story is so clever it's interesting from the get-go. . . . *Bees in the Butterfly Garden* should appeal to cozy mystery fans and historical romance readers alike. . . . It's a very promising start to the series."

CROSSWALK.COM

The Great War Series

"[*Look to the East*] teems with conflict. . . . Lang's novel is a cautionary tale as well as a romance within an exciting framework of war, secrets, and blissful reunions."

PUBLISHERS WEEKLY

"A story of love and courage that uplifts and inspires. Lang brings an element of inspiration and beauty to the story that renews the reader's faith in mankind and the power of love."

FRESHFICTION.COM ON *LOOK TO THE EAST*

Tyndale House Publishers, Inc.
Carol Stream, Illinois

All in

God

time

MAUREEN LANG

Visit Tyndale online at www.tyndale.com.

Check out the latest about Maureen Lang at www.maureenlang.com.

TYNDALE and Tyndale's quill logo are registered trademarks of Tyndale House Publishers, Inc.

All in Good Time

Designed by Stephen Vosloo

Edited by Sarah Mason

Published in association with WordServe Literary Group, Ltd., 10152 S. Knoll Circle, Highlands Ranch, CO 80130.

Unless otherwise indicated, all Scripture quotations are taken from the *Holy Bible*, King James Version.

Scripture quotations marked NKJV are taken from the New King James Version.® Copyright © 1982 by Thomas Nelson, Inc. Used by permission. All rights reserved.

All in Good Time is a work of fiction. Where real people, events, establishments, organizations, or locales appear, they are used fictitiously. All other elements of the novel are drawn from the author's imagination.

Library of Congress Cataloging-in-Publication Data

Lang, Maureen.
  All in Good Time / Maureen Lang.
    pages cm. — (The Gilded Legacy)
  ISBN 978-1-4143-6447-6 (sc)
1. Prostitution—Fiction. 2. Bankers—Fiction. 3. Seduction—Fiction. 4. Denver (Colo.)—Fiction. I. Title.
  PS3612.A554A55 2013
  813'.6—dc23   2012041000

Printed in the United States of America

19   18   17   16   15   14   13
7   6   5   4   3   2   1

For my daughter, Torie—
You revealed your heart for others at a very young age, when a
baby on television cried and instantly inspired you to cry along.
In that, you and Dessa have much in common.

Acknowledgments

My RESEARCH of 1880s Denver was made easy and enjoyable because of the work and help of Jay Moynahan, retired professor from Eastern Washington University. Not only did I benefit from Professor Moynahan's own publications, but he generously pointed me in the direction of pertinent material he used during his decades of work. Without his recommendations I'd have been far less informed about society's vices so common in many frontier towns, including Denver.

I'd also like to thank Massimo Duraturo for his help with Mrs. Gio's Italian, and my friend Jeff Gerke for the introduction. Jeff is a perfect example of the wonderful generosity found in the Christian writing community.

And as always, I'm indebted to my critique partner, Siri Mitchell, and to the amazing talents of the Tyndale team: Karen Watson, Stephanie Broene, Sarah Mason, Beth Sparkman, Stephen Vosloo, and the marketing and PR support of Babette Rea and Maggie Rowe. It's so easy to possess a grateful heart when surrounded by people who deserve to see one.

My brethren, count it all joy when you fall into various trials,
knowing that the testing of your faith produces patience.

JAMES 1:2-3, NKJV

PROLOGUE

Mosquito Range, near Leadville, Colorado, 1875

"BE SURE to send my gratitude and affection to Mr. Wells and Mr. Fargo," said Henry Hawkins.

The stagecoach driver's hands shook as he offered Henry the contents of the lockbox—a box Henry had coerced the driver to blow open, providing the right mix of explosive and mud to adhere to and destroy the lock without harming anything inside the box. Heaven knew Henry had practiced enough times to get it right.

A quick glance assured Henry he'd gotten what he'd come for. He was three times a robber, three times of the same coach. Each time he'd been certain of the lockbox's contents; otherwise it wouldn't have been worth the risk. Today the familiar green pouch nearly burst with gold fresh from Colorado mines and smelted pure in Leadville. Accompanying that was a stack of greenbacks and banknotes, all of which Henry received while still aiming his rifle at the familiar but wide-eyed driver—the only man Henry had left unbound.

Henry stashed the goods in his own pouch. "Get over to the side, Zeb," he ordered the driver, whom he'd met on his two previous holdups. "You know the routine by now. Hands high so my boys won't fire on you. That's it." He let his grin of confidence speak for itself, but truthfully he could barely contain his mirth. His "boys" were nothing more than roughly hewn, perfectly straight lengths of wood. Placed at just the right angles amid boulders above them along the narrow pass, they looked as if they were the ready rifles of his gun-toting partners in crime.

Henry avoided meeting the gaze of only one man in the party, the one he'd ordered Zeb to secure first. He'd rather not have waylaid a coach with Tobias Ridgeway aboard, but it couldn't be helped, not with the amount of gold and cash Henry knew would be transported this time through.

His mother's brother was known from Leadville to Denver as straight and trustworthy, outspoken but earnest, an honorable sort every boy wished he could claim as a father—as Tobias was in surrogate form to Henry.

Except today Henry wished he didn't know him at all.

Even now, with a false beard and mustache—fairer in shade than any Henry would have naturally grown with his jet-black hair—and his lanky form thickened by the padding he wore beneath his shirt, Henry dared not look his uncle in the eye. Unfortunately, Uncle Tobias was standing right next to a man Henry must address: a courier in the employ of Leadville's largest mine. He routinely rode the coaches between Denver and Leadville and was this very day carrying a considerable amount of gold. Henry knew this because the man was a regular customer at his mother's mercantile, and Henry had overheard him boasting more than once about being trusted with such an important task.

"I'll take the nuggets from the mine." He kept his voice to a raspy whisper, staring at the other man through the eyeholes of his mask.

The man's eyes nearly popped from their sockets, but then he let his gaze slip upward, as if wondering how accurate Henry's cohorts might be. Evidently he decided not to take the risk of running. "I don't . . . know . . . what you're referring—"

Henry poked him with the muzzle of his rifle, pushing aside his jacket lapel. "No one will get hurt if you just keep steady." Then with one hand he fished inside the man's jacket for the pouch containing the best output from his employer's mine: gold ready to be converted to specie in Denver. Henry ripped it away with less trouble than he'd expected.

"Your reputation is too kind, sir," Uncle Tobias rumbled. "Rumor has it the recent robberies along here didn't create any unnecessary suffering."

"And it's still true," Henry said softly, aiming his response at the man from whom he'd taken the pouch. "It was never really your money, now, was it?"

"I'm available if you need help spending that," invited the red-headed woman who'd been ordered to stand off to the side with the men, though Henry had spared her the indignity of bound wrists.

In spite of his need to hurry off, Henry shot the woman a grin, the unfamiliar beard tickling his cheek. "I'll keep that in mind."

He turned his attention back to the stage driver. "It's been a pleasure doing business with you, Zeb." He backed away from the coach. "Rest assured me and my boys will not be delaying you again. I bid you farewell and good tidings for a prosperous future, along with profound apologies if my mischief has resulted in any trouble for you."

With that, Henry darted beyond the bushes and boulders that lined this portion of the road. As before, he shot into the air once he was well away—mostly to hasten the coach in its departure, but even to his knowing ears, the echoes sounded as if his "guns" from above might be going off.

The rough, loose, rocky terrain once again aided him. He was confident none of the passengers would risk the wide gullies, treacherous incline, sharp granite, and precariously balanced boulders threatening any crossing. It was a terrain Henry had practiced navigating both on foot and by horse.

The whistle of a bullet proved his confidence wrongly placed. Instinctively Henry ducked. Without looking back, he shifted his route to the most dangerous path of all: a trail on the other side of the ridge barely wide enough for the elk, deer, and bighorn sheep that were the only creatures sure-footed enough for such a spot as this. It took Henry in the opposite direction from his horse, but he figured to circle back once he lost whoever was tracking him.

Even as securely as he'd fastened the brown muslin covering him from the top of his head to the bridge of his nose, with holes cut wide enough to let him see, he needed every bit of his sight to navigate the treacherous path that loomed above the deepest of all the ravines. At the bottom, the icy force of the mountain's winter snowmelt churned mightily.

He tugged the mask away, too late realizing his grip wasn't secure as a breeze ripped the material from his hold. There was no time to retrieve it. And why bother? Even if found, the bit of muslin couldn't be connected to him. Or to his mother, from whose sewing box he'd stolen it.

It wasn't long before the detour served him. By the time he reached the curve in the deer path, he looked back to find it empty.

Nonetheless, Henry lost no time returning to his horse by circling around and downward to the tree line. Having gone this route meant he couldn't retrieve his wooden "rifles." It was a good thing this was Henry's last robbery; the secret that he'd acted alone would be out as soon as investigators returned to the pass.

No matter now. He found his horse just where he'd left him, hidden in a cluster of bristlecone pines. It had taken only a few minutes to reverse the horseshoes into prepared holes in the horse's hooves. A casual tracker would think him going the opposite direction altogether; a closer, experienced inspection would at least delay any chase.

It was near dark by the time Henry returned to town, minus

his disguise. He stopped at the smithy, once owned by his parents, that now stood next to his mother's mercantile, pretending concern over the horse's shoes as he slipped them back into their proper positions. Not much later, he walked home, leaving his horse behind. No one would ever know what was hidden in his saddlebags. Tomorrow he would return to his special spot: a hole in the ground that no miner would be able to find, and no bear, goat, or snake was likely to occupy thanks to the pungent coal tar he'd applied to the walls as thickly and lovingly as it had ever been applied to a roof.

He would add today's catch to the stash he'd already buried. Once that was done, Henry knew his work as an outlaw was finished.

Just as fast and easily as he'd planned.

1

Twelve years later

DENVER, 1887

Henry Hawkins watched the smoke cloud hover, then disperse over the head of Lionel Metcalf, who was not only one of his biggest investors but one of the most influential men in Denver, the Queen City of the West. That Lionel allowed Henry to invest his funds—the legitimate ones, at any rate—was no small accomplishment on Henry's part.

"We could use a man like you, Henry," Lionel went on. "Established, not too young but not too old, either. Smart, well spoken. Not bad to look at, and still a bachelor at . . . what? Thirty years old? We might not let women vote, but don't forget for a moment that they influence the men around them who do. You represent what every man in this town wants to be: successful, respected. Free to do as you please. They'd listen to you."

Henry had started shaking his head before Lionel was half finished with his sugary words. He didn't even look at Tobias Ridgeway, who was not only Henry's uncle but also, as of five years ago, his bank manager. This bank was a large step up from the more modest banking and mercantile Henry had begun with, and he had needed a man he could trust.

Lionel was a scout sent ahead to test the political waters that Henry had no intention of jumping into. That was all he'd need, a bunch of spies prying into his personal life. Henry's present life might be pristine compared to the corrupt politicians too often

1

found in public office, but his past life was something he would rather not have investigated.

"No, Lionel. As flattering as all that sounds, my answer is still no, just as it was when you wanted me on the city council. Colorado has two fine senators already, and I expect both to run for reelection. You don't need me muddying the water."

"But that's nonsense!" Lionel said as he puffed his cigar. He leaned forward, exhaling and waving a palm as if the smoke were in the way of his words reaching Henry. "We can always use new talent. Bowen's term is nearly up, and I have it on good information that he likely won't win even if he does run for reelection. Which is why we must get someone on the ballot who can."

"Interesting, Lionel. But I'm still not your man."

"Think of where it could lead, Henry. From senator to governor, or bypass governor altogether and go straight to president of this entire nation. It's time the president was chosen from a Western state, isn't it?"

If Henry laughed more often, if he hadn't grown so unaccustomed to doing it, he might have laughed at the notion of his being in the White House. Instead, he issued one of his rare smiles, along with the not-so-rare shake of his head.

"If you don't take the offer, Henry, we'll go to Turk Foster."

Henry stiffened, abandoning whatever trace of a smile he'd managed to extend. It was exactly the kind of threat that could tempt him into making a foolish mistake. Pulse pounding in his ears, he very nearly spoke before Uncle Tobias did.

"It would be a sad day for Colorado to have the likes of Mr. Foster running for the Senate," Tobias said with a jovial laugh. The huge man was more often cheerful than threatening; even his insults sounded friendly.

Henry's moment of temptation passed. Tobias was right. Foster, on a similar path to prosperity as his, might be ambitious and clever, but his sins were far more visible than Henry's. He would have a tough time getting elected, even in Denver, where the veneer over corruption was thin, but there nonetheless.

Henry stood just as a tap sounded at the door. Before responding to the summons, he said to Lionel, "It's your job to choose the best man. I know that man is not me, but I also doubt it's Foster." Then Henry walked around his desk to open the sleek, paneled hardwood door of his considerably sized office.

Mr. Sprott, his clerk, stood there with a somewhat anxious look on his face. "An appointment for Mr. Ridgeway, sir." One of the man's nervous habits was to adjust his clothing—a tie, collar, cuff, or anything handy—as if he wasn't used to formal office attire. That was likely true, since most of the Denver workforce consisted of former miners, failed fortune seekers, or railroaders. "He asked me to let him know when his appointment arrived, and she has."

She? Henry wondered what kind of appointment Tobias had with a woman.

"Thank you, Mr. Sprott," Tobias said. He stood, excused himself from Lionel, and offered a brief glance toward Henry.

Henry watched him leave, seeing nothing more than the back of a slender woman clad in the deepest purple from hem to hat. She followed Mr. Sprott into the smaller office Tobias used, adjacent to Henry's.

Henry frowned. It was likely the same do-gooder Uncle Tobias had mentioned yesterday, a woman whose application the bank had recently received. She wanted a loan in order to coddle those who'd have been better off back East, where life was unequivocally easier.

If Henry didn't have Lionel waiting to continue this unnecessary meeting, he'd have followed Tobias into his office and shown the woman to the door.

But Lionel didn't appear ready to be put off so quickly.

Dessa Caldwell stepped inside the small bank office and raised a gloved hand to check one more time that her hair was still swept up neatly and her hat wasn't askew. The Lord had chosen her for this task, and she meant to represent Him well.

She looked around the office. One tall, barred window let in ample light, but other than that, the room was rather spartan. It offered a serviceable, solid wood desk scattered with paperwork, as well as a sturdy chair of matching varnish. Two chairs in front of the desk were also wood, stained a similar dark color. A clock and a calendar hung on one wall, but there was nothing to identify this office as belonging to anyone in particular.

At least the bank didn't waste money on opulence. The exterior of the building itself was impressive enough: three stories high and boasting tall white pillars flanking the doorstep. Inside, the half-dozen busy employees she'd passed presented every indication of a successfully run bank. And the vault—what little she'd seen of it on her way in—was more than intimidating. Surely those were all good signs.

Dessa placed her parasol beneath an arm to adjust one of her gloves. This was only the fourth bank she'd tried for her loan, and she was determined not to let the first refusals dampen her confidence. After all, her inspiration came from something more than *just* confidence, didn't it?

"Good afternoon," greeted a jovial voice behind her.

Dessa turned, automatically mirroring the smile offered to her. The man possessed a mix of gray and brown hair, fair skin, and a round, pleasant face. His size could have landed him a position as bouncer at any one of the disreputable establishments Dessa knew existed on the darker side of town. For some reason that comforted her, even though she'd never once needed a bouncer's aid or even met such a person.

As he passed her on the way to his desk, he reached out to shake her hand. She accepted without hesitation.

"Mr. Ridgeway?" she asked.

"That's right. Tobias Ridgeway, at your service. And you're Miss Caldwell; is that correct? Please, have a seat."

She did so, leaning forward despite her desire to not appear too eager. There was something immediately inviting about this man, so warm and friendly as he sank into his chair and gave her another smile. Nothing at all like the last bank clerk, who barely gave her a moment's attention before sending her away. Loan money to a woman! It simply wasn't done.

In this first instant of facing Mr. Ridgeway she knew he would do no such thing. Pushing caution aside, she let his smile inspire a lighthearted bubble of optimism.

"I see from your application that you would like a loan." He pulled familiar papers from one of the stacks on top of his desk. She recognized her own handwriting and the many questions she'd been asked about the intentions and risks associated with the loan she had in mind. "Quite a substantial amount. Hmmm."

"Yes, it is quite a sum, Mr. Ridgeway. As you can see, we've tried to foresee every need. But as you'll also see, I've raised a fair amount in donations from churches as well as from the Ladies' Benevolent Society. Beyond that, once Pierson House opens we intend to sell textile goods. Children's clothing, linens, quilts, and blankets. Several stores and churches in the area have agreed to help us sell our goods, so distribution won't be a problem."

She could have named a number of investors, like the owners of White's Mercantile, who had provided a roof over her head since last fall, or the wealthy Plumstead family, who had pledged a hefty monthly donation for the next four years. There hadn't been room on the application for such details.

He looked up from the paperwork. "You said 'we,' Miss

Caldwell, and yet it is only you here before me. There is no man to help you invest, to help guarantee the loan with a steady income?"

She refused to allow her bubble of hope to be broken, despite a pinprick of annoyance. From what she knew of men, they were just as likely to bring woe to society as progress or prosperity. "I intend to offer promise of a reciprocal income, the same as any small business would do. With confidence of profits to come."

"Yes, so you say. But it depends upon a number of things: The reliability of continued donations. The success of reaching prospective residents. The talent of those residents and their willingness to work once you've attracted them to your home. Have you a number of clients ready to be welcomed into your establishment?"

That was the one question she would rather not answer . . . at least not yet. "I'm quite an able seamstress myself, if you don't mind my saying so," she told him. "It's a talent easily taught to anyone with a reason to learn. And women in the circumstances I wish to help will certainly have a reason."

Mr. Ridgeway referred back to the paperwork. "Yes, about that. It says here that you hope to offer women of all backgrounds and situations safe refuge, a place to live—at least temporarily—when shelter is needed. That you would offer this to young women— girls, even—who find themselves in a business not easily discussed in polite society."

Dessa's heart picked up a beat. That was indeed an important part of her purpose: to serve the most vulnerable population in a state where more prostitutes than wives could be found. Though the railroad had brought families, the prospect of gold and silver had attracted even more men to the mining camps throughout the state. It was an undeniable fact that many were more than willing to pay for the intimate services of a woman without thought of marriage.

"There are a great many women right here in Denver who need

the protection of a home such as I'm proposing. Women who, if they only had the chance, could find a happier life than what circumstances have forced them into."

Dessa noticed his fair skin had turned a bit pink, as if the conversation made him uncomfortable. And while she found that somewhat amusing coming from a man of his age, his attitude was part of the problem. Too much of "polite society" wished to ignore the facts altogether.

"Men in this rugged territory," she added softly, "have been able to carve out a place for themselves whether or not they strike it rich. And as able-minded as my sisters of the fairer sex are, it remains true that we are often at the mercy of those stronger than us. If a woman falls into desperate circumstances, she'll often need extraordinary kindness to free her."

"And this Miss Pierson for whom your home will be named? Where is she?"

"I came to Denver with Miss Sophie Pierson two years ago. We'd traveled to many other cities over the years, speaking to groups, hoping to help women at nearly every social level. But nowhere did we meet more needy women than right here in Colorado. Miss Pierson worked tirelessly with churches and benevolent societies in the hopes of gaining support to open a refuge, but she succumbed to typhus late last fall. With God's help, it's my goal to see her wishes become a reality."

Although Mr. Ridgeway continued to look at Dessa, he did not speak, as if expecting her to continue. She wondered in that moment what he contemplated. Certainly his thoughts weren't unpleasant, as he had a look on his face of near admiration. Still, it was hard to know if his approval of her ambition might extend to an actual loan.

He seemed reluctant to look away but did so after a moment, straightening the papers in his grip. "I've read your application thoroughly, Miss Caldwell, and I'd like to commend your work. Your goals are, to my way of thinking, admirable. But this sort of loan isn't easily made. I assume you've exhausted your other avenues? From the churches and societies you mentioned?"

She nodded, although thoughts of Sophie's five-year goal came to mind. *"Raise the majority of the funds first,"* she'd said, *"and then if more money is needed, a loan might be the last resort."*

But why wait so long if Dessa could garner a loan now to speed the process? She needed to get into the very neighborhood she wished to reach, and the only way to do that was to become part of it. Ever since the house near Market Street had come to her attention, Dessa had known it was just the right location for Pierson House.

That was why she would try every legitimate bank in Denver, no matter how long it took. When she exhausted that list, she would start over again and keep asking until she received the money she sought.

Mr. Ridgeway patted the neat stack in front of him. "I'll need to consult with the bank's president, of course. I wanted to meet you in person first, to confirm what I guessed from your application and letter."

He stood, extending his hand once again. "Return tomorrow morning at ten thirty, Miss Caldwell, and I'll have an answer for you."

Dessa shook his hand with renewed enthusiasm. The answer wasn't no!

Mr. Ridgeway walked around his desk. "Allow me to escort you out. Do you have a carriage, or can I have someone hail a hansom cab for you?"

"I have a friend waiting, thank you."

"Then I'll bid you good day."

"Thank you, Mr. Ridgeway, for your time and consideration."

She extended her hand again but saw that his gaze was arrested by something behind her. Dessa turned to catch sight of two men emerging from another office closer to the vault.

"If you are a praying person, Miss Caldwell," said Mr. Ridgeway, his voice lowered nearly to a whisper, "and I sense that you are, that's the man you need to mention to God. Mr. Henry Hawkins."

Surely he meant the one who was staying, not the older man who'd just placed a hat upon his balding head and was even then walking toward the door. But how could the president of such a large and prestigious bank be so young? He couldn't be much older than Dessa herself. And, she couldn't help but notice, a more handsome man she had never seen.

But the look he possessed as he turned back into his office held none of Mr. Ridgeway's friendliness.

Dessa's smile faded. Indeed, as he enclosed himself inside his office without noticing her at all, Mr. Henry Hawkins looked every bit as cold as the banker who'd shown her the door only two days ago.

"If you could join me in that prayer, Mr. Ridgeway," she whispered back, "I would be most appreciative."

2

ALTHOUGH IT WAS barely past eight, the sun had already set behind the mountains, casting Denver into its habitually early evening. Henry Hawkins let himself inside and latched the door behind him, greeted as usual by the quietness of his own home. Twice a year this house burst with light and guests and noise—one investors' dinner party in winter, another in summer, to impress depositors—but for the other 363 days, the house was closer to a mortuary than a home.

He used to welcome the lack of noise, but tonight this house on the established but still fashionable Fourteenth Street felt hollow and empty.

"Barron! Mr. Barron!"

Instead of his butler, the cook answered his call. Mrs. Giovannini was a marvel at breads and sauces, but she was not the kind of servant—or company—Henry needed at the moment. He'd never employed a housekeeper, wanting to keep his staff at a minimum. Barron was butler, valet, and head of the staff and was paid accordingly.

"Where is Barron, Mrs. Gio?" He refused to spend so many syllables on a single name and so had never called his cook by anything but the shortened version. He'd been told her Christian name was Giovanna, which together with her last name might sound lyrical, but Henry wasn't in the habit of singing for anyone.

"Barron—he go to . . . how you say? *Fratello!* He go see

11

fratello . . . you *non qui* . . . we think you not home *molto in ritardo*, so he go see his *famiglia*. You see?"

Henry nodded, though he did not see at all. It was simply easier to let the conversation end.

"You want *cena*? Dinner, yes, Mr. Hawkins? I bring you dinner. You sit. You rest. You tired."

That much he did understand, and she was right. Loosening the high collar on his shirt, he stepped farther into the wide foyer and for the barest moment didn't know whether to turn left into the dining room or right into the parlor. No doubt Mrs. Gio had kept his dinner hot; she was prompt at serving him a full meal no matter what time he arrived.

But he opted for the parlor despite such thoughts. She could serve him in there, with a tray at his most comfortable chair. There was no question about it; Henry felt tired beyond his years.

He didn't welcome the realization. Admittedly, Henry had been in a hurry to grow up most of his life, but he hadn't thought to skip his youth for old age. His own father, at age thirty, had worked over the blaze of a smith's shop from dawn until dark. He'd pounded and forged, creating everything from mundane horseshoes and work tools to the intricate designs of fancy residential gates that graced more than a few houses like the one in which Henry now lived.

His father's idea of slowing down had been to sell the smithy and open a mercantile next door. Promptly one year into the reduced physical labor, he'd dropped dead. To this day, Henry's mother still worked long hours in that very shop. What right did Henry have to be tired after a day spent sitting behind a desk?

Only one man could be blamed for wearing Henry down. His uncle, Tobias Ridgeway. The man was like a tick on a dog's ear, dug in for the duration. Ever since Henry had given him a job at the bank, the man hadn't stopped bringing in projects for investment.

Some had been interesting, like a product called celluloid to be used in place of ivory for billiard balls. A practical idea, until Henry learned that fire and moisture damaged the product. Since anything from a lusty sneeze to a spilled beer or dropped cigar could wreak havoc on what should be a perfectly smooth surface, it soon lost its appeal to even the most frugal billiard hall owners.

Lately Tobias had grown more charitable in his recommendations, something Henry found unaccountably irksome.

Just as Henry settled in his chair, a rap at the door echoed through the empty foyer. He grumbled, recognizing the force behind that rap. Only an arm the size of Uncle Tobias's could produce such a sound.

He let Mrs. Gio answer, listening through another round of attack on the sturdy, carved wooden door before Mrs. Gio's halting English welcomed Tobias in. Tobias's familiarly firm step soon crossed the foyer ahead of his escort, and there he stood, all six burly feet of him. He glowered as if Henry had done something wrong.

"I hava your dinner," said Mrs. Gio once she caught up to Henry's guest.

"Thank you, Mrs. Gio," Henry said briskly, then looked at Tobias. "You're welcome to half of whatever is on this tray. Mrs. Gio always brings too much."

"I've eaten already," Tobias said, though even as his mouth uttered the words, Henry could see his nose signaling an altogether different sort of response as Mrs. Gio passed him with the tray.

"Bring another plate, will you, Mrs. Gio?" asked Henry. "And another tray. We'll stay in here rather than the dining room. I won't be leaving this chair until I go to bed this evening."

Mrs. Gio looked pleased at his offer to share the bounty she'd brought, though he guessed she would bring Tobias a tray every bit as filled with the fragrantly spiced and sauced eggplant and plenty of bread to soak up every drop of what she called gravy.

"You left the bank without seeing me." Tobias used the phrase as an accusation. "Did you forget there was something I wanted to discuss with you?"

By this time in the day, Henry had less patience than ever. Being anything but direct only wasted time. "I assumed it was another attempt to convince me to get involved in the charity work you've become enamored of lately. Is it?" A single glance at Tobias's face told Henry he'd guessed correctly.

It was one thing to offer Tobias a job—out of old affection mixed with an irreducible residue of guilt. Keeping him on had proven a good idea, because other than this occasional lapse into civic risk he was a sound investor. Loans from his desk almost always proved reliable.

But it was something altogether different to go along with every idea Uncle Tobias presented. Henry had built his bank, his home, his reputation, his very life upon things Denver needed. Businesses that provided goods like mining tools or, more recently, household necessities. Still other loans provided farmers with seed for crops or grain for livestock. Necessary ventures, nearly all of them.

A rest home for prostitutes was not a sound business investment, even if they euphemistically called it a home for wayward girls. Such things were best left to the churches, where charity was meant to originate. Henry had a business to run, and that meant enjoying profits without suffering unnecessary—or quite predictable—losses.

"This so-called charity idea might be just what your soul needs, Henry." Tobias looked around, raising a palm to encompass their surroundings. Henry looked too, despite knowing exactly what he'd see: a sensibly appointed room with the highest-quality furniture. He owned no knickknacks or sentimentalities, just a clock on the mantel and an oil lamp in case there was trouble with the recently installed electricity. One portrait hung on the wall, of a man Henry had never known. His mother had told him that man was her father, making him Tobias's father as well. It was all they had of him, a canvas she'd rolled up and taken with her from Manchester, England, when she and Tobias had come as little more than children. Tobias said Henry resembled him, but Henry didn't see it.

In truth he wasn't like his grandfather, or his parents, either. *They* had worked as hard as he did, or harder, but had little to show for it. Still, the portrait offered investors the human side of Henry, since he had little other family to show them.

"There's nothing wrong with my soul, Tobias—not that it matters, since it won't be needed until that's all that's left of me. This loan you're so eager for us to issue is untenable. Have you told the party to seek out the church's help as I instructed?"

"As *I've* said before, the church has given all it can. The girls— perhaps even an occasional young mother-to-be . . . Well, the idea is to turn no one away, so not all churches are eager to help."

"Here is your supper, *signore!*" said Mrs. Gio, her cheerful voice a stark contrast to Tobias's awkward tone. "Ah, you always bring a good *appetito*, Signore Tobias. *È buono! È buono!*"

Tobias had the grace to set aside his annoyed frown over the interruption, an annoyance that was evidently forgotten once a full plate was settled before him. His smile turned serene.

"Thank you, Mrs. Giovannini," he said, sitting at the table nearby and using it rather than his meager lap.

Henry took another bite of the savory meal and thanked Mrs. Gio on her way out of the room.

A few minutes of silence followed as Henry ate, watching Tobias do the same. As usual, the man ate with gusto, his only sounds an occasional moan of satisfaction over one taste or another. Henry would have been amused if he wasn't still irritated by the one trait he both admired and detested in Tobias Ridgeway, depending on whether or not they agreed about an issue: Tobias lived with tenacity.

"There are places for such people already," Henry persisted finally. "Poor farms, I'm told, won't turn away someone in need. Surely there are already such places within a reasonable distance of a city as large as Denver."

"True enough, but there are a great many needs those of us who are blessed should not ignore. Much is expected from those who are given much, Henry. And you have been given much."

Henry washed down the bread—flaky and white, rubbed with garlic butter on its crust—with a glass of the wine Mrs. Gio made and stored in the cellar. He leveled a stare at Tobias. "You're paid a generous wage, aren't you? Isn't everyone employed at my bank given a wage that's the envy of nearly all other bank clerks in Denver?"

"Yes, you're a generous employer."

"How I choose to donate discretionary funds is my personal business, but I'll not authorize bank funds for something that will undoubtedly bring not a cent in return."

"But that's just it, Henry. Miss Caldwell explained how she plans to turn a profit, along the lines of the very poor farms you cited yourself. She intends to teach the girls to sew linens and such to help with the expenses. It'll not run entirely upon charity, only the initial investment—"

"Which hasn't a hope in heaven to be repaid." Henry shook his head and wiped his mouth at the same time. Once his mind was made up, he never changed it. Surely Tobias knew that by now.

"Perhaps not repaid in money, but in satisfaction? In knowing you've helped the lives of those less fortunate? Your mother would be proud if you made such a decision."

"I'll thank you not to bring my mother into it. As it pertains to bank matters, the relationship between you and me is strictly business." Henry set aside his tray, as tired of the food as he was of the company. "Go home, Tobias. Aunt Etta is no doubt waiting for you."

"No worries there; I stopped in before I came here."

"And ate her dinner as well?"

Tobias shrugged one hefty shoulder, then took another mouthful of the eggplant, squeezing his words out around the food. "There is another reason I think you ought to get involved in this particular project."

"Any benefit would be hard-pressed to outweigh the sheer nonsense of the proposal."

Tobias took the last of his bread and scraped it around his empty plate, scrubbing up the last bit of the red sauce. He popped the bread in his mouth, took a final swig of wine, then wiped his mouth as Henry had a moment before.

But when he began to speak, a hearty burp came out instead. Tobias smiled, satisfied with himself. "Pardon me, but that was a delicious meal. I'll be sure to stop in the kitchen and tell your Mrs. Gio before I leave."

"You were saying, Tobias? About the benefits of whatever loan you want me to extend? Finish your argument so I can have some peace and quiet."

Tobias set aside the wine and the napkin, then placed both palms on his brawny thighs with a thud. "It's this, Henry. You're a miserable, lonely old banker trapped in the healthy body of a much younger and viable man. I don't know what's made you build a vault around your heart and soul and life, but because of a promise I made to your mother, it's become my goal to see it blown to smithereens."

Henry cocked his head. "My life? Blown to smithereens?"

Tobias laughed loud. "No, just the vault around it. Once you're free, I guarantee you'll be a much happier person."

Henry might have declared himself happy already, but even he knew that apart from the satisfaction of a successful business, there wasn't much evidence for such a claim. "And what has this to do with offering a bad loan that will no doubt tarnish the sensible reputation I've spent all these years building for my bank?"

Tobias stood, approaching Henry and leaning over him so their eyes were level. "If the goodness of Miss Dessa Caldwell cannot ignite the dynamite it'll take to do the blasting, then I'll give up hope for you altogether."

"By giving up hope, do you mean you'll stop hounding this soul of mine that you insist I acknowledge?"

Tobias stood full height again, adjusting his jacket, patting his rounded stomach. "Let's just say I'll reconsider my tactics should I fail in this venture."

Henry leaned his head against the plush leather chair. He closed his eyes, eager for peace. "Off you go, Tobias. If the goodness of Miss Caldwell is so extraordinary, I'm sure she won't have trouble finding the money she needs at her church. Or at another, less practical bank."

"No, Henry." Tobias's oddly stern voice, deeper than usual, caused Henry to open his eyes again. "I came here tonight to tell you this: I put through the necessary paperwork to approve Miss Caldwell's loan, based on my authority. You can give me my walking papers if you like, but tomorrow morning when she visits your bank, she'll be taking with her every penny she requested."

❧

Dessa wiped her brow with her wrist, careful not to touch her bloodstained fingertips to her hair or face.

"By God's mercy," she said, cradling a small, wet infant, "you've only to deliver the after-matter now, Cora."

Dessa, with no more training than from books and her role as a silent witness to a number of births Sophie Pierson had assisted, had watched over the delivery of three such infants on her own since Sophie's death. She didn't doubt the regularity of needs like this around here, where even midwives refused to come.

Today Cora's young friend had taken over the role Dessa used to play at Sophie's side. Now that the child was delivered, the girl's eyes weren't quite so frightened. Not like they'd been when she'd shown up at the back door of the mercantile where Dessa lived, well after it had closed for the day. She hadn't stopped pounding until Dessa answered.

Dessa was surprised anyone knew she was living in the upstairs corner of White's Mercantile, especially someone who never frequented the store. But the girl said she'd heard of Sophie Pierson, who'd been everything from suffragette to midwife, wherever support of women was needed. Quickly introducing herself as Nadette, with little more than a plea about helping to birth a baby, she'd pulled Dessa out of the mercantile and led the way—at least a mile—to this forlorn building in the city's Fourth Ward.

Dessa had yet to spend much of her time in this neighborhood— the very one she hoped to serve. Hobnobbing with potential donors from the more respectable end of town was the only avenue toward establishing the mission Sophie had envisioned. Dessa hadn't yet graduated beyond that step.

She hadn't been afraid to follow Nadette here—she knew God was at her side—but she'd taken the opportunity to look around. Not just because she'd likely have to find her own way home. She'd be living in this neighborhood sooner than even Sophie had hoped if everything went well at the bank tomorrow.

"You've delivered a fine, healthy girl," Dessa told Cora now, but as quick as the words were uttered, she turned away from the exhausted young woman, taking one of the cloths Nadette offered and bringing the infant to the washbasin in the far corner of the small room.

The newborn was dark haired, matching the inky hair of her mother. Unlike some of the women Dessa had met while traveling the country's best—and worst—neighborhoods, Cora didn't live up to any of the advertisements the more expensive brothels might circulate. She had crooked teeth and a bent nose, a sure sign that this was no fancy parlor house where the madams employed only the prettiest girls. Cora, even now, was too thin in body and face for a calling like this.

Calling. The word caught in Dessa's mind. This life was no calling; it might not be hell, but it was certainly close.

Dessa gently washed the squirming infant. Such a sweet child, only whimpering to show she was alive, allowing herself to be wiped clean without protest or demand.

"Are you sure you want to give the child to me, Cora?" she whispered, despite her fears that there was only one way this evening could end happily, and that was if Dessa could take the infant to the woman she'd met some time ago who arranged adoptions.

From the bed Cora turned her face away, with not so much as a whimper to match her daughter's.

Dessa wrapped the child in the cleanest rags that were left, pulling open one of the drawers on the nearby dresser—it was almost empty but for some kind of wispy material—and settling the child there while she turned back to the basin to wash her hands one last time.

"I'll take care of Cora now, Miss Caldwell," Nadette said calmly, already taking away the afterbirth and gathering the warmed bandages for Cora's abdomen and thighs, just the way a midwife might have done. "She'll be all right with me."

Dessa left the towel by the basin, pausing a good long moment in hopes of finding a crack in Cora's demeanor. Would she send a quick glance the baby's way? Was there indecision on her brow?

Any sign could be enough—perhaps through her child Cora might be persuaded away from such a life.

But there was none of what Dessa sought. Cora had known what she was doing when she'd sent for Dessa. She'd been summoned to help deliver the child and take her away, out of this house, out of this neighborhood. To a better life.

If only Dessa could have offered Cora shelter, a taste of life in a safer, more hope-filled environment. Wouldn't she then long to keep her baby?

Visions of all Pierson House could mean filled Dessa's mind. Soon she would have the power to offer that very thing to women like Cora. She must have misread the hardness on Mr. Hawkins's face earlier today—and even if she hadn't, God could soften any heart. *Any* heart, even that of a man whose face offered not a trace of compassion.

For now, though, Dessa could only wish the young, now-childless mother well, and then take the baby with her to the woman who would find new parents.

God, oh, God, have mercy on us all!

3

HENRY HAWKINS tipped his hat to each clerk as he passed by on the way to his office. Clerical desks took up one row to his left, while tellers' cages lined the wall to the right. At the opposite end and closest to his office stood the massive bank vault, built with no expense spared by the best manufacturer in the country and delivered all the way from Cincinnati. Thirteen by eighteen feet, with walls three feet thick, a two-and-a-half-ton outer door, and a fifteen-hundred-pound inner door. Safe from explosives, burglary, fire, or mobs. Safe even from young and foolish masked men with rifles.

Henry's pride assured him that such a vault wouldn't fail to inspire a sense of security in anyone who banked with him. He even employed an armed guard twenty-four hours a day, something other banks thought a needless expense for an impregnable safe.

Henry slipped wordlessly past his personal clerk, Mr. Sprott. Like Henry's home, the office in the corner of the bank was well furnished yet not ostentatious. The quality and size of his mahogany desk spoke of importance, confidence, success, and longevity, without appearing excessive. Other than the hook upon which he hung his hat—and in winter his coat and scarf as well—there was no sign of personal belongings. He discouraged that throughout his bank. This was a place of business, where personal lives were not to be seen.

He sat behind his desk in the light from an arched window, placed high for safety, the panes crossed with iron bars. Because it was an outside wall and farthest from either of the two huge furnaces that heated the radiators, the room tended to be chilly in winter. But Henry didn't mind; if his office was too comfortable, visitors might linger too long.

As usual when Henry arrived midmorning, Mr. Sprott had left the mail in the center of his desk. The desktop was neat and clear of clutter, offering only a pen and inkwell, blotting paper, a silver-handled ivory letter opener, and an olive-wood string dispenser. Anything confidential or of value to the bank was secured each night: seals and pending letters, account ledgers, and bank stationery.

After unlocking his desk, Henry took a cursory glance at the mail. He found the usual correspondence from his directors, reference inquiries regarding former or prospective employees from cashiers to clerks, a letter he expected from the state outlining banking regulations. Near the bottom of the stack was an invitation from Lionel to a charity event that Henry had no intention of attending.

As he tossed one envelope aside, a smaller note that must have been stuck beneath fell to the floor. Thinking the size identified it as yet another social invitation, Henry picked it up with the intention of discarding it. He made it a practice never to attend social functions, not even for charity. Because he was universal in his refusals, no one could feel slighted. And because he was one of the richest men in the city, everyone on his guest list attended his semiannual gatherings despite not having him attend theirs in return.

A single slip of onionskin fell out of the envelope—the kind of paper Henry forbade his employees to use since it invited the accompanying use of carbonated paper and risk of forgery. Besides, such paper was too thin for easy use, especially for his bold pen stroke, and so delicate that even water could destroy it.

The writing was simple, almost childlike in its printing. He read it once with profound confusion, but even before the words took meaning his pulse began to speed.

There are no secrets from God.
Set your affection on things above, not on things on
the earth.

The note itself was neither directed to him nor signed. He looked again at the envelope; it bore his name and the bank's address, but there was no return, not even a postage mark over the stamp.

Henry sprang to his feet, sticking his head around the door. "Mr. Sprott," he called. "Come here a moment, will you?"

The young man—who couldn't be much older than Henry had been when he'd returned from college in Chicago—straightened an already-straight tie, then pulled at the cuffs of his shirt beneath his jacket. "Yes, sir?"

"Did you leave the mail on my desk this morning?"

"Yes, of course, sir. As usual."

"And did you go through it first?"

"Yes, sir, and removed anything that wasn't addressed directly to you."

Henry returned to the other side of his desk, holding up the unsealed envelope. He had slipped the contents into his pocket. "This one, this small one—was it delivered as usual, or was it brought here personally? It was already opened and you can see the stamp was not canceled."

Mr. Sprott reached for the envelope but Henry kept it between his thumb and forefinger.

"Yes, I see that now, sir. I opened the envelope as usual, but I hadn't noticed the stamp wasn't canceled. Shall I complain to the mailman?"

Henry contained his impatience. "No, Mr. Sprott. I only wondered if you knew who delivered it."

"The mailman, I suppose. It was with everything else he brought to my desk this morning."

"Thank you, then. That's all for now."

With a request that Mr. Sprott close the door on his way out, Henry sank into the leather chair behind his desk and pulled the note from his pocket once again.

Innocuous enough, but for that reference to secrets. A prank? What sort of prank, and to what end? Was the reference to God meant to spur him to church—with hopes of his bringing a tithe? What sort of evangelizing was this, anyway? Was Henry the only one to receive such a thing?

God knows my secret.

The words repeated themselves in his mind, far louder than the rustle of the sheer paper as he crumpled it. He walked to the corner of the room, to the pitcher and water glasses, then stuffed the paper into one of the glasses, poured water over it, and watched it dissolve.

❧

Dessa marched through the center of the bank, her gaze on the door to Mr. Tobias Ridgeway's office. She was afraid to look anyone in the eye for fear of seeing rejection there.

Lord, Your will be done.

With barely more than a glance, she asked the clerk between the only two enclosed offices to let Mr. Ridgeway know she had arrived for their meeting.

The door to his office opened before the clerk even stood to knock.

"Miss Caldwell!" He emerged from his office and greeted her warmly, holding out his hand to take one of hers with something more than a handshake. This was just the kind of greeting she'd hoped for . . . and yet she imagined Mr. Ridgeway was the sort of gentleman who might be too kind to issue even a rejection any way but considerately.

"It's good of you to be so prompt," he said. "I was just coming out to Mr. Sprott's desk to see if everything I asked for is in order, and then you can be on your way without delay. I'm sure you're eager to let the property holder know you'll be proceeding with your plans."

Dessa's head went so light she was afraid she would faint—she who had never swooned in her life. She was close enough to Mr. Sprott's desk to reach for its corner, a solid object with which to steady herself. "Do you mean to say . . . that is, my loan has been approved?"

With a grin on his round face and a gentle touch to one of her elbows, as if he knew she needed a reminder she wasn't in a dream, Mr. Ridgeway nodded. "Yes, Miss Caldwell. You'll soon have what you need to take ownership of the property you have in mind." He turned to Mr. Sprott and received an envelope the other man held.

"Oh, Mr. Ridgeway!" To her embarrassment, she felt the hot sting of tears in her eyes. Hardly the most professional reaction to a business transaction! She fought them back, grabbing one of Mr. Ridgeway's hands in a heartier handshake than a moment ago, even as with the other she received the thick envelope, no doubt containing paperwork along with the banknote she needed. "Thank you!"

Mr. Ridgeway waved away her gratitude. "It's Mr. Henry Hawkins you should thank. Without his consent, this institution would not be contributing to your endeavors."

Dessa pressed her fingers to her mouth in an attempt to hold back more flowery words of thanksgiving. She cleared her throat, determined to fit the picture of a woman who'd never doubted for a moment that this loan was deserved. "May I extend my gratitude to him, do you suppose? I wouldn't take more than a minute of his time."

Mr. Ridgeway's brows rose approvingly. "I think that's a fine idea! Come with me, won't you?" Without delay, Mr. Ridgeway led Dessa past the clerk's desk and to the adjacent office. He tapped once, then before waiting for an answer, opened the door wide enough for Dessa to see the bank president standing in front of a tea cart holding a crystal glass of water.

"Henry!" Mr. Ridgeway greeted him, leading Dessa inside.

She nearly floated toward Mr. Hawkins, her feet felt so weightless. She held out her hand, hoping he wouldn't notice the unsteadiness in her breathing or the tremble in her fingers. Though she reminded herself there was nothing personal about this introduction, she couldn't help but be struck once again by the look of him. Perhaps he wasn't as young as she'd guessed from across the room the day before. There was a settled look to his features that seemed on the brink of lost youth, though there wasn't a wrinkle to be seen. Nearly as tall as Mr. Ridgeway, Mr. Hawkins was half the other's width. Still, his shoulders were broad and his chin well carved, giving him the look of slender strength.

As he accepted her hand in his and she looked into his face— into the darkest eyes to match the darkest hair—she was hard-pressed to summon a coherent thought about her mission, her calling, or her vision to help others. In that moment she was simply a woman meeting a man—not a servant meeting a godsend— for the very first time.

"Henry, may I present Miss Dessa Caldwell, whom I mentioned to you just yesterday."

Mr. Hawkins didn't look as though he heard the introduction, or if he did, the announcement didn't seem entirely welcome. He issued the most unexpectedly intense—and unfriendly—glare.

"Perhaps I've come at the wrong time," Dessa said, her heart pounding so hard that she wondered if he felt its beat through the tips of her tingling fingers. She withdrew her hand.

"Nonsense," said Mr. Ridgeway. "Henry, you can spare a moment, can't you? Miss Caldwell has come to speak to you."

"Oh yes," she said, the warmth of gratitude washing over her once more, leaving no room for uncertainty. "I'm so very grateful for your approval of my loan. In fact, I wish to extend an invitation to you—and Mr. Ridgeway as well—for one week from today. I'm eager to show you the home your generosity will help me to establish."

Mr. Ridgeway filled the slightest gap of silence created by the lack of response from Mr. Hawkins. "Yes, of course; we'd be delighted. One week from today, you say? Will that be enough time to get yourself settled?"

Her enthusiasm, only slightly dampened by Mr. Hawkins's steely silence, burst upon her again. He'd approved her loan, hadn't he? He must believe in what she was doing; she only wanted to fortify his faith in her. "I have so many household donations only awaiting collection! I won't rest until the doors to Pierson House open." She shifted her gaze back to Mr. Ridgeway and his welcoming, friendly face, sparing only a glance at Mr. Hawkins before finishing. "Would you care to come at lunchtime? That is, to share luncheon?"

"Delightful!" Mr. Ridgeway said. He placed a hand on her elbow, directing her with his other hand away from the office in which Mr. Hawkins stood.

Dessa moved to retrace the steps they'd taken only moments before, but confusion stopped her. She turned back to Mr. Hawkins and conquered what she suddenly realized had been disappointment, not just at his reception but at the general lack of welcome in his demeanor. She'd taken his approval of her loan far more personally than she realized.

"Mr. Hawkins, if you have any doubts about the loan, or about me, I'd like to assure you your trust is well placed. This home will be a shelter for women in need, a place of refuge not otherwise to be found in our lovely but all-too-human city. If you'll visit me, I can show you exactly what I mean."

Another silence followed her words—one that even Mr. Ridgeway dared not fill. Mr. Hawkins's gaze was neither harsh nor friendly, but she could not fathom what thoughts lay behind that piercing look of his.

"I'll be there at noon," he said at last. He started to turn away but stopped to assess her a moment longer. "One week from today."

Rather than a simple acceptance of an invitation, it seemed almost a challenge.

But Dessa refused to dwell on it. She miraculously held the banknote in her hand. Nothing short of death could pry it away until she gave it to the seller of the home she wanted. Now she had all she needed to finish the transaction for Pierson House, to begin the mission God had placed on Sophie Pierson's heart—and through her, upon Dessa's.

Soon—very soon—Mr. Hawkins's loan would produce all the fruit it was intended to bear.

She let Mr. Ridgeway lead her from the office, closing the door behind them.

"All right, then," said Dessa, taking in a breath she seemed to have forgotten she needed. She looked from the closed door to Mr. Ridgeway, whose face shifted quickly from concern to an eager and now-familiar smile, and held out her hand to him. "Thank you,

Mr. Ridgeway. I look forward to seeing you and Mr. Hawkins one week from today."

She clutched her handbag and walked from the bank, conscious that clerks and tellers alike watched every step she took.

4

Dessa stood on the cement porch of the home on Nineteenth Street that she now had every right to claim as belonging to her. Well, to her, the bank, and the many who contributed cash donations both past and future.

She went inside, an echo and a prayer of thanksgiving following each of her steps as she made her way through the vacant parlor. It was easy to envision the donated furniture that now awaited only collection and delivery. Not every room would be filled just yet, but she had no doubt all her needs would be met soon.

Sophie Pierson herself hadn't expected to open such a home for another two years, and that at the very earliest. She'd been prepared to work toward it for five!

But here it was. What had once been the home of a Market Street merchant would soon boast the name Pierson House. Mariadela White had been the first to hear it was for sale for far less than it was worth, and Dessa quickly pursued the opportunity. Yes, opium dens and gambling houses had encroached on the neighborhood, which was why respectable families had moved farther from Cherry Creek and the railroad yards that had sprung up in the last decade. They'd left behind those Dessa's heart ached to serve.

This was precisely where Pierson House needed to be. Surely even Sophie would have followed this quicker plan, despite her caution about borrowing. Hawkins National might have refused her as easily as those first banks had done. But considering the relative ease with which Dessa had procured the funds, she couldn't help believing God had hurried the schedule for a reason.

Even though at the moment Dessa had not a single girl committed to joining her. That was to have been the next phase in Sophie's plan, once the funds were raised—actually getting into the neighborhood, even in a rented room or storefront, to befriend the residents. Dessa's plans had bypassed that step altogether. Certainly it would be far more appealing for women to find immediate shelter in such a comfortable home!

Dessa knew she had work to do, but it was work she had no doubt God would bless.

≈

On his way home from the bank, Henry instructed his driver to go well past his house and to slow once they reached Nineteenth Street in the Fourth Ward. He wanted plenty of time to assess the building that Tobias—and through him, Henry himself—had allowed to pass into the hands of one young and obviously optimistic young woman.

Seeing the house, he acknowledged it looked sound enough, with a roof that appeared in fine condition over a brick structure that would last many years to come. Fire had taught the city well.

Still, the trim was in need of paint, and he wondered if Miss Caldwell had taken on more than she could handle. Not that any of the homes along this street looked as though their owners took much pride in the neighborhood. It was far too close to the worst vice in the city. Everything was for sale around here, from women to gaming to cheap liquor to opium beds.

Nor was it far from the edge of another section, the one that mimicked respectability. A place where people like Turk Foster attracted a better-dressed clientele to his gambling den.

Miss Caldwell's house was the filling in a sandwich made of the worst elements of society, and from what he'd seen of her, she wouldn't last long.

Derision filled him. How long would it be before the darkness around here blotted out the foolish light that had filled Dessa Caldwell's eyes?

It was a shame, really. He wondered if she would be so pretty once the realities of the harsher side of life snuffed out that light.

One last thought trailed along with Henry as the driver continued their slow progress down the street. It was a wonder Uncle Tobias wasn't fretting over a woman left so vulnerable in a neighborhood like this. Tobias mustn't know.

The thought only irritated Henry, because now he wished he didn't know either.

5

DESSA FAIRLY COLLAPSED onto her bed, well after dark. In the past week she'd scrubbed, painted, hefted furniture, and unpacked crates of donations in between sewing and hanging curtains and cooking for helpers. Whenever she sat, she worked on a collection of linens to be sold at White's Mercantile in the hope of starting an income separate from expected donations. All of which left precious little time for sleep.

Yet even as she rested her head on the pillow, a smile spread once again across her lips. She was doing it. Not alone—the proprietors of White's were her biggest donors and best friends since Sophie's death—but it was hard not to feel satisfied that Sophie's vision was becoming a reality so quickly. She'd carefully budgeted the expenses for the next three months, and if everything continued as expected, she could use that time to welcome new boarders and build up an inventory of items to sell.

As Dessa drifted off to sleep, she assured herself that tomorrow's luncheon with the investors from Hawkins National Bank and, soon after that, a dinner for her biggest donors would prove nothing but successes. They would see she was ready to open the doors to those in need.

If only women were already applying for the help she'd advertised in every corner of the neighborhood and beyond. . . .

Perhaps she dozed, though it felt only a moment later when

something awakened her. Disoriented, she looked toward her bedroom's freshly curtained window. But it was still dark.

She listened. Around the corner, Holladay Street—now known as Market Street since the Holladay family no longer wanted to be associated with what was sold along the avenue—came alive after dark. She'd heard music from pianos and fiddles meant to draw people in from the boardwalks. Dessa had tried countering with a song of her own on several nights since she'd moved in. Sitting on her porch singing a favorite hymn was quite different from the invitations to cribs and bawdy houses that paid protection money so authorities would ignore what the women were really trying to do. From balconies at the parlor houses or doorways of the cheaper, one-room cribs on the frayed fringes of the neighborhood, women flaunted their wares amid raucous music.

But sitting up in her bed, Dessa realized the streets had gone quiet. Surely she must have slept, because the younger the night, the noisier the neighborhood.

Turning over, she hoped to get a bit more rest before another busy day ahead. She had fresh bread to make in the morning, and a pie. Thankfully, Mariadela White would come early to help—

A crash sent Dessa's heart to thumping. She threw off her covers and sprang to the cool wood floor. Had she locked the front door before coming to bed? It was her habit to leave the door wide open during the day; although she had yet to receive her first visitor, she wanted curious neighbors to come calling, to ask what their new neighbor was about if they hadn't seen her flyers. But at night, while she slept, she'd taken the precaution of locking the door.

Yet she'd been so tired she couldn't recall if she'd done so tonight.

Ear pressed to her bedroom door, she listened again. Whatever the crash had been, it had come from the floor below. That gave her some comfort. The stairway creaked at nearly every step. If someone were coming up the stairs, she would hear him or her.

In a moment, though, she heard something else. Singing. Loud, off key. And decidedly male.

"In Dublin's fair city,
Where the girls are so pretty,
I first set my eyes on sweet Molly Malone,
As she wheeled her wheelbarrow
Through the streets broad and narrow,
Crying, 'Cockles and mussels! Alive, alive, oh!'"

With a prayer on her lips, Dessa listened a moment longer as the singer evidently forgot the next verse and filled in with a "la-la-la." Whoever was downstairs must certainly be lost, and perhaps drunk.

And she must be rid of him.

Grabbing her robe, Dessa donned it while opening the door and rushing to the top of the stairs. There, she stopped once again just to be sure she heard only the one voice, then crept down to determine the best plan to send away whoever had come calling.

The stairway was hidden in a hall of its own, set to the back of the parlor so the wall space was not shorted. She peered around the edge of the staircase hall, noticing first that the chair donated only yesterday was toppled over. Beside it, flat on his back, was a shadow that did not belong—somewhat reminiscent of the smooth, rounded tops of the foothills. His hat had come askew and covered all but his mouth, from which he picked up the tune of "Molly Malone" with a thick Irish brogue.

With a glance around the rest of the parlor to be sure he'd arrived alone, Dessa stepped into the room. The parlor floor was every bit as cool to her feet as the stairs and bedroom floor, despite what had been a warm July day. Less frightened now than annoyed, she was prompted by the feel beneath her bare feet to think about garnering some rugs before winter.

"What are you doing?" she demanded. "You mustn't sleep here!"

"What's that?" The man struggled to sit up, slipping from the wobbly support of his elbow and back to the floor, inspiring Dessa to help him to his feet. Between his size and unsteadiness, the task was no less challenging than moving the heaviest of deliveries, but she wrestled him to the settee nonetheless. Thankfully, it accepted both his weight and her own when she fell beside him.

"Many thanks, young Molly Malone," said the man, the unpleasant scent of strong drink on his breath.

Dessa popped back to her feet, clutching together her robe. "I'm afraid you have me confused, sir. This is Pierson House, and there is no Molly Malone here."

He laughed, loud and hearty. "To be sure, little lady, that I know. Molly Malone is long dead, if 'twere true she ever lived a'tall."

She extended a palm toward the door behind them. "Then can I help you out?"

He made a move to stand but fell back on the settee, which creaked to accept him yet again. "Ah, now, miss, I heard a rumor this is just the place for someone in need."

"But only for women, sir! You must go now."

He fought for his footing once more, stumbling back, sighing, stumbling again with a laugh until Dessa grabbed his arm to hold him steady.

"Are ya sure ya can't allow me the night? What's left o' it, at any rate?"

"Now, sir, what would the neighbors say if I permitted gentlemen where only ladies are allowed?"

He issued another hearty laugh. "Around here they'd say only, 'Welcome to the neighborhood!'"

"Yes, but I wish to live in this world yet not be part of it," she told him, throwing his arm around her shoulder to haul him closer to the door. He wasn't so rotund as she'd first imagined, his jacket and vest having been rumpled. Yet he was sturdy nonetheless, square of build like a tugboat. It was no easy chore to move him, even with his tottering help.

"Perhaps I might find a place on the porch . . . out of the rain?"

"It isn't raining," she said, glancing outside through the open curtains of the parlor window.

"Ah, but it was and will again!"

"Not tonight," she said with a grunt to keep him moving, when he stopped altogether.

Then, as if she were no more than a child, he brushed her hands away and turned back. Though he nearly toppled with his first step in the opposite direction, he righted himself and continued through the parlor, past the stairway, and into the kitchen.

"I came round the back first," he told her. "That porch overlookin' the yard—it suits me." He grabbed the edge of a kitchen chair as if the floor had lurched beneath him. But then he continued on his route.

The house had a covered porch, though it offered no amenities. Dessa imagined working out there in the warm afternoons, taking in the fresh air. Perhaps canning there in the fall. Never once had she imagined it as this man obviously did, as a sanctuary for drunken slumber.

She'd left a pile of rags and blankets, ones that had been used to cover the wood flooring while she and volunteers had painted the inside walls. It was to that pile this man headed.

"This will do—ah, yes—just fine for me." He fell to the floorboards with a thud, softened only by the discarded materials.

"But you can't stay here!" Dessa told him. "You must go home . . . or wherever you spent last night."

Her only answer was a deep sigh, followed shortly by a snore.

She bent over him, lifting one of his solid arms. "Oh, no you don't!" She tugged on him despite knowing she would have no success without his help. "You must wake up!"

To that he pulled his arm free, rolled away, and placed his hands beneath his face, eyes still closed, obviously content to stay where he was.

She shook his shoulder, demanded yet again that he go, grabbed the only arm she could reach, but all to no avail. Looking around, Dessa wondered if she had anything she could use to lift him. On a dolly, the way she'd seen one rather small man lift the heavy new stove that had been delivered earlier in the week?

But there was nothing to be done. With a moan of frustration, she returned to the kitchen. At least he wasn't inside the house. She shut the door, locked it, and for good measure dragged one of the kitchen chairs over and tilted it under the knob. Afterward she went to the front door and did the same, this time using one of the chairs from the dining room.

There would be no more surprises tonight.

Dessa rushed to open the front door upon hearing Mariadela White's voice. It had taken so long to fall back asleep that she'd spent half the night without rest. When she finally did sleep, she'd gone an hour past the time she wanted to start the day.

Pulling the chair away from the door and unbolting it with a twist of the lock, Dessa ushered her friend inside.

Mariadela looked from Dessa to the chair, a curious expression on her face. Mariadela might have been beautiful when she was younger, but age had softened her into what could only be called matronly. Her olive-colored skin was still smooth, but her dark hair was streaked with gray and her middle had thickened. Even now, with an amused smile on her face and a sparkle in her dark-brown eyes, she had the look of a woman who could be almost anyone's mother. "Isn't the lock enough?"

Pulling the chair back to the dining room, Dessa spoke over her shoulder. "I had a visitor last night. Let's go see if he's still here."

"He!" Raised brows accompanied the repetition. "You mean a man came here in the middle of the night?"

Dessa had barely finished pinning up her hair and tucking her shirtwaist into her skirt. She checked both on their way through the dining room. "I'll tell you all about it after we make sure he's out of here."

"You should have a telephone installed, Dessa," Mariadela said as she hurried behind. "You could have called us and I would have sent William over."

Dessa started to say that if she could afford it, she would love such a luxury, but she had decided days ago not to speak to Mariadela about money anymore. Even though it had been Mariadela who'd told Dessa about the bargain this house had been, she had a feeling Mariadela thought she'd hurried things in pro-curing the home with the help of a bank instead of waiting for donations to cover the full amount.

The back door not only had a glass window in the top half but was sided by matching windows overlooking the porch. Once Dessa moved the chair out of the way, she peered through first one window, then another, to scan nearly all of the porch and the yard as well. She immediately spotted the pile of blankets, but there was no sign of her late-night visitor.

She unlocked the door, opening it slowly.

He was gone.

"Thank You, Father in heaven!"

"He's gone?" Mariadela asked.

Dessa nodded, looking out to the small yard just to be sure. There was nothing much to be seen beyond weeds and hardy grass, no trees or flowers, only an old water pump they did not have to use thanks to indoor plumbing. An abandoned wood-framed carriage house took up most of the area, a structure that had somehow survived every fire she'd heard about from the city's past. A fence marked the rear of the lot. Beyond that she could see the backs of other buildings: another carriage house—that one brick like all the others—and the side of a small restaurant.

"What happened?" Mariadela asked.

Dessa glanced at the watch that dangled from a chain around her neck. "Let's just say I needed all the protection God had to offer last night. I'll tell you as we work." She'd already lost precious time this morning, and they had a lunch to prepare. An important lunch—one in which she needed to impress not only Mr. Ridgeway but perhaps more especially Mr. Hawkins. If a good meal and all the improvements weren't enough to validate their faith in her, then God Himself would have to intervene on her behalf.

6

HENRY DIPPED THE RAZOR back into the washbasin, then finished shaving with a final swipe to his chin. His skin was anything but smooth anymore, as the scrape of the razor attested. So different from the skin of a child, for example. Or a woman.

He pummeled his face with a towel, disgusted by thoughts that refused to go away despite his continual efforts to banish them the moment they arrived. Yes, the do-gooder Tobias had so foolishly lent the bank's money to undoubtedly possessed soft skin. So did nearly every woman in the world, at least softer than his. So what?

He pretended for a moment not to remember her name, but it was useless. Dessa Caldwell. Was she daft, or just a zealot who clung to some kind of faith—either in God or mankind—to the point of foolhardiness?

Either way, it didn't matter. If Henry found the slightest reason to think the whole thing a mistake, he would order Tobias to do something he'd expressly forbidden in the past: reverse the entire process and work toward getting the bank's money back. He might first contact the house's previous owner and see if it could be handled nicely. If not, Henry would give strict orders to foreclose the minute she was late with a payment. Better to try reselling the property than let it deteriorate in the too-full hands of a woman who would likely be better off elsewhere.

Henry needed to be rid of this business transaction, if only to return his full attention to the bank. Where it belonged.

꙳

"The blueberry pie!"

Dessa grabbed the oven door handle, too late remembering how hot to the touch it would be. She pulled back her smarting fingers and waved them in the air to cool, as Mariadela stepped between her and the Monarch oven.

"You're as nervous as a new bride cooking for the first time." Mariadela opened the oven door with a towel to protect her own hand, pulling out a perfectly golden pie. She smiled, holding up the triumph in baked goods. "Your guests this afternoon might be bankers, but they're men first. Judging by my own husband and boys, they'll eat just about anything."

Dessa wanted to believe her friend, but recalling the stern look on Mr. Hawkins's face the day she'd received the happy news about her loan made her wonder if he would be easily pleased. Somehow the thought did nothing to ease her skittishness. She wished she'd had a rested night; being overtired didn't help her nerves.

"I just want the meal to be a good representation—"

"I know," the older woman cut in. "A good representation of the Lord's work."

Dessa offered Mariadela an apologetic smile. "Have I said that before?"

"Only about twice a day, every day, for the two years I've known you."

The Whites had been among Sophie and Dessa's first supporters, and Mariadela one of Dessa's closest friends since losing Sophie. Since then, the Whites had even provided Dessa with a rent-free room above their mercantile—despite the expansion of their store to the second floor. They were likely glad to have the space back for their burgeoning business. That had played no small role in Dessa's decision to speed along the opening of Pierson House. This was as much a shelter to Dessa as it would be to other women in need.

Mariadela set the pie on the marred wooden table behind them. The table was a donation that could have used a good sanding and a new coat of varnish had Dessa the time. "I didn't need the reminder of God's involvement in this place," Mariadela added, "not since I found out where your loan came from."

Dessa nodded. "I shouldn't call it a miracle, but I do. Yet Hawkins National is a bank, after all. That's part of what they do. Loans to businesses."

Mariadela's laugh sounded something between a scoff and genuine amusement. "Not to *this* kind of business. I've known Mr. Hawkins since he was my husband's biggest competitor, when he opened a store fresh out of college from back East. He may be a banker, but he's a merchant first, through and through. Fair, maybe. But generous? Compassionate? No. If you shake him hard enough, you'll hear gold coins rattling in that chest of his, not a heartbeat."

"Perhaps he's changed." Dessa didn't realize until speaking the words that she wanted them to be true.

"If he has changed, it's because of that Tobias Ridgeway," Mariadela said as she began to gather the vegetables they would serve. "The man is a saint, and married to a saint as well." She looked around the kitchen and smiled. "But for whatever reason Mr. Hawkins extended you the loan, he won't be disappointed. Look at all you've done, and in so short a time! You've been in only a week and you've increased its value already. It's a home fit for anyone now."

Dessa looked at the kitchen, with its imperfect but fully functional table, mismatched chairs that were nonetheless made to last, and a variety of cookware, dishes, and cutlery. Not a single piece would have graced even the servants' quarters of the home in which Dessa had served in St. Louis, but being able to call it all her own made each and every piece lovely.

The house itself had proven as sound as the seller claimed. Working plumbing, solid flooring, steady gas for cooking and lighting. The now-dust-free rooms smelled fresh and clean. Nearly every wall in the house had been painted, thanks to supplies donated from Mariadela's store and a volunteer workforce from the railroad mission school. There was also a good deal of furniture already in place. Upstairs, besides the bedrooms offering beds and clean linens, was a variety of clothing that had been donated from the church Dessa attended with the White family. Down here, the dining room boasted a somewhat nicer table than the one in the kitchen, along with six chairs that matched. Even the parlor wasn't empty; it was furnished with a side chair and matching settee, each cast in the French Louis XVI style. The oval stitchery on the seats showed wear, and the gilt wood of the scantily padded arms was scratched, but it hardly mattered to Dessa. Not only had all of it come from generous hearts, hearts directed by no less than God Himself, but last night's visitor had proven the furniture sturdy.

"All we need are the residents," Dessa said. Her voice lacked the confidence she normally added but at the moment could not summon.

Mariadela patted her hand. "They'll come. No need to worry. They're out there; they just need to know they have an alternative."

"I was so sure they would come immediately—I've distributed flyers and applications everywhere, all along Market and Blake between Nineteenth and Twenty-Third Streets. I know I haven't gotten to know many in the neighborhood yet, but I've seen the number of people who do their business around here. Surely there are some women without a roof over their heads at all. How can anyone prefer no roof to this one?"

"It will only take one of them to be brave enough to leave behind what she knows. Then others will follow. You'll see."

How Dessa wanted to believe her, but it was difficult to avoid the niggling disappointment that her start hadn't already been as successful as she'd expected. Yet she was more than tireless in her effort. And God's timing was always perfect, wasn't it?

Mariadela was right. They would come. It was just a matter of time.

🌿

Henry looked out his carriage window, largely ignoring whatever Tobias was saying. From Henry's first investigation, he remembered their luncheon destination wasn't far. How well had Miss Caldwell survived this first week living so near the city's riffraff? With any luck, she would be eager to give back the bank's money and have this silly venture ended once and for all.

"Henry?"

He was suddenly aware that Tobias had called his name and was looking at him expectantly. "Yes?"

"We've arrived."

Henry's gloved hands gripped his walking stick as he moved to the carriage door Tobias held open. Jumping onto the pavement, Henry looked around, starting with the house in front of him.

To his surprise, the trim on the brick structure had been painted a clean beige, unremarkable if not for the darker trim at the windowsills. An outward improvement that might help him resell the place.

Not far away was a restaurant with living quarters above, and on the other side of that a single-story tavern, with a sign in the window advertising a pawnbroker on the premises. Likely it wasn't just a tavern, though they probably did sell drinks. Pawnbrokers went hand in hand with gambling rooms. Not exactly the worst of the businesses to be found within a few blocks, but definitely not intended to meet the needs of polite society.

"This is where you invested the bank's money." Henry's words were as flat as the roof on a yet-to-be-demolished structure across the street, victim of a fire. A charred sign, which once advertised massages, hung at an odd angle.

"As Miss Caldwell explained," Tobias began, while Henry took immediate satisfaction in seeing that he looked doubtful too, "she needs to be near the population she wishes to reach."

"How will staying in this neighborhood free any one of them from what she hopes they will leave behind?"

"A good question, Henry. Let's ask her, shall we?"

Tobias was already up the half-dozen stairs to the freshly painted threshold.

To Henry's surprise, it wasn't Dessa Caldwell who answered. It was Mariadela White, from White's Mercantile.

"Come in, gentlemen!" she greeted them warmly, far more warmly than Henry would have expected, given their history. He'd never intended to damage White's business all those years ago by offering his goods at a rate even Henry could barely afford. And it wasn't generosity, either. It had been good, sound business practice for the plans he'd had in mind.

"Dessa will be down in a moment, but please, come inside. Let me take your hats."

She did so, setting the items aside on a hook provided next to the door. The room was sparsely furnished—only a settee, a side chair, and a small table holding an oil lamp—but he could see an adjoining dining room that offered a table and more chairs. Nothing yet hung on any of the walls, but like the trim, these walls were recently painted, here a dull but unblemished gray. A carton sat off to the side of the dining room, next to the table. It appeared to be half-full of linens.

"What a pleasant surprise, Mrs. White," Tobias said as he, like Henry, looked around. "We didn't expect to see anyone but Miss Caldwell."

"I've been helping her when I can."

Though Henry said nothing, he recalled she had several children who, almost ten years ago, had been constantly underfoot and into mischief—part of the reason he was sure customers had preferred his quiet establishment just across the street. Likely those same children were valued employees by now.

Before Henry could think of a greeting of his own—one he wasn't overly eager to extend anyway—the moment was lost in the warm welcome of Dessa Caldwell as she swept into the room from a hallway opposite.

"How happy I am to see both of you! Do you know Mrs. White?"

"Yes, of course," Henry said, offering her a brief glance. "Though she banks with a competitor."

Tobias laughed. "Yes, but we won't give up hope, will we, Henry? It's always a pleasure to see Mrs. White. Tell me, how are William and the family?"

A few moments of conversation followed, words Henry knew he was bound to forget before too many minutes passed, so he occupied his thoughts elsewhere. He could see the dining room was set for five. Evidently Mrs. White was to stay, which didn't surprise him, but he wondered who the fifth would be.

"May we show you around, Mr. Hawkins?" Miss Caldwell asked.

Henry turned his full attention on her at last. His memory hadn't exaggerated her loveliness—if anything she was more so. Her light-brown eyes were merry, her smile comfortable and easy. Her hair, just like the darkly burned gold he'd imagined, looked soft to the touch.

Why had he come? This whole ridiculous loan had been Tobias's idea. Henry had already counted the money as lost. He should have let Tobias receive this warm welcome on his own.

But then, if he wanted the loan to come to a quick end, he would have to do it himself.

"The furniture has all been donated," Miss Caldwell said. He noted her voice was somewhat breathless, as if she was nervous. "There are five rooms upstairs. Besides my own, only two are ready, but it won't be long before we have beds for the rest. Mariadela's husband is fashioning bed frames already, so we'll need only mattresses."

She led them into the kitchen, where, despite Henry's determination not to enjoy himself, the scent of some kind of soup and bread tickled his nose, along with a fragrantly spiced main course.

A pie sat on the edge of a stove, which momentarily distracted him from the equipment beneath it. Though he was no expert on household goods, he remembered from his own merchant days that a Monarch was among the best stoves on the market. He looked around again, wondering just how old this structure could be. Not as old as he'd assumed?

"Was the stove in the building when you arranged to take ownership?" he asked.

"Why, no, Mr. Hawkins." She seemed pleased he'd noticed. "Isn't it lovely?"

"Expensive," he said. "Or was it, too, a donation?"

She looked from him to the stove, as if surprised. He was sure her look held a hint of guilt, convincing him she'd very likely spent some of the bank's money to purchase it. Had she so little regard for how much it cost? "It was a necessary part of our investment. Offering a good meal, well prepared, is a sure way to draw those in need. Sometimes God uses the stomach as well as the ear to convey His message. Something I hope you'll learn when we serve lunch." The last words were uttered with such a confident smile it was all Henry could do not to abandon all his good sense and smile in return. Even though she'd just called a stove an *investment*.

Back in the dining room, he learned the carton he'd thought yet to be unpacked contained items going with Mrs. White when she left. Linens, as he'd guessed, but to be sold at White's Mercantile. The first income against her loan. Henry refrained from smirking. It would take a lot more than a few tablecloths to repay the money she owed him.

"You've done a fine job getting settled so quickly, Miss Caldwell," said Tobias. "Now all you need are your guests. How soon will you be welcoming your first client?"

Client. Leave it to Tobias to recall the diplomatic term. Still, Henry was glad he'd asked. He looked at Miss Caldwell for her answer, and for the first time since their arrival she seemed unsure of herself.

"I'd expected some girls initially," she said.

"I'm not sure anyone believed Dessa's vision would be a reality so quickly," Mrs. White said. "They'll be here just as soon as they know the door is open."

Miss Caldwell's brows—fine, long brows that got involved in each of her expressions—now gathered. One brow, he noted, curled slightly toward the bridge of her nose when she frowned, as she was doing now.

"I'm a firm believer in absolute honesty." She said the words plainly but at the same time did not meet his eye, or even Tobias's eyes, which were as always far more inviting than the average banker's. "While I fully expect several clients to join me *soon*, I admit I'm surprised by this initial reluctance. It's understandable, of course, to have some hesitation about entirely changing one's life."

Henry folded one hand over the other. It would be within his rights to demand if she truly knew the sort of person she seemed intent upon helping. Had she not researched other institutions like the one she was trying to establish? He would be fully within reason to blame Tobias for not having been more diligent about the sort of expectations that should be fulfilled.

Just when he might have begun such a lecture, Miss Caldwell took the smallest step closer to him. Henry wanted to step back but knew he was too close to the table to do so. He had no choice but to look at her, though he wished he didn't have to.

She was truly beautiful. If she had something to say, she waited an extended moment to study him in the way he wanted to study her in return. They might have been alone for all Henry cared about either Tobias or Mrs. White, particularly when he saw the look of utter gratitude on Miss Caldwell's face.

He tried pulling his gaze away but failed. He didn't want her gratitude. He should tell her without hesitation that he'd never been in favor of this loan. If it hadn't been for the fragments of loyalty Henry still harbored for Tobias, he'd have sacked him for his insubordination. A foolish loan was a foolish loan, no matter how lofty the intentions. Or how lovely the borrower.

"I know Pierson House is off to a humble beginning, Mr. Hawkins." Her voice was soft, easy to listen to. "But the need is here. Right here. I'm so very grateful for the chance you've given me, the confidence you've shown me, the generosity you've proven in such a tangible way toward the vulnerable women of this city. Thank you."

She extended one hand, and Henry knew if he touched it he would swallow the words he might have used. He had not the slightest hint of confidence in her, nor a smidgen of generosity.

But something—some idiotic, childish, primitive force inside him—made Henry raise his hand to take hers in his own.

❧

Dessa had never seen eyes quite like Henry Hawkins's. Gray, like those of a newborn baby whose parents would have to wait for their child to unveil which way the color would go: blue or brown. How was it possible his had stayed so thoroughly gray, not even tending toward hazel?

He'd been reluctant to accept her hand, but now he held it firmly. His touch couldn't help but broaden her smile. Each day since the loan had been approved, she'd wanted to assure him he'd been right to trust her. Somehow, wanting to prove herself to him had become more important than she'd expected. He was, after all, just a man. And men could prove so troublesome.

He cleared his throat, and she withdrew her hand. She hadn't realized she'd held it overlong.

"Lunch will be on the table in a moment," she said softly. "Won't you—" she glanced at Mr. Ridgeway—"both be seated?"

"I can't help but notice there is another place set," Mr. Ridgeway said in his familiar friendly tone. "Are we expecting someone?"

Mariadela was already in the kitchen, so Dessa answered. "We'd hoped William White could join us, but he sent a message that he'll be here only for dessert. We'll leave the plate, though, just in case."

"Ah, dessert," said Mr. Ridgeway. "I spotted that pie right off."

With a laugh, Dessa hurried away to help Mariadela bring in the food, everything from a cool gazpacho soup with hearty bread to an herb-crusted chicken she'd been enthusiastic about preparing.

In the kitchen, she wanted nothing more than a moment to ask Mariadela what she thought of Mr. Hawkins's attitude, but her friend was already laden with a tray, and so there wasn't time. Had Mariadela even noticed his frown? Did she know if he was always so serious? Dessa grabbed the covered tray of fowl from the oven and followed Mariadela back to the dining room.

If the success of a luncheon could be measured solely by the taste of the food served, then Dessa's was a resounding triumph.

If measured by polite and interesting conversation, some might call it enjoyable.

But if success were measured by the look of Mr. Henry Hawkins, then this luncheon was an uncontestable failure. He spoke only when Dessa asked him direct questions. Would he care for more vegetables in his soup? *No.* Was the chicken to his liking? *Yes.* The weather had been fine this summer, except for the afternoon showers. *Yes, so it has.* It seemed from Mr. Ridgeway's description that his bank was always as busy as Dessa had witnessed during her own two visits. *Yes, it is.*

Dessa was determined to ask him a question that would draw more than the briefest of answers. "Mariadela tells me you were once in the mercantile business yourself, Mr. Hawkins."

"Yes, I was."

She held back a sigh. "But you found banking more to your liking?"

He sipped the water she'd served with their meal, then dabbed his mouth with a napkin—a napkin she'd sewn. "I opened the mercantile as a forerunner to my bank. To build trust among my customers, most of whom already used my crediting services as a bank. I'd never intended to stay in the mercantile business."

"Which was fortunate for my husband and me," Mariadela said. When Dessa looked at her friend—having heard a hint of hardness in her tone—she saw immediately that Mariadela regretted her words. Or perhaps only the resentment she'd hinted was behind them. She smiled over the frown her own words had produced on her face. "You were a worthy competitor, Mr. Hawkins."

He gave a quick bow with his head, as if she'd saluted him.

"I'd say White's has done quite well," Mr. Ridgeway said, "converting that second floor from storage to customer merchandise."

Mariadela's smile became pleased. "Yes, my husband is very proud of trying to keep up with the city's growth."

"Your bank has certainly done that," Dessa said to Mr. Hawkins. "It's one of the finest buildings in Denver—ahead of most others of the city, even."

She'd meant it to be a compliment, but he looked at her with his frown renewed, as if she'd described the bank as too lavish. Could she say nothing right in front of this man? The only subject he'd spoken of with any interest had been the stove. . . . Did he believe she'd made an unwise investment in that silly stove and think it as extravagant as the Roman pillars on his bank?

"Speaking of being ahead of its time," he said slowly, letting his gaze travel the room, "what of this place? Perhaps your lack of clients is a sign that our time—or society—is not yet ready for what you have in mind."

Dessa's pulse quickened, not just from his words but because he'd voiced fears she herself had been trying to avoid. "I'm sure Denver is ready to join the ranks of the best cities in the country, Mr. Hawkins, and not stay stuck with a reputation for wild ways. Buildings like your own and the opera house and countless lovely churches all attest to that." She knew she was teetering on rambling, but his face remained so stoic that the words kept coming. "Pierson House is a bridge, offering those who might be stranded in the old ways a chance to join the new. There are so many more jobs available now, even for women. New hope, new lives. Restoration."

"The oldest cities in America—I'd venture to say the world—still offer those wild ways, Miss Caldwell. How is it you think you can change that?"

"If we reach one person at a time, we'll have done far more than just turning our backs with indifference or pretending there aren't real lives at risk. There are women out there who want a better life but don't know how to get it. Some of them are little more than trapped children who can't find their way."

"Have you ever considered they might not want another way?"

"Is there a child on this earth who dreams of growing up to be enslaved by another, or by opium or alcohol? Or perhaps thrust aside by an employer after making the mistake of trusting one of the family members with favors he had no right to demand?" She set aside her fork, reminding herself—perhaps too late—that she was indebted to this man. "Pierson House hopes to answer the plight of those less fortunate, from all walks of life."

"I would think everyone who believes themselves less fortunate would be at your door already."

From the way he spoke, the way he acted, Dessa finally saw that it was entirely possible—no, it was likely—Mr. Hawkins would have been another banker showing her to the door. How foolish she'd been to think Henry Hawkins an answer to her prayer, when it had been Mr. Ridgeway all along. She suddenly wondered if Mr. Ridgeway might have risked his job to push through this loan without Mr. Hawkins's approval. How had he managed to do it?

Neither Dessa's doubts nor Mr. Hawkins's mattered. What mattered was that Pierson House was a vision God had given to Sophie, the godliest woman Dessa had ever known. Surely God would bless her efforts—if not for Dessa, then certainly for Sophie!

"I think what you're implying, Mr. Hawkins, is doubt that Pierson House can succeed. Perhaps you and I have a different definition of success, but I believe to the very core of my soul that it can, and will."

He scanned the dining room, sparing a glance over his shoulder to the bay window that faced the street. When he turned back to her, the look in his eye was openly skeptical. "Right here, near the center of the very spot you hope for them to escape? What makes you think they'll change their ways if they aren't required to leave what they know? Why come here at all if they're not really leaving?"

She bristled at his condescending tone, feeling the last bit of admiration she might have felt for him slip away. "To catch fish, you must go to the water. Pierson House is a freshwater holding pond, a place to make the transition. I have no doubt it's only a matter of time before God sends us those who will accept His help."

In the pause that followed, Mr. Hawkins leveled a stare at her that seemed anything but convinced. Just as she contemplated more words to further her side of the argument, the front door opened, a sound drawing everyone's attention.

Expecting Mariadela's husband, William, Dessa looked up, and whatever feeble hope that she'd at least given Mr. Hawkins something to think about dissolved. Scrambling to her feet, she rushed to forestall the man from entering—the very man who had come to her in a drunken stupor in the middle of the night.

She stopped him just inside the door. A glance in Mr. Hawkins's direction, closest to the window, gave her hope he hadn't yet seen the newcomer from his vantage.

"I'm afraid you're in the wrong place, sir," Dessa said quietly—calmly—taking one of his arms to turn him back to the door.

"Naw, I remember precisely. And I never forget me debts. Here ya go, missy. For last night."

To her horror he extended a bill in his hand, one she immediately pushed away. With her free hand she grabbed the edge of the door he'd left open, hoping not only to hide him from the others but to get him to leave before anyone nearby noticed something so terribly amiss.

"You owe me nothing, sir," she whispered. "Please go."

"But you showed me a kindness, and I wanted to repay—"

"Is there something wrong?"

To her horror, the words spoken just behind her came from Mr. Hawkins. She closed her eyes in a moment of desperate prayer for guidance, then did the only thing she could—turned around to face the very curious and obviously disapproving banker.

"No, nothing is wrong," she said lightly. "I was just saying this gentleman is confused about where he is."

The man laughed, removing his hat—crumpled with wear—and placing it in the same hand as the dollar bill. He then extended his free hand to Mr. Hawkins, who made no move to accept the friendly gesture.

The man pulled back his rejected hand, wiping it along the side of his stained and dirty jacket. "I don't blame ya, sir, for not takin' me hand. Your kind and mine don't mix very often, now do we?" He winked at Dessa. "He's a fine-lookin' one for sure, missy. You can tell he'll pay ya and pay ya well."

"He's not—"

"Just what happened here last night?" Mr. Hawkins pressed.

Both Mr. Ridgeway and Mariadela now stood nearby, Mariadela looking as mortified as Dessa felt, and Mr. Ridgeway considerably more curious than condemning.

"I can explain that, sir." The caller once again held out the dollar bill, which Dessa still refused to accept. He faced Mr. Hawkins, taking in what looked to be a deep, fortifying breath. "'Tis a fact, me boy, that I was a victim of me own undoing. Ah, but it was a *strong* drink that got me last night. Like a torch going down me throat and straight to me empty belly. When I needed a spot to curl up and sleep, I found me way right here to this very room, because rumor has it to be a refuge of a kind. And this wee slip of a girl helped me to a bed, so I wouldn't be left in the gutter."

"On the back porch," Dessa said, her words barely making it beyond her embarrassment. "To a pile of rags."

"Still, 'twas a soft pile, and I was out of the night wind, off the pavement so to speak. I came to offer me thanks, and me money. Though . . . if it isn't too much trouble, might ya make change for me? I have but this single bill, and don't ya know I can get a bed down the street for half this. So would two bits be a fair price for a porch, do ya suppose now? A porch not even used 'til I got here, so late as it was?"

"Keep your bill, Mr. . . ." Dessa stopped, not knowing what to call him but having no wish to find out. She grabbed the door once again, hoping he would take his leave. But he was looking beyond them to the dining room, where remnants of lunch only needed clearing away.

"Now that looks as if 'twere a fine meal. Fine indeed."

Dessa released another breath. She knew what she ought to do—knew, too, that Mr. Hawkins's disapproval would only increase. Yet she would not ignore the prompting to do right, no matter how deep the banker's frown.

She went to the table, grabbed two slices of bread and a hefty slice of chicken, then returned to the man at her door.

Handing the sandwich to him, she said, "I must ask you to go now, sir. But let me make it clear since you're of sobriety. This is a home for women *only*. Please don't come here again."

Accepting the sandwich with a grin wide enough to reveal crooked and graying teeth, he placed his hat back upon his head, pocketed his dollar, and with a zealous bite, he gave her another wink before going out the door.

"Feeding him will only bring him back," Mr. Hawkins said.

"I simply forgot to lock the door last night," Dessa told him, her spine so rigid it ached. "It won't happen again."

With a mix of relief and disappointment, she watched Mr. Hawkins step past her to the hook beside the door. Placing the hat on his head, he faced her, so close she could see for the first time that there was a mix of light- and dark-gray flecks in his eyes. If his hair ever turned gray, it would likely match.

"Banks have a way of foreclosing on loans that are not repaid on a regular and timely basis. If he was an example of the clientele you're attracting—" he held out a palm in the direction of the modest box of linens nearby—"and if that is the source of your repayment fund, Miss Caldwell, then I suggest you prepare yourself for foreclosure."

Then he walked through the front door, calling Mr. Ridgeway's name over his shoulder.

7

"Was that really necessary, Henry?"

Tobias plopped his considerable girth on the seat opposite Henry, jostling the entire carriage. He had a look of purest irritation on his normally jovial face.

"Go back if you like," Henry said, looking out the carriage window. But as the vehicle rolled forward, they both knew it was too late.

"If I'd known you were going to threaten her with foreclosure, and this before her first loan payment is due—"

"The loan was a mistake, Tobias; even you must see that now. She's a fool to live in this neighborhood, if men like that drunken Irishman are the only people who want anything to do with her. She's just sitting there sewing and cooking on that stove, and she's obviously already tapped anyone who will give her the charity she needs. How is it we've been foolish enough to make this home a reality before either she or the neighborhood is ready for it?"

"You don't know that! And you must give her a chance. She's obviously worked day and night to get settled, and I have no doubt she'll do exactly as she hopes."

Henry spared his uncle a glance. Doubt was all over Tobias's face, despite his words. "At least it'll be easier to sell, with the improvements she's made on the place."

"Huh," grumbled Tobias, then grumbled again. "Fine and well for you to sit there, hoping she fails. Huh."

It was nothing to be proud of; even Henry knew that. He attempted a halfhearted smile. "You're just angry we didn't get any of that pie."

"Of course I am!" Tobias said, grinning at last. "Aren't you?"

The funny thing was, in spite of telling himself his actions had been justified, Henry realized he was indeed missing that very thing.

"Why don't you suggest she open a café?" Henry asked. "She has the kitchen for it."

"I cannot believe you begrudge her the purchase of a stove. You heard what she said: appealing food is part of the investment."

"Yes, if it *were* a café. I want you to tell her that."

Tobias leaned forward and Henry felt his stare even though he continued to look out the window.

"Tell her yourself."

❧

"Shh, hush now, Dessa," soothed Mariadela, having pulled her chair around the table, close to Dessa's.

"The whole luncheon was a disaster! He—he didn't have to be so . . . so mean!" Dessa knew she sounded like a child, but that's exactly how she felt. Chastised as if she'd done something foolish.

The worst part was she still couldn't help wondering if she'd been every bit as foolish as Mr. Hawkins seemed to believe. The thought brought a fresh supply of tears. "Oh, Mariadela! What if he's right? I thought—" A hiccup interrupted her; then another sob overtook her. "I thought women would be eager to find a safe place under this roof! And there isn't one, not a single one, who came!"

"They will," Mariadela said. "They will."

A new thought came to mind, one Dessa hadn't even entertained before now. "And what if the donations don't continue as regularly as expected? Why, if a single donor decides to go elsewhere, I won't be able to make the payments. Because Mr. Hawkins is right! I can't pay back that loan just from linen sales."

Dessa used one of her carefully sewn napkins to wipe away tears that were only replaced by more. "What if I've misunderstood what God wanted me to do? Why didn't I wait and work toward more donations the way Sophie would have done, so I wouldn't have to borrow so much?"

Thoughts of Sophie brought inevitable grief, something Dessa carried despite the nearly nine months she'd been gone. Visions of Sophie going off one day, as she so often did, to the county hospital—better known as the pesthouse—not far away on Wazee and Sixteenth, where poor and indigents came for treatment of any contagious disease. Sophie had gone there often, never with a thought to herself. They couldn't have guessed God would allow her ministry to end because of one of those visits. Conditions in the almshouse—the greater part of the pesthouse—were what had inspired Sophie to open an alternative in this very neighborhood.

Dessa had never cared for the irony that Sophie died in a city known for its crisp, clean, dry air that promised healing for so many of the infirm.

"If only Sophie were still here," Dessa whispered, wiping again at her tears, relieved they were beginning to wane. An idea rose that made the last of them stall. "I need to visit her grave. I've always been able to imagine better what she would do when I'm near her."

"Yes, that's a good idea. When William arrives, he can take you."

Dessa sighed as they cleared away the remnants of the meal. At least the men had eaten everything on their plates, including seconds.

"William will be pleased there's more pie left for him," Mariadela said with a wink.

But the smile Dessa afforded in return was anything but genuine.

Denver City Cemetery wasn't far from Brown's Bluff—the spot designated as Capitol Hill after years of delays and disputes. Building had begun on the state capitol just last year. Dessa had visited the cemetery often since Sophie's death, having fought Sophie's family for her right to be buried where she wanted—not back in St. Louis in the prestigious family plot, but right here in Denver, with those relegated to the edge of the cemetery, where the remains of the lower classes from respectable to criminal could be found.

At Sophie's graveside, tears replenished themselves in Dessa's eyes. She knew Sophie wasn't here, that this grave was nothing more than a testament to the way Sophie had lived her life trying to help those less fortunate. And yet standing here never failed to bring Dessa closer to her dear friend's memory.

Sophie hadn't just been helping those who didn't seem able to help themselves. She, like Dessa, had carried a sort of obligation to set something right—though in Sophie's case the wrongdoing had not been her own. But Sophie had felt the need to make up for the wrongs done by a Pierson. Her brother had compromised more than a few women's virtue. Including Dessa's.

"Did I fail you, Sophie? Did my impatience once again spoil your plans?" She wiped at a fallen tear, not feeling the dampness on her fingers for the thickness of her glove. An unexpected smile tugged at her lips. "I haven't forgotten the times my impatience got the best of us. That horrid mail express carriage we took from Greenville to Louisville, or the shortcut we took in Chicago that ended with us hopelessly lost. My fault, both, and you missed important meetings because of my foolishness. Yet you were able to fix it all, weren't you? And never blamed me, not once."

A meager laugh escaped, but her tears weren't banished altogether. "Oh, Sophie, I knew you would comfort me. I didn't think I'd be able to laugh today, not after the way Mr. Hawkins made me feel." She hugged her arms to herself. "I know I've made mistakes. I know impatience is one of my biggest faults. But this time . . . it's more than just impatience. Did I misunderstand God's will? Was I to put your dream in other, more capable hands than mine? I wish I knew."

If Mr. Hawkins's visit had done anything, it had surfaced every doubt Dessa had secretly harbored since her unhesitating start. She'd been so convinced no one but she had the same amount of passion and pure doggedness to get the job done that she hadn't stopped to think she might not be the right person to implement Sophie's vision.

Sophie had loved even those who'd turned their backs on God, not seeing their sin the way so much of society was wont to do. She saw the weakness and weariness that forced so many into a life that came with pain and loss of choice. Choice, at least, was something Sophie strove to restore.

Raised until she was seven in an institution for orphans and indigents, Dessa knew firsthand how it felt to be bereft of choice. Upon her seventh birthday she'd been sent by train to work. Her brother went to a farm while Dessa was placed into service with the Pierson family in St. Louis. A place that Dessa herself had eventually needed to escape—an escape Sophie provided.

Coming here today had been the right thing to do. Renewed resolve filled her. Even if opening Pierson House had been premature, even if Mr. Hawkins thought it a mistake, it wasn't. It couldn't be. Who knew better than Dessa the heartache and loss of everything from faith to dignity when a person was denied all choice, all hope?

It was up to Dessa to prove Mr. Hawkins—and her own doubts—wrong.

8

"SIR! SIR!"

Henry had barely climbed out of his carriage before a scrawny youth stepped in his way on the bank steps. He waved an envelope in Henry's face so fiercely that Henry raised the handle of his walking stick to put some distance between himself and the offending item.

"What is it, young man?"

"You're Mr. Hawkins, ain't ya?"

"I am."

"Then this is for you." He slapped the envelope to Henry's chest.

To prevent it from flying in the wind, Henry grabbed the item as the boy raced off down the street. "Wait just a minute!"

But the youth had already gone too far and obviously had no interest in answering Henry's call. Henry found that odd; most boys who delivered notes—even those who'd been paid on the front end—expected a tip upon delivery.

Henry slipped the envelope into his pocket with an undeniable sense of foreboding. He wished he'd had the quickness to grab the boy by the collar and demand to know who'd hired him for the delivery.

Once inside the privacy of his office, before even hanging up his hat or putting aside his walking stick or removing his gloves, Henry pulled out the note he wished to ignore.

He should light a match to it without opening it.

Instead, he tore open the envelope, and a small piece of familiar onionskin floated out. On one side were scrawled the words:

False face must hide what the false heart doth know.

Henry crumpled both the paper and the envelope, wishing once again he'd detained that boy. He must find out where these intolerable notes originated.

Dessa held the note in her hand, her heart dancing, fingers trembling. A prospect!

The note wasn't signed, but it had a clear purpose. A purpose Dessa was only too eager to fulfill. She glanced at the watch she wore like an adornment every day. Eleven o'clock. She had enough time to finish the embroidery on a handkerchief, then hire a hack to take her to City Park, where she was to meet by two o'clock the woman who'd authored the note.

Dessa was used to seeing women from various parlor houses and brothels paraded through the city in open carriages—it was a form of advertising that Denver's growing, more respectable population might resent but had no recourse against. And City Park, set beyond Denver's limits—and therefore beyond its jurisdiction—was a natural magnet for anyone who wanted to leave behind the city's noise and stench of smelters' coal smoke along with its laws and judgments.

Yet as she left the hired cab at the park gate, she wasn't sure what to look for. The note said only to identify the author by a red flower on her hat. It didn't name the person as someone from the sporting end of town, a maid who might be in trouble, or even the daughter of one of the donor families Dessa had met in the last two years. Manner of dress could be quite different depending on one's station.

Dessa paid the driver, instructed him to wait, then clutched her handbag and set off along the open, grassy parkland.

There weren't many amenities to this park, though officials promised a future in which patrons would visit a water garden, monuments, and a variety of trees and flowers. So far, though, the park boasted little more than squatters and surrounding farmland.

But Dessa wasn't alone as she paced herself to stroll as if she were only taking in the fresh country air. Though she saw few families, there were a number of adults—both men and women— taking advantage of a view of the mountains on the horizon that Dessa never tired of.

She saw no one wearing a red flower, on her hat or otherwise. Dessa walked along, wishing the note's author had been more specific. The parkland was fairly extensive. Suppose Dessa had come to the wrong end? She had no choice but to keep looking.

A breeze cooled the air today, but under the warmth of the sun Dessa was comfortable. She occasionally stopped, looking before and behind, breathing deeply. Whenever a new carriage came along, Dessa would stop and wait. Either someone rode off or new visitors emerged. None of them wearing a red flower.

A half hour passed, and Dessa considered returning to the hired hack and going back to the city. If the girl was serious about meeting Dessa, she would make another attempt. If only Dessa knew where she could contact the girl; she wasn't the least bit afraid of going to her rather than meeting in a public place.

Still, she walked a bit longer, surveying the area, occasionally turning her gaze westward toward the mountains. A squall erupted in the sky but too far off to pose Dessa any threat. She watched the rain paint vertical gray stripes on the horizon.

Once she saw a man who, from a distance, looked like Mr. Hawkins, but she quickly dismissed the thought. Even if it were he, torn away from his beloved bank, she hardly wanted to acknowledge him. He wouldn't welcome her anyway. She wished thoughts of him didn't haunt her, but if she imagined seeing him at every turn, she couldn't deny the fact that he remained on her mind.

At last, convinced whoever had sent the note was indeed not coming, Dessa returned to the carriage that had waited all this time—for an extra charge. She couldn't afford to wait longer.

The ride back to the city seemed quicker than the journey out to the parkland. An hour wasted, when there was so much to do at the house. Dessa alone couldn't produce enough textile goods to cover the loan. But she wouldn't have help until she reached the women that so far seemed bent on avoiding her.

Dessa's footsteps on the front stairs to the porch were far slower and heavier than they had been earlier at the prospect of meeting with her first potential client. *Have I misunderstood, Lord? What am I not seeing? What have I done wrong?*

Thoughts of Mr. Hawkins's judgment made her steps nearly unbearable.

The door was, as usual, left unlocked. It was said that these few square blocks near the tracks were the only ones in the city where the few upstanding citizens left needed to lock their doors. Dessa refused to do so. If someone was so desperate as to break into her home, a home that offered little as far as earthly possessions, then they were in far greater need than she.

After removing her gloves, hanging her hat on the hook, and wishing once again she could afford a small table for such things as gloves and pocketbooks and handbags, she stuffed the gloves inside the hat, laid the handbag on the dining room table, then headed to the kitchen. Although Dessa enjoyed cooking, she had little desire to prepare anything for herself. A cheese and tomato sandwich would do for dinner.

But at the kitchen threshold, all thoughts of food disappeared. Dessa wasn't alone.

9

"HELLO," DESSA SAID, half to cover her surprise and half because she had no idea what else to say. At the kitchen table, eating the very sandwich Dessa had planned to assemble for herself, was a woman still garbed in jacket and hat. A hat without a red flower. Cheese and a slice of tomato peeked out between two slices of bread left over from yesterday's baking.

"You the gal who runs this place?" The woman spoke with her mouth half-full, swiping her chin before taking a drink from the cup in front of her.

Dessa approached the table, seeing upon a closer look that the woman was perhaps twice her age. Although her hair was unkempt and the tight-fitting, low-cut jacket over her equally low-cut dress was somewhat rumpled, her fingernails were clean and her skin marred only by the fine lines of age.

"Yes, I'm Dessa Caldwell." She smiled. All she'd needed to do was leave the house and someone was finally seeking her! "Welcome to Pierson House."

The woman smiled, but it was crooked in a way that might have had something to do with the food still in her mouth. "I heard you're willing to take in women in trouble."

Dessa felt her eyes widen. "Are you . . . in trouble?"

The other woman laughed so loudly Dessa winced. The laugh went on, long and hearty, so that the woman had to set her sandwich on the napkin in front of her and hold her side as if it would burst if she didn't.

At last she drew in a long breath, exhausted by mirth. "Any monthly irregularities in me is due to age, girlie, and not any contribution from the male persuasion." Then she frowned as quickly as the laughter had erupted a moment ago. "Though I did have a baby once. A long time ago." She studied Dessa with a tilt of her head, eyes narrowing to reveal new wrinkles. "Would've been about your age by now, I guess. Twenty years?"

"I'm twenty-four."

"Hmm. That old and no husband? You the sportin' kind yourself, girlie?"

Dessa shook her head, approaching the bread and other items the woman had left out on the end of the table. She'd just as soon join her as have the woman eating in front of her. Taking a plate from the nearby cabinet, she returned to the table to assemble her own sandwich.

There was a single slice of tomato left, but before Dessa could add it to her cheese and bread, the woman grabbed it. She ate it in one quick bite, smiling afterward without a trace of compunction.

Dessa lifted a brow but said nothing, settling for the cheese and bread alone. "How did you hear about Pierson House, Miss . . . ?"

"You can call me Belva. It's what everybody calls me here in the city."

Dessa wondered if Belva kept her identity a secret to protect a family somewhere, or to keep anyone she once knew from finding out how she earned money. Or was it more personal than that? Sophie had once mused to Dessa that some women might hide their names to protect that secret part of themselves they never wished to sell.

"Did you find one of my applications?" Dessa poured herself a glass of lemonade from the pitcher Belva had taken from the icebox. "I've left them in the kitchens of every house that would let me, but I'm afraid they weren't very well circulated or I'd have had more response by now."

Belva laughed again, though this time it seemed more with derision than amusement. "I heard about them applications. You think any of them you sprinkled here and there actually got passed to the people you want? You know what would happen to a girl who tried to get away from one of them houses, let alone take someone else with her?"

"I see the girls on the street all the time. They seem free to do as they please." Sophie had once told her about some foreign women, mainly Chinese, who had been brought in for the Chinese men working on the railroad. Slaves, so it was rumored. But that didn't happen in other areas as far as Dessa knew. "Aren't they free?"

Belva pushed away her napkin, now empty of her own sandwich, then leaned back in her chair as if to find a fuller picture of Dessa. "Is anyone? Free, I mean?"

Dessa offered a quick, silent, barely noticeable prayer of thanksgiving for the food before biting into her sandwich. Then she allowed another moment of silence rather than acknowledging the question she doubted Belva thought answerable anyway.

The journal Sophie had left behind, one chronicling information she'd gathered from other institutions that helped fallen women, said that the older the woman, the less likely she was to reform. Dessa didn't know if that was true, or true in every case, but somehow because of that, she'd never expected someone older than herself to seek her help. Was this a person Dessa *could* help?

She pushed away her doubt. Belva was here, wasn't she? That meant she must want to try what Pierson House had to offer, and Dessa wasn't about to refuse anyone.

Besides, it might be that Belva could help Dessa as much as the other way around.

"How do I reach more women, then?"

Belva looked surprised by the question. "You want my help? Ha." But even as she revealed her surprise, she hung one arm on the back of her chair and folded her hands like a swing. She leaned closer, and the ruffle of her bodice fell onto the soiled napkin on the table. "This is what you do, girlie. You pack up and leave. Ain't nobody gonna come here; you may as well know it right now."

"You came. Aren't you here to stay?"

Belva laughed again.

Dessa placed her sandwich on her plate. "But why not? Why would women rather end their sporting career by poisoning themselves with a dime of morphine or throwing themselves from the fifth-floor staircase at the Windsor than come here?"

"At least either one of those is permanent." Her words, harshly spoken, were followed by a lift of her brows and a look around the kitchen. "Say, you got anything to drink? Other than that horrid lemony stuff? Like wine? Or better yet, whiskey?"

Dessa shook her head.

Belva huffed. "That's the first thing you ought to do, then. Get something here they want. Strong drink, for one."

"I have good food," Dessa said. "Did you like the bread?"

Belva dismissed the question with a wave of her hand. "Look, I like you, kid. You remind me of what my own daughter might have looked like, if she'd lived a minute past birth." Her brows drew together so quickly that the expression of sadness seemed almost unexpected to Belva herself. "It was just as well, I guess. I couldn'ta given her anything but heartache and shame."

"But that's just it, Belva," Dessa said. "Wouldn't it be better to get away from a lifestyle that makes you feel that way?"

Another disgusted *pfff* came from her lips. "Listen, them girls don't want to come to a place that'll only remind them of the shame. 'Specially the ones who are settled into the choices they made. I know what you do-gooders do best, and that's dole out the judgment. We ain't no frail sisters nor fallen angels, because we ain't frail and we certainly weren't never any angels."

"But I don't want to 'dole out the judgment,' as you say. Who am I to do that? My father died in the war without knowing I was on the way. My mother died the day I was born. My brother was three and we were sent to an asylum. Do you know who gave us the only love we ever knew in that place? Women just like you, Belva. Until the officials sent us away to work. I haven't any judgment against you, because I might just as well have had to earn my living the same way."

Dessa stopped her story far before it was finished, but even that much was more than she'd told anyone since coming to Denver, even Mariadela. Somehow thinking of it reminded her of a lingering cloud she found easy to ignore only when working her hardest. Memories of the day she'd turned twelve and learned her brother had been killed in an accident were darkest of all. Fallen from a hayloft, which shouldn't have killed anyone, except somehow he'd landed so that his neck had been broken. That was the last day she'd ever dreamed of reuniting with him when they were grown, to live like a real family did.

Maybe Dessa ought to have known from that day on that she hadn't been destined for family life. Her own mistake, not many years later, had closed that option for her.

Belva stood. "I gotta go." She looked away, perhaps unwilling to see the tears stinging Dessa's eyes. "Thanks for the vittles."

Then she left the kitchen and walked to the door in the parlor.

Dessa ran as far as the dining room. "But . . . are you sure you don't want to stay?" she called after Belva. "You're more than welcome! Always!"

Belva didn't even turn back as she walked out the door, leaving Dessa alone with only an urge to cry.

10

HENRY DIDN'T KNOW what he was waiting for. He'd chanced to spot Miss Caldwell out at City Park, where he'd taken his brisk constitutional at midafternoon, having been expected at the bank too early to do it before going in. Sitting behind a desk wasn't to his liking in many ways, a rare negative aspect of the banking career he'd sought nearly all his life. The park suitably answered that need, drawing him as it did many who were more comfortable away from the city.

Having seen Miss Caldwell lingering, he'd almost approached her. But the circumstances of the luncheon still sat heavily, so he'd walked in the opposite direction and circled back to his carriage. Then he'd waited, reading through an entire issue of the *Denver Sentinel* while he did so. Obviously this was no pleasure visit to the park for her, no taking in the air or simple enjoyment of the mountain view just beyond the plain. She was waiting for someone. Another drunkard?

But she never met anyone.

Despite his better judgment he'd instructed Fallo, his carriage driver, to follow her hired cab. As expected, it took her back to Pierson House. Why he waited any longer he did not know, except for a niggling suspicion he wished to banish. He wanted to be sure the business for which she'd borrowed money was indeed everything she'd described. That meant women going in and out of this establishment—and *no* men.

It wasn't long before his patience was rewarded. The front door opened, but instead of Miss Caldwell, another woman emerged. Someone he'd not seen before. Henry leaned back in the carriage, out of view from the window, and waited until she'd traveled some distance before deciding to follow.

He watched the woman walk—strut—down the street, away from Pierson House. From the cut of her gown to the sway of her hips, she was no doubt headed back toward the Line: that row of bordellos along Market Street.

He bumped his cane on the roof of the carriage and his driver pulled forward, according to Henry's signal. He would see where this woman went.

Not since his youthful days before college had Henry been so beset with foolishness. He knew his suspicions were ground-less. Miss Caldwell was an innocent. An idealistic do-gooder. But the thought of her dealing alone with that drunkard—and in the middle of the night, no less—had alternately annoyed and impressed him. Annoyed him for all the obvious reasons. If a lamb ventured into the slaughterhouse, it had no one but itself to blame for its demise. On the other hand, Miss Caldwell had not only chosen to reside within the narrow radius of the state's most noto-riously sin-packed district; she also apparently believed this was exactly where she belonged.

Evidently this woman of ill virtue was exactly the kind of per-son Miss Caldwell sought. Why did she seek them? Did her faith blind her to all sensible reasoning?

When the woman slowed her pace just down the street, Henry leaned forward. Though she did not stop, she paused before a neat, sturdy brick structure. Henry needed only glance at the two finely dressed women lounging on the wide front porch, a little white poodle on each lap, to guess it was a parlor house. Those poodles they paraded with them throughout the city came with such an obvious label that no respectable woman in town dared own one.

He looked again at the building. It was no doubt a more expensive place of prostitution but offered the same services nonetheless.

Despite a wave from the women and a friendly yap from one of the dogs, the woman Henry followed kept walking. At last she turned at the second corner, and he tapped the carriage ceiling again—three quick raps for a right. It mildly surprised him that this woman went right rather than left. Her clothing, from what he could tell, was more likely to grace the halls of a two-bit joint than something in the nicer neighborhood she headed into now.

Two blocks later, she crossed in front of the carriage and Henry gave a quick knock instructing the driver to stop altogether. Then, moving from one side of the carriage to the other, he watched her walk down the lightly traveled street. It was late afternoon, an hour when gambling dens and dance halls were still tightly closed. These streets wouldn't come alive again until after the sun set, and then they'd be abuzz with activity until nearly dawn.

There was one place on this street Henry hoped she would pass, but something in his gut told him that was exactly where she headed.

To the Verandah. Turk Foster's dance hall, named for its wide balcony spanning the entire facade on the second floor. Neither the name nor the rented rooms upstairs gave a clue that inside was one of the most profitable gambling dens in the city.

Henry guessed this wasn't the only business Foster owned, though for public record it was the only one he acknowledged. As a dance hall it was technically legitimate, even though it quietly attracted some of the wealthiest gamblers in the city—patrons of the so-called arts. The variety theater kind.

But something about this woman didn't match. Certainly no one employed at the Verandah would dress in such a humble fashion, not even on an errand of her own. So what was she doing, marching right inside as if she lived there? Had she sneaked out to investigate a place like Pierson House for herself? Would she leave behind the splendor of Foster's and dress in the lowest fashion she'd falsely presented just now?

Or had Foster sent her for some reason? It made sense that he wanted to keep an eye on what went on in his little corner of hell, a kingdom he undoubtedly ruled—to the extent the other miscreants and the law allowed. But why take any interest in a place like Miss Caldwell's? It wasn't exactly his competition.

Henry shook his head, exasperated as much with himself as with the questions. He rapped on the carriage roof again and the vehicle rolled on, this time in the direction of the city center. He didn't breathe easily until reaching his own neighborhood, whose residents might visit Turk's ward from time to time but nearly always refused to admit it.

※

"So she didn't stay longer than that?" Mariadela asked. She and Dessa worked in the kitchen, cutting vegetables for a pickled salad they would serve the following day at another meal, this time a dinner party. The gathering was to be held for those who had donated to Pierson House—far more willingly, Dessa knew, than had at least one guest of the luncheon two days before. And although Mr. Ridgeway had been extended an invitation, Mr. Hawkins had not. He likely would not have accepted anyway.

"No. She stayed barely long enough to finish her sandwich. The whole conversation was unsettling." Dessa paused from chopping the carrots in front of her to look out the window with a sigh. "She made it seem as though the girls will never choose to leave what they know."

"They'll come, Dessa. You did the right thing. You told her you weren't here to judge them, just to offer them refuge."

Although Dessa had told Mariadela that Belva seemed convinced a bed in Pierson House automatically came with judgment, she hadn't talked about the rest of the conversation. Some memories were best forgotten, even ones that had been not only pivotal in her willingness to help Sophie with her vision but the reason she'd been chosen to do so in the first place.

"Besides," Mariadela added, "she wasn't the woman with the red flower in her hat; you said so yourself. Perhaps that one will show up on your doorstep any moment now."

"I hope so." Dessa sighed again. "Being unable to draw women here will jeopardize future donations; it could end them altogether if the rooms upstairs are empty much longer. It was hard enough to garner the amount of money we raised in the first place."

"Every mission takes time to get established."

Now Dessa paused over the vegetables to frown. "I worry about the Plumsteads' not accepting tomorrow's invitation."

"Stop worrying! They simply had another engagement, and besides, it gave you the opportunity to invite Reverend Sempkins and his wife instead. They've brought in more donors than anyone else we know."

Dessa didn't want to worry, but she couldn't deny how desperately she depended upon the Plumsteads' support. Without their monthly pledge, she'd be unable to meet her regular payments to the bank. And until proving Pierson House a success, it would be impossible to attract new donors. She must fill those beds!

"Listen, Mariadela." Dessa's heart thumped with anticipation to share an idea Belva's visit had ignited. "What if we expand our expected clientele?"

"What do you mean?"

"Belva reminded me that older women in the brothels aren't apt to come to a place like this. And I've been going through

Sophie's journal again, where she mentions what she thought were the failures of other missions like this one. Things she wanted to avoid."

"You've already made clear on the applications that Pierson House is a place of refuge for all women in distress, regardless of past or present circumstance."

Dessa nodded. "But what if we sought the youngest girls? Ones who haven't yet taken up the sporting life but might be tempted to it because of the money? The ones who are working at a factory for pennies a day, either on their own or with families who can barely afford to live? Or . . . what if we found a way to reach those who've been brought to such a life against their will? Sophie interviewed more than one woman who started out by being tricked into such a lifestyle."

"That's fine, Dessa," said Mariadela, although her tone sounded anything but inspired. "But how would we find these girls, except the way you've already tried? By distributing the applications to the very spots such a girl would show up—at the back door of every brothel or crib in town."

"I plan to go to the factories, too, where girls are paid so little."

Mariadela nodded. "A good idea. I'll send my boys with you to help."

"And then there are the Chinese women who've been brought here as slaves. We could—"

"Stop right there." Mariadela set aside the peas she'd started shucking and stared grimly at Dessa. "For one thing, white society doesn't mix with the Chinese—like it or not, that's the way it is. The quickest way to stop donations is to interfere in a culture we know nothing about. A culture that, rightly or wrongly, was blamed not all that long ago for taking jobs from whites when they crossed the railroad workers' picket lines. You weren't here during the riots with the Chinese. I was."

"But what do girls who have been brought here as slaves have to do with all that?"

"No, Dessa." Mariadela's tone and gaze were stern. "It's too dangerous. Listen to me on this. You know it's hard enough to find support for the kind of women you want to help. How much easier it would be to raise funds for anything else—orphans or men still disabled from the war . . . or even abandoned puppies. But Chinese women? You may disagree, but your Mr. Hawkins won't be the only one wanting foreclosure on this house if we take in women from Hop Alley; I guarantee you that."

Dessa heaved the deepest sigh yet. *Why, Lord, is life so unfair?*

11

HENRY STARED at the oblong sign Tobias held across his lap on the carriage seat opposite him. Carved from one of the many pines Colorado was known to grow so well and etched with the words *Pierson House*.

"How many people do you suppose will be attending tonight?" Henry asked. He already regretted agreeing to go along. Hopefully there would be enough guests that he could ignore those who would readily ignore him in return.

Tobias shifted in his seat, and the sign nearly fell to the floor of the carriage. "Oh, I don't know. How many would her table sit? Six? Eight? Perhaps ten at the most."

Something in his uncle's demeanor made Henry redirect his gaze from the view beyond the carriage. Was it his imagination, or had the always-honest Tobias Ridgeway done something that made him nervous?

"I'm surprised she wants me anywhere near those who willingly emptied their pockets for such a place."

Tobias smiled, but his eyes darted away too quickly for Henry to be satisfied. "It'll be good for you to spend time with people who believe in her." His voice held all the enthusiasm Henry was accustomed to hearing from him, especially when involved in something with which Henry disagreed. "You may come away tonight with an entirely new perspective."

That Henry doubted, wondering yet again why he'd chosen to accept this particular invitation when he'd easily refused so many in the past.

⚜

"You don't think William will be late, do you?"

Mariadela's face didn't offer very convincing assurance. The mercantile closed early on Tuesday evenings, which was why Dessa had chosen tonight for the donors' dinner. But having known the Whites for the past two years, she'd seen how many times both of them had been held late with work or seeing to the needs or demands of a lingering customer.

Fortunately Mariadela had brought her oldest two daughters to help with last-minute preparations—though Dessa had been working all day and Mariadela had helped most of yesterday, too. If the girls had waited for their father to bring them, there would be no one to offer the punch before dinner or to serve the meal itself. But the sad fact was, having his best two workers away from the shop meant closing time for William might take that much longer.

"Everything will be fine, Dessa," Mariadela said at last. The table was set, Mariadela's daughters were in the kitchen donning crisp aprons straight from the mercantile, and every aspect of the meal—from the vermicelli soup to the braised beef to the apricot soufflé—had turned out to perfection. The new stove was everything Dessa had hoped it would be, allowing cooking and baking to be a pleasure.

"I love what you did with the leftover trim paint," Mariadela said, looking at the stenciled decoration Dessa had added to both the parlor and the dining room. They couldn't afford the more fashionable wallpaper, so Dessa had improvised by adding a pineapple pattern to one wall in each of the two rooms. That was all she had time for, but she thought it might be enough.

Dessa wanted to be pleased by the compliment, but her thoughts couldn't be drawn from the evening ahead. Mrs. Naracott had sent a note earlier in the afternoon saying she and her husband would be bringing an extra man—their sturdiest coachman—with them tonight. Their driver would take the carriage to a safer neighborhood to wait for them, but if Dessa agreed, they would leave the coachman to stand guard on the porch so they could eat in complete comfort inside, knowing they were safe. He wouldn't, of course, be expected to sit at the table, so Dessa was not to worry about food or a place setting.

Even Reverend and Mrs. Sempkins sent a note inquiring if a luncheon might have been a better choice to introduce Pierson House. Was it safe to come to such a neighborhood after dark?

Dessa had reassured them that she'd deliberately scheduled the meal for six rather than eight so they could feel free to leave before the sun had set.

Mr. Ridgeway was likely to notice the temporary guard lingering on the front porch. Hopefully he wouldn't think she'd spent money that should go to the bank to hire the man on a permanent basis!

She'd extended tonight's invitation to Mr. Ridgeway's wife as well, but quickly received a note back that she was up in Cheyenne with her sister. Though Dessa had been disappointed that she wouldn't be able to meet the woman tonight, it was probably fortunate that Mrs. Ridgeway wasn't able to come. At least Dessa's table would be evenly set. One of the new dangers she faced as an unmarried hostess was juggling the number of guests to accommodate a balanced table.

When a knock sounded—fifteen minutes before the invitation prescribed—Dessa's heart twittered as she hurried through the dining room to answer the door.

But it wasn't anyone she expected. Instead, she found a boy holding the largest bouquet of flowers she'd ever seen.

"Delivery for you, miss." He shoved the flowers toward her.

"How lovely! But where did they come from?"

"Compliments of Mr. Turk Foster. And with a friendly welcome to the neighborhood."

Then, before she could hope to find a nickel or even a penny to tip him, he ran off.

"What's this?" asked Mariadela, removing the apron from around her waist.

"A boy just delivered them. He said they were from someone by the name of Turk Foster."

Mariadela's brows shot up with such surprise that the delivery might have been a prickly cactus rather than a colorful array of flowers.

"I'm not sure I've heard that name yet," Dessa said as she walked back to the kitchen. The flowers were too tall for the dining room table, but wouldn't they look nice in the parlor, to brighten up the table in the corner? She could move the oil lamp to the floor. No need of that tonight, with the old house's gas lighting in fine working order. "But if he's from the neighborhood, he must be someone I should get to know."

"As far as I know, he's one of the richest gamblers in Denver. Why he should send flowers is beyond me."

"The boy said they were to welcome me to the neighborhood." As she spoke, Dessa rescued an empty paint can from the porch. She lined it with a towel to keep any paint residue from the stems, then added water from the faucet and returned to the parlor with the attractive arrangement. There was such an array of upright and cascading flowers that they hid the can altogether.

Mariadela huffed behind Dessa. "Pierson House isn't exactly a rival for Mr. Foster's dance hall. I don't understand why he would single you out with flowers. I'm sure he doesn't welcome other businesses here on any regular basis. Why would he?"

"No matter," Dessa said lightly. "Perhaps he was used of God and doesn't even know it. Our dinner party needed something like this to make it special."

A knock at the door sounded again and there was no time for Dessa to consider the reason behind the delivery. Perhaps God really did have something to do with it! The sentiment inspired exactly enough confidence for her to greet her first guests with a welcoming smile.

❧

The door and windows to the two-story brick home were all open as Henry's carriage pulled up. From his seat he could see straight into the parlor and spotted a number of people standing and holding beverages.

Dissatisfaction formed in his chest. It seemed an entirely busier place than the way it appeared in the middle of the day. Henry wasn't at all sure he liked the transformation.

But then, how else was it to look when a party—even a respectable dinner party—was to be held?

Surprisingly, Uncle Tobias let himself out of the carriage first. He seemed in somewhat of a hurry as he nearly bounded up the few stairs, past a man lingering on the small cement porch. A closer look revealed the man on the porch to be a servant of some kind, by the polish of his boots and the bow he offered. Had Miss Caldwell been able to hire protection for the evening? But why, when for the first time she had ample company to keep her safe? Surely she didn't want to present to her guests the truth about the dangers of this neighborhood.

Nothing made sense when it came to this woman.

Miss Caldwell herself greeted Tobias at the door, a look of pleasure and welcome making an already lovely face that much lovelier. For a moment Henry wished the expression wouldn't end when she looked at him, but he prepared himself for the inevitable.

Her frown appeared, as expected. What he didn't expect was the surprise that accompanied it, tinged slightly by what looked almost like horror. Had his behavior at their luncheon so thoroughly revealed how little he believed in this mission of hers?

If so, he should turn around right now.

"Mr. Hawkins." Her voice was more welcoming than her initial expression had been, so he had to give her credit for a speedy recovery. "How very nice to see you again."

Henry tipped his head her way as he removed his hat. A moment later she took the hat from him, along with his walking stick and Tobias's accessories. Glancing around the room, he saw an older couple he recognized as the Naracotts. They were on his investors' dinner guest list every year as influential participants in the financial world, and they attended faithfully. The Clarks, who banked with him, were present too. A glance past both of the men to their wives revealed surprise similar to Miss Caldwell's.

"Well, Hawkins!" said Homer Naracott. "We didn't think we'd see you here tonight."

Leland Clark approached as well, offering a raised brow and a laugh. "I've often wondered what it would take to get you to accept a social invitation. Evidently the secret is for the request to come from a lovely and available young woman."

Henry had little patience for their fun. Just as another man approached, someone Henry did not know, he excused himself to follow after Miss Caldwell. Little did he care that such an action only reinforced their banter. He may host two parties every year, but even so he'd never overpracticed social niceties. He wasn't about to start now.

✻

"What are we going to do?" Dessa fretted to Mariadela, who was seeing to last-minute details of the meal.

Her friend was frowning but hardly appeared as rattled as Dessa felt. Mariadela had the presence of mind to perfectly slice—with a very sharp knife—the bread they would serve with the meal.

"Not to worry, dear," said Mariadela. "We'll just add another plate when William arrives, as if he's the unexpected addition. No one will be the wiser that we didn't expect Mr. Hawkins."

"Then I suppose we should start the meal right away," Dessa said. "Before William arrives. Is everything ready?"

She would have turned to the oven to see for herself, but a shadow at the kitchen threshold caught her attention, the very object of her distress. How long had he been standing there?

"Mr. Hawkins," she greeted him again, approaching to lead him out of the kitchen. "If you'd like some punch before we sit down to dinner, Mrs. White's daughters are serving in the—"

He was already shaking his head and appeared in no mind to follow her direction to leave. "You didn't expect me tonight, did you?"

"Why, we had every hope . . ." The polite lie died on her lips as she saw one of his brows skeptically rise.

Mariadela came between them with a basket of sliced bread in her hands. "Mr. Hawkins, even I know you never attend parties. If that isn't enough, it was clear from the day you came here that Tobias Ridgeway approved the loan, not you. Can you blame her if she didn't send you an invitation?"

Mr. Hawkins crossed his arms, looking between the two women. "I want to be perfectly clear. Not only did you not expect me, but you never even extended an invitation to me?"

Evidently Mariadela felt as Dessa did; silence was confirmation enough.

If Dessa had not expected him, even less did she expect a sudden burst of his laughter. Yet he issued a deep, hearty bellow, one that seemed to have been trapped inside him for quite some time and had just now found a way to emerge.

Dessa exchanged a glance with Mariadela, who looked equally confused.

Before long Mr. Hawkins leaned against the doorframe, laughter fading, arms still crossed. Then he stood taller, unfolding his arms, and gave them a brief bow. He was back to the formal banker so quickly Dessa might have doubted he'd departed from his typical image, even for that brief moment of mirth.

"The truth is I haven't found anything so funny in years. Do you know how many social invitations I've ignored since setting up business here in Denver?"

Dessa shook her head.

"Nor do I, actually. Countless. Tonight I accept an invitation, only to learn one wasn't even issued. I find that funny. Don't you?"

Now it was Dessa's turn to fold her arms. While she thought him even more handsome when he smiled, she wasn't at all sure she should be amused. What was she to say to the others? How could they possibly add another plate to an already-crowded table when William arrived and not have it seem the social mistake that it was?

Another question emerged above her concerns. "Why did you accept this invitation, then—if one had come?" Perhaps embarrassing her before her biggest donors was something else that might amuse him.

"That's a very good question," he said softly. "Would you rather I left?"

"No, of course not." Her answer was hasty, but she was surprised to realize it was every bit as sincere as it was swift. If he stayed, perhaps he could see for himself the confidence her donors had in her.

"But if my count is correct, there are three couples—six people—in your parlor right now. Mr. and Mrs. White bring that total to eight. Including yourself, Miss Caldwell, along with my uncle, if I stay there will be eleven required to sit at a table that will barely seat ten. I'm afraid my one venture out to a society party has created more trouble than it's worth."

"There is only one solution," Mariadela said, and Dessa turned her attention to her gratefully, since she hadn't a clue what to do. "I'll stay in the kitchen. No one has seen me yet anyway, just my girls who are helping out. Everyone will think I never intended to sit."

"But what about William? You would have him sit at the table without you? And what of your gown? You look dressed to attend a party, not to serve at one."

"Nothing an apron won't hide. We'll easily explain he could never be trusted to help serve a dish, so we had to put him at the table or he'd have gone hungry."

Dessa wanted to hug her. "Oh, Mariadela!"

But Mr. Hawkins was shaking his head. "It hardly seems fair to you if I take your place, Mrs. White. I can easily leave through the back door and be forgotten in a moment."

Mariadela laughed now, with pure amusement. "Not since they've seen you. I'm sure your arrival made an impression."

Without further discussion, Dessa led the way back to the parlor, where she announced dinner would be served just as soon as their final guest arrived. No sooner had she spoken than William entered with an apology for keeping hungry people from a meal.

❧

Henry folded the napkin beside his plate. One thing the meal reminded him of: if Miss Caldwell hoped to draw people to this place through her cooking, she was well equipped to do so. He'd had a second helping of that apricot soufflé, after he thought he couldn't eat another bite.

He could barely believe what he felt inside as he looked around the dining room. Here, at this table filled with people from whom he'd so long hidden himself, he found a sense of community. Something that was sadly absent at the obligatory dinner parties he held.

Even as it was surprisingly pleasant to be reminded of such a feeling, he wondered what any of them would say if they knew the truth about him. Not only that he hadn't a bit of their belief in Miss Caldwell's mission, but the truth of his past. He may not have hurt anyone all those years ago, but his crime certainly hadn't been victimless. He'd stolen money he had no right to take. How would any of them feel if he'd stolen from them?

He wondered yet again if there was some connection between those bothersome notes he'd received and his crime. Asking around to see if other businessmen had been targeted, perhaps by a church trying a new method of attracting members, had led nowhere. Without revealing the existence of the notes, there seemed no way to investigate in any depth.

He needed, once again, to leave all that behind him. It was impossible that anyone should know what he'd done so long ago. Impossible.

Besides, Henry could console himself with the knowledge that five years ago he'd made an anonymous repayment to both Wells Fargo and the mine from which he'd taken the money. The banking portion of his business had succeeded by then, as he'd always been sure that it would. Repaying the illegal loan had suspended some of the guilt he'd carried.

Still, Henry had denied himself any life apart from his work because of that secret. Even after restitution, he realized secrets never really died. Those notes proved it, whether or not the two were connected. Secrets only hibernated. If the truth came out, his bank would fail and Henry knew it.

Anyway, he was so set in his private ways that he didn't want to change anymore. Not even for what he'd found at this table. It was too late.

"Yes, I noticed the man outside on the porch," William White was saying. He sipped his coffee. "I thought you'd been able to hire someone."

"As grateful as I am for Mrs. Naracott's coachman tonight," Miss Caldwell said with a gracious smile at the other woman, "I've been safe on my own. Except . . ." Her gaze landed briefly on Henry. "I did have a man well into his cups come visiting here in the middle of the night once, but he was easily directed to the porch, and after that I was more careful about locking the doors at night."

"Goodness!" said the reverend's wife, Mrs. Sempkins. "I'm sure I don't know what I'd have done."

"Likely leaving him alone would have been enough," Miss Caldwell said. "He was well past all sensibility or harm. I'm really fine here. In any case, I own nothing anyone would want to steal. Except for the wonderful new stove that cooked this meal." To Henry's surprise, she smiled at him, and he found himself unable to do anything but offer a small one in return. "And that would be rather hard to get out of the door, if I can judge by its delivery."

He'd have wondered if she were trying to coax a reaction from him, but her face lacked all malice. So he let himself enjoy the private jest between them as others complimented her use of that kitchen stove.

"It's too bad you don't have dear Miss Pierson here to live with you," Mrs. Naracott said. "At least two might be safer than one."

"Yes, I miss her every day of my life," Miss Caldwell said. Had she purposely avoided acknowledging the censure in the other's tone?

"She was so sensible," Mrs. Naracott went on. "Not to mention a formidable person in her demeanor and forthrightness. I recall her saying, though, Miss Caldwell, that she didn't plan to move into the neighborhood for a few more years, allowing the two of you to establish friendships and trust first. What made you decide to move in so soon?"

This time, not surprisingly, Miss Caldwell avoided any eye contact with Henry. "How many girls might be lost in the next few years if we waited?"

"But if they haven't the trust, as seems obvious from your lack of clients, perhaps the opening might have been better served by Miss Pierson's plan."

Tobias raised one of his hands to attract the eyes now focused on an increasingly uncomfortable-looking Miss Caldwell. "If I may say so, Miss Caldwell's research was thorough enough to compare experiences from two other such missions. It's not uncommon to begin modestly, then multiply. I have no reason to believe that pattern won't be repeated right here."

"Miss Pierson never expected immediate success," Miss Caldwell added, sounding less confident than she had before the conversation took such a turn. "Patience was one of her many virtues."

One that, perhaps, Miss Caldwell lacked? Henry didn't have to voice the question to see he wasn't the only one wondering.

🌿

The sun was barely setting behind the mountains by the time Dessa said good night to many of her guests—only the Whites and Mr. Ridgeway remained. And Mr. Hawkins.

Like the servants whose roles they'd taken that evening, Mariadela and her daughters whisked away the dishes, insisting Dessa leave the cleaning to them. Although she'd spent the majority of her years doing those things for others, she knew that until the two bankers left, she had little choice but to continue playing the hostess.

Ever since Mrs. Naracott had voiced her doubts, Dessa had thought of little else. Only when the conversation took on a lighter tone did she force herself to listen. They talked about an electric trolley that promised to revolutionize the movement of people all over the city. People needed no longer live, work, and die within the same small radius once such a marvelous thing came to town.

With so few of them left in the parlor, Mr. Ridgeway asked William White to accompany him out to the porch to help affix the sign he'd brought as a gift to Dessa. Delighted that the sign would be hung so quickly, she hurried off to find a hammer, hooks, and nails. Then she moved to follow them outside.

"No need to come out until the task is over, Miss Caldwell," Mr. Ridgeway said. "The night's surprisingly chilly."

She might have argued—she found the temperature quite comfortable—except William claimed he worked best with a partner but without an audience. So since she hadn't the energy to go against both of them, she stayed inside.

Unfortunately, with the girls and Mariadela busy in the kitchen, that left Dessa alone in the parlor with Mr. Hawkins. The very person she'd hoped to avoid speaking to, now that he knew he wasn't alone in his doubts about her plans.

She told herself not to be nervous; after all, he hadn't rescinded the loan, and even though his quiet presence hadn't given much of a clue as to whether or not he'd enjoyed his first social outing in years, he hadn't been the first to leave. Maybe that meant something.

Before she could ask, he spoke. "I told Tobias that you should consider opening Pierson House as a café. After two excellent meals here, I no longer take those words lightly. You could, you know."

Her heart skipped a beat. Was that what he thought she should do with his bank's money? "It's the soul, not the belly, I'm hoping to see filled." Then, because she didn't want to risk reigniting the sour mood she knew him capable of showing, she added a smile. "Even with the best stove in the neighborhood."

He held her gaze, and for a moment seemed younger than he normally appeared. When he'd laughed earlier, so unexpectedly, he'd looked young then, too. Hiding behind that banker's facade might be a man who could attract many a woman—well, at least ones unlike Dessa, those who hadn't the benefit of a mentor like Sophie to show them there were other things besides marriage that a woman might reach for.

"I saw you the other day," he said without looking away. "At City Park. You appeared to be waiting for someone."

She nodded. So she hadn't imagined seeing him there. "I'd received a note from a woman who said she wanted to meet me. But she didn't arrive after all, much to my disappointment. I'm confident she'll reach me again, though."

"There was at least one person here tonight, Miss Caldwell, who was surprised that you haven't yet housed any of the women you hope to help. Has it surprised you, this slow start to your mission?"

"Anything slow surprises me, Mr. Hawkins."

※

Henry let his gaze linger on her again, for the first time wondering if they had something in common. How many times had impatience gotten the best of him? Starting with the way he'd gathered his own investment money.

But he didn't allow those thoughts to progress. The differences between them were vast and varied. And the fact remained that though he might have offered restitution for his past, a man with a secret was still a man who couldn't count on a secure future. Or offer to share such a tenuous future with anyone else.

"I have faith Pierson House will be everything God wants it to be," Miss Caldwell said. "Sometimes I try to get ahead of God's plans, I admit, but we're nearly always going in the same direction. I hope you aren't worried about the loan, because I assure you this place will be filled with a force of needleworkers in no time at all, and each bed that's used will inspire even more donations to keep us going."

He didn't believe her for a moment, and right then he wasn't sure she believed herself. But he could afford to offer her some comfort, thanks in no small part to having just partaken of another of her excellent meals. "I have no desire to foreclose on this property, Miss Caldwell." He allowed himself another look around at the freshly painted walls, taking in the décor she'd cleverly added with a paintbrush. "This house is already worth more than what you paid for it, even considering its proximity to a less desirable neighborhood. I'd rather not take it back. If we counted you out, the only type of buyer to be found in this neighborhood would likely be a madam. Brothels aren't the kind of business my bank wants to invest in."

"I'll never sell to such a place!"

The passion behind her statement surprised him, and he studied her for a moment. "Is it possible, Miss Caldwell, that you hate this neighborhood, after all?"

"Not the neighborhood, Mr. Hawkins. Just the businesses that trap women inside of them."

Just then William White entered from the front door, eager to show Miss Caldwell where he and Tobias had hung the sign.

Nonetheless her words—and her obvious passion against a major portion of her surroundings—left him wondering if she wasn't so blind to this neighborhood's faults as he'd believed.

12

DESSA PUSHED AGAIN on the bar that boarded the doors to the empty carriage house. It was either such a tight fit inside the latch that it stuck, or it had been sealed somehow. Most likely the doors hadn't been opened in years; certainly they hadn't been opened since she'd moved in. Glancing around for something to pry apart the wide double doors, sparing her fingers in the process, she found a slim and sturdy stick that might have been fashioned for just such a task.

Fearing that even the stick wasn't strong enough, she was about to give up when the board popped out of place. The doors sprang free, nearly hitting her in the face in their eagerness to open.

She peered inside the old building, only half surprised to see the sun lighting the area from above. Looking up, she spotted a hole in the roof just as she heard the scampering of some small animal in the opposite corner. A squirrel with fat cheeks flicked a curly tail. It ran one direction, then the other before disappearing under an opening beneath one of the walls.

She needed to find some kind of suitable wood in here to add to the sign Mr. Ridgeway had brought. Looking around, not immediately finding any prospects, she pondered prying a wallboard loose if nothing else was available. One at the rear appeared to be hanging precariously already. Obviously the rickety shelter offered little protection from wildlife, so removing a board would make little difference.

When the doors had opened so violently, they'd loosed what she guessed to be years of dust and dirt from their crevices. But now that her eyes had adjusted to the relative darkness, she realized the carriage house was far more orderly than she would have expected of a place with a hole in the roof and wild animals living inside. There was even a cot set off to the side, narrow but complete with a pillow and blanket. An old jacket was cast over the foot.

The dusty floor was empty except for a rusted and abandoned hitch, a few broken pieces of wood that may have come from the roof, and a curiously placed bowl in the corner, near the spot where the squirrel had been hiding. If she didn't know better, she'd say it had been storing nuts there, from the few left in the center. Didn't squirrels bury nuts and seeds?

Deciding against taking the wallboard—at least having it in place, even if it was wobbly, gave a brief impression the building was still sound—she fought with the doors to close them again, then brushed her gingham skirt free of soil as she made her way back inside the house.

She would speak to Mr. Ridgeway about where he'd acquired the wood for the sign he'd given her. It was likely best to have her addition match his anyway, if she was to attract anyone with it.

❧

"Come in," Henry responded to the knock at his office door.

As expected, Mr. Sprott stuck his head around the door, though he did not step inside. "There is a Mr. . . . Smith . . . to see you, sir. He doesn't have an appointment." Then Mr. Sprott entered after all, leaving the door open behind him as he stepped closer to Henry's desk. "He's quite young and seems a bit nervous," he whispered, "and asked to speak to the bank president alone. Should I send him off?"

Henry did not need to leave his desk to give the visitor the benefit of a glance. He could easily be seen just outside the open office door, staring intently in the direction of the vault.

The boy was slight of build and did indeed look as nervous as Mr. Sprott claimed, with one hand in his pocket and the other twitching now and then. He was narrow-shouldered and couldn't be more than eighteen years of age by the smoothness of his chin. Though it was a somewhat shadowed chin. Dirt? Surely he was too young to have much of a beard. By the simple black cap that covered him from nape to crown and the rough cut of his jacket, Henry guessed whatever business he had with the bank was inconsequential at best. Another miner looking for an investor, no doubt. One so scrawny wasn't likely to go far.

Henry was about to tell Mr. Sprott to send the boy on his way when he spotted Miss Caldwell going into Tobias's office.

The sight of her simultaneously intrigued and alarmed him. There was only one reason he could imagine for her visit to his bank, and particularly to Tobias's office. She probably wanted to borrow more money.

"Send him in," Henry told his clerk. If the boy wanted anything of the slightest interest, he could provide the excuse Henry needed to make his way into Tobias's office before Miss Caldwell left.

⁂

"Yes, that's right," Dessa told Mr. Ridgeway, who had immediately, even happily, ushered her into his office. "I'd like it hung just below the one you've already provided."

"And it's to say what, exactly?" Mr. Ridgeway picked up a pencil.

"'Free Beauty Lessons, Tuesdays at Two.' Would that be too many words, do you suppose? Can it easily fit on a piece of wood roughly the same size as the Pierson House sign?"

"Oh yes, yes, I'm sure my man can make it to your specifications." Still, he looked baffled. "But why would you want to offer such lessons? Won't that . . . well, won't it encourage women in the business you're trying to *dis*courage?"

She leaned forward, allowing her smile to broaden. "That's just it, Mr. Ridgeway. The beauty lessons I'm proposing will be to beautify the soul. Because after all, God has the power to make everything beautiful, hasn't He? We've only to look at what He's created to see that. I'm willing to stoop to whatever ploy I need to get them inside the door. How do you like my idea?"

He stroked his smooth double chin. "Well, of course I have so little experience with such . . ." But before he'd even finished his sentence, he offered her a smile with a twinkle in his eye. "It's worth a try, Miss Caldwell. I'll have the sign readied immediately and come by to affix it myself before the week is over. Will next Tuesday be soon enough to offer your first lesson?"

Dessa stood and extended her hand to him. "Oh yes, and thank you, Mr. Ridgeway! God has blessed me through you once again. I'm very grateful."

He led her outside his office, one hand politely at her elbow. "I'm sure you're full of wonderful ideas, Miss Caldwell," he was saying, but just then his gaze left hers for a spot beyond her shoulder.

Dessa turned to see what he was looking at. She'd hoped not to run into Mr. Hawkins, but there he was, just emerging from his office. A shorter man, and younger—surely no more than a boy—held Mr. Hawkins's arm at an odd angle, nearly behind his back. That Mr. Hawkins would allow such contact was curious indeed, until Dessa saw the desperate look on the young man's shadowy face, glimpsed only when he twisted his head from side to side to see beyond the brim of a hat that was too large.

"Stand back!" Though no one had approached, the boy yelled the words anyway, waving a glass vial above his head. His high-pitched voice alone betrayed his youth. "Everybody! Stand where you are. Don't move!"

Mr. Hawkins held out his free arm, palm down, as if to offer what comfort he could. Though he appeared stiff, on edge, he was not in a panic.

The youth pushed Mr. Hawkins forward, and the banker obliged by walking steadily toward the vault. Neither Mr. Hawkins nor the boy with the strange glass vial ever looked Dessa's way.

Whispers sprang up in every direction. Mr. Sprott, the clerk Dessa had met on previous visits, stepped forward, but Mr. Hawkins shifted his palm upward to halt the clerk's progress.

"He has nitro, Mr. Sprott," Mr. Hawkins said, far more calmly than the boy at his back had spoken a moment ago. His pronouncement sparked such stark terror in the mild clerk that even before the words registered in Dessa's mind, she felt his fear. "You'll want to stand still so you don't startle this man into dropping the vial. All of you." Mr. Hawkins raised his voice, but only in volume, not in alarm. "Just let him go about his business and it'll be over in a moment. That's it. Calmly."

Dessa watched, heart thumping, as Mr. Hawkins opened the bars that stood as the first deterrent to entering the massive vault behind them. During business hours the money was evidently rather easy to access, based on the mere moments it took Mr. Hawkins to fill a bag while the young man dangled the glass vial of powerful nitroglycerin—a substance that could easily bite away chunks of the Rocky Mountains to uncover gold and silver hiding within.

What would happen if he dropped that vial here? Surely the vault, and everyone around it, would be blasted to the sky. Including Mr. Hawkins.

Mr. Ridgeway, at Dessa's side, took a small step forward—but only far enough to stand in front of Dessa. She peered around his shoulder to watch as the boy received a bag filled with notes and greenbacks—perhaps even some gold, judging from the heavy appearance of the bag.

Then, in possession of what he'd come for, the youth turned on his heel and ran toward the bank door.

Only to trip and land sprawled on the floor not three feet from freedom.

Dessa was sure she wasn't the only one to close her eyes in sheer terror, preparing for impact. She raised her hands to cover her face—but nothing, absolutely nothing happened.

Before even the first shriek sounded, Dessa saw Mr. Hawkins chase after the boy. The youth had barely regained his footing before the banker seized him round the waist, tackling him to the floor and directly into the small puddle of whatever innocuous liquid had been in that vial.

The bag of money tumbled from his grip, spewing its contents much as the vial had.

With the would-be thief already down, people gathered round, Dessa among them. A clerk gathered up the loot, replacing it in the sack.

Mr. Hawkins's jacket was askew, his hair fallen down over his brow, but he was the first to his feet. Somehow he managed to keep hold of the boy's collar, and as the guard who evidently was just outside the building was summoned, Mr. Hawkins thrust the thief toward the confines of his office. They both disappeared inside.

"You'll excuse me, won't you, Miss Caldwell?" Mr. Ridgeway had clearly been disturbed by the incident, as evidenced by the beads of sweat on his forehead and upper lip.

"Oh, of course! But may I stay? It's all such a blur. . . . I need a moment to catch my breath."

It wasn't entirely the truth, since she'd left out her urge to assure herself that Mr. Hawkins was unharmed. Though why that was the first thought on her mind she did not know. How heroic he'd been, to catch the thief that way!

"Yes, of course," said Mr. Ridgeway. "Come with me, if you like. It appears we weren't in any danger after all." Then, pulling a handkerchief from his pocket and briefly rubbing his face, he followed the path the bank's security officer took to Mr. Hawkins's office.

Henry could still feel the blood pumping madly through his veins, amid a swirl of leftover fear. Fear that was being replaced by relief, triumph, and anger.

But looking down at the boy—who surely must be near the age Henry was when he'd more successfully tried the same line of work—that anger suddenly transformed into a mix of wrath and guilt. It was the first time Henry had felt what those on the coaches must have felt all those years ago.

"That was the most rattle-headed attempt at a bank robbery I've ever seen," he told the boy. "What's your name?"

"S-Smith."

Henry shook his head. "No. I want your real name."

The boy slumped in his chair, as if he'd just now surrendered to the fact that he'd failed. "Murphy."

"Well, Mr. Murphy, do you know the punishment for attempted bank robbery?"

He nodded but kept his face lowered so that his large hat hid most of it. "I saw a man hung for robbing banks. In Nebraska."

Henry patted the boy's shoulder, only now realizing he was even slighter than Henry thought beneath a jacket several sizes too large. If he hadn't been so fooled by that vial of water, he'd have seen this whelp thrown out the doors in no time at all. The boy was built for neither mining nor robbing. "One failed attempt is more likely to send you to jail than a hanging, boy. Unless you've made other, more successful attempts in the past?"

He shook his head slowly. "No, sir. This is my first time."

"Well, Henry, I didn't expect to hear you comforting the rascal. Who have we here?"

Henry looked up to see his uncle, followed by his security guard, Mr. Wilson, and Miss Caldwell. A swell of emotion followed. Regret that Miss Caldwell had to witness such a scene, relief that they were all spared, a touch of unexpected pride that she'd been there to see him best the boy instead of being a victim of such a prank. And frustration that it mattered.

"This is Mr. Murphy." He addressed his security officer. "I want you to make sure this boy is confined here in my office while we find out if he has family, Mr. Wilson. Then, if he does, you'll bring his parents here."

Murphy's eyes rounded so wide that Henry noticed the boy's face for the first time. Indeed, it *was* dirt along his jawline. And his eyes were feathered by thicker lashes than he'd have expected. "You aren't . . . sending for the police?"

Henry stared down at the boy, pleased when he cowered. "Do you want to go to jail?"

"No, sir."

"Then you'll cooperate by telling Mr. Wilson and me what we want to know, won't you?"

"Yes, sir."

"Start by taking off that hat." But when Henry reached for it, the boy raised his hands in defense, as if Henry had been about to strike him. "I just want a look at you, boy."

Tobias stepped forward. "Show some respect for those who have the power to send you to jail, will you? He only wants you to remove your hat."

"I—I'd rather keep it on, if you please." He kept his face averted and a hand at each side of his hat, staring at the floor again. "But I'm grateful to you, sir, for not sending for the police."

Henry looked away from him to allow a glance in Miss Caldwell's direction. He might have felt embarrassed over the pleased—albeit surprised—smile he saw on her face. Perhaps she was glad he wasn't intent on sending the youth to jail, where he belonged. But a new commotion at his office door drew his attention before he could ponder those thoughts. Mr. Sprott was there, followed quickly by Ed Ruffin, the policeman who regularly patrolled the neighborhood. Henry frowned anew.

"What's this I hear about an attempted robbery?" Ruffin asked, stepping around Mr. Sprott to stop before the boy's chair in front of Henry's desk.

"No need to bother you with this, Ruffin," Henry said. "It was just a prank. A foolish one by a foolish youth. Nothing more."

Ruffin shifted the billy club hanging on his belt, looking now at Henry, this time with confusion. "You don't want me to arrest him?"

"No, Mr. Ruffin. That won't be necessary." Then he glowered at the boy again. "Not this time, at any rate. If I learn he's tried this before, or if he tries it again, my charges can be made then."

Murphy lifted his terror-filled face, a face Henry was beginning to see in a whole new light. "I promise you I've never done anything like this before. And I won't again; I swear I won't."

"Yes, well, so far you haven't given me much reason to trust your word, so we'll see whether or not you're telling the truth. Get comfortable, Murphy. It's going to be a long afternoon."

Henry directed everyone from his office, though he had an idea to keep Miss Caldwell behind. When she paused at the door, he knew she had something to say, even though she seemed hesitant to utter it.

"Yes, Miss Caldwell?" he prompted. Perhaps she wouldn't mind staying a moment longer, at least until he could prove or disprove what he suspected of Murphy. For one, why he was so tall but possessed a voice that was yet to change. . . .

"It appears you believe as I do after all, Mr. Hawkins," she whispered. "Everyone deserves a second chance."

"You may be a bit generous toward me in your assessment, Miss Caldwell. I wonder, though, if you might stay a moment?"

Her brows rose. "Yes, of course, if there is anything I can do."

Henry lowered his voice. "I wonder if you might be more successful in asking Murphy to remove his hat?"

Now her brows drew together, as she turned from him to gaze at the back of Murphy's head. She approached the boy's side. "I wonder, Mr. Murphy, if you would take off your hat?"

He stared at the floor again, but shook his head.

"Is there some reason you don't want to remove it?"

He shook his head yet again.

Henry's impatience grew by the moment, so that he was nearly tempted to forcefully pull away the offending garment and see for himself whether his suspicions were founded in fact or fancy.

But before he could do so, Miss Caldwell knelt before the boy and laid a gentle touch on his hands. No sooner had she done so than her eyes widened and she sent a surprised glance Henry's way. Then he knew he wasn't wrong, and she'd figured out what Henry guessed.

"Is Murphy your first name or last?" Miss Caldwell gently inquired.

"Last."

"And what's your first name? The name your mother calls you?"

"My mother's dead."

"And your father?"

He swiped at his face with a sniffle. "Dead too. Just last month."

"Well, what did they call you before they died?"

"Jane."

Then the girl who was dressed as a boy burst into tears.

13

All the newspapers carried the bank story, though only the *Rocky Mountain News* found it spectacular enough for the front page, if only at the lowest corner well under the fold. The fact that it had been a girl who attempted the caper brought in some sensationalism, but because it was described as a "prank"—the very word Mr. Hawkins had used—rather than an attempted robbery, the newspapers treated it as such.

No doubt if Jane had been successful, if they'd never learned the vial she'd waved in the air had only contained water and she'd run off with a sackful of money, or if she'd blown up the bank and half the employees with it, the story would have garnered headlines in every paper in Denver and beyond.

Dessa sat at the kitchen table reading the accounts from the two newspapers she'd gone out to purchase early that morning. She wanted to show them to Jane when she rose, though Dessa wondered if the girl would welcome or bristle at the notoriety.

Sipping her morning coffee, Dessa settled back in her chair, undeniably satisfied to be sheltering her first client. From what little she knew of Jane, she was certainly in need. Sixteen years old, brought West by parents who were after the same thing everyone else came to find: a new life. Rocky Mountain fever had taken her mother within months of their arrival, and her father had been killed in a factory accident a few weeks ago. Jane did have a job until recently, but she had been let go from the textile factory after she'd been sick a day, then fainted at her sewing table on the day she'd returned.

Dessa thought it was a wonder the girl had any strength at all once she learned how long she'd gone without much to eat. The ten-hour-a-day job hadn't earned enough to pay the rent, let alone many visits to the grocer. Jane said the only way she had the stamina to plan what she'd done at the bank had been by stealing from the open fruit bins at Birks Cornforth over on Fifteenth.

Jane's desperate action had seemed her last and only option, unless she wanted to go to the poorhouse. Or worse.

Ever since yesterday's fiasco at the bank, Dessa hadn't stopped thanking God that their paths had crossed.

She had to admit the entire episode left her with some confusing thoughts about Mr. Hawkins, though. Before yesterday, she'd grown used to thinking ill of him. It surprised her that she was so pleased to learn he had a heart after all, instead of only those coins rattling about in his chest as Mariadela once claimed.

"Good morning."

Dessa set aside her coffee with a smile at Jane's greeting. She rose from her chair to offer Jane the one opposite, then went to the coffeepot. Jane was fully dressed in a walking skirt topped by a somewhat outdated but nonetheless fine-quality basque from the donation box upstairs. They'd gone together to reclaim the pitiable amount of possessions at the tenement house Jane had been about to be evicted from, but the clothing she hadn't sold or bartered away consisted of only two tattered dresses and a pair of shoes without laces. When Jane had seen the donations Dessa had to offer, she'd readily agreed to toss her old dresses in the waste bin where they belonged.

"Coffee?" Dessa asked.

"I don't know. I've never tasted it." She took a seat. "My mother said it wasn't good for me, and Father said we had better things to spend our money on. Luxuries like food, for example."

Dessa smiled anew. "Well, we don't have many luxuries here,

as you can see, but we have plenty of food, a solid roof over our heads, soft pillows to sleep on. God provides all our needs."

Instead of coffee, Dessa poured Jane a glass of milk. Then she set about frying some eggs and bacon.

"I recently circulated invitations to Pierson House at most of the factories," Dessa said, "trying to reach girls just like you before they got to such desperate straits. Did you ever see one?"

Jane looked away, an unmistakable look of discomfort on her face.

"You did, didn't you, Jane? Do you mind if I ask why you didn't come here, instead of doing what you did at the bank?"

Jane pushed away a stray strand of hair—long, richly vibrant brown hair that had been necessarily hidden inside that cap. One look at it and her gender would have been immediately clear. "I thought I could get by on my own."

By stealing? The words were on the tip of Dessa's tongue, but the one thing Sophie Pierson had drilled into her was that judgment had no place under the roof of a refuge.

"And so you will," she said instead, turning back to the frying breakfast. "Maybe you can get your job back at the factory now that you'll be eating properly, or find another job. Or perhaps you'd like to go to school? At least you know you'll have a place to stay with no fear of being tossed onto the street until you settle on something suitable. You'll find you do have options, Jane, and I'm here to help as long as you need me."

As Jane accepted the full plate of food, she glanced up at Dessa, brows raised. "Do you mean I get all of this? For myself?"

"Of course. I've already eaten."

"Oh my! I haven't eaten so much since . . . ever!" She laughed. "A girl could lose her figure around here, if she had one."

Dessa returned to the coffeepot to refill her mug. "Eating three healthy meals a day will be good for you, inside and out." She took her seat again. "Which reminds me. I'll be posting a sign outside in just a few days, about beauty lessons I'm offering each week. Would you care to help me with my lessons?"

Jane laughed. "Me? I think there's a reason I fooled everyone at that bank into thinking I was a boy, Miss Caldwell. I'm not exactly what you'd call pretty, or even feminine. I'm too tall, too skinny, and my face . . . well, I'm not pretty. I know that."

Dessa studied her. Though on Jane the secondhand gown sagged at various unfilled curves, it already lent some appeal because of her tiny waist. It was true that the loveliest thing about Jane was her hair, but there was nothing wrong with her face— nothing that a bit of confidence wouldn't improve. Her brows were perhaps a bit too thick, but that could easily be fixed if she had the desire. And she had a distinctive look to her short nose, one that could be called delightful. Besides, she was too young to determine whether or not her face would mature into beauty.

"Beauty starts on the inside, Jane. That's the kind I mean to teach."

"Oh. You're talking about God again, aren't you?"

"You don't believe in God?"

She shrugged, still eating. "I don't know much about Him. My mother took me to church, but after she died, my father never went back. And to tell you the truth, God must not have missed me much because He sure didn't help when I needed Him."

"Oh, Jane," Dessa whispered, "don't you know? It was God's foot that tripped you in the bank yesterday. He's the One who made sure you dropped that vial. He did it to send you here."

"Yoo-hoo! Dessa! Are you here?"

Dessa and Jane were upstairs, going through a crate of material Dessa had stored with the charity clothes in one of the empty bedrooms. Jane had assured Dessa that even though she'd been sacked by the textile company, she could indeed sew. They'd been about to gather material for a new set of pillowcases when Dessa heard Mariadela's call from downstairs.

"We're here! But don't come up; we're coming down."

They found Mariadela at the base of the stairs, where Dessa made the introductions.

"I read about the excitement at the bank in the newspaper this morning," Mariadela said, waving a copy at Dessa. "You couldn't come by the mercantile to warn me not to miss the story? It says your name right here, that you'd taken in the—" She suddenly stopped herself and glanced at Jane, then held up the paper again. "It calls you a prankster. No name."

Dessa laughed, leading them all to the dining room, which she'd long envisioned doubling as a sewing room. The table was just right, and the lighting was fine, particularly in the afternoons when the sun filtered through the front bay window.

"Isn't it wonderful they mentioned we'd taken her in at Pierson House? We can certainly use the free publicity!" Dessa settled the material on the table. "I was going to bring Jane to meet you this afternoon. I know you're busy in the mornings. As I've been." She smiled, adding, "With a client, for once."

"I don't think either of us is too busy for you to tell me that my closest friend's life has been in danger." Then she spared another glance at Jane. "I'm sorry. I know you didn't mean—"

"It's okay. I was worse than a prankster, and it wasn't just a dumb thing to do. It was cruel to everyone who was there. I didn't think of that ahead of time."

"It was Mr. Hawkins who suffered the most, I think," Dessa said as she unrolled the material they would cut and sew. "But he never panicked, not for a moment."

Jane nodded and smiled along. "He was so kind the whole time, even before he knew there was only water in that vial. I've done nothing but regret trying to make him a victim."

"Kind? Henry Hawkins?"

"Of course, Mariadela!" Dessa said. "He didn't press charges, did he?"

"That's what the newspaper said. I thought it was because the prankster was a girl."

"Oh no, that wasn't the reason at all," Dessa said.

"He was going to let me go even before he knew I was a girl," Jane added.

"Hmm. Well, if I didn't know better, I'd say Mr. Henry Hawkins just restored his place as one of Denver's most eligible bachelors."

"What?" Dessa knew she shouldn't be so shocked. He was, after all, a fine-looking man, one of considerable means. And not all that old.

"Every girl and her mother were after him for years," Mariadela said. "But eventually everyone accepted that he's the living representation of Mr. Dickens's Scrooge, before any of the spirits came to haunt him back to humanity. He wants to be left alone, and so that's what we do. No one talks about him anymore, except for two things: banking matters and those dinner parties he holds to keep and impress investors."

Then she sighed. "But that may change now. Everyone coming into the store this morning couldn't stop talking about how heroic he was to save the bank, and then make sure the—well, you, Jane—didn't go to jail. It's made him human again."

For some reason the notion of every young woman in Denver, not to mention their matchmaking mothers, being after Mr. Hawkins made the hairs on the back of Dessa's neck stand up.

❧

"No, Mr. Sprott. None of them. Not a single one."

"But, sir, this woman has refused to leave for the past hour. I believe she's stubborn enough to wait until you exit your office at the end of the day and waylay you then."

Henry sighed. He was beginning to think he'd have been better off if Jane's vial had contained nitroglycerin after all. Invitations, telephone calls, and notes had been arriving all day. Some were disguised as gratitude from bank shareholders, but he knew the invitations to dinner parties were schemes to introduce to him one young woman or another. He'd seen it all before, escapades that he hadn't missed in the least during his years of isolation.

"Very well. Send her in. But—" he called after Mr. Sprott—"you are to return to my office in precisely three minutes and tell the woman I have a pressing engagement. I'll not tolerate her company a moment longer than that."

"Yes, sir."

Mr. Sprott left, only to return with a stout woman in a cream-colored gown and the tallest, most ridiculously feathered hat Henry had ever had the misfortune to see. She waddled toward him, both hands outstretched.

"Thank you for seeing me, Mr. Hawkins! You do recall inviting my husband, Samuel Hamilton, and me to your lovely home this past winter? My husband has been trying to get you to join the Denver Club—it's attracting all the best men of the city, I assure you. And I represent the Women's Anti-Saloon League. Both organizations would be happy if you would visit—"

Though Henry had politely risen to his feet upon her arrival and accepted one of her extended hands in a brief greeting, he now took his seat again, despite the fact that she had not yet done so herself. If she were as meticulous as he guessed, she would see it as the slight he meant it to be.

"I'm terribly sorry, Mrs. . . ."

"Hamilton. Mrs. Samuel Hamilton. Esther, if you like."

"Yes, well, Mrs. Hamilton, I'm very sorry but my responsibilities here at the bank leave me little time outside the office. You understand, of course."

"Oh, but you must eat, mustn't you, Mr. Hawkins? I'd be— that is, my husband and I would be ever so pleased to have you to dinner. We'd love for you to meet our daughter! A true beauty, so says everyone who meets her. Can we plan for you to come, then? Saturday evening? Or perhaps Sunday afternoon? Surely you don't work every day of the week! Even someone as dedicated as yourself must take time for rest. It's not good for the soul to work all the—"

"Mrs. Hamilton," Henry said, in a tone so firm he was pleased to see her mouth clamp closed, "if your daughter has recently become of marriageable age, then I am far too old for her. If she has been of marriageable age for some time, then I shall be blunt and tell you she is far too old for me. In any case, I am not in the market for a wife. Good day, Mrs. Hamilton."

"But I don't understand, Mr. Hawkins. What would be the right age?"

Thankfully, Mr. Sprott came through the door just as she finished her question, sparing Henry the need to extend an impolite answer.

14

"I'D BEEN LOOKING FORWARD to this task myself all week, in fact," Tobias said to Henry as he settled a sign across Henry's desk. "But Etta's train is due in from Cheyenne at last, and I'm eager to greet her. You understand, don't you, Henry? She's been gone an entire month, after all. So you'll do it—if not for me, then for your dear aunt?"

"Is there some reason you can't deliver the sign tomorrow? Why must it be today?"

"Because it's Friday! And as you can see from the sign itself, the first lesson will be on Tuesday. If Miss Caldwell is to have the benefit of advertising, even a single day could be a lost opportunity."

For the first time since Tobias had placed the sign on his desk, Henry looked down to see what it said. "Free Beauty Lessons, Tuesdays at Two." He harrumphed. "What's this all about, anyway? Is she trying to rescue the kind of girls who frequent that neighborhood or just make them more profitable?"

"The former, I assure you. She's attempting to beautify the soul. Something we could all benefit from."

The latter words were somewhat mumbled, and Henry knew to whom his uncle referred. He harrumphed again.

"Enough grumbling, Henry," said Tobias. "You'll do it, then? Perhaps if you accomplish the task before lunch, and you're nice enough, she'll offer you a meal in the bargain, or at least a piece of pie. She's owed you one, you know, ever since we left that luncheon without dessert."

Henry doubted Miss Caldwell would see it that way, though he couldn't help but admit to himself the reluctance he exhibited was entirely fabricated. He wanted to see if her first client remained under her roof—a client his bank had inadvertently supplied. At least some of his money was going to a cause he might find worthwhile: saving someone from repeating the same kind of stupid mistake he'd made.

"Very well. I suppose I can affix it to the bottom of the other sign whether she is there or not. Have you the tools? A hammer?"

"Miss Caldwell has everything you'll need."

Henry eyed his uncle suspiciously. If he didn't know better, he would say Tobias was beginning to sound like one of those mothers eager to arrange a meeting with their daughters.

"And, Henry?" Tobias said as he opened Henry's office door to exit. "Take my advice and go just before lunchtime. That way you'll have a better chance of being offered something to eat."

Whatever doubts Henry had a moment before disappeared with that suggestion.

Not that he had any intention of following through with his uncle's ploy. He wouldn't allow himself to arrive on her doorstep waiting to be fed like some stray cat.

Henry stepped from his carriage, taking the sign with him—along with the hammer and nails he'd stopped to purchase. Instructing Fallo, his driver, to wait, Henry stared at the home Miss Caldwell and his money had purchased. It was quiet, like the rest of the street at this time in the late morning.

Not wanting to do exactly as Uncle Tobias had suggested by waiting until lunchtime, Henry had set out for supplies not long after Tobias left his office, just after midmorning. But the process of leaving his office and searching for the right materials had taken longer than he'd expected. First he'd been detained by Mr. Sprott, then again at the bank entrance when one of his biggest investors had stopped by. Then the mercantile he'd hoped would provide the kind of hammer he wanted hadn't had one in stock, so he'd ended up going to White's. It had taken him a full five minutes to decide whether to go inside or look for another store. Despite having sat at the same dinner party with William White the other day, Henry had been avoiding the man for years and planned to continue doing so. It was hard not to recall just how close their competition had once been, when Henry nearly drove White's Mercantile out of business.

William, however, had been unavoidable once Henry went inside. Even so, he was every bit as welcoming. Particularly when Henry handed over the money for the hammer and box of nails.

So here it was, nearly lunchtime after all.

Spotting the sign Tobias had affixed next to the open bay window, Henry approached. Tobias had found a way to drill hooks into the caulking between the bricks supporting the window. All Henry needed was to attach this sign to the bottom of the one already hanging. There was ample room to do so and still have this addition visible from the street.

Henry held up the sign to center it, but just as he did so, he overheard voices from the other side of the open window.

"My mother always said a woman should dress modestly. To her, that meant just plain ugly, I think. Dresses hung on her even worse than they hang on me. I guess that's why I thought God must want women to dress in a way that hides everything."

Henry stopped. He recognized Jane Murphy's young voice and anticipated hearing Miss Caldwell's in return. He took a step back. He should leave. If he made any more noise they were sure to hear him and would likely come outside to investigate.

"But you don't have to look any further than a sunset—or a bird, or a fish, for that matter, if the scales shine in the right light—to know God delights in beauty! And we're made in His image, so of course we're naturally attracted to beauty."

Henry started to back farther away from the window, aware that his indecision about whether or not to make his presence known did not give him permission to eavesdrop. But he heard Jane respond and stopped to listen.

"I know men like beauty. Some think almost any woman is beautiful. I guess that's why there are neighborhoods like this one. They're looking for a beautiful woman, or for a drink that might make one of them beautiful."

Miss Caldwell's brief laugh coincided with the slight movement of the curtain on the breeze. "For a while, anyway."

"Do you think everybody who . . . well, who lives in this neighborhood is going straight to hell for their sins?"

Hellfire talk. Worse, hellfire mixed with women talk. Still, he was curious to hear what Miss Caldwell said about that.

"No, I don't. God tells us outright that some behavior is sin, and other behavior seems to be punishment enough without having it named a sin. But no matter what people do, have done, or will do, God's seen it before. He went to the cross so we don't have to be punished."

Now Henry really should go, but his feet would not obey.

Instead he lifted the sign in place as noisily as he could, then gave it a good whack just for the sound of it, without even a nail. It occurred to him at that moment that he might have sent Mr. Sprott to perform this task, or even employed Fallo to do it. And yet here he was, about to make a fool of himself if he didn't complete what he'd come to do.

"Oh! I wonder what that is."

Two inquisitive faces soon appeared at the center pane, the

filmy curtain pulled aside. He looked up but only nodded an acknowledgment, putting a couple of nails between his lips so he wouldn't be expected to speak.

"Hello!" Jane Murphy's pleasure at seeing him was unmistakable in her tone, aside from the broad smile on her face. How had he been fooled, even for a moment, that she was a boy? She looked every bit the girl today.

Beside her, Miss Caldwell looked every bit the woman. Her hair was piled atop her head, soft and loose, with a few curls framing her face. Her shirtwaist, what he could see of it, was pure white and close fitting. Just now she offered him a smile he couldn't help but return. He nearly dropped one of the nails, so he let them fall into his palm.

"I came to hang the sign Tobias had made for you. It won't take long, and then I'll be on my way."

"But it's lunchtime!" Jane said, looking from him to Miss Caldwell. "Isn't it?"

Dessa tilted her head and considered him with pleasantly raised brows. "Have you eaten, Mr. Hawkins? We're having leftover chicken pie, and there's more than enough for all three of us."

Chicken pie wasn't exactly the blueberry he'd missed from that first luncheon, but it was a fine substitution. He nodded before the refusal already forming in his mind would deny him what he really wanted to do.

❧

Dessa took up the used plates from the kitchen table, glad that the meal seemed to have pleased Mr. Hawkins despite the informal setting. He'd eaten enough to prove that; the chicken pie was gone.

Jane had done most of the talking—Dessa found the girl to be a pleasant chatterbox, but a chatterbox nonetheless—and Mr. Hawkins had answered her many questions, though he'd done so in his usual one-syllable way. Had anyone else ever tried robbing his bank? *No.* Was that because of the guard he hired? *Yes.* Did he like working with money? *Yes.*

When Jane spoke of her father, saying he'd been a clerk at a warehouse back in Nebraska, a shine of love came over her face, followed by unmistakable grief. She said she thought he'd have been better off working in an office here in Denver instead of at the smelting factory. But it was the only job he could find after his try at mining failed, and so he'd done his best until the day he died.

"He was a wonder at numbers and taught me everything I know," Jane said. For a moment she looked ahead with a smile as if she could see his face, then back at Mr. Hawkins, her expression earnest. "I can add and subtract without paper and pencil, and I'm faster than most. I saw an arithmometer at the textile factory, and oh, how I wanted to try it. Do you have any at the bank?"

"Yes."

"Do you need any more help in the bank? Another clerk?"

"No."

Dessa caught a glance from Mr. Hawkins and wondered if he'd had enough questions for the day. "Speaking of the bank, I'm sure Mr. Hawkins must return to his duties." She let her gaze meet his. "It was so kind of you to make the time to hang the sign for me."

He stood, obviously having taken her words as a prompting to leave—when all she'd really meant was to spare him more questions that he obviously didn't enjoy answering.

But before leaving the kitchen, he turned back to Jane. "Work hard at whatever you choose to do, Jane, and maybe someday when you're a bit older you'll find a place in my bank."

From the opposite side of the table, Dessa sent him a smile over the back of Jane's head. How could she have doubted he had a heart?

Both Dessa and Jane escorted Mr. Hawkins to the front door.

Jane held out her hands and asked him to wait, then hurried to the mostly wilting flower arrangement still sitting in the corner of the parlor.

"You can rescue the last of the flowers, Mr. Hawkins!" She boldly took hold of his lapel and looped a flower into the empty buttonhole provided for such things. "My father always told me wearing a flower on his coat reminded everyone around him to smile." Then, looking rather sheepish, she turned to Dessa. "I hope it's all right?"

Dessa smiled. "Perfectly. That was the last one holding any freshness. I meant to carry them out this afternoon."

"Still from the dinner party?" Mr. Hawkins asked.

She nodded. "A Mr. Turk Foster had them sent over. Do you know him?"

"Foster." The single name came with more than a frown; it came with obvious dislike. "I do know him. Do you?"

She shook her head. "I can't imagine why he sent the flowers, except the boy who delivered them said they were to welcome Pierson House to the neighborhood."

Mr. Hawkins turned to take his leave, but hesitated. He looked at Dessa. "Miss Caldwell, you may rightly think I have no business offering you advice, but let me assure you, Mr. Foster's interests aren't likely to be compatible with yours."

Then he placed his hat on his head, bid them both a good day, and left the house.

15

"MISS CALDWELL? Miss Caldwell?"

Dessa stirred at the sound of her name. It took a moment to realize the voice was not at her door, but came from the open bedroom window facing the back of the house. Throwing off her covers, she glanced at her watch on the bedside table to see that it was just past two in the morning. With some alarm, she went to the windowsill and knelt beside it to look out.

A girl not more than fourteen years old stood on the weedy grass that grew between the laundry-line poles and water pump. "Oh, Miss Caldwell! You remember me, don't ya? Nadette. I took ya over to Cora, to help her with her baby? I'm still deliverin' the laundry to places like hers 'til I get me a spot in the business."

Dessa had been hoping Cora might turn up to ask about her baby—safely placed in a good home—but so far she hadn't. Perhaps Nadette had come to find out.

"Cora's baby is just fine, Nadette. Living in a home with two fine parents right here in Denver."

"That's good. Cora woulda liked that."

"Would have?"

"She's dead. Swallowed the carbolic she used to ward off the syphilis 'stead of usin' it like it shoulda been used. Found out it didn't work to prevent syphilis anyhow, but it worked all right to kill her."

Dessa sank back on her heels. "Oh no. That's just awful, Nadette. Why didn't she come here instead?"

"Why would she? You couldn'ta helped her get rid a the burn."

"No, but . . ." Dessa, fully awake now, wanted to scream at the pain and waste, but only allowed herself a swipe at her tearing eyes. "Why don't you come in, Nadette? You can live here and never join the Line at all."

"You got yourself a pie-ano in there?"

"A piano? No, I'm afraid not. But maybe someday we will."

"Well, it don't matter anyhow. I come because there's somebody else who might want to stay here, not me. Only she ain't ready just yet. She don't—I mean doesn't—want nobody to know she's even thinking about coming. She's only three doors down from here, Miss Caldwell! She promised to put in a word for me over there if she ever left, and so I'm trying to hurry it up. If I get to talkin' better, I can take her spot straight off, and as you can tell, I'm workin'—work*ing*—at it. You reckon those beauty lessons you're startin' might teach me how to talk better? Or is it just for lookin' prettier?"

"It's for inner beauty, Nadette. Come on Tuesday and find out all about it."

"I don't know if I can, 'specially if it won't make me prettier on the outside. . . . So you'll go and see my friend tomorrow, then? Right down the street? She goes by Miss Remee, only she ain't no madam like the name sounds. She's just a sportin' girl, same as I wanna be."

"No, Nadette! Come here instead. I'll find a job for you, and pretty clothes, and you'll have a safe place to live."

But Nadette was already shaking her head. "You want me to be some kind of shopgirl? Pshaw, I'd make barely twelve dollars a week, and I don't talk good enough for that anyways. You can't get me a job that'll bring in the kind of money I can make at one of them nice houses—like the one down the street! That Miss Remee can make *fifty* dollars in one night. I aim to hold out 'til I can get me a spot like that. A nice place with a pie-ano, too, 'cause I can play anything I hear. And besides the money, the madam buys the girls all the pretty dresses they want. They got candy there too."

Dessa had folded her arms halfway through Nadette's tirade. "She buys those dresses without expecting to be paid back?"

Nadette shrugged. "If you're in the business, it's all the same. Pretty clothes on the girls bring in men with more money, and that's what I want. So, you gonna do it? Visit Miss Remee?"

"But if she doesn't want anyone to know she's thinking about leaving, my visit won't—"

"That's just it, Miss Caldwell! You don't hafta convince her; you could get her in *trouble* with a visit. Why, they're apt to throw her out on her—well, toss her right out on the street any day now. Nobody talks to her but me, she's so uppity. But the men like her, so Miss Leola keeps her on. If she's tossed out, she won't have noplace else to go but here. She won't go down to the cribs, let me tell you that! She's likely to leave the business altogether. She just needs a little push, is all."

Dessa drew her bottom lip between her teeth. "I don't know, Nadette. I don't want anyone to get into trouble. I'm here to help, not make things harder."

"But she wants to leave; she just won't admit it to nobody but me!"

"Why doesn't she come here herself, then, if she wants to leave the business? The reason I'm here isn't any secret, especially to the place down the street. I've dropped off my applications there."

Nadette threw up her hands. "What kinda help are you gonna be if you don't follow up on a tip like this? I tell you there's a girl who wants to leave the business, and you're standin' up there with all kinda excuses to do nothin'. You gonna do it, or what?"

"I'll see, Nadette. I want to pray about it first."

Nadette looked as if she might say something else but instead just nodded and turned away.

Dessa surveyed the dining room table, where she'd placed lace-edged hankies and little white cards with a verse printed in calligraphy on one side. To the handkerchiefs she'd easily added a small, embroidered teardrop in the corner to match the verse from the Fifty-Sixth Psalm: *Put thou my tears into thy bottle.*

"Do you think anyone will come?"

Jane asked the question innocently enough, but it nonetheless sparked in Dessa the very thing she hoped to dispel in others: insecurity. If the announcements she and Jane had distributed to various brothels around the neighborhood had been received the same way the Pierson House applications had been, the afternoon was doomed to failure.

Dessa refused to contemplate such thoughts. "Of course they'll come! We only have to let out the scent of those fresh scones we have baking. We mentioned free refreshments on the flyer. Come, let's open those windows."

Before long the table was complete with teacups and plates, along with napkins Dessa had also embroidered.

"Everything looks beautiful, Miss Caldwell."

Dessa smiled, glancing at her watch necklace. It was exactly two o'clock. This had to work. It must.

In light of the note Dessa had received earlier today, she could barely deny she was more desperate than ever. Last week she'd invited Mrs. Plumstead to come to today's inaugural beauty lesson, since she and her husband had been unable to attend the donors' dinner party. But Mrs. Plumstead's regrets had come this morning.

Was it another scheduling conflict, or was one of Dessa's biggest donors second-guessing her pledge of support?

Holding out her hand to Jane, Dessa led the way toward the door. "Let's wait on the porch, shall we? The banisters on each side of the steps should do for seating, don't you think?"

The day was glorious, with endless sunshine and the cool, dry air Denver had become known for. Even the unpaved street out front was free of mud or puddles and the boardwalks along the sides easily navigated. Nothing, absolutely nothing, stood in the way of visitors today.

They sat in companionable silence for a while, and when the first pair of ladies—of questionable virtue from the cut of their bodices—walked by, Dessa smiled broadly and called a hello.

But they ignored her and kept walking.

"I guess they have someplace else to go," Jane said softly.

Dessa nodded. She looked down the street again, seeing it was empty. She did hear voices nearby, female voices—a laugh now and then—but not a soul appeared on the boarded walkway.

A carriage rolled by and even slowed down as it neared Pierson House. Dessa's heart rate picked up. It was a covered carriage, so she couldn't easily see who was inside, but when it kept going, it no longer seemed to matter. Dessa saw the brim of a flowered hat and knew a woman was in the carriage. But evidently that lady, too, had someplace else to go.

She sighed. *Oh, Lord, what am I doing wrong?*

Dessa glanced once again down the street. She knew where those voices came from: the porch of the brothel situated so close by. Where someone who called herself Miss Remee might even now consider leaving, if only she found the courage to do so.

Dessa hadn't visited her, much as Nadette might have liked. She had indeed prayed about what to do, but received not a trace of peace considering the possibility of getting someone into trouble.

As eager as Dessa was to help women, she knew this was the kind of decision that couldn't be forced . . . or hurried. Not if it was to be a lasting one.

And yet . . .

By two thirty Dessa had to admit—to herself and to Jane— that no one would come. She wasn't sure which shameful emotion she battled more fiercely: anger or embarrassment over her obvious failure. She should stride right down to that nearest bawdy house and demand to know exactly what it would take for them to stop ignoring her.

She shook her head at her own thoughts. *Dear Lord, what would Sophie have done? She was so much better at listening to You than I am. . . .*

No sooner had the prayer been uttered than Dessa had an idea. "Come with me, will you, Jane?"

Dessa marched into the kitchen, where she grabbed the basket she used at the market. After shaking it upside down over the sink to make sure it didn't have any leafy remnants or crumbs from past purchases, she went to the linen drawer of the built-in cabinet in the corner and took out two of the largest napkins she owned. Each boasted a pretty flower pattern, just the look she wanted.

First she lined the basket with one of the napkins. Then with the other she wrapped the scones, placing them inside.

Next she found the ribbon box she stored in a lower cabinet and went into the dining room. She'd painstakingly folded each handkerchief to show off the lace edges, but she could easily tie them with ribbons and fan out the lace for a look every bit as attractive. She could tuck the card with her pretty calligraphy— and a verse that so aptly explained the reason for the embroidered teardrop—inside. After showing Jane how to do it, they had the dozen handkerchiefs finished in no time.

"We're going to make a special delivery, gifts to the girls down the street."

"You mean we're going to see . . . soiled doves?"

"Yes, Jane. That's exactly the kind of girl Pierson House is available to. If you'd rather not come, that's all right. I just thought it might help for them to see that I'm not entirely on my own anymore."

"Oh no, I'll come. Poke me if I stare, though. I've only ever seen one woman up close who made her living that way."

"They're just like you and me," Dessa said as she went to the doorway to find her hat and gloves. The unwanted memory of Bennet Pierson came to mind. *Well, perhaps a bit more like me than Jane.*

The female voices grew louder as they approached the house three doors down. Three girls sat on wicker chairs on the porch, laughing and talking. Two of them held matching little white dogs on their laps. When Dessa and Jane turned from the boardwalk onto the short cement walkway leading to the porch, both of the dogs yipped and one of the girls stood, putting her dog on her hip.

"You lost, girls?"

"We're neighbors from just down the street," Dessa said cheerfully, pointing in the direction of Pierson House. "We have too many scones from this morning's baking and wanted to share them with you." They looked so skeptical, Dessa added, "As a gift."

She held out the basket.

"What kind of scones?" one of the girls still seated asked.

"Blueberry. And I have a couple that are plain, with a bit of sugar on top."

Dessa glanced at Jane, hoping she might say something, and found the girl was indeed staring, just as she'd feared. Dessa elbowed her.

"They're good!" Jane said immediately. "I've already had three myself."

The dogs still barked, but once Dessa and Jane were on the porch, they stopped. Two of the girls stepped closer as Dessa pushed aside the handkerchiefs to unveil the scones.

"I don't eat anything made by someone I don't know," said the third girl, still seated. She stared straight ahead, looking at neither the visitors nor her housemates, just petting the dog on her lap.

The other two girls laughed and reached in to take a scone apiece.

"That's how she got here!" one said as she took a bite. "A piece of cake made with opium and she was one of us before morning. Isn't that right, Min?"

"I'd be happy to split one with you," Dessa offered, "and eat half right here in front of you so you'll know it's safe. I made them myself."

"Ooh, they're good!" said the one holding the other dog. The animal caught a crumb in midair that fell from the corner of the scone, then looked eagerly for more.

"You're from that Pierson House down the street, aren't you?" the second girl standing asked as she ate her own scone.

Dessa nodded.

The girl still seated held her dog closer to her chest. "You'd better leave before Miss Leola sees you here."

Dessa offered a smile anyway. "I suppose I am bad for business, but that's why I've come midday. I don't want to get in the way. I just wanted you to know I'm here. If you ever need a friend, I'm close by. And—" she lifted the basket—"I wanted to bring gifts for the girls. Handkerchiefs."

The girl who'd first addressed them laughed. "You're sure trying hard, I'll grant you that, Miss Pierson."

"Oh, I'm not Miss Pierson. My name is Dessa Caldwell, and I'm pleased to meet you."

"We saw that sign about beauty lessons. What kind of beauty lessons?"

"To talk about how God made all of us in our own wonderful way. He thinks we're all beautiful."

"Yeah, sure, he's a man, then," said the girl who didn't hold a dog, though she'd saved a bit of her scone and tossed it to the one at her side. Then she reached for the basket, looping it over her arm and taking out one of the handkerchiefs. Untying it, the card flew free and she bent to retrieve it. "What's this about tears?"

Dessa smiled again. "It goes with the little teardrop on the handkerchief. I like remembering that God must think even our tears are beautiful, if He cares enough to keep track of them—in a bottle for each of us. I suppose He thinks anything can be beautiful if it brings us closer to Him."

"You'd better take your gifts and your scones and go back home, Miss Pierson—or Miss Caldwell," said the girl still seated. "Before somebody you don't want noticing you notices you."

"Miss Leola?"

"Did someone call me?"

The new voice from the door was rich and commanding, curious and intimidating all at the same time. Dessa looked to see the woman who was obviously the madam of the house. She was splendidly dressed in a golden gown, cut low to amply reveal the charms she encouraged men to buy, pinched tight at the waist and pleated to the floor.

She came out to the porch, taking the basket one of the girls had accepted and handing it back to Dessa. "We have all the food we need, Miss Caldwell. And more." Her cool smile grazed Dessa first, then Jane. Her smile did not quite reach her eyes. "So allow me to return your generous offer. Should either of you be in need of help, we're also here night and day."

"I know you," Jane said slowly. "You came to the factory a few times with that other lady, to talk to girls on our way home. You even offered me a job once."

Miss Leola looked Jane over, brows rising. "Did I now?" Her voice, so smooth and cultured, felt almost like a caress. "Well, the offer still stands. We enjoy a generous and robust market, with all the pretty dresses and money you could ever want."

Jane averted her gaze, looking down at the ground.

"Miss Leola," Dessa said, knowing if she cowered now she'd have failed again, "I don't want to hurt your business. I just want your girls to know if they ever need someplace to go, they can come to Pierson House. Wouldn't that be better than some of the ways the girls leave the business?"

"I assure you my girls are all quite happy here." Miss Leola put one hand on Dessa's shoulder and the other on Jane's, encouraging them to turn. Jane did so, but Dessa tried not to comply.

"Can I at least leave the handkerchiefs for you? And the scones?"

"As I said, we have more than we need here. Good day, ladies."

Then Dessa knew she had to go; there was nothing more she could say.

Feeling once again a failure, Dessa led the way home. Visiting the house had been an idea inspired by God, she was sure of it, but she must have done something wrong.

Back in the kitchen, where she emptied the basket, she was glad for the moment that Jane was quiet. Perhaps she felt the failure too.

Would Dessa ever be of any help to those in this neighborhood?

She put the handkerchiefs in a pile and went to find a plate for the scones. Watching Jane straighten the handkerchiefs neatly, Dessa wondered how the embroidered hankies would ever be used if the girls for whom they were meant refused to accept them.

She sank to the nearest chair, another prayer on her lips.

"Oh!" Jane's voice was pleasantly surprised.

Dessa looked at her.

"One's missing. We brought all twelve, didn't we?"

Dessa nodded, leaning forward to make her own count. Finding only eleven, she let her gaze happily meet Jane's.

It was a start.

16

HENRY WALKED BRISKLY through the bank following his early morning constitutional out at City Park. He nearly smiled at Mr. Sprott as he passed the clerk on his way into the office.

So when Tobias called to him, obviously having waited to spot him, Henry turned without a trace of annoyance, although he was still somewhat peeved at the older man. Henry had learned his aunt Etta's train hadn't been expected until Saturday, a full day after Tobias had sent Henry on that fool's mission last week to hang the sign at Miss Caldwell's. Tobias claimed to have gotten his days mixed up.

"I've had a talk with Etta and your Mrs. Giovannini," Tobias said, "and we've all decided your summer dinner event should come a bit later this year. Instead of one month from today, we think it should be held five weeks from Sunday."

"And why is that?"

"Because we've just gotten word the Verandah is having another of those disgusting masquerades, and much as we hate to believe any of our investors would attend such a thing, the truth is they do. Foster's party would be held on the same night as your dinner, unless we change."

Whatever good cheer Henry had enjoyed a moment ago dissolved at the news. Foster again. Those masquerades ought to be outlawed now that Denver was so far on its way to becoming one of the nation's premier cities. But Henry knew that was a useless hope. He'd heard New York City itself had similar parties, or worse. Hosted by no less than brothel madams.

Not that Foster was much of a cut above that.

But why should Henry change his date to accommodate Foster's party? It would serve any of his nearly two dozen investors right to be suspected of attending a socially unacceptable alternative. Anyone not showing up to Henry's event would be left open to the worst doubt, which should make attendance to his dinner all the more desirable—at least for the sake of one's reputation.

Yet as tempted as he was to insist, Henry had little desire to expose anyone else's sins. He had enough of his own to keep hidden.

"Fine, then," he said, turning back to his office. Gone was any desire to smile, replaced by the more familiar urge to scowl.

"Oh, and Henry," Tobias said, following him to his office door. While Henry hung his hat and removed his gloves, Tobias stood at the threshold. "I've taken the liberty of ordering the invitations printed individually with the names of your guests, in anticipation of your agreement. And I've added one more name to the list."

Going to his desk, Henry spared a glance but did not prompt his uncle for a name. He already had a guess of his own.

"I'm eager for Etta to meet Miss Caldwell," Tobias said, "and what better opportunity than this?"

Suspicion confirmed, Henry sat in his chair to attend to his work. Tobias took his silence as agreement, as he so often did, then left his office.

As Henry studied the ledger in front of him, he couldn't help but notice that the addition of Miss Caldwell's name to the guest list had restored his former good mood.

"Where did you learn to do all this, Miss Caldwell?" Jane asked while sitting at the dining-turned-sewing table. "You can cook and sew, and I've never seen a neater bed than the one you make."

"I was a maid from the time I was seven until I started working with Miss Pierson. That's how I met her, as a maid in her parents' house."

"Oh. I thought . . ." She averted her gaze, a crimson tint rising to her cheeks.

Dessa smiled. "Did you think I might be a reformed soiled dove?"

Jane shrugged. "I guess I did wonder why you want to help them so much."

Dessa hesitated a moment. She mustn't be so afraid to reveal her past, especially with the clients who might come to reside with her. At least . . . some of that past. "Because, but for the grace of God, I might have become one of them."

Jane's eyes widened. "But you just said—"

"I said I wasn't one, and I wasn't. Weren't you tempted, even for a moment, when Miss Leola offered all those gowns and money?"

Jane tended to her sewing again. "Maybe I was. But I don't think you could've been. You've told me more than once that everything in this house belongs to God, as if it doesn't matter whether you own any of it or not."

Dessa wasn't sure how much to reveal, particularly to someone as young and inexperienced as Jane. She was used to keeping at least one secret, and with Jane it didn't seem necessary to talk about all the twists and turns that clouded Dessa's past. It wasn't necessary, was it, to explain that Sophie's own brother had been the catalyst that prompted Sophie to choose Dessa as her partner in the work she'd dedicated herself to?

"I'm not saying you were tempted to the work of a sporting girl, or the money that might come with it," Dessa said. "But there can be a security of income, even from things God wouldn't approve. Sometimes we allow ourselves to do desperate things if we don't trust God to take care of us."

Suddenly there was a crash at the window—the noise so close Dessa and Jane simultaneously dropped their sewing to lift their arms and protect their faces.

Then silence.

"What in the world?"

A glance at the other end of the dining room revealed the window broken through the center—and a rock the size of Dessa's palm teetering on the end of the table.

"Stay here, Jane," Dessa ordered. She ran toward the front door.

Commotion down the street drew her attention. A man had a boy by his tattered collar, not far from a carriage stopped behind the most magnificent pair of black horses Dessa had ever seen. The door was wide open, as if the carriage had been hastily vacated by the man who even now yelled and shook the boy. The captive flailed his arms in a futile attempt to free himself.

When the man caught sight of Dessa, he shoved the boy in her direction, keeping hold of the collar in case the boy had any ideas of fleeing. With his free hand, the tall, slim man managed to tip his hat Dessa's way. "Is that your home, miss? The one this boy chucked a rock at?"

"Yes!"

Stopping only a few feet in front of her, he gripped the child by both shoulders, forcing him to stand at attention before Dessa.

"Here he is, ma'am. Caught in the act—I saw him myself. I can take him down to the police station if you like. That's my carriage right there."

"Oh no, please don't." She looked at the youth, who couldn't be more than thirteen or fourteen. He was only a bit shorter than she, and dirty from head to toe. "Why did you do such a thing, young man?"

"I—I just did, that's all." He glared at her. "Go ahead, have him take me to jail. I don't care."

"But I don't want to be responsible for someone so young being sent to such a dire place," Dessa said. "Tell you what. Why don't you come inside and help me clean up the mess? I'll give you a cookie. Then the next time you feel like throwing rocks, you might remember the cookie and pick another window to smash. Or maybe you won't throw any rocks at all. Would that be all right with you?"

He wiped his nose with his sleeve. "What kind of cookie?"

"Shortbread."

"What's that?"

"You'll have to come and see. They're my favorite; that's why I make them." She smiled. "I have a feeling you might like them too."

She thought he might smile back, but he looked away instead. He did, however, nod.

"Are you sure you want to take this urchin inside, miss?" asked the tall stranger, still holding one of the boy's arms. "He's probably a thief as well as a vandal."

"It's quite all right, sir," Dessa said. "I haven't anything worth the trouble of stealing. Won't you come inside as well? Tea and cookies are the least I can offer to repay you for your help."

The man and boy exchanged a somewhat bemused glance, which Dessa found oddly amusing. They looked as though kindness wasn't to be found in this neighborhood, something she was here to prove wrong.

Inside, Jane had already set about sweeping up the broken pieces of the window. The boy, evidently eager to fulfill the duty he'd been assigned, grabbed the dustpan she'd left nearby and held it steady for her to collect the shards.

"Hello there," Jane said to the boy as she continued the task with his help. "What's your name?"

"Ryan. But everybody calls me Rye."

"Rye and Mr. . . . ." Dessa turned to the man beside her inquisitively. He was staring at Jane and for the moment seemed to be assessing her in a way that suggested he knew what sort of neighborhood he'd ventured into. She'd have to assure him he wasn't in the kind of place he either feared or had been looking for.

He was appealing in a rugged sort of way, with a scar splitting one eyebrow. Between the broad expanse of his shoulders and the sharp line of his jaw, she thought he might have been the inspiration behind any one of the frontier-tale dime novels she knew girls back East regularly devoured. She'd read more than a few herself when she could afford them and had the time.

"I'm sorry," she said, "but I don't know how to introduce you to my friend, or to welcome you to Pierson House. You're inside a mission to help those in need."

"Indeed?" he said, the brow with the scar rising curiously. "A mission . . . of what sort?"

"God—and a group of generous donors—have made it possible for Pierson House to open its doors to girls who find themselves in need of a safe place. If you've heard of the YWCA, it's like that."

"I see." He held out his hand toward Dessa. "Actually, I did know you were new to the neighborhood, but I wasn't sure of your purpose. The rumors around town aren't always reliable. My name is Foster. Turk Foster."

Dessa pulled back her hand ever so slightly before pushing it forward again. She hoped he hadn't noticed that her first response to his name was to recoil. How silly! It was a reaction based only upon the input of a stodgy, stingy old banker. Well, not so very old. But most definitely stodgy and stingy.

Mr. Foster accepted her hand, and she shook his warmly. "Oh, Mr. Foster! Thank you so much for the flowers you sent to welcome us to the neighborhood. How did you know they were needed on the very day I hosted a dinner party for some of my most important donors? The flowers brightened up the parlor nicely."

He smiled, then without letting go of her hand, he pulled it upward to kiss her fingers. "It was my pleasure. And it is again now, to see they brought you a smile."

Rye stood by with the full dustpan, and Dessa reluctantly pulled her gaze from Mr. Foster's friendly eyes. She directed Rye to follow Jane to the kitchen.

"Won't you sit in the parlor, Mr. Foster?" Dessa asked. "I'll bring in some tea and a plate of cookies—"

"Oh, no, no, Miss Caldwell. Don't go to the trouble." He glanced at the window. "I'll send someone round this afternoon to repair your window before dark—at no charge to you or to your donors."

"How very generous. How can I thank you?"

He placed his hat back on his head, going to the door. "I've an idea. You could accompany me to the opera house on Tuesday night. That's how you can repay me, if you insist that you need to at all."

Desire to agree mingled with her inevitable answer. "I—I'm not sure what to say, Mr. Foster. Except to apologize that I couldn't possibly go. I haven't proper attire for an opera, for one thing. My lifestyle is far simpler than those who usually go to such places."

He stared at her a moment, making no attempt to conceal a light of appreciation. His blue eyes were clear and bright and at the moment searing right into her. "The more formal opera season won't start again until fall, Miss Caldwell. If you accompany me on Tuesday, there will be a light musical revue, one that's sure to entertain even as it requires no formal attire."

Instead of being embarrassed by her lack of experience with

high society's seasons, Dessa offered an unabashed laugh. "There, you see? I've been inside many lecture halls throughout the country, Mr. Foster, but never once as a patron of the arts. I am a woman of work, not leisure."

His smile nearly mesmerized her, accompanied by his avidly attentive gaze—as if he were trying to see inside her soul. It made her feel as though she was the only living person who existed for him at that moment.

She broke the gaze, reminding herself she'd seen such a thing before. *We're all attracted to beauty and charm . . . but it shouldn't blind us to all else.*

He wasn't deterred. "All the more reason for you to taste the theater as it was designed to be. For music and . . . did you say this mission—" he glanced around—"is from God?"

She nodded.

"Then if music is from the gods, you shall hear it as you've never heard it before."

"There is only one God," she said, embarrassed when her words came out as little more than a whisper. Rather than looking at his eyes, now she couldn't seem to take her gaze from his mouth.

"Say that you'll come with me," he said, and his voice, too, was low. Intimate.

"I . . . I don't normally—"

"But I assure you," he said with a smile, "this will be anything but normal. It will be an experience you'll never forget. Shall I call for you at eight, then?" He let his gaze leave her face, doing so with such eager appraisal she nearly welcomed the sensation as he scanned her from head to toe. "What you're wearing today is certainly presentable. Any man would be proud to escort you, and I shall count myself honored."

It was on the tip of her tongue to agree. It would have been so easy. But an image of the sugar-tongued Bennet Pierson rose to an unlikely rescue.

"No, Mr. Foster. I'm afraid I cannot go." Dessa took hold of the doorknob nearby, grateful that it was cool to the touch. She nearly leaned her forehead against the door itself. "I'm very grateful for your help today, and if you would be so kind as to send someone to repair the window, please tell them I'll provide a very pleasant meal in return. I haven't any money to pay for the glass, but I'm a good cook and would count the service as a great favor."

Mr. Foster turned to the door. "Then I shall accompany my man for the job and share the meal as well." He winked at her. "One way or another, Miss Caldwell, I intend to enjoy your company."

He tipped his hat in farewell and saw himself out the door.

Closing it behind him, Dessa leaned against the solid wood and folded her arms against herself. It had been a long time since a man had paid her any attention; she'd nearly forgotten what it was like.

It wasn't only that she hadn't allowed the time to get to know any of the men she'd met across the country; she'd been inspired by Sophie.

Sophie had never once let a man turn her head. She'd been far too sensible, and more importantly, entirely dependent upon God and His direction. She'd never expressed a void in her life for not having been loved by a man. She was, instead, loved by the many she helped.

And Dessa meant to be just like Sophie. Charming as Mr. Foster might be, she must never forget that she'd once been so desperate for the admiration of a man that she'd freely given away what the women in this neighborhood sold for a fee.

17

"So you'll come, won't you?" Dessa asked Mariadela. After Mr. Foster had left, after Rye had been given first a sandwich and then the promised cookie, Dessa had nearly run all the way to White's Mercantile in search of her friend's advice. She would stop at the market on the way home for what she would need for dinner guests—Mr. Foster and his glass man, and Mariadela and William, too, if they could both get away.

But Mariadela was already shaking her head. "We have a buyer coming this afternoon from Cheyenne and a salesman due to arrive any minute all the way from Chicago. I must be here for both. The order from Cheyenne is important, and the salesman from Chicago is bringing sewing samples. William depends on me to know what we need in such matters." She frowned. "Why do you think you need me there, anyway? Jane is with you now; you won't be alone."

Dessa sighed, looking momentarily at the ceiling but seeing right through it all the way to heaven. How could she explain that Turk Foster reminded her of her greatest failure? One that had very nearly ruined her life? "You know Mr. Foster—"

Mariadela shook her head again. "I know *of* Mr. Foster. I don't know him personally."

"That's more than I know! Mr. Hawkins told me I'd have little in common with the man's interests. And believe me, from the few minutes I spent in his company, I think I already know the kind of man he is."

"What kind of man is he?"

"One who knows how to get a reaction out of someone else—particularly a woman."

Mariadela's brows shot upward. "Don't tell me he got a reaction out of *you*!"

Dessa looked around to be sure neither William nor any of their children were nearby, then whispered, "Tell me, Mariadela: What would you do if a handsome man made you feel as if you were the only woman in the world?"

"And that's how he made you feel?"

"Let me just say I know that's what he's capable of making a woman feel." Unlike a certain banker who might be every bit as handsome, only he made her feel as though he'd rather be with anyone except her.

Mariadela grinned. "If it's Mr. Hawkins who warned you about him, then why don't you go to him for help? Invite him to tonight's supper."

"Oh, Mariadela," she said, exasperated.

Her friend patted her hand. "I wish I could help you, honey. But I just can't get away. The best I can do is to try to stop by afterward. You can make it clear that I hope to join you for dessert. Would that help?"

Dessa nodded slowly, though she wasn't at all sure. This was, she knew, ridiculous. She'd learned her lesson, hadn't she?

Bennet Pierson was the only male heir to the Pierson name and money—and as smooth-talking a man as Turk Foster. Bennet had gone through one maid after another, even after his marriage. When it had been Dessa's turn—just after she'd reached seventeen—she'd been foolish enough to welcome his attention. He was not only older, wiser, and handsome; he was so important, so respected. And he'd chosen *her*! A girl of no means, an orphan.

She couldn't deny dreaming that she would last longer than the others, if she ever had a chance.

It had only taken one time for Dessa to realize she'd been as much a fool as the others who'd believed themselves to be special recipients of his attention.

Thankfully, Sophie had learned what happened and rescued Dessa from ruin by taking her along on her travels. As Sophie used to say, it was God who had rescued Dessa, since He'd inspired the mission to help women in need. Given Dessa's experience in the Pierson family's employ, as well as in the orphanage, she had been the perfect choice to understand some of the girls they would encounter.

But this was neither the time nor the place to tell all that to Mariadela. Perhaps the memory of Bennet Pierson was all Dessa needed to remind her how shallow were the promises of some men.

Even so, when her favorite market stop took her within a few blocks of Hawkins National Bank, she couldn't help going out of her way to pass by. Without conscious effort, her steps slowed. Perhaps she'd overreacted to Turk Foster's visit. Had it only been Mr. Hawkins's warning that made her so wary of Mr. Foster? And what did it matter what Mr. Hawkins thought, anyway?

It didn't, of course. And yet Mr. Hawkins was the kind of man she knew she could trust, even if he'd never offered her more than disapproval over both her mission and how she'd spent his bank's money. He was an honest man, if a bit curmudgeonly.

She had half a mind to go in there and invite him to dinner, just as Mariadela had suggested.

Yet she knew she would not. She kept walking, the grip on her market basket all the tighter. She was no longer that young, naive girl Bennet Pierson had taken advantage of. She could take care of herself—and she would.

Henry, at one of the tellers' cages to oversee a rather large with-drawal, spotted Miss Caldwell on the sidewalk outside, slowing in front of the bank. He lost count of the money in his palm. Would she come in?

But then she continued at a faster pace than before. Surely this street wasn't on her normal route for errands. Had she intended to come inside but changed her mind? Why? And why would she have wanted to come here in the first place?

He nearly dropped the money he was distributing to go out after her.

But instead, knowing not only his duty but that such an action would have been hard to explain—a banker chasing down a woman on the street?—he went on with his business, just as he always did.

Perhaps, though, he would have Fallo take him home by way of Pierson House this evening. It was several blocks out of the way, but it wouldn't be the first time he'd done so.

It didn't take the glazier long to install a new pane of glass, and when he neared finishing, Dessa went to the kitchen to check on the last-minute preparations for dinner. Duckling, new potatoes, peas in turnip cups, and dinner rolls she had made yesterday. For dessert, she would serve a silver cake that was just like a golden one except she'd siphoned off the egg yolks—which she would use tomorrow for a vanilla pudding recipe.

The duckling only needed to cool a few minutes before she could slice it and serve dinner. After asking Jane to fill the glasses with water, Dessa made her way back outside.

Although the glazier had told her he came at Mr. Foster's request, Mr. Foster himself had not yet arrived. Dessa wondered if she would be relieved or disappointed if she had only the friendly, middle-aged glazier to share her dinner. She should definitely be relieved . . . and yet, she wasn't entirely sure that was all she felt.

However, when she arrived outside to let the glazier know his promised dinner would be served as soon as he was ready, she saw that he and his wagon were already gone.

In the wagon's spot was a fancier carriage, the same one she'd seen earlier that day. Mr. Foster's. She knew because it was pulled by a pair of shiny black horses with long and thick matching manes—a uniquely attractive pair.

Mr. Foster was just alighting.

"That's what I like," he said with a broad smile, "a woman so eager to see her guest that she comes out to the curb to meet him. As long as I am that guest, of course."

Dessa looked around. "Your glazier must have just left. I was about to tell him dinner is ready."

Mr. Foster gently took her arm and looped it through one of his, leading her toward the Pierson House porch. "He's been well compensated, I assure you. But he has a family waiting at home and a wife who would rather he ate dinner only at her table. You understand, of course. This neighborhood has a way of making a woman want to see her man at home, if you know what I mean."

Dessa nodded, though she couldn't deny feeling her pulse speed. It was certainly a reasonable excuse, one she hadn't consid-ered. "I should have extended the invitation to her as well, then. Perhaps she would have enjoyed having someone else cook for both of them."

"No need to worry. Today's job brought him a nice little bonus, and my compliments." He glanced to the repaired window. "Is the work to your satisfaction?"

"Yes," she said, though she didn't look at the window. She looked down the street instead, wondering if the glazier was close enough to hail back. She could ask him to return with his wife. Certainly she could keep the duck warm in the oven. . . .

But instead of seeing the wagon, Dessa spotted another familiar carriage turning onto the street. Surely that was Mr. Hawkins's coachman atop that black lacquered clarence? What in the world had brought him into this neighborhood?

She smiled to herself. Perhaps it wasn't anything in this world at all.

"Oh, Mr. Foster, you'll excuse me, won't you? I believe we have another guest for dinner after all—one of the parties responsible for helping me to open Pierson House."

Mr. Foster's gaze followed the direction of hers, though she noticed his scarred brow—the only apparent flaw on his otherwise handsome face—pulled downward into a frown.

She offered a contrasting smile. "Perhaps it's fortuitous that your glazier couldn't stay. We have just the right number of plates already at the table."

"Indeed."

※

Henry looked down the street as his carriage turned the corner. If all appeared normal at Pierson House, he wouldn't instruct Fallo to stop. How could he? How would he possibly explain a visit? He'd made it clear from the start that he had no real interest in Miss Caldwell or her mission. Stopping by for a neighborly visit was something Tobias would do. Not Henry.

But Henry knew why he'd had his driver go this way and despised himself for his weakness. He simply wanted to see Dessa Caldwell; he'd be a fool to deny how often she came to mind. Seeing her hesitate in front of his bank today had dismantled any power to resist driving by.

It did no good to tell himself men with a past did not pursue polite women who were looking for honesty and a sound reputation in the men they might consider fit to share a future with. His reputation, his fortune, his banking institution were all built upon a foundation of glass. One whisper about how it all began would see it shattered.

Glancing out, the first thing that caught his eye was the carriage stopped in front of Pierson House: a black barouche with the hood drawn over the top, along with a pair of matched Friesians. If the carriage itself wasn't identifiable, the horses were. Turk Foster was known to ride one of those long-maned horses throughout the city—rumor had it that was how he'd seduced more than a few young women. They'd been attracted first to his horse.

Henry's jaw tensed. What was Foster doing at Pierson House? Chasing after a runaway girl from his dance hall, or looking for a new recruit?

Abandoning all thoughts of driving on, Henry tapped his walking stick on the roof of his carriage and Fallo slowed behind Foster's barouche.

"Why, Mr. Hawkins, how nice to see you!"

At the unexpected hail, Henry's driver stopped altogether. Henry hadn't seen Dessa Caldwell on the other side of Foster's carriage until now, but as he hurried to exit his own coach, his gaze fell briefly—disapprovingly—on the man behind her.

Henry tipped his hat. "Good evening, Miss Caldwell. I . . . trust all is well with the sign I hung the other day?" He forced himself to look beyond her to the shingle still affixed to the house. "It's been some time since I trusted my handiwork and had my man drive us by to be sure it was still in place."

To his astonishment, she left Foster's side to thread his arm with her own. "It's as sound as can be, and I'm so very grateful for your help. Do you know Mr. Turk Foster?"

Henry offered his hand, though any warmth he might have

felt a moment before quickly evaporated. Foster took it, appearing every bit as cool as Henry himself.

"Won't you stay for dinner, Mr. Hawkins? It's the least I can do for your trouble. The dinner will be one of gratitude all the way around. To you for the sign, and to Mr. Foster for his help earlier today."

"What help was that?" He hoped his suspicion didn't show through the inquiry.

"One of the street kids threw a rock through her window," Foster said as they walked up to the porch. "I happened to be passing by at the time and offered to have the window repaired."

Henry looked over at the window beside the sign he'd hung. It appeared intact, though now he noticed a few glistening shards on the ground beneath.

"It was fortunate for Miss Caldwell that you happened by," he said. *If it was a coincidence. . . .*

Inside the house, Henry removed his hat and gloves as Foster did the same. Despite being convinced he had been right to drive this way—and right to stop, which had forced a dinner invitation from a woman whose goal in life seemed to be to feed anyone who came by—all Henry felt was irritation. For all the male visitors to this house, a casual observer might think the place fit right into the neighborhood.

Another unwelcome thought crossed Henry's mind as he followed the others to the dining room. Had Foster been approached to run in next year's Senate race, as Lionel had indicated? If Foster had been foolish enough to agree, wouldn't someone like Dessa Caldwell be just the right kind of wife to capture the votes Foster's blemished reputation would scare away otherwise?

"Oh, Mr. Hawkins!" Jane's surprised voice reached him from the direction of the kitchen door. She held out her hand as she approached. "How wonderful to see you."

Henry accepted her handshake while Miss Caldwell spoke.

"Jane, you already know Mr. Hawkins, but I didn't get a chance to introduce you formally to Mr. Turk Foster. Mr. Foster, this is Jane Murphy, who lives here with me at Pierson House."

Henry recognized the interested glint in Foster's eye, creating in Henry an unexpectedly strong sense of protection.

"Dinner will be served shortly, gentlemen," said Miss Caldwell as she left them to approach the kitchen. "Jane, perhaps you could show our guests to the table and have them choose where they'd like to sit."

Miss Caldwell disappeared behind the kitchen door.

"So, Jane," said Foster, "how is it that you're familiar with the elusive Mr. Hawkins? Rumors have always proclaimed him to live in a rather small social circle. A circle of one, if I may say so without offense." He bowed his head Henry's way.

"No offense taken," Henry said, then stepped toward the dining room table with the sincere hope that Jane was too embarrassed to admit how they'd met. If Foster hadn't read about the incident in the newspaper, there was no sense enlightening him. She should put all that behind her, where it was best left.

"Mr. Hawkins and I met at his bank," Jane said without a trace of the chagrin Henry had hoped for.

"That's right," Henry said, and caught Jane's eye with the slightest shake of his head. "Now then, Jane, where will you be sitting? I assume Miss Caldwell will want to take the place closest to the kitchen."

"Oh." She looked momentarily confused, then motioned to the chair on the far side. "I'll sit there."

Henry found his way to the end of the table, opposite where he knew Miss Caldwell would sit. Foster appeared to be contemplating something; otherwise Henry was quite sure they'd have had a race to the seat he now claimed.

"At the bank . . . You're too young to work there, too young to do business there." Foster looked at Henry with a new light in his eye before turning that gaze back to Jane. "You must be the girl I read about, the one who came into the bank and threatened Mr. Hawkins with the false nitro?"

Jane looked abashed at last. "Yes, I'm afraid so." She moved closer to the kitchen door. "I believe I'm needed in the kitchen before we sit."

"So," Foster said, his full attention on Henry now. "I thought there was something curious about that story. You called it a prank, but she clearly intended to rob you."

Henry placed his hands on the chair in front of him, staring at the table rather than at Foster. "It was a prank, nothing more."

"Only because she didn't get away with it. And you let her go. Why? Because she's a girl?"

"She's a child. Children make mistakes."

"I'd say she's a bit more than that," Foster said with a glance toward the kitchen door. Though he'd kept the comment to little more than a whisper, Henry heard the appreciative tone. Perhaps some of the girls on Foster's stage were as young as Jane.

"She has a home here," Henry said, hoping the reminder would keep any thoughts of exploiting the girl far from Foster's mind.

He shrugged, then returned his gaze to Henry. This time Henry did not look away, though the other man's scrutiny went on longer than he thought necessary. "Curious about your letting a would-be thief go, Hawkins. Knowing you by reputation, I'd have said you thought money far more important than forgiveness for a prank, even one from a girl."

Just then Miss Caldwell came through the swinging kitchen door, and Foster's face changed from dubious to welcoming faster than Henry could take his next breath.

Henry might have been out of practice at social gatherings, but he meant to participate in—and direct—this conversation.

He smiled at Miss Caldwell. "I couldn't help but notice the table is set as if you'd expected me. Am I taking someone's place again?"

Miss Caldwell laughed, a sound he found all too pleasant. "I'd invited the glazier who did the work on the window this afternoon, but Mr. Foster said he was unable to attend. So you see? With or without an earlier invitation, Mr. Hawkins, you were meant to sit at this table."

Henry kept his gaze ahead, afraid if he did so much as glance Foster's way, he'd look like the strutting peacock he felt like inside.

"Jane," Henry said after they'd been seated, after Miss Caldwell's prayer for the meal, and after she'd begun filling the plates, "have you decided yet whether or not you'll return to school?" He wasn't above revealing his familiarity with the girl to make it appear to Foster that Henry had more right to sit at this table than he.

"Miss Caldwell and I have discussed it, but I have the rest of summer to decide." She looked hopefully in Henry's direction. "What do you think I should do, Mr. Hawkins? Go back to school, or get a job?"

He was about to answer—school, most definitely—but he'd barely opened his mouth before Foster spoke up. "I can offer you a job starting tomorrow, over at my theater. The Verandah. Have you heard of it?"

Jane shook her head slowly.

"It's the finest concert hall in Denver. I'll admit there is some gaming that goes on, but I assure you—and you, Miss Caldwell— that it's a fine, upstanding venue for variety theater. It's really a happy place! People come every night of the week to laugh and enjoy music and escape the worries of their day." He winked at Jane. "Have you ever wanted to be on the stage, Jane?"

"I . . . hadn't thought of it before. I can't sing." She glanced at

Miss Caldwell. "At least not like Miss Caldwell. I'm good at math, though."

Foster laughed and looked to the head of the table. "You're both welcome to my stage at any time." Then, as if he'd guessed the offer wasn't stirring interest, he raised his glass in a toast to Jane. "Mathematics, eh? I've always admired a smart girl. To perfect the old French proverb that says only men and queens can afford to be ugly, there is nothing more desirable than a girl who is both smart and beautiful."

Jane's cheeks turned instantly pink, and Henry lifted a brow at the man's easy charm. He was clearly everything Henry was not.

The thought prompted him to glance Miss Caldwell's way. Did she think Foster charming? How could she not?

"I'm sure we can find suitable work for you, Jane," Foster went on, "perhaps helping my assistant with the books. He's always appearing overworked and would probably welcome the help of a pretty assistant."

As Jane's brows rose with interest, Henry's gathered in concern. If Miss Caldwell had any idea what Foster was proposing, she'd be protesting already. Get the girl in a place like that and she'd lose any chance in polite society—the kind of society Miss Caldwell would want her to be part of.

"There is an academy over on Seventeenth Street that offers an extensive mathematics course," Henry said. The school was looking to build a larger facility, which required more funds. An exploratory committee had contacted Henry some time ago, trying to sell him on the merits of their faculty. Unfortunately for them at the time, he'd refused to get involved. It was a school exclusively for girls. Until meeting Jane, he'd thought only boys needed the rigorous environment of such a school. "It's called Wolfe Hall. They have scholarships available for young women such as you. Would you be interested?"

"Oh yes, Mr. Hawkins!"

With a mix of satisfaction and secret embarrassment, he turned his attention back to his meal. Scholarships, indeed. He had no idea if they offered such a thing. What he did know, however, was that he'd sooner spit into the wind than have the likes of Turk Foster snatch away a girl he'd already saved from jail once.

Surely an anonymous scholarship fund for the girl could be arranged.

⁂

Dessa sipped the water in her glass, looking at Mr. Hawkins over the brim and trying to hide her astonishment. Was this the same Mr. Hawkins sitting at this very table, the one who had previously offered little more than yes or no to any given question? He was a veritable chatterbox today.

Surely it had been God Himself who'd sent Mr. Hawkins by this evening!

Sometime later, when she saw both gentlemen to the door, after Mr. Foster had kissed her hand in a lingering way that pushed politeness to its rim, she watched Mr. Hawkins place his hat on his head and turn to the door for a silent departure.

But then he turned back to her. "May I say, Miss Caldwell, that the stove has proven to be a fine investment for you?"

Dessa couldn't contain her broad smile. "Why, Mr. Hawkins, that's the nicest thing you've ever said to me."

She was amused at the curious look on Mr. Foster's face as he followed Mr. Hawkins from her house. He was charming, indeed—but she didn't deny that sharing a private exchange with Mr. Hawkins was more delightful than it should be for a woman intent on staying a spinster.

18

Dessa filled the trash bin with the remnants of breakfast: orange peels, the scrapings from her bowl of oatmeal, a few crumbs from the soda biscuits she'd baked. With the food trash separated from the rest, she took it all out to the two bins the garbage wagon would empty on Wednesday.

Outside, she expected the air to be fresh—but as she approached the side of the carriage house where the bins were kept, she smelled something other than the clean air or the trash. She smelled smoke.

Heart pounding, she looked back at the house but saw nothing suspicious, not even from upstairs, where Jane still slept. Turning around, she looked along the yards in both directions.

Nothing.

The smell seemed to be stronger as she approached the covered trash bins. Could someone have tossed in a match?

Instead of lifting the lid on either the food or the regular waste bin, she felt the sides first. Neither was hot.

Yet that smell . . . She looked at the carriage house. It was old and dilapidated, that was true. But the scent seemed stronger now that she was so near the building.

Setting aside the buckets, Dessa approached the door she always had such trouble opening. It took several minutes to pry it loose, even as she tugged it back and forth. Once again it sprang open most unexpectedly.

The scent of smoke was stronger than ever, though she saw

nothing unusual. Stepping inside, she found her eye drawn to the blanket on the bed—more specifically, to a rather large and black circle burned right through to the hay mattress beneath.

Rolling up the rest of the blanket and pressing on the marred center to be sure there were no flames left, she felt dampness instead. Someone had started this fire . . . but just as surely, someone had extinguished it.

Dessa turned around to study the space. There was noplace to hide; she knew she was alone.

Walking back to where the boards were loose, she pushed one. The plank slid easily out of the way, wide enough for her to slip her head outside. Two loose planks, side by side, would allow a person of some girth to pass through. Someone *had* been here! And this was how they were coming and going.

There was no one in the area now, though. Turning back again, she searched for any sign of regular occupancy. There were no clothes, no leftover food, nothing but the burned blanket and a discarded bowl. She realized it was the same one that last time held nuts for that squirrel.

"Oh, Lord," she said aloud, "if someone wants a roof over their head, why won't they come to my front door?"

Determinedly, she left the carriage house to return to the kitchen, where she found the same hammer and supply of nails Mr. Ridgeway had used to hang the sign beside her dining room window. She would show this person, whoever it was, they needn't resort to poaching. They were welcome inside.

She pounded nails in the planks until they were firmly in place—a task that took far longer than she expected. Jane came in search of her and offered to help when Dessa found several more loose boards, all the way around the structure. Between the two of them they sealed sixteen planks—a few of them crookedly, but firmly all the same.

"Now all we have to do is write a note."

"A note?" Jane said, following Dessa inside.

Dessa brushed a loose tendril of hair from her face. Between the morning's exertion and the heat of the sun, she wanted to take a bath. But that would have to wait. "We're going to invite whoever was living here to come to the door."

"But you don't know who it was! It could be anybody. A criminal, even!"

"Then they probably won't take advantage of the offer. But I don't want someone staying here without knowing who it is. They must come to the door to find welcome under either this roof or that one."

Dessa wrote the note, then nailed it to the first plank she'd righted, at the back of the building.

Just as she returned inside the house, her thoughts on that bath, someone knocked at the front door.

🌿

Henry stepped out of his carriage and approached the door to his bank, but something prompted him to take a look around. It had been a long time since he'd felt a pang of nervousness that someone was watching him. Those pangs had faded once he knew he was no longer liable to go to jail for his youthful mistake, particularly after he'd repaid the money he'd stolen so long ago.

But there it was again, the feeling that someone had followed him out to City Park and was even now watching him walk into his bank.

Memories of those two notes came to mind. He'd received only the two, so he'd preferred to forget about them. Until now.

On the top step leading to the door, Henry turned around, pretending he'd forgotten something in his carriage. But instead of going back to the carriage, he scanned the street again. There were a few pedestrians walking on the other side of the road, coming out of the market. A boy ran from one doorway to another, while a delivery wagon sat outside. Nothing unusual, no one even remotely shady.

He shook his head, then continued on toward the bank's entryway.

❦

Dessa opened the door just in time to see the back of a woman dressed in one of the loveliest gowns she'd ever seen. It was far more ornate than something Dessa would wear, the shade a pink of the ripest watermelon, with shirred sleeves that were pulled low off the shoulders to complement a satin basque fading into a pleated skirt drawn tightly at the back. When she turned, Dessa's eye was immediately drawn to the low and wide cut of the square décolletage, made almost decent by a threadlike trim along the edge.

"Hello!" Dessa said, opening the door wider. She wished she hadn't exerted herself quite so much this morning; she felt soiled and ugly next to this light-haired beauty. "Come in, won't you? I'm Dessa Caldwell."

The young woman looked momentarily indecisive, as if she might turn around again. She clutched a velvet pouch so tightly that Dessa saw her knuckles were nearly as white as the handkerchief sticking out the side of one hand.

Dessa neared her. "Is that one of the handkerchiefs I made?"

The woman held it out, not so much to hand it back as to simply show it. "I stole it from another girl."

It didn't matter. "Come in, won't you?" Dessa nearly whispered the invitation, but it was enough. As she held the door, the other woman came inside. "Can I get you something? Tea, perhaps? Would you like breakfast, or perhaps an early lunch?"

She shook her head. "No . . . I don't know why I came." She

turned back to the door, but Dessa still stood near it. "I need to go."

"Oh, but do stay!" Dessa insisted. "Just for a visit."

Dessa led the woman to the settee in the parlor just as Jane joined them from the kitchen. Dessa introduced Jane, though she couldn't offer the name of their guest in return.

Jane looked between the visitor and Dessa. "Do you want me to keep sewing those pillowcases?"

Dessa nodded, grateful the girl had noticed the other woman's tension. "Yes, Jane. There is more material upstairs. Take your time finding something suitable, all right?"

With Jane gone, Dessa turned her attention fully on the woman who sat on her settee. "Are you quite sure you wouldn't like something? Tea?" Dessa gave a quick smile as she watched the woman twist the ribbon on her little pouch. "I don't like tea much myself, but I've always welcomed it when I'm looking to do something with my hands."

The woman's light eyes took on a hint of what could only be relief. With that simple observation and admission, Dessa had broken through, tipped the woman's indecision in favor of staying. The woman burst into tears, and Dessa moved immediately to a spot next to her so she could put her arms around her.

"Oh!" She leaned back from Dessa's touch.

"I'm sorry," Dessa said gently, settling her hands back in her lap. "I only wanted to offer comfort."

The woman stood, but thankfully did not go near the door. She moved to the chair Dessa had vacated. Then she wiped at her tears, using the handkerchief in the very manner Dessa had hoped it would be used. "It's been a long time since anyone's touched me without wanting something."

"I shouldn't have assumed you'd welcome such contact," Dessa admitted. "I'm so very sorry."

The woman shook her head, then wiped away another tear and offered an unexpected, brief laugh. "I'm a little nervous, but I suppose that's obvious." She took a moment to compose herself, closing her eyes, stiffening her shoulders. Then she opened her eyes and looked at Dessa curiously. "Do you know that we can hear you singing those hymns at night? Here you are, singing to God while Miss Leola curses you. She's just happy you go to bed early, or you'd ruin her business altogether."

"I never meant any harm. Is my voice so unpleasant?"

"No, not at all," she said. "It's *what* you're singing, not how you're singing. Men don't tend to stop in when they hear words like 'Sinner, come home.'"

"I suppose I should offer an apology," Dessa said with a smile, "but it wouldn't be a very honest one."

"Miss Leola always has the piano player play his loudest while you sing, so anyone who makes it past the door won't be bothered. I suppose she should apologize for that."

Dessa thanked her, then said, "Do you mind if I ask your name? I'm so glad you've come, but I don't know what to call you."

"I'm known as Miss Remee to everyone around here. You've probably guessed I live at the bordello down the street."

Dessa nodded. "You're most welcome here, Miss Remee. For as long as you like."

Miss Remee looked around the room, her gaze settling on the stenciled wall. "My mother used to have curtains in the kitchen with pineapples on them. A symbol of welcome, she used to say."

"That's what I hoped they would be here, too."

Miss Remee's delicate brows tried to gather, but her forehead was too smooth for such an expression to mar her appearance. Her eyes were a lovely shade of amber, nearly gold, and just now they seemed to be swimming in a pool replenished with diamonds.

"My mother's kitchen wasn't very welcoming, though. Not once it was obvious I wouldn't attract a suitable husband."

"Does your mother live here in Denver?"

She wiped her eyes again, dabbed at her nose. "My folks are in Indiana. Far enough away, even with the railroad."

"Sometimes distance is just what we need."

"That or a shotgun." She smiled at Dessa's raised brows. "Say, do you have a family you left behind somewhere?"

Dessa shook her head. "Plenty of bad memories, though." Then she asked, "Are you sure you wouldn't like some refreshment?"

Miss Remee hesitated, but a slow smile soon appeared. "I overheard a couple of the girls claiming you bake a good scone."

19

A LOUD BANGING roused Dessa from a deep sleep. She sat up with the sense that before she'd even awakened, her heart rate had quickened. The pace only multiplied when she heard Jane's frightened voice.

"Miss Dessa?"

Dessa jumped from her bed and opened her bedroom door, ushering in the girl.

"Did you hear that banging? There! Someone's trying to come in. And it's not even sunrise yet!"

Dessa looked at the watch she kept by her bedside, lit by moonlight streaming in from the open window. It was just before four in the morning, and the sun was nowhere in sight.

"Stay up here, Jane. I'll see who it is."

"But, Miss Dessa!" Jane grabbed her hand. "Aren't you afraid?"

Yes, she wanted to say. But she shook her head, though she was sure it did little to convince the girl. At the top of the stairs she met Miss Remee, who'd taken residency in the third bedroom.

"Has this ever happened before?" Remee asked, pulling closed a robe provided from the donation box. She'd left behind all of her fancy gowns and nightclothes as payment for what she owed Miss Leola, bringing with her only one small satchel of belongings.

Fortified by Miss Remee's presence—even in the few days

175

since she'd joined them, Dessa had learned she was as tough as mutton—she answered with a voice far more brave than she'd felt a moment ago. "Only once. A drunkard. Perhaps it's him again."

Downstairs, Dessa approached the door while Remee went to the window to peek out. "Do you see anything?" Dessa whispered.

Remee shook her head.

"Who is it?" Dessa shouted through the door.

"It's me, Miss Molly Malone. Fergal. Fergal Dunne. I have your note."

"My note?"

"The one from the carriage house, don't ya know?"

Miss Remee joined Dessa at the door. "That's Fergal Dunne, all right. I'd know his voice anywhere. Let him in. He's harmless."

Dessa shook her head, having recognized the Irishman's voice too. "And drunk, no doubt. I can't let a man in here. Donors would stop their support the minute they found out." Thankfully the Plumsteads had sent the donation she'd feared would not come, and she'd been able to make her first bank payment. But that didn't mean such a thing would continue if the reputation of Pierson House were compromised. The Naracott donations were every bit as vital, and Dessa still worried their support could easily waver.

Remee reached past Dessa to pull open the door. "Then they won't find out."

A moment later the same drunken man who'd shown up shortly after she'd moved in was once again tottering into Dessa's parlor.

"Why, Miss Remee!" He swayed before the other woman, his eyes blinking as if to clear his vision. "I heard a rumor ya might have come down here. And here ya be!"

"Yes, it's true. But what are you doing here? Why aren't you at Miss Anabel's?"

"Got sacked." Fergal Dunne wandered unsteadily to the chair

nearby and plunked himself down. "Ah, 'tis a sad day when a man canna hold a job." He looked up at them, swiping a sleeve over his mouth. "'Tis the drink, you know. It's me ruin; it has an evil grip."

Dessa stepped closer. "So you're the one who's been living in the carriage house, Mr. Dunne?"

He pulled off his hat and attempted to bow while still seated. "Only between—" he burped—"jobs."

"And what is it you do?"

"He's a bouncer," Remee said. "Only no one keeps him on because he drinks all the whiskey meant for the girls and patrons. And when he promises to stop, the moment he has any money he goes out to buy his own. What kind of bouncer can barely keep on his feet, Fergal? It's no wonder you can't hold a job."

He placed his hat over his heart and closed his eyes. A week's worth of stubble lined his chubby chin, and his hat was every bit as crumpled as it had been the first time he'd visited.

"Too true, all." Then he opened his eyes, took a moment to focus as his drunken gaze sought Dessa. "Which is why I shall be needin' the use of the carriage house, if ya please. I've noplace else to go. Perhaps I might be the bouncer here, since ya have a few girls with ya now?"

Just as he asked the question, Jane peered around the wall separating the parlor from the staircase—wide-eyed but without the fear she'd exhibited earlier.

"I'll work for meals," Mr. Dunne offered. "Meals and a roof . . . such as it is in the carriage house, with more than a wee bit of a hole up there."

Now Remee and Jane both looked at Dessa, as if wondering whether she could turn out someone in such obvious need.

She folded her arms against the chill. "Only until you find other employment, Mr. Dunne. And only as long as you stay sober. Do you understand? You'll find no strong drink here, and I want none of it in that carriage house."

He wobbled to his feet. "Ah, bless ya, bless ya indeed. 'Tis a true saint's heart ya have beatin' in there, Miss Molly Malone."

"Miss Caldwell," she corrected him but doubted he'd heard or would care, at least not until he was sober.

"And no cigars, either, Mr. Dunne," she said as she steadied him on his way to the back door.

"So that's how ya found me out," he said over his shoulder. "Cigars and whiskey. Never was there such an evil pair. . . ."

Dessa shook her head, wondering all the way to the carriage house if taking him in was what Sophie Pierson would have done.

Somehow, she doubted it.

❧

Henry sat at his desk, having arrived earlier than usual since rain had gotten in the way of his morning walk. He stared at the paperwork before him but saw not a bit of it. Too many thoughts were in the way. Wasted thoughts, useless ones. All centered around one person.

To his surprise and Tobias's delight, Miss Caldwell had delivered her first payment in person. Henry had missed the momentous occasion, having been in an investment meeting, but Tobias had told him about it with a gleam of pride in his faded-blue eyes.

Irritated with himself for wasting a full five minutes simply staring rather than working, Henry leaned over his desk once again. But nothing could make him concentrate, not even his irritated impatience.

Such preoccupation was what came of being dragged back into society. He'd been happy enough on his own before this, hadn't he? Well, perhaps *happy* wasn't the right word. Certainly content. At least he hadn't been *un*happy living withdrawn from the world, detached and dispassionate. It was a life he'd been resigned to ever since the day he left Chicago. It was there he'd realized the choices he'd made before had allowed business success but destroyed any hope of success in personal matters.

When Tobias rapped on the door as he opened it, Henry was relieved at the interruption.

For the first ten minutes as Tobias went over various reports he'd brought with him, Henry kept his mind where it ought to have been all morning. No more visions of Dessa Caldwell—or worse, Turk Foster calling on Dessa Caldwell. Perhaps he would have a productive day after all.

When Tobias rose from his chair to leave, he shifted his paperwork from both hands to one, then put his free hand into his pocket.

"Henry," he said, as if unsure of his next words. He pulled something from that pocket—a familiar handkerchief, although it was an odd shade for anyone's taste, a lackluster beige. Henry had seen that particular slip of material before, when Tobias had stuffed it into one of the drawers of his desk. An odd handkerchief, indeed, that he seemed strangely protective of. "I wonder if I could have a word with you."

Henry looked up at him, not annoyed but not interested, either. "I thought that was what we've been doing?"

Tobias shook his head. "No, this is rather more personal than business. It's just . . . I'm not sure how to approach the subject, or if it's my place to do so."

Henry folded his arms over his chest. "Neither of us has time to stutter and stumble through some awkward uncle-to-nephew conversation. Why don't you go back to your own office, and once you've figured out what you want to say—and if you still want to say it—come back and have done with it."

Tobias opened his mouth, once again tugged on the material

from his pocket, only to return it to where it had been. Then he shook his head, turned, and walked to the door. "No."

"No?"

He turned back at the door. "I haven't any peace about it just yet. Perhaps the subject is unnecessary, after all. Good day, Henry."

Henry glanced at the clock on his wall. "Good day? Are you leaving, Tobias? The day's barely begun."

But Tobias didn't answer; he walked from the office, not bothering to close the door on his way out.

Henry watched his uncle as long as he could, but Tobias disappeared once he rounded Mr. Sprott's desk.

Henry scowled as he tried shifting his attention back to his work. He knew exactly what Tobias wanted to talk to him about. They may have settled into a bank-president-and-manager relationship over the years, but the fact remained that Tobias was the only relative Henry still had any contact with. As Henry's uncle, perhaps he felt it his duty to speak up about Henry's choice to live the life of a social recluse. Heaven knew he'd tried many times to draw Henry out. Those dinner parties he held to impress investors hadn't been Henry's idea.

And now Tobias probably suspected Henry's growing, unwieldy infatuation with Dessa Caldwell. Tobias had already tried nurturing it, and he'd no doubt push them right down the aisle if he could. Why not? Wasn't his nephew like every other healthy young man, wanting home, hearth, and family?

And Henry did. Oh, how he did. He wasn't foolish enough to forget the fact that he was getting older. If he didn't marry soon, obtaining a wife and having children would become more a burden to them than a blessing. What wife wanted an old husband? Worse, what child wanted a father who more resembled a grandfather? Henry knew what it was like to lose a father; it wasn't something he wished upon his own children.

There was only one question that trumped all of those. What wife, what child, wanted a man who might very well be destined for financial and social ruin?

Unfortunately for Henry, even the most somber answer did not keep him from devising possible reasons to see Miss Caldwell— even without Uncle Tobias's interference.

20

DESSA HAD WORRIED that having a man sit at their breakfast, lunch, and dinner table would invade the privacy and female camaraderie she was trying so hard to build between herself and her two new boarders. But Fergal Dunne was more like an eccentric old uncle than an interloper—and he never ate breakfast, leaving at least one meal each day just for the ladies. Plus, through the first week, Fergal had stayed sober.

It was a week of hope and laughter under the Pierson House roof. Over various sewing projects Dessa had designed, they got to know each other. Jane had set a tone of chatty openness earlier in the week, revealing more about her growing-up years in Nebraska, where all her happy memories had been left behind. Since coming to Colorado, she'd found nothing but heartache, at least before she'd come to Pierson House.

Why her father had suddenly left his stable job as a clerk in an Omaha warehouse she would never know. He'd always been so reliable back home . . . not unlike Mr. Hawkins, she'd added. That was how she preferred to remember her father. As a clerk, not as a gold-seeking dreamer, a dejected miner, or a frustrated smelter who'd died far too young.

Miss Remee was slower to reveal her past, at first saying only that she'd left family behind in Indiana. But today, just after lunch when they'd enjoyed a companionable silence for a while, she started talking without even being asked.

She told them her father had never forgiven her when the man she was supposed to marry broke off their engagement because of rumors he'd heard about her. Rumors that were mostly true, about disappearing from a party for several hours with the dashing cousin of her best friend, a young man from New York who dazzled everyone he met. Including and most especially Remee—although it had broken her heart to learn he hadn't thought her worthy of marriage, not even when the rumors about them spread like dust on the wind.

It hadn't taken long for her misplaced trust to destroy her reputation as well as her future. So she'd left home to find an independent life in the West, leaving her past far behind her. But like Jane, she'd found the respectable jobs didn't pay enough to live on. At first she'd supplemented her income only now and then, arranging to meet certain men for a certain price. Eventually, though, full-time prostitution had provided the best financial security she could find.

"I thought I was lucky to get into Miss Leola's," Remee finished. "I had my regulars and most of them weren't too bad." She lifted her gaze to stare straight ahead, but Dessa could tell from the hardness on the other woman's face that the memories were anything except pleasant. "But some of them wanted more than what they paid for. I don't know what was worse: suffering a slap now and then or some pitiful soul begging me to pretend I loved him. They were just renting my body. What right did that give any of them to think they should have something more from me?"

Dessa listened, as did Jane, as Remee talked on. She told of women who had been abandoned by their husbands and forced into the sporting world to take care of the children they sent to boarding schools. About women who ran off from homes where they were ill-used, only to suffer another kind of ill use by society.

Women with no trade other than their bodies, foolish young girls who'd been tricked into believing a sporting life was easy and profitable, women who turned to alcohol or opium to lessen the burden that came not only with social ostracism and contempt, but with the deep-down knowledge that they sold something most people believed was never meant to be used in such a way.

"You want this place to attract women like me, Miss Caldwell? You get them here with the promise of making money." Remee looked at the embroidered pillowcase in her hands. "Not the pittance we can make with things like this. You find a way for a gal to support herself without selling her body, and you'll see a line of women eager to get in. And when you figure that out, you ought to say something about earning money in those flyers you pass around."

When a knock at the door sounded, Dessa rose to answer it, sorry that the interruption had cut Remee short. She was no doubt right about the financial needs of women in her situation. But how could Pierson House promise anything but living off the generosity of sympathetic donors?

Opening the front door, she found Rye with a bouquet of flowers so wide he had to hold it with both of his scrawny hands.

"For you, Miss Caldwell. From Mr. Foster."

Dessa had been about to receive them when the name stopped her short. She should have guessed. This was the third time he'd sent her flowers, along with a note asking once again to escort her to the Tabor Opera House. Would the man never give up?

It also meant she would probably be seeing him sometime soon; the last time he'd sent flowers, just a few days ago, they had served as a prelude to his arrival.

"Come inside, Rye," she said, not entirely pleased by the pretty bouquet or the note accompanying it. "We have scones on the kitchen table."

"Yeah?" he said, passing her for a quick jaunt to the kitchen.

At the dining room table, Dessa addressed Jane. "Perhaps you might pour him some milk to go with the scones?"

Jane nodded, but her gaze was on the flowers. "Mr. Foster again?"

"Yes, I'm afraid so."

"I don't know what Foster is up to," Remee said, looking at the delivery with raised brows. "From what I hear of him, he's not the marrying kind. But if you ask me, you're lucky to have caught his attention."

"Was he a regular visitor to Miss Leola's?" Jane asked from the kitchen door. Dessa was glad the girl had stayed long enough to ask, because she wanted to know too. "Is that how you know him?"

"No, I never once saw him there. Let's just say lots of girls would've been happy to give him their services for free. As if he were a mac."

"A mac?" Jane repeated.

Remee smiled. "I don't think Miss Dessa would approve of educating you on sporting terms, Jane." She slid a glance Dessa's way, then continued despite her words. "Maquereaux like to call themselves 'one lover to many ladies,' but they're nothing but salesmen sampling the wares they sell. And what they sell are the women they've likely seduced into the trade."

"Oh, you mean a pimp?"

"Jane!" Dessa said, surprised the girl knew the term and hoping Rye hadn't heard from the other side of the door. He might not be much younger than Jane, and he no doubt knew a lot from living on the streets, but Dessa had no desire to add to his education.

The girl's cheeks pinkened, but she raised her brows in indignation all the same. "I worked in a factory, Miss Dessa. You don't work in one long before you learn a *few* things."

Dessa looked again at Remee once Jane closed the kitchen door behind her. "Do you think Mr. Foster is invested in prostitution?" That was just what Dessa needed, to be inadvertently involved with a man who kept the very business going that she wanted most to fight! "Is there anything I should know, considering Mr. Foster has been here under our roof?"

"I never made it a point to get too involved in anyone's business but my own, so I don't know much about Mr. Foster. Except that he's popular with the ladies on or *off* the Line." Remee cocked her head to one side. "Any gal would brag if she'd been to Foster's place. Lots of deep pockets on the patrons there! If Foster had let us, we'd have attended there every night in the hope of finding rich lovers."

"He says his place is all perfectly respectable."

Remee laughed. "It's a theater, but it's mostly women who sing and dance on his stage. Everybody stops whatever game they're playing to watch the shows because they're so good."

"But it's respectable?"

Any trace of a smile on Remee's face disappeared with Dessa's persistence. "Look, Foster's Verandah is as respectable as it gets. It's not a brothel, if that's what you want to know."

Dessa looked again at the flowers and the note. "It's just that I heard he's . . . well, I guess you'd call him of the snake variety. Not taking no for an answer suggests he might just be a snake after all. A polite person would stop asking after a time or two."

"If he *is* a snake—and I don't think he is—then he's a rattler." She winked. "That's a gentleman kind of snake. Warns its victim first, you know?"

Later that afternoon, Dessa stopped by Mariadela's for a variety of plants divided from those in the Whites' garden. But the lovely greens couldn't lift her spirits once Mariadela told Dessa her news.

"The Plumsteads are leaving Denver?"

"I'm afraid it's worse than it sounds, Dessa. They're going back East to live with family. The donation they made a few days ago will be their last."

They were on the porch overlooking Mariadela's yard, where the plants had been neatly tucked in a burlap sack, awaiting Dessa's pickup. Thankfully there was a set of wicker chairs nearby, because Dessa needed one to sink into.

"Couldn't they wire their donations here? Or . . . leave something behind, a fund of some kind? Perhaps Mr. Hawkins's bank could arrange—"

Mariadela was already shaking her head and joined Dessa on an open chair. "I'm afraid they're leaving because they've lost their income. I don't know the details, but apparently the mine Mr. Plumstead invested in has gone dry. I'm so sorry, Dessa, but we can't count on them for further donations. Mr. Plumstead even came by this morning to see William. I heard him hint that he hoped to get back the funds he gave us."

"You told him that's impossible, I hope! I've already handed it over to the bank."

"I heard William say that very thing. Mr. Plumstead was likely too proud to come directly to you, but he's known for some time that things were going bad. The truth is they haven't a penny to spare, especially now."

Dessa's chest felt so weighted she could barely breathe. "But what are *we* to do?" The moment she heard her own words she wished them back. "Oh, I'm sorry. I can't imagine how difficult this must be for them. Yet . . . it puts Pierson House at risk."

Tears heated the rims of her eyes, but she refused to cave in to them. She stood, taking up the burlap bag. There was no sense sitting here wallowing in her worries.

"I know you'll be praying with me," Dessa said over her shoulder. "Don't stop until we have the answer."

Dessa should have taken a hansom cab but knew sitting still was impossible. She needed to move, to spend some of her nervous energy. Once she reached Pierson House, she didn't go inside.

She wasn't yet ready to face Jane or Remee. Leaving the burlap bag in front of the house, she went round to the porch for a garden hat, gloves, and small shovel. She'd never stored such things in the carriage house, not with its faulty door, and since Mr. Dunne had taken up residence in there she was glad not to have any need to go in.

Mr. Dunne. He would have to leave too if they couldn't afford Pierson House anymore. Her leaden heart sank even lower.

But she refused to give in to the desire to sit down and cry.

It was well into summer, and these plants needed planting. Certainly they would make Pierson House all the more appealing with a garden of its own to greet every visitor. She swallowed the lingering lump in her throat. She'd actually looked forward to this task, but now it came with a sense of desperation. She must make this place at least *look* like it would succeed!

Oh, Lord, please open some funds from somewhere to help us!

There wasn't much room between the house and the street, but Dessa meant to make the most of what soil she had to work with. She should have been tired after the long walk from Mariadela's, but she still had plenty of energy. She dug into the ground without mercy.

The first cuttings went in easily, but she had little sense of satisfaction. Money, she decided, was more trouble than it was worth. Why must she always worry about it? If only the value of a service, not its popularity, determined revenue.

"Good afternoon, Miss Caldwell!"

Dessa turned from her task, the effort to rid her face of a scowl nearly more than she could handle.

Dismounting from horseback was Turk Foster. Apprehension

flared in place of her temporarily squashed worries. Setting aside the hand shovel, she removed her dirty gloves and watched him tether his fine, shiny black horse to the hitching post near the curb. The animal—one from the pair he'd used to pull his carriage—possessed an incredibly long mane that, at least for a moment, calmed her senses with a vision of God's artistry.

"How do you do, Mr. Foster?" she asked as she accepted his extended hand—a gesture he drew out to simply hold her hand. "Your horse is certainly lovely."

Still not letting go, he looked over his shoulder at the mount. "Yes, she's a beauty, isn't she?" Then, both hands covering hers now, he added, "I'm a great admirer of beauty, which automatically makes me a great admirer of yours."

Pulling her hand from his gentle captivity, she murmured her thanks, glad when he turned his attention to her work behind them.

"And what have you embarked upon today?"

"It doesn't look very appealing yet, I admit, but before many days have gone by, I'm hoping this will be the brightest spot on the street."

Mr. Foster returned his gaze to hers and tipped his hat. "I'm sure it's that already, Miss Caldwell." He winked. "Quite sure, in fact."

She offered a smile before looking away again. Perhaps he wasn't a rattler, after all. More like one of those snakes a charmer used, that stared before striking. "I hope you won't mind if I don't neglect my work. I really ought to get back to it."

He looked toward the house. "Are you all alone? No more boarders?"

"Oh no! Jane is still here, of course, and I don't believe you've met my newest guest." Then, as an afterthought, she added, "Actually we have two new boarders. One of them is in the carriage house."

"The carriage house? Your rooms are full already?"

"We have room for several more ladies, particularly if we put more than one to a room. So if you know of anyone, please tell them about us." Surely her tone hadn't matched the desperation in her heart. It wasn't too late to fill up the rooms, and in so doing attract new donors.

"Sounds like you're creating a nice little family here." Then he frowned. "Well, except for the poor creature in the carriage house. Why have you banished one from the house? Someone from Hop Alley, maybe?"

"No, that boarder is a man. I'm not at all certain we should have agreed to take him in, so his stay may be brief. But he has noplace else to go for the time being."

"And who is this man? Perhaps I can help out, take him off your hands."

Her brows rose. If Mr. Dunne secured an income, they might ask him to contribute toward the loan payment! "It would be so helpful if you could give him a job. Only . . . I must warn you he has a taste for drink. But if your theater doesn't sell alcohol, it could work out wonderfully."

"I'm afraid alcohol flows rather freely at my establishment—to offer my patrons every enjoyment of their choosing, of course." He grinned. "After a glass of wine or two, all my performers become incredibly talented."

She supposed she should have been amused by his attempted wit, but the brief moment of hope so quickly burst wouldn't allow her encouragement of any kind. She shook her head. "Then having my boarder join you can't possibly work, since Mr. Dunne readily admits he cannot stay away from strong drink."

"Mr. Dunne?" he repeated. "Fergal Dunne?"

"Why, yes. Do you know him?"

"Yes, I'm afraid I do. And you'd be wise to tell him to leave.

He'll find a way to drink, Miss Caldwell, and be a pest until he does."

"I'm sure you're right, but I can't seem to get him to seek help elsewhere. He insists he doesn't want to leave the neighborhood."

"Why leave the land where alcohol flows out of nearly every spigot?"

Dessa pulled on her gardening gloves again. "Thank you for your concern and advice, Mr. Foster."

Instead of taking his leave, he placed a hand on each of her arms, effectively forcing her to look at him again. She knew such contact wouldn't be permitted in polite society but reminded herself she wasn't sure that was where she lived anymore . . . or belonged.

"Miss Caldwell." He freed her arms and smiled abashedly over his touch. "I came by to issue yet another invitation to the opera, this time in person, with the hope that you'll see on my face how eager I am to have you accept. Is there any particular reason you continue to refuse me?"

"I thought I explained already, Mr. Foster. I rarely attend social events unless they're connected to raising donations for Pierson House." She'd looked away, but now sent him a quick, exploratory glance. "And if I may be even more personal than that, I don't participate in behavior that can be described as . . . courting."

"Now that, Miss Caldwell, is a travesty." He'd caught and held her gaze steadily, and she did not doubt his sincerity. She shouldn't let it warm her heart, but it happened anyway, burrowing its way right through her downtrodden mood. "You are a lovely young woman of virtue and generosity. Any man on earth would be pleased to court you."

Nor should she let him look at her that way. . . . She turned, wishing either Jane or Remee would walk out the front door. Perhaps Dessa should have learned by now how to refuse a man, except that she had encountered so few of them while living her nomadic life with Sophie, and her frantically busy one since settling in Denver.

"Thank you for your kind words, Mr. Foster, but I really must get back to work on my garden."

Still, he made no move to depart. "You know where that leaves me, don't you?" The timbre of his voice was light, appealingly playful. Flirtatious. "With no alternative but to arrange a fund-raising opportunity for you."

Dessa's weary heart picked up a beat. "What sort of opportunity?"

"To do exactly as you wish: raise money for Pierson House. Why not? I have a theater, don't I? A business that can be dedicated—at least for one special day—to a cause more worthy than fattening my own pockets?"

Caution tempered her interest, but interest definitely ignited. Urgently. "Here, in this neighborhood of the Fourth Ward? Raise funds for an alternative to . . . well, to certain kinds of businesses this area of the city is known for?"

"You'd be surprised how those on the polite edges of the ward claim one thing while doing another. I'm sure we'll soon have everyone in Denver talking about your Pierson House."

"You're willing to do this just because I won't go to the opera with you?"

"Opera is not the point. I simply and honestly want to spend time with you. What better way than to work toward the same goal—together?"

Dessa continued to eye him. He was eager, all right. And a theater was a viable venue to raise a significant amount of money. But was it proper? She recalled how Remee had described Foster's Verandah. As respectable as this end of town could get. What did that mean? More importantly, what would it mean to other donors supporting Pierson House?

But how could she not consider the opportunity, especially in light of losing the Plumsteads' support? Was it just a coincidence that Mr. Foster should come along on this very day and present her with such an idea? Or was it all in God's timing? God was known for answering prayers nearly instantly . . . and in unusual ways too.

Together, she and Mr. Foster might raise enough not just for next month's payment, but to pay down a good portion of her entire debt to the bank. To Mr. Hawkins. Would Dessa's impatience to open Pierson House be forgotten if she could pay off the loan without complete dependence upon the regular donors?

She removed one of her gloves again and extended her hand. "All right, Mr. Foster. Your offer is too generous to refuse. Come inside, won't you? Perhaps we can start planning right away."

21

On Sunday morning, Henry ordered breakfast a full two hours earlier than usual for the only day of the week he did not go to the bank. He then summoned his driver, Fallo.

"To the City Garden, sir?" Fallo asked as he opened the carriage door. He never called it City Park or Denver Park as others did, but rather what the city hoped it would become one day: a vast garden to attract respectable citizens and discourage those who only wanted to escape the city's laws.

"No, Fallo. No walk today, at least not for now." He handed Fallo a slip of paper with an address scrawled on it, the same slip Henry had been given yesterday afternoon by a man he'd hired to bring him information. It hadn't taken long to figure out where Reverend Sempkins was the pastor, and just as quickly he had verified that Dessa Caldwell attended there regularly, along with the White family. Henry even knew where they sat.

As Fallo looked at the address, he uttered a cough no doubt meant to cover a gasp of surprise. Henry settled himself in the carriage without so much as a glance Fallo's way.

Henry knew what this meant, this venture into society. What more common way was there to join a community than to attend one of its churches? Every habit he had nurtured since he'd settled in Denver protested this as the wrong thing to do. This sort of action would undoubtedly have people thinking he wanted to get to know them. He'd likely receive more invitations to social events, to dinners. All things his diligently private lifestyle had diminished, despite the brief period of resuscitation Jane's prank at the bank had created.

Besides the obvious potential to inconvenience his entire life, he also knew this could be seen as a first step in making known his personal interest in Miss Caldwell. How could anyone see it otherwise? How could *she* not recognize it for what it was?

It was insane, this whole idea. Henry very nearly rapped on the carriage ceiling to have Fallo turn around. But instead he gripped the tip of his walking stick as if it were alive and he needed to subdue it.

The truth was, Henry wanted this chance. Maybe he wanted it more than he wanted to protect himself.

Only Jane accompanied Dessa to church on Sundays, riding with her in William and Mariadela White's carriage. Although Dessa had invited Remee and Mr. Dunne as well, they chose to stay at home. She knew Mr. Dunne had a few books in the carriage house that he'd scrounged up somewhere; she'd seen him on that cot, passing the time reading. If only she could get him to read one of her favorite collections of sermons, or the Bible itself.

Perhaps she ought to stipulate church attendance as a requirement for staying at Pierson House. What harm would it do? It had never occurred to her that someone wouldn't want to go to church, since it was a highlight of her own week.

Dessa had planned to speak to Mariadela about Mr. Foster's offer for a benefit on their way to church that morning, but the opportunity didn't easily arise. She might have been more determined to bring up the issue, but the truth was Dessa felt as nervous as she was excited about the arrangement. Raising funds in a new way certainly made sense, but would the tactic appeal to Mariadela, who resided outside the Fourth Ward?

Jane had yet to learn about the plan, but Remee had been in the parlor when Dessa brought Mr. Foster inside. She'd been pleased enough to meet him, though she hadn't offered more than a nod at his introduction. However, she'd shown quick enthusiasm about partnering with his Verandah. Not only would such an event create much-needed attention for Pierson House; Remee was sure it would bring in a considerable amount of money.

Not long after taking her place in the pew the White family normally occupied, Dessa joined the congregation in one of her best-loved hymns.

> "'Tis so sweet to trust in Jesus,
> Just to take Him at His word;
> Just to rest upon His promise,
> Just to know 'Thus saith the Lord.'"

As usual when Dessa sang, her surroundings soon faded as she relished the words and melody. She closed her eyes after the first chorus, letting the next verse become a prayer that took her spirit to the presence of God. Heart soaring, she wished the moment would last forever.

Shuffling sounded behind her, calling her attention back to her surroundings. It wasn't unusual for worshipers to continue arriving even during the first few songs of the service. There were always latecomers, and very often the only seats left were those toward the front, where she and the White family always sat. She ignored the slight noise and continued singing . . . until the voices around her began to fade. Soon she felt as if she were the only one in the pew still worshiping.

Dessa opened her eyes, looking down the row to see Mariadela's wide-eyed gaze aimed beyond her. On Dessa's other side was Jane, but she was looking behind her as well and Dessa couldn't see around the girl's poke bonnet. Curious, Dessa turned to see what could possibly be of such interest to have stopped them from singing.

Mr. Henry Hawkins stood in the pew directly behind Dessa. He looked straight ahead, his entire being stiff, as if he were aware he'd been the cause of the disturbance and wished to avoid further attention. The congregation gradually regained its voice.

> "Jesus, Jesus, how I trust Him!
> How I've proved Him o'er and o'er!
> Jesus, Jesus, precious Jesus!
> Oh, for grace to trust Him more!"

It took a moment for Dessa to join back in, but not before realizing her heart was once again soaring—though not in an entirely spiritual way.

Henry heard not a word of the service until halfway through the sermon. Before then, he'd stared sightlessly ahead, feeling every bit the fool he was. What was he doing here? Why had he thought, even for a moment, that he could thrust off the shackles of his past?

But when Reverend Sempkins spoke about a man being different once he had the Spirit of God inside him, Henry couldn't help but listen. God's presence was bound to change a man. To the reverend there was no doubt about it.

God knew Henry needed to change. Other than his servants, the only companions Henry had these past years were guilt and fear. On occasion, Uncle Tobias buffaloed his way past the gates Henry had built, but he was the only one who tried anymore. Henry had not visited his mother, nor had she visited him, in over two years. It was too much to endure their stilted conversations and her pained, searching gazes amid the effort of acting like anything but the stranger he'd come to be. And so he'd stopped visiting altogether, convinced if she knew the truth about her only child she would have nothing to do with him.

There was no evidence of any personal relationships in Henry's life. Who, other than Tobias, even called Henry by his first name? A few investors, that was all. It had been so long since he'd heard a woman refer to him as anything other than Mr. Hawkins that he'd forgotten what his name might sound like in a female voice.

And yet . . . the words from the reverend assured him that God made everything new—made people new. What He did on the cross blotted out the past. The thought—this notion that Christ had paid for Henry's sin—demanded pondering, something Henry found himself hoping to do.

No sooner had such thoughts tempted comfort than a new one besieged him: *Heavenly forgiveness is one thing; earthly quite another.* Someone knew his past. What other meaning could those two notes have had than to carry a threat? How much the author of those notes really knew might be doubtful—but evidently he or she knew enough to be suspicious of Henry and his character.

He looked around, a renewed sense of panic settling on him. It was too much, this battle inside him. He'd been wrong to assume he could do anything more for society than what he did at the bank.

The truth was, he had no chance—not at rejoining society, and especially not with a woman like the high-minded Dessa Caldwell. She deserved far better, and he deserved far worse.

So before the final chord from the last hymn sounded, Henry slipped out of the pew and hurried to the back of the sanctuary, out the door, and to his carriage without saying a word to Fallo, who soon had them carried away from the church.

When the last chord of "Holy, Holy, Holy" drifted from the organ, Dessa opened her eyes and, with a smile, turned to exit the pew in the hope of catching Mr. Hawkins's gaze.

Only to see the spot he'd occupied was vacant.

Filing from the sanctuary, Dessa fought her disappointment. What had made him leave? And what had made him show up in the first place?

One glimpse at Jane told Dessa that she, too, had hoped to speak to him. She was peering through the crowd, this way and that, but Dessa could see from the girl's matching disappointment that he was nowhere to be found.

"Well, that was a short-lived thrill," said Mariadela as she took hold of Dessa's arm to walk toward their carriage. William and Mariadela always went out of their way to pick her up. There was not enough room for the whole family in the carriage and the church was closer to their home, so the children walked, rain or shine.

Dessa made no pretense not to know Mariadela's meaning. "You did see him, then. It wasn't my imagination?"

"If it was, that imagination spread throughout the entire congregation. Mr. Hawkins in a church! I don't think that's something any of us have *ever* seen."

"Then why did he come today, only to arrive late and leave early, with no chance to be welcomed?"

"Likely for that very reason. He's never been the social type, as you well know."

"But he came!" Jane said, her brows high. She grinned Dessa's way. "And he sat just behind us, of all the other places he might have taken. I think he meant to join us, only he got shy at the end."

No, *shy* was not a word Dessa would associate with Mr. Hawkins. *Taciturn, abrupt, opinionated . . .* and *kind,* too.

As they settled in the carriage and William directed the rig back toward Pierson House, Henry Hawkins continued to fill Dessa's mind. How wonderful it would be to have no worries about paying down the loan, if the benefit was as successful as she hoped! She could hardly keep herself from imagining what it would be like to pay off the debt entirely, and far sooner than expected.

Dessa guessed that Jane thought of Mr. Hawkins as well, from the way the girl's gaze roamed, perhaps in search of his carriage, as they left the area of the church.

When at last the White carriage pulled up in front of Pierson House, Mariadela jumped from the rig to follow Dessa and Jane to the porch, telling William she would only be a moment.

"You realize this is an extraordinary opportunity, don't you?" Mariadela said.

Dessa shook her head. "No, I don't. What do you mean?"

"There was only one reason Mr. Hawkins came to that particular church today, and why he chose to sit in that particular seat. To see you, and for you to see him."

Jane nodded along eagerly, as if her agreement was all that was required to convince Dessa of the truth.

Dessa's gaze went from one hopeful face to the other. Did she understand them correctly, that they wanted to see some special sort of . . . friendship . . . develop between her and Mr. Hawkins?

Even as she felt the blood heating her face, she needed to look away to hide what surely must be a spark of interest all too ready to jump into her eyes.

"Perhaps he's been meaning to attend, only . . ."

But Mariadela was already shaking her head. "You know what you need to do, don't you? Encourage him to return to church. Invite him to take you." She glanced William's way. "Tell Mr. Hawkins my William is tired of leaving so early to pick you up every Sunday, and if Mr. Hawkins plans to return, it would be a great favor if he could bring you in his carriage." She touched Dessa's hand. "It wouldn't be improper because Jane would be with you. And it would reinforce his reason to go to church. All good things. Right?"

Dessa wanted to nod, to fall easily into Mariadela's line of thinking. But instead she spared a glance William's way. "Is he really tired of picking me up? I know it's out of the way—"

"Oh, you great goose! I offered that as an excuse for you to talk to Mr. Hawkins about it. William's never once complained and isn't likely to, either. He loves you like a sister, or at least like *my* sister. So you'll do it? You'll go to the bank and talk to Mr. Hawkins?"

Jane was already offering a smile of encouragement, the twinkle in her eye the very picture of what Dessa fought. How could Dessa possibly hesitate if it meant bringing a man to church—a place he might find the best of the society he'd been ignoring? Church was likely the very thing Mr. Hawkins needed, not only to find friendship with others, but with God as well.

More than that . . . the idea that *she* had been the reason behind Mr. Hawkins's extraordinary arrival today had ignited an ember of warmth and hope—so clear and strong even the array of doubts already forming to discourage her weren't enough to deny what she felt.

But how could she, with her past, encourage him—or any man—in such a personal way?

"I—I'll think about it," she said; then to both Mariadela's and Jane's obvious surprise and disappointment, she turned from them and walked into the house.

She had all week to figure out the right thing to do. But that might not be the same as what she wanted to do.

22

"Miss Caldwell! Miss Caldwell!"

Dessa looked up from the sewing project in front of her, hearing her name through the open dining room window. She recognized Nadette's voice and knew Remee did as well from the half scowl on her face.

Remee continued with her own sewing. "Why doesn't that girl come to the door instead of making a scene?"

Dessa reached the windowsill just before Jane did and held open the curtain. She waved to the girl. "Come inside, Nadette."

But Nadette shook her head. "You ain't told that Miss Remee what I said, didja?"

"She's right here, Nadette. I'm sure it'll be fine if you join us. Come in, won't you?"

Although the girl appeared conflicted about what to do, Dessa dropped the curtain and went to the door, along with Jane. She heard Remee follow them from the dining room.

"What was she saying about me?" Remee asked.

"She hoped you would put in a good word for her at Miss Leola's."

"Oh, that," Remee said with disgust. "I told her I would, but it's no use. Miss Leola won't take in a ragamuffin. Nadette's not even alley cat material, let alone fit for a place like Miss Leola's."

"Thank heaven for that," Dessa said, before pulling open the door. "I don't think she'll settle for anything less."

Nadette still lingered out front, not even on the porch.

"Come in, Nadette. Have something to eat, at least," Dessa added.

"You got a pie-ano in there yet?" Nadette called.

"No, but I have some muffins. Would you like one?"

The girl chewed her bottom lip all the way to the door. Then, inside, she looked around as if she expected the roof to cave in. When her gaze landed on Remee, she crossed her arms and glared. "You didn't tell Miss Leola about me, didja? I bet you didn't even forget—you just didn't wanna do it."

"That's right, Nadette, I didn't." There was not a hint of remorse in her voice. "It's for your own good."

"You said ya'd do it, but ya didn't. I guess you might lie to a *customer*," she said with disgust, "but not to another gal in the business."

"You're not in the business," Remee said.

"I wanna be!" Nadette pulled at the dress she wore, its pattern marred by stains and its sleeves and hem tattered. "You think I wanna wear castoffs from a Chinaman's laundry? This is the best they can do for me. It'd be better if I just went around naked. Might make some money that way, anyhow."

Dessa put an arm about the girl's thin shoulders. "We might have something upstairs you can have, Nadette."

But Nadette shrugged off the contact. "I'll make my own way, thanks. I only came because I wanted to tell ya somethin'. 'Bout a girl the Chinamen over in Hop Alley are bringin' in."

"What girl?"

Nadette wiped at her nose. "I wouldn'ta come 'cept I promised one a them girls at the China Palace that I'd do what I could." She glared at Remee. "*I* don't go back on my word."

"What about this girl, Nadette?" Dessa asked.

"I want ya to help me get her out, soon as she's delivered. Before . . . ya know, before someone gets his hands on her."

"Delivered . . . you mean she's being brought to a brothel against her will?"

Nadette nodded. "It's Liling's baby sister, Mei Mei, grown up to fourteen now. They say it's her turn to come here, but Liling don't want her to have to do the same thing they brought her here for—ya know, for all them railroad Chinamen. She don't want Mei Mei to be no *baak haak chai*." She lifted her chin as if proud she knew a second language. "That's—"

"One hundred men's wife," Remee finished. "Most of us have been called that in just about every language there is."

Dessa recalled Mariadela's warning against getting involved in a culture not her own. . . . And hadn't she heard there was some kind of halt on legal immigration of Chinese? That might stop the trouble before it even began.

"If she's coming from China, they won't be able to bring her into the country, Nadette. They'll be stopped at immigration, and she'll be sent back."

Both Nadette and Remee laughed at that.

Nadette added a sneer. "You think they'd do anything legal like bringin' her through immigration?"

Dessa sighed; she should have known. And if a fourteen-year-old girl was being brought here only to be a prostitute—too young to decide for herself—wasn't it Dessa's duty to see that she be spared such a fate? There must be a reason God had cleared the way for this information to reach Dessa. "When is the girl supposed to arrive?"

Nadette lifted her hands. "I dunno! But I know it's soon, 'cause I heard 'em talking about it myself. Everybody knows about it— the more they talk, the higher the price goes for her first customer. Even my soaper's wife is worried he'll make a bid for her! Liling is real pretty, and they say her sister must be even prettier, 'cause she ain't been used like Liling. Yet."

Fury sprouted roots around Dessa's heart. That such a thing

ALL IN GOOD TIME

should be planned as if a girl's virtue—her entire future—could be bid on like some kind of *thing*. This was a human being made in the image of God—and just a child!

"You tell Liling if she can get her sister here, I'll hide her."

"Okay!"

Then Nadette spun on her heel and left before Dessa could call her back for the muffin she'd promised.

Closing the door, Dessa turned and her gaze landed on Remee's somber one. The other woman shook her head. "You have no idea what you're doing, do you?"

That, Dessa could not deny.

23

Mr. Foster had already visited Pierson House twice more, and during the first of these he and Remee had discussed ideas and details without even waiting for Dessa to return from the kitchen with tea. During his second visit Mr. Foster had announced that his theater manager fully supported the musical revue they planned to present, and if they used their current talent, they could be ready in a couple of weeks. As far as Dessa was concerned, the sooner it was held, the better.

To Dessa's surprise, Mr. Foster asked if she might consider performing as well. If Remee's judgment could be trusted, along with Jane's opinion, Dessa would be just what the show needed.

But she'd refused; she couldn't fool herself into thinking that singing before an audience, even for a cause dear to her heart, was proper. She admitted she knew nothing about theater shows and was glad to leave the details entirely in the hands of Mr. Foster and his employees. She asked only that the songs performed would be respectable.

Later in the week, Mr. Foster arrived with an artist's preliminary poster that, once printed, would be pasted all around the city as soon as possible to advertise the new revue benefiting Pierson House. She was amazed at the speed Mr. Foster worked; everything was moving so *quickly*. And yet it was exciting, knowing soon she would have a substantial amount of money to pay down her loan. Wouldn't Mr. Hawkins be pleased by that!

She had to admit the poster was striking. On Sunday the twenty-first of August, it claimed, all profits of the Verandah would help keep Pierson House going. Since Dessa had insisted that no alcohol be served—something both Mr. Foster and Remee initially objected to—it would allow the Verandah to be open on a Sunday. Not that most businesses in the Fourth Ward adhered to Sabbath day closings anyway, but Dessa was glad to have gotten her way on this.

The exact function of Pierson House wasn't mentioned, and there was a bare-shouldered woman drawn along one edge of the poster, obviously singing. But overall the advertisement was in good taste with bold, clear printing and a pretty scalloped design decorating the border. Remee had gushed over it at first sight. All Mr. Foster needed before going to print was Dessa's approval.

Dessa couldn't help being impressed by Mr. Foster's eagerness and attention to detail. He was obviously well versed in planning—and promoting—whatever went on in his theater.

He always stayed for a cup of tea, a time during which Jane disappeared to her own room but Remee stayed. That was fine with Dessa. She had no conscious desire to be alone with Mr. Foster, even if he was as charming as ever. Yet if she were honest, at least with herself, she was immune neither to those charms nor to every engaging expression Mr. Foster aimed her way. His smiles were warm, and when he laughed, his brows lifted in delight. The brow with the scar could catch her attention, but no less than the apparently sincere admiration she saw in his gaze.

What was it about a man's admiration that was so difficult to ignore? Was it some need inside Dessa that she'd ignored all these years as she attempted to emulate the focused life of her mentor? She wondered if Sophie had ever wanted the attention of a handsome man, though she couldn't imagine her ever losing a moment's sleep over such a thing.

But before Dessa drifted off to sleep each night, after reading her Bible, after the prayers that kept her mind where she wanted it, it wasn't an image of Mr. Foster that she struggled to keep at bay. More often it was the face of Mr. Henry Hawkins. She thought of him sitting at her dining room table, or laughing outright in her kitchen, or sitting in church on Sunday as he'd tried so desperately to disappear from everyone's stare.

Not that she welcomed visions of Mr. Hawkins any more than those of Mr. Foster. Despite the hopes Mariadela and Jane had inspired after Mr. Hawkins's church visit, romance wasn't for Dessa—and marriage certainly wasn't. She'd given away that opportunity even before she'd decided to take up where Sophie had left off.

As the week went by, Dessa knew that as honorable as it might sound to invite Mr. Hawkins to church, it wasn't proper for that invitation to come from her. She would be pleased to bring him a large sum of money after the benefit, but she wouldn't indulge the personal feelings that were all too eager to command her attention.

However, on Friday morning, when an invitation arrived to none other than the Hawkins National Bank investors' dinner, to be held in Mr. Hawkins's home, every wish of spending more time in his company was renewed. The thought of visiting his house, seeing him there, intrigued Dessa more than she should allow.

Dessa was certainly not an investor; in fact, she was just the opposite. She'd borrowed money that Mr. Hawkins himself had expressed doubts she could repay. She was the last person in Denver whose name should appear on that invitation list. And yet he'd either allowed it . . . or thought of it himself.

She scanned the invitation again. "You are cordially invited to attend the semiannual Hawkins National Bank dinner gala on Sunday, the twenty-first day of August."

Sunday, the twenty-first day of August . . .

The very same date as the benefit for Pierson House!

The disastrous timing was clear: the biggest investors of the city would be busy at the Hawkins dinner—and unavailable to attend any event benefiting Pierson House.

And somehow worse, though certainly not as important, Dessa would be unable to attend both events.

Dessa clutched the invitation to her chest, calling immediately for Jane, who'd gone upstairs to rummage through the material box in search of something suitable to replicate a hair band she'd seen in a catalog. New hair ornaments were among the girl's favorite fashions. No sense alarming Remee with the conflict, at least not yet.

By the time Jane answered Dessa's call, Dessa was already putting on her gloves. "I have an errand to run, Jane. Do you think you could see about dinner preparations for me? I'm not sure how long I'll be gone."

Because, indeed, she might have to make two calls this afternoon. One to the Verandah, and the other to the bank.

At the Verandah, Dessa found each window as well as the ornate double doors wide open to let in fresh air, but inside it was nearly empty—at least of patrons. Various employees bustled about the huge, gilt hall. She saw immediately that for a theater there were precious few chairs. More common were tables, where employees now brushed felt-draped surfaces of various heights and lengths; round wood tables were being dusted, along with a couple of elongated tables that hosted a sort of box elevated in the center with neat squares cut out in a curious pattern. A few of the tables had high sides and white squares painted on each end while their centers held glistening circles with red and black numbers etched along the edges.

But the most impressive feature was a polished bar along one wall, complete with spittoons strategically placed along a brass foot rail. Behind it hung a huge, glittering mirror that reflected the electric chandeliers dangling from the ceiling.

Was this a theater, or a drinking establishment?

Dessa's heart sank with each step, particularly since the stage on the farthest end of the room was the last thing she noticed. Though a green velvet curtain was pulled back to reveal an ample performance platform, it was more than clear that the theater was anything but a focal point of the Verandah's business.

Dessa gripped her handbag even tighter as she approached one of the workers.

"Excuse me," she said, and the man stopped brushing one of the tables to face her. "Can you direct me to Mr. Foster? Can I find him here . . . so early in the day?"

The man grinned, giving her a glance that lasted too long and traveled too far. "Sure, he's here. See that door, over there in the corner?" He pointed to a door inset with paneling and a small plaque centered at eye level. "You want me to go over there with you? I'll knock for you and announce your name if you tell it to me."

"No, that won't be necessary." Then, after a single step away, she glanced back at him with a tight smile. "But thank you for the offer."

He grinned again. "Ain't you the polite one? Quite a difference from what we usually see around here."

Dessa found her way through the maze of tables. How could anyone call this a concert hall, with so few chairs? At the moment those chairs were placed in a meager stack to the side while the floor was being cleaned. The only places for them would be at the various tables interspersed throughout the room. How could patrons enjoy whatever performance was being presented when some of their backs would no doubt be facing that stage?

The brass plate affixed to the door warned that whatever lay behind was private. After a moment's hesitation, Dessa knocked, but it wasn't Mr. Foster who answered. Rather a tall man, solidly built, opened the door only wide enough to see Dessa, blocking her either from entering or from seeing beyond his broad shoulders. The surprise on his face was quickly replaced by a large smile.

"Can I help you, miss?" As he asked, he relaxed his hold on the door, opening it a bit farther.

"I'm looking for Mr. Foster and was told I might find him here. My name is Dessa—"

"Caldwell," the man finished for her. "I know who you are, miss. I drive the carriage for Mr. Foster and been by your place."

Before he finished his admission, Mr. Foster approached from behind, his face full of delight.

"Miss Caldwell! What an unexpected surprise. Come in, won't you? Can I offer you refreshment? I'm afraid I don't have any tea, but I could send Thomas to find some cider for you."

"No, no," she said, shaking her head, "please don't go to any trouble. I cannot stay. I came to ask you something that couldn't wait until your next visit to Pierson House. Tell me, have you arranged for the posters announcing the date of our benefit to be printed?" Even as the question came out, she couldn't ignore the weight lingering in her stomach. A benefit for Pierson House—here!

Mr. Foster stood a trifle taller, brushing aside the lapels of his jacket to tuck his thumbs beneath the suspenders he wore. "Printed yesterday and being pasted around the city as we speak. One day ahead of schedule."

"Oh . . ."

He frowned. "But I thought you'd be pleased."

"Oh, I am—by your diligence. Only . . . well, it's what I came to ask you. It's too late, though. No matter." The words came out, but inside she knew it did matter, at least to her, a great deal. "Thank you, Mr. Foster. Your enthusiasm is admirable, as usual."

He reached out a hand to detain her but stopped short. Still, his fingers grazed the sleeve of her basque.

"Tell me what's troubling you, Miss Caldwell," he said softly. "Perhaps there's something I can do."

"No, no, it's nothing. A scheduling conflict has come up, but there's nothing to be done about it if the announcements have been posted." *Nor anything to be done about the venue. . . .*

Now he took her elbow, guiding her farther inside the room. Plush settees and chairs were clustered in small groups near another ornately carved bar. This one was also replete with a mirror reflecting bottles of various height and width set along its lower edge, though there was not a spittoon in sight.

Despite the opulence of the furnishings, Dessa couldn't banish her uneasiness. This wasn't at all what she'd expected of a *respectable* theater. Why, oh why, had she so hastily allowed Mr. Foster to arrange this benefit?

She summoned a feeble protest in an attempt to rally her spirits. Should she have refused *any* help if it would benefit Pierson House? Remee had reminded her more than once that the business side of supporting Pierson House was at least as important as the spiritual side. Righteous indignation tried to stand up against Dessa's queasy apprehension. It had seemed such a reasonable idea at the start. . . .

Nearly without her knowing, Mr. Foster had deposited her in a chair deeply upholstered in red velvet. She knew she mustn't stay. No matter how generous the offer, the fact remained that the Verandah was no theater; it was a drinking and gaming hall. She oughtn't have agreed to the offer—or even entered such an establishment.

She must go to the bank. She'd thought she'd have to tell Mr. Hawkins that she wasn't free to attend his party, much as she would have liked to. But now . . . perhaps she ought to confess her concern about her involvement with the musical revue.

While it was possible she might not be required to attend the revue Mr. Foster and Remee had designed, how rude would it be for Dessa not to show her gratitude? Yet how could she be seen to support the venue?

It had all happened so quickly.

"Tell me about this scheduling conflict," said Mr. Foster. "I admit it's only a week after an annual ball the Verandah hosts, but that one is purely for entertainment purposes, without a penny of expense to my invited patrons. With a week in between, I assure you my clientele will be ready to empty their pockets, especially for a good cause."

"A . . . ball?"

He waved away her inquiry, as if he regretted having mentioned it, and took a seat opposite her, in another of the fancy chairs.

A glimmer of hope, nearly too small to be felt, came to life inside her. If he hosted a *society* ball, perhaps he did draw the kind of wealthy people she hoped could be most generous, from the broad and respectable population that grew every day in Denver.

"What sort of ball?" she persisted.

"Nothing for you to concern yourself over, Miss Caldwell. It's a business obligation for me; otherwise you'd have been my very special guest, I assure you. But it's not likely to be the kind of ball you would be accustomed to."

Accustomed to? She'd never in her life been to a ball, and though the Pierson family had hosted many, all it ever meant to the staff, including Dessa, was a change in routine, added duties, and more often than not every bedroom in the house filled with demanding overnight guests.

"But if there will be Denver business patrons attending—"

Mr. Foster's handsome face set ominously. "No, Miss Caldwell. This one's not for you."

She let out a resigned sigh. What was she thinking, anyway?

How could she tell him it wasn't so much a wish to attend as a wish to know how respectable was his guest list? She hoped the ball might give her some assurance that aligning the name of Pierson House with the Verandah wasn't the complete mistake she'd suspected a moment ago. But evidently she would have to trust Mr. Foster entirely.

She stood, holding out her hand to bid him farewell. "Thank you, Mr. Foster."

He stood as well, taking a step that put him a bit too close. "Don't you think you might call me Turk, Miss Caldwell? Dessa? After all, we're friends now, aren't we?"

His inviting gaze held her attention. This wasn't the first time he'd asked her to address him so intimately, but it had never seemed proper. Here, seeing the Verandah for what it was, the prospect of such friendly and familiar terms seemed even less so.

She pulled her hand from his. "I'm sorry, Mr. Foster. I do think it's best to keep our relationship formal. I hope you understand."

Taking her elbow again, he guided her to the door, where his driver still stood guard. Though the man stared straight ahead, he'd obviously heard the entire exchange. He opened the door to let Dessa out, and both of them followed her all the way to the street.

"May I offer you my carriage?" Mr. Foster asked. "It's not a long walk to Pierson House, but the sun is a bit warm today, isn't it?"

She might have accepted his offer before today, but every aspect of his help had become somehow clouded. "No thank you, Mr. Foster."

She spotted a hired hack just up the street. That would do, even though she was watching her pennies.

"Surely you aren't considering taking a hack somewhere?" he asked, evidently having followed her line of vision. "When my carriage is so much more comfortable?"

"I need to run an errand, actually," she admitted.

Before she could say another word, Mr. Foster waved Thomas forward. "My carriage sits idle and ready right next door. I would accompany you myself except I'm waiting for a shipment I need to sign for."

"But really, Mr. Foster, I wouldn't want to impose—"

He laughed and took one of her hands, patting it. "What kind of imposition do you imagine this to be? I'll be sitting in my office the rest of the day. My horses will appreciate being able to trot along the street; they always do. And Thomas will be back before I have need of him. I insist."

Then he kissed her hand, and she saw that Thomas had already turned the corner of the building to do Mr. Foster's bidding. Surely the carriage had already been hitched, because only a few moments later the magnificently matched pair so unique to Mr. Foster's rig emerged from beneath the arch of the attached carriage house.

Casting aside every ounce of hesitation—which felt strangely reminiscent of being carried away—Dessa thanked Mr. Foster for his generosity, then let him play the footman as he pulled down the carriage step and assisted her inside.

"It gives me great pleasure to help you in any way I can," he said, leaning on the step and inside the carriage, close to where she'd settled. "All that's required is that you let me."

She felt the smile on her face before she could hold it back. He lived on the very boundary of polite society; she knew that now. A very dangerous place to be, especially for someone like her who depended on respectable donors' generosity. But even with all she'd just discovered, resisting his charm was impossible.

Mr. Foster folded the step and closed the door, giving her a friendly wave as the carriage rolled forward. What harm could one ride, alone, do? She was simply accepting the generosity of a friend—a friend at least to Pierson House, if not to her personally.

24

"You there!"

Henry stepped down from his carriage, eager to return to work after his brief absence for lunch. Hearing his uncle calling after a youth—who was now running away from Tobias at full speed—caught his attention.

"Did you see that scalawag?" Tobias demanded of Henry as he approached.

"Only the haste of his escape. What's happened?"

"I stopped to look at that new poster—something I think the boy was working on, if I can judge by that paste bucket and brush I saw him with. I wanted to ask him about it, but he rushed off before I could speak to him." Tobias turned back in the other direction and extended his palm toward the corner. "You need to see this, Henry."

From the pucker of Tobias's brow, Henry guessed whatever it was couldn't be good news.

He followed Tobias a few steps down the block, toward the corner where a telephone pole held up the lines along the street. "It shouldn't be difficult to find out who sponsored the poster if you wanted more information," Henry suggested as they walked.

Tobias was already glaring at the newest advertisement affixed to the pole.

Henry saw the image of a woman drawn along the edge of a generously sized poster. It reminded him to petition the city council once again to establish an ordinance to restrict such advertisements. Some were undoubtedly in poor taste, although this one didn't seem to be. Worse, when the paste dried or the wind got hold of a loose corner, they tore and inevitably littered the street. Besides that—

"Pierson House?" The words jumped out at him, and he gripped his walking stick as he closed in on the pole. "A benefit . . . at the Verandah? For Pierson House? How can this be?"

He was blathering like an idiot, but at the moment that was what he felt himself to be. Other than a brothel, he simply could not comprehend a less likely establishment to be connected to Pierson House.

"And look at the date, Henry."

The conflict only compounded Henry's speeding pulse and quickened breath.

"This is outrageous. It's madness. It's—"

His own carriage had pulled from the curb, but another was now pulling into the vacant spot in front of the bank. Henry's quick glance lengthened when he recognized the long-maned pair of horses.

Turk Foster. Speak of the devil.

Henry tore the poster from its spot, and it came easily— wetly—away. He held it clear of his jacket and shoes and advanced upon the carriage just as the driver jumped down to hold open the door and lower the stair.

Standing stiffly, walking stick in one hand and poster dangling from the tips of his fingers in the other, Henry had no clue as to why Turk Foster might be in this neighborhood. But he wouldn't be leaving before hearing an earful.

The skirt annoyed him first. Foster must not be alone.

Then he saw her.

Dessa Caldwell allowed the driver to assist her, then took

the spot before Henry on the street with a broad—albeit slightly abashed—smile upon her lovely face.

"Good afternoon, Mr. Hawkins. You're just the person I was looking for."

Swallowing a lump of embarrassment over having been seen in Mr. Foster's carriage—something she might not have felt so acutely had she not just learned all she had about the Verandah—Dessa intentionally widened her smile. But when she caught sight of the familiar poster hanging disdainfully from Mr. Hawkins's fingertips, her embarrassment multiplied to something more closely resembling alarm.

Mr. Hawkins offered only a glare in return for her dwindling smile—amid a warning she couldn't help but catch. Even Mr. Ridgeway glowered, making her heart sink under such obvious censure. So she *had* been an utter fool to link herself to the Verandah—and they weren't about to overlook that foolishness.

Squaring her shoulders, clutching her handbag, she glanced again at Mr. Hawkins. "I wonder if I might have a word with you?" How brave she sounded, how sure of herself. How positively righteous, when she was, in fact, utterly wrong. And he obviously knew it.

Mr. Hawkins stepped aside, though his visage did not soften in the least. "A word, Miss Caldwell, is exactly what I was about to request of *you*. Shall we?"

She led the way into the bank, past all the desks and teller cages, sure each and every bank employee knew she marched toward some kind of punishment. Abject fear quickened her breathing.

Mr. Sprott popped from his seat in time to open the office door for her. Once the three were inside—Mr. Hawkins, Mr. Ridgeway, and herself—Mr. Sprott pulled the door shut without having to be told.

Somehow, having Mr. Ridgeway present brought some comfort. Small though that comfort was, because he, too, looked so utterly disappointed.

Mr. Hawkins dropped the now-curling poster into the waste bin beside his desk. "I see that you've disregarded my advice about Turk Foster," he said as he rounded his desk. He remained standing, though Dessa nearly fell into one of the chairs before his desk. Perhaps she should have remained standing as well, the way he towered over her. But her limbs refused to hold her.

"If I might explain—"

"There is no possible explanation you could offer that would justify a partnership between Pierson House and the likes of Foster's Verandah."

"Let's all sit, shall we?" asked Mr. Ridgeway. Though his tone was serious, Dessa found further comfort anyway. Perhaps she was too eager for it, but she hoped he wouldn't let her down. "How about a glass of water? Anyone?"

Neither Dessa nor Mr. Hawkins accepted the offer, but a moment later, after Mr. Ridgeway was seated, Mr. Hawkins sat as well. That helped, though minimally.

"Do you know what you've done?" Mr. Hawkins asked. "Have you no sense at all? How do you expect to keep donations coming in from the kind of people you're currently depending upon in society if you partner with the dregs of it?"

"I only thought—"

"Don't," he interrupted. "Don't tell me you've thought for a moment about what you've done. You can't have, or you wouldn't have done it. I warned you against Foster, Miss Caldwell, and yet before I know it, you allow his name to be linked to your cause. A cause that is so contrary to his that it would be laughable if it weren't so pathetic."

"Now, Henry, we can't blame it all on Miss Caldwell, can we?

It was likely a scheme of Foster's all along. He's the one who would benefit by having Pierson House fail."

Mr. Hawkins smirked. "Oh yes, why don't we blame the spider entirely for the fly's demise, when the fly flew directly into the web." He made no attempt to hide his disgust.

That was enough to strike a defensive chord in Dessa, even if she did build that defense on a foundation of her own folly.

She stood, enough of her energy restored to hold herself erect. "Mr. Hawkins, I admit I should have investigated the business that's carried on at a place like the Verandah. Until this very day I thought it a theater, not a thinly disguised—if not outright—gambling hall. But when Mr. Foster offered to donate the entire proceeds of one designated day to benefit Pierson House, what was I to say? Was I to refuse such generosity? He's promised that the venue for the day will be respectable. What reason had I to doubt him? What reason, even now, do I have to doubt his word?"

Mr. Hawkins stood as well, leaning over his desk with a scowl. "He's not likely to welcome any reform to that end of town, not when he has a hand in so many of the profits. What could be better than to see you fail? Especially when you so easily cooperate."

"I know Pierson House won't *end* what goes on down there. Everyone knows that! I only want to offer a place of refuge, to help those who might want to get away, to be a stepping-stone. Even those who live in the neighborhood should want to support such a place, shouldn't they? Instead of watching another woman die at her own hand or in an opium bed? Why wouldn't Mr. Foster allow it—even support it—as he claims he wants to do?"

"We'd like to think he's been honest with you, wouldn't we, Henry?" asked Mr. Ridgeway, who took to his feet now too. But he shook his head sadly. "It's just that it's unlikely, Miss Caldwell. I'm afraid I must agree with Henry. I'd say Foster would rather see you closed than help you. Have you thought about what the regular donors will do when they see you're involved with the Verandah? That's probably what Foster has in mind: to ruin you with your regular donors."

She sank back to the chair, all strength abandoning her, and aimed a glare at Mr. Hawkins. "What harm could a little concert bring? That's all it's to be."

"In a gambling hall, in a place that regularly welcomes the kind of women you most want to help."

"Oh no, Mr. Hawkins!" She stiffened her spine. "The Verandah's not a brothel!"

"No, it's not a brothel—but if he welcomes such women to arrange business there, then it's little different."

His derision was barely tolerable. If he was right, she'd been more a fool than she realized.

Dessa stood again, not daring to look at either one of them. "I came because I realized the date conflicted with the date of your dinner party, Mr. Hawkins. And now I'm afraid, under the circumstances, I would not be attending, even were I free."

꽃

Henry watched Miss Caldwell retreat to the door, knowing he hadn't spoken a single untrue word. Yet he felt as defeated as she must be at that moment.

He saw Tobias turn to him, a panicked look on his face as he silently motioned to Henry.

Stop her. Go after her. Don't let her go.

All of which Henry should have ignored.

Or at least he should have thought of it himself first.

"Wait."

The single word echoed before Miss Caldwell reached the door. Henry looked briefly at Tobias. "Leave us for a moment, won't you, Uncle Tobias?"

He probably shouldn't have broken his rule about referring to Tobias in such a way—a rule most staunchly adhered to under the bank's roof—but it was done and there was no changing it.

Tobias seemed only too pleased to comply and made no reference to the lapse in how he'd been addressed.

Thankfully, perhaps a bit surprisingly, Miss Caldwell complied too. She stood steady, her back still facing him, still rigid. She was looking at the floor rather than watching Tobias leave as he closed the door behind him.

Henry left his desk, approaching her silently.

"I owe you an apology, Miss Caldwell." He spoke to her back. "I had no right to be so abrasive with you."

She said nothing, her unyielding posture revealing only resistance.

"You must realize the source of my concern," he added softly. If only he could tell her his concern had nothing to do with business, his or hers. He'd bungled this whole confrontation, and there wasn't a thing he could do to take back the words.

"I know that you're concerned about the repayment of my loan. I don't blame you for that."

Money being the furthest thing from his mind might have surprised him a few weeks ago. He stood not three feet from her, wishing he could close the gap altogether. How easily he could take her into his arms, if she would let him.

"No, Miss Caldwell. My concern is not about the loan."

There, a subtle crack in the armor she'd donned the moment he'd confronted her on the street. The line of her shoulders softened ever so slightly, though she did not turn to him. He stepped even closer. Two feet from her.

"I want you to succeed, actually," he whispered. "I hope you believe that."

She turned at last, her movement causing them nearly to touch. How he wanted to kiss her then—and she was so close, close enough to follow through on his wish. His gaze traveled her face, the face that visited so many of his thoughts, both awake and asleep.

Henry couldn't help himself. He moved his lips toward hers. For a moment she stood still, even lifting her face to his. Could it be? Would she accept such a kiss?

But then, before contact was made, he pulled back. He still had his secrets and wasn't at all sure he was ready to share them. He knew the vulnerability a kiss produced. Among so many things, it brought with it the need for honesty.

Belatedly, Dessa knew she should have been the first to resist this very real confirmation of Mr. Hawkins's feelings. She had her secrets, after all, and if he knew her past he would likely not offer to kiss her at all. Not when a kiss could mean so much—if indeed it would mean more to him than it had to the man who'd kissed her first so long ago.

Yet if he hadn't pulled away, there was no denying that she would have willingly—delightedly—received his kiss. More than received it, she would have fully and happily participated. Even now, having been denied that kiss, a keen sense of disappointment tugged at her heart. How could this be, when she'd resolved to follow Sophie's path?

Common sense accused her of not being rational; a moment ago he'd had every right to take her to task. Perhaps the memory had kept him from following through on the kiss. Perhaps he had reason to regret letting her suspect he harbored interest in her at all.

She turned away once again, offering him only her profile. "I accept your apology, Mr. Hawkins. I hope that you'll accept mine as well. I shouldn't have spoken in anger, because you're the one in the right. Not me."

Then she fled from his office.

25

"I BLAME MYSELF," said Mariadela, seated opposite Dessa at the kitchen table. They hadn't eaten; none of them had. Dessa couldn't muster the energy or the interest in food, not when her roiling stomach couldn't possibly accept a bite. There were no complaints from Jane or even Remee—though she wondered how long it would be before Mr. Dunne came inquiring about lunch.

Her friend's words sparked Dessa's frustration. "Please, don't blame yourself! It was my own impatience, my own lack of foresight. And it all went forward so quickly!"

"But if I'd known," Mariadela said gently, "I'd have told you what kind of place the Verandah is. I expect Jane didn't know, but why didn't you say something, Remee?"

Though Mariadela spoke the words without anger or malice, Remee lifted her chin and looked away. "The Verandah is respectable. To me. All kinds of police and politicians go there, factory bosses and owners. A lot of respectable people mix there."

"Anonymously, yes," Mariadela claimed.

Remee shook her head. "No. They might go to Miss Leola's anonymously, under the cover of darkness even, but everybody knows everybody at the Verandah. There aren't any secrets there."

"And that's why they all wear masks to that annual ball?" Mariadela said with a lifted brow of skepticism.

That piqued Dessa's interest. "Mr. Foster mentioned that ball. It's a masquerade?"

Both of Mariadela's brows now lifted in horror. "He didn't invite you, did he?"

"No, in fact he made it clear I wouldn't fit in."

"Well, that might be the only honest thing he's ever said to you, Dessa. That ball is . . . it's said to be a night of decadence. Drinking and opium and girls." Mariadela's gaze fell on Remee, who averted her eyes and remained silent. "You've been to one, haven't you?"

She only shrugged. "Maybe I have."

"And that didn't warn you that a Pierson House benefit wouldn't be well served there?" Mariadela lifted her hands as if discharging all her own guilt.

"Look here," Remee said. "I may not have officially run Miss Leola's place, but I did the books—I know how much it costs. Pierson House is going to need a lot more money than what we can bring in with our sewing. This was a business deal, and would have been a sound one."

Mariadela's face gave no hint of understanding. "Once our donors see those posters or hear about this benefit day, they'll stop sending in money. Pierson House will close, and you'll go right back to Miss Leola's."

Remee glared across the table. "Right back where I belong, do you mean?"

Dessa put a palm over Mariadela's hand that rested on the empty table before them. She raised a pleading look Remee's way. "No one thinks that, Remee. Please don't think that's what any of us want. And I refuse to believe this is the end of Pierson House." She folded her arms tightly. "To start with, I'll speak to Mr. Foster. I'll tell him that while I appreciate all he's done, I've realized I cannot be involved in this benefit. I won't attend the event at all, and if he continues with it, I'll refuse the money he raises."

Remee scoffed. "Refuse what might be the last bit of money you see for a while? That's ridiculous."

"I can't possibly accept it if it will alienate my consistent donors. I'll ask Reverend Sempkins to invite the donors to a meeting, and I'll admit my mistake and beg their forgiveness. That's what God's love is all about, isn't it? Forgiveness? If they can't find it in their hearts to forgive my foolishness, then perhaps Pierson House wasn't meant to succeed." She shook off an urge to cry. "At least not under my direction."

"Now, Dessa," said Mariadela, "you needn't think so drastically. No one has been more dedicated to helping others than you."

Dessa pressed her thumb and forefinger to the bridge of her nose in the feeble hope of stemming her tears. "I've been a fool to think I could take Sophie Pierson's place. Who am I but a maid, with no education except what was given to me in the service of others?"

"Oh, Miss Dessa!" Jane's face was wet with her own tears. "If I thought I was no better than my last job, I'd be in jail. You've said right along God can use me, no matter what I've done or not done. It's true, isn't it? For you, too?" She glanced toward Remee. "For all of us?"

Remee leaned forward. "If I didn't believe you could handle Pierson House, Dessa, I'd have left already. I know I'm to blame for all this. I went along with it from the start and put you at ease about it."

"No, Remee. I should have at least checked the venue, and I didn't."

Mariadela scooted her chair even closer to Dessa's. "It doesn't matter anymore who's to blame. The important thing is that we all believe in what God can do here at Pierson House."

Dessa had the unexpected urge to laugh through her tears. Wiping away the dampness on her face, she looked at each one of them gratefully. "It's times like these that Sophie always reminded me of Balaam's donkey. If God could use an animal like that to speak and spare someone's life, perhaps He can use me after all."

Once Dessa had contacted him, Reverend Sempkins told her that he would arrange for the major donors to linger after the church service this coming Sunday. Dessa wasn't looking forward to the meeting but knew it was unavoidable. Just like tonight's meeting with Mr. Foster.

She'd sent a note asking him if he would come by on Saturday—after dinner, since hosting a meal seemed far too friendly for what she was about to do.

He was due any moment. Jane and Remee both assured her they would be well out of sight, upstairs in their rooms. In a way, she wished they would stay for support, but she knew this was something that had to be done without their help. And for Mr. Foster's sake, she thought it best done without an audience.

He was, as usual, both punctual and polite. She'd already set out the tea service, knowing it wouldn't cool before the appointed time of his arrival. But after she'd divested him of his hat and gloves and poured the tea, she couldn't help realizing the sharp contrast of this simple parlor visit to how he must usually spend his Saturday evenings.

"Thank you for coming on such short notice, Mr. Foster," she said. "I assume Saturday is one of your busier days at . . . your place of business."

"Nothing that can't take care of itself." He sipped the tea with a smile.

"I'm afraid the reason for this visit isn't likely to be one you'll welcome." She paused, even though she'd rehearsed exactly what she would say. Somehow, face-to-face, it seemed impossible to tell this man that not only were his efforts to help unwelcome, but as far as Mr. Hawkins and Mr. Ridgeway—and she suspected

Mariadela as well—believed, they might be nefarious. Every one of his smiles seemed so sincere.

"I welcome any reason to spend time with you, Miss Caldwell. Haven't you've guessed that by now?"

She set down her teacup with a slight rattle. "I realize I don't know how to say what I've been practicing all day. Quick and short is probably best."

He set aside his tea as well. "That sounds ominous, combined with the stricken look on your face. Is something wrong?"

She took in a quick, fortifying breath. "Since seeing the venue of your benefit for Pierson House—since seeing the Verandah—I find it's not in Pierson House's best interest to be involved after all. I'm afraid I'll have to bow out completely, with my profound apologies for the trouble and expense you've already incurred."

"What? Bow out? Why?"

She folded her hands, avoiding his intense and obviously confused stare. "Pierson House enjoys the regular support of a number of donors. If they believe there is any connection—friendliness, so to speak—between this place and a place like the Verandah, they'll likely withdraw their support altogether. And while I'd welcome the help of new funds from your patrons, I can't afford to lose the support of the community that's invested in me all along. I've worked hard building their trust since coming to Denver." She looked at him at last. "I hope you understand."

He shook his head. "No, I don't. Not at all. Does it matter where the support comes from, so long as it's there? Because I assure you, there is money to be found for you through the event at the Verandah."

"People want to be sure that what I hope to do here doesn't get muddled. I'm already in closer proximity to the Line than most people want, but I've always believed it was important to be right here, close enough for someone in trouble to reach before changing her mind. But because of that, investors are wary. If they think I'm becoming too much a part of the society I want most to change . . ."

"I see."

Dessa couldn't miss the disappointment in his voice and expression, perhaps even regret that there was such an impenetrable barrier between his place and hers. For a moment she wanted to thrust aside all doubts she had about his motives, doubts planted by Mr. Hawkins. Surely Mr. Foster truly did want to help her!

"I'm sorry, Mr. Foster."

And she was.

❧

"I agree it's an unfortunate time of day to be entering a neighborhood like this," Reverend Sempkins said to Henry, having dismissed Henry's suggestion to wait until just before the investors' meeting tomorrow to speak with Miss Caldwell. "But if she's to have the best chance in the morning, we'll need to advise her on what to say. Having your support will be a great help to ease the donors' minds."

Henry looked out the window of his carriage. He hoped so, but he doubted his presence would make much of a difference. He wasn't exactly in the same circle of influence when it came to compassion and generosity.

"If she had a telephone, we could have called ahead," the reverend went on. "But as it is, she'll likely welcome our visit regardless of advance notice."

❧

"I don't see why you won't accept the money at least," Mr. Foster said. "I accept that you may not want to be there for the revue. I should have realized myself everything you've just told me. I often forget many of my patrons have two lives—one on each side of the city. I'd hoped they could mix. But the money could still be yours if we proceed."

Dessa shook her head. "If my donors saw any link, it wouldn't be welcomed. I'm sorry for my mistake in all of this. It's best not to carry through with it at all."

She started to stand, to bring this sadly uncomfortable meeting to an end, but when he reached for her hand from the end of the settee where he sat, she stopped.

"So this is it? You'll send me on my way, and I'm not to see you again?"

His gaze captured hers, but she managed to nod. "You have no need of me or what I'm trying to do here, Mr. Foster. I should be surprised you wanted to help at all."

He gave a brief laugh. "I didn't—at least not at first. What you do is contrary to all the businesses around here. We're all linked— the taverns, the dens, the gambling halls, and the brothels. We all appeal to that same side of people. The one that wants to keep us all in its grip. Pleasure or profit, so long as we ignore what people like you think of us."

That he'd lumped her in with a judgmental group of others should have come as an insult, but his tone had been too gentle. And if he knew the truth of her past, he would realize she wasn't like those who cast stones. Those without such universally inexcusable sins as her own. What she'd done may not be unpardonable by God's grace, but she knew there were those not so willing to extend the same grace.

"Then you *don't* have a reason to help Pierson House, do you?" Had Mr. Hawkins been right after all?

"That's just it. I want to help you in whatever you do, even if it means a change to my own life." He raised his hand to caress her face. "I've never known a woman like you. Someone so thoroughly good."

She averted her gaze. "I assure you, Mr. Foster, I'm not so thoroughly good. Any goodness in me is because of God's help."

He took both her hands in his and pulled her to her feet along with him. "That's what I mean. You won't even take credit for your own fine qualities. That's astonishing. And irresistibly appealing."

He wrapped his arms around her, and before she could push him away, his lips were coming down on hers.

❧

"Oh! Heaven help us!"

Henry looked to see the aim of the reverend's gaze—peering through the window of Henry's carriage and directly toward the window of the Pierson House parlor. Since the curtains were pulled aside and the lamps fully lit, it was easy to see inside.

Henry's heart stopped, then skittered in his chest. Dessa—he forgot to call her by anything but the intimacy of her given name, since he felt so intimately violated—was kissing none other than Turk Foster.

He scrambled to the carriage door before the reverend had even reached for the handle.

❧

Dessa pushed at Mr. Foster's shoulders and pulled her face away, in the process nearly falling back into the chair behind her. "Mr. Foster!" She held one arm out to keep him at bay. "I must ask you to leave. Immediately."

She wasn't sure what he'd have done—reached for her again or stepped back—but when someone pounded at the front door, he stood stiff and tall and did nothing to detain her from answering.

Not that she needed to open it herself. Before she'd even taken a step toward the door, it swung wide. To her mortification, Henry Hawkins stood there—and without a doubt he'd seen what had just transpired.

"Is this what goes on here every Saturday night?" he demanded. "Because if it is, I fail to see the difference between Pierson House and any of the brothels you claim you want to empty."

"It's no business of yours, Hawkins," said Mr. Foster. He stepped to the middle of the room, as if inviting confrontation.

Mr. Hawkins seemed more than happy to accept that invitation. He stomped toward Mr. Foster and the two faced off. "More than half the money for this place came from my bank, Foster. I'd say that makes it my business."

"Perhaps what goes on professionally, but not personally."

Mr. Hawkins turned to Dessa. "Around here the lines are blurred between personal and professional, and everyone knows it. I demand to know what's going on."

"I—I was just telling Mr. Foster that I'm excusing myself from the benefit."

"That's not what it looked like when we pulled up."

Dessa was about to ask about the "we," but when she heard the voice behind her, her already tormented heart increased its pace even more. Painfully so.

"Mr. Hawkins," said Reverend Sempkins, "I think you missed an important part of what just happened. You were at the door when Miss Caldwell refused this man's obvious advance." He looked from Mr. Hawkins to Dessa. "That's how it appeared to me, at least. His action *was* unwelcome?"

She nodded, embarrassed to the core—and made worse when she heard footsteps on the stairs behind the parlor. Now everyone would know; there was no avoiding it. Private behavior made public once again—it was no easier this second time in her life.

Mr. Foster passed Mr. Hawkins, then the reverend. He took his hat from where Dessa had hung it and placed it on his head. His irritation seemed to rival Mr. Hawkins's, who watched the other man leave with unconcealed contempt.

Mr. Foster ignored everyone but Dessa and aimed a brief bow her way. "I beg your forgiveness, Miss Caldwell. You won't be troubled by me again."

Then he left by way of the open door.

❧

Henry sucked in a calming breath. There was no sense denying it, even to himself. He was an idiot. Whether that kiss had been welcomed or not, what right had he to hurl himself in as if he were some kind of knight, there to save the damsel? Or worse, to barge in like a witness to cast ready censure? Is that what she thought? Was that what he'd done?

Now he could barely stand to have her looking at him, although one quick glance in her direction made him doubt she wanted to meet his gaze anyway.

"Reverend," Henry said as he approached the door, "if you could speak to Miss Caldwell about why we came, I would appreciate it. I'll wait in the carriage."

Without even bidding Miss Caldwell good night, he followed in Foster's wake.

26

DESSA WOKE GROGGY the next morning, after a mostly sleepless night. When she had dozed, her dreams were filled with women dancing on a stage before an audience who only pointed fingers of shame at them.

Mr. Hawkins was in her dream too, overlooking it all with grim disapproval, ultimately becoming the first of the audience to turn his finger from the stage to her.

She dressed carefully this morning, making sure her gingham gown was free of soil and wrinkles and that her hair would stay in place in a tight coil. She might not be facing a jury today, but that was what it felt like.

She did thank God for Reverend Sempkins. He'd assured her last night that he believed her about Mr. Foster's unwelcome advance, and that as far as he was concerned, nothing had changed. He expressed hope that none of the donors had noticed any of the posters plastered about the city, and forewarning them would avert much of the damage. If Mr. Foster was as good as his word about ending any collaboration, he would likely see they were removed as quickly as possible.

Dessa planned to make sure that happened, even if she had to pull down every single poster herself.

It was Mr. Hawkins who invaded most of her thoughts. She told herself it shouldn't matter what he thought of her person- ally; it was only his professional opinion that mattered. Perhaps having him believe she was less than the honorable woman she presented herself to be was for the best. After all, she had no hope of romance—and until meeting him, she hadn't struggled much with that surrendered dream.

But it was still important that he think her qualified to run Pierson House, and if she couldn't restore herself in his estimation, then she had little hope she could keep the confidence of other donors for long, no matter how willing they'd been originally.

Before going to bed last night, she'd asked Remee and Mr. Dunne if they would attend church services with her and Jane in the morning. Even if their presence wouldn't help change any minds, having them there might remind her she'd done some little good, at least.

She was relieved to see both of them already at the kitchen table with Jane when she came down. She was late and had no intention of eating anything before they left, but she could see that they had already cooked and seen to the dishes, judging by those left to dry on a towel next to the sink.

"Thank you," Dessa said to them all.

Then she turned to lead the way outside, where they would have to walk a few blocks in order to catch a hansom cab. Last night she'd asked Reverend Sempkins to stop by the Whites' to let them know there would be too many leaving from Pierson House for their carriage, and she would arrange other transportation.

"Dessa," called Remee as she followed her through the dining room.

Dessa stopped, pulling on her gloves.

"Are you sure it'll help if I come along?"

Dessa raised a surprised gaze to meet the other woman's. She laid a hand on Remee's arm. "If nothing else, it'll help me to have you there. And you'll be welcomed, Remee. I *know* the people in this church."

Remee looked away. "Not from my perspective, you don't. You can't."

That Remee had stayed away from church because of shame astounded Dessa, creating yet another dent in her already-abused confidence. Had she done nothing to restore Remee's feeling of value? She and Jane might be the only two students in her weekly beauty classes, but she'd hoped the lessons had been more effective than this. Remee still didn't understand how beautiful God thought her.

Dessa blinked back tears that were too ready to collect. "Oh, Remee, no one should keep you from worshiping God if that's what you want to do. If they do, it's *their* sin, not yours."

Jane took a step nearer, having been close enough to hear the entire conversation. "It'll help if you have Miss Dessa on one side and me on the other, won't it? If anybody frowns your way, we'll meet them with a smile times three. That'll be like heaping hot coals of kindness on them, just like in the Bible. Right, Miss Dessa?"

But Mr. Dunne, just opening the door, spoke before Dessa could. "A smile times four, if ya please."

He winked and ushered them out the door.

Henry sat in his carriage, staring across at the empty seat opposite him. Despite assuring himself this was the right thing to do, he wasn't at all sure his effort would be accepted.

Suppose Miss Caldwell remained as embarrassed as he was? Suppose she didn't want his help? Suppose she thought he believed less of her, regardless of how she'd received Foster's kiss?

When he'd left Pierson House so rashly last night, he'd convinced himself he ought to wash his hands of this whole mess. Dismiss the loan as a lost investment, should it come to that. Not get involved in trying to save the place, and only hope from afar that it survived.

But he knew he couldn't do it. If today's struggle was ultimately one of pride, it was a foolish struggle. Perhaps what he felt wasn't only embarrassed regret over the way he'd broken into her parlor, but fear that his own would-be kiss had been just another of its kind. From what he recalled of the moment in his office—and he recalled it in detail—she'd have accepted his kiss. Had he misread her? Had Foster done the same, in whatever had taken place before *he'd* kissed her?

The slowing of Henry's carriage drew his attention from such unpleasant thoughts. He looked out the window, seeing he was still more than a block from Pierson House.

Just as he wondered why Fallo was stopping the carriage, he spotted a foursome walking along the sidewalk. At this hour on a Sunday morning, and on this end of the city, there was little activity to attract attention. He saw immediately that among those four walking were Jane Murphy and Dessa Caldwell.

It seemed as if he would face his embarrassment a few minutes earlier than expected.

❧

"Oh, look! Isn't that Mr. Hawkins's carriage?"

Dessa wasn't sure who had spotted the carriage first, she or Jane. But Jane's call commanded Remee's attention as well as Mr. Dunne's.

Dessa stopped just as the carriage came to a halt before them, but her heart rate picked up as if extra blood flow were needed for a sprint. She'd convinced herself she wouldn't be seeing him this morning. Not after last night. If he'd meant to come to church today in support of Pierson House, she was sure that had ended the moment he'd burst into her parlor.

She didn't flatter herself to even think jealousy had been the cause of his reaction. Wounded pride, perhaps, was the most personal motivation she should ascribe to him. She hadn't forgotten their own near kiss, and there she'd been, fully accepting the kiss of another—or so he obviously thought.

Mr. Hawkins jumped from his carriage, and she knew she had no choice but to face him. It couldn't be a coincidence that he was here, in her neighborhood. That realization alone brought a faint glimmer of hope.

"Thank you for stopping, Fallo," Mr. Hawkins called up to his driver. Then he stepped closer to Dessa. If last night had embarrassed him at all, she saw not a trace of it now. "I came to offer my carriage. Although . . ." His voice dwindled somewhat as he took in the four of them. "I'll sit atop with my driver, so the four of you will easily fit."

"I haven't any objection to sittin' up top, sir," said Mr. Dunne. "Never been inside such a fancy rig anyway—wouldn't know how to sit in one."

"All the more reason you should sit in one now." Replacing his hat, Mr. Hawkins climbed to the driver's seat while the driver himself offered assistance to the others.

So he was embarrassed after all. He may have been kind enough to offer transportation today—or perhaps it was his way of assuring that she would face the trouble her errors had created—but he couldn't bear to sit in the same carriage with her.

At the church, Mr. Hawkins once again sat directly behind Dessa. Although her concentration was somewhat divided, she knew her prayers were answered, particularly when Remee afforded her a smile. No one had so much as lifted a condemning brow in her direction.

Those who were interested in meeting about the future of Pierson House funding were invited to remain in the sanctuary after the service ended. Reverend Sempkins began the discussion with the facts. To one or two gasps, he revealed one of the posters that were even now being taken care of. Mr. Hawkins stood to assure everyone that his Mr. Ridgeway had hired an army of boys to search the city and remove every one of them.

Then Mariadela stood. "If any of you wish to cast blame, I shouldn't be spared from receiving some. Denver has been my home nearly all my life. I know what goes on at the Verandah. Until Friday, Dessa didn't." She lifted her chin ever so slightly. "If I hadn't been so busy at the store, I'd have prevented this whole mistake. Not that I think it was that, entirely. Mr. Turk Foster likely knew exactly what he was doing."

As grateful—and humbled—as Dessa was, she could not remain silent while Mariadela made her offer to share the blame.

"Ladies and gentlemen," she said, standing as well, "please don't cast blame anywhere but at my own feet. It was foolish of me to risk the good—but new—name of Pierson House. I didn't realize how foolish until seeing the Verandah for the first time. If I have any excuse, however feeble, it's to cite the speed with which the plans went forward. Mr. Foster came to Pierson House a little more than a week ago and offered his theater as the venue for a musical revue. That was all I knew. I know ignorance is hardly an excuse, but unfortunately that's the truth. The arrangements accelerated so fast, all I could think was not to refuse a donation—of any kind. The apostle Paul himself once said so long as the gospel was preached, he was happy. I'm afraid I used that to soften whatever qualms I might have had. If the funds were garnered legally, then I was willing to accept them."

Mrs. Naracott stood, gloved hands folded tightly in front of her. "That's just it, Miss Caldwell. Any funds you might receive from a place like the Verandah would be quite illegal. How could you not know that?"

Dessa turned to her in surprise. "But . . . the Verandah operates openly. I realize Mr. Foster calls his business a theater and more goes on there than just musical entertainment, but—"

Mrs. Naracott cut in. "It's still an illegal gambling den. *Illegal,* Miss Caldwell."

Mr. Hawkins, who'd kept his seat behind Dessa, now stood as well. "Everyone knows the ordinances against gambling are ignored. How many residents in Denver are gamblers themselves? Wasn't your father a silver miner, Mrs. Naracott? What are miners, except gamblers?"

"That doesn't make the money raised in a place like the Verandah legal."

"No, of course not, but if Miss Caldwell believed it to be one kind of place, only to learn it was another, she can't really be blamed, can she?"

Though Mrs. Naracott had looked away when Mr. Hawkins raised the origin of her family's wealth, she now squared her shoulders and stared directly at Dessa. Dessa had all she could do not to cower, feeling once again like the maid she'd been reared to be. It didn't matter that Mrs. Naracott's father hadn't inherited his wealth; Mrs. Naracott had, and with such an inheritance came audacity that Dessa had seen before.

"With Pierson House's name and reputation yet to be firmly established, and so thoroughly dependent upon the goodwill of others, you are obligated to keep your motives clear and your efforts free of anything remotely scandalous." Mrs. Naracott's gaze fluttered over the small crowd of fifteen or twenty people seated around them. "How do we know something like this won't happen again?"

"I assure you it won't," Dessa said quietly, looking submissively toward the floor, just as she'd been taught when addressing anyone of wealth or status.

But Mr. Hawkins evidently wasn't finished. "Has anyone considered another fact? Something Mrs. White alluded to? This might not have been a mistake of Miss Caldwell's as much as a plan of Turk Foster's. What of his motives? Does anyone find it remotely suspicious that he approached Miss Caldwell such a short time ago and within a few days put an entire musical program together, then plastered advertisements all over the city? Should we ascribe this to altruism, or does his haste speak of something else? A desire to cause the very kind of trouble we're having right now? Wouldn't he wish to see a place like Pierson House closed?"

Reverend Sempkins nodded. "I do recall those days when one alderman or another tried to shut down the gambling halls. Mr. Foster was the biggest protestor. I suppose having a haven like Pierson House is a reminder of virtue he'd most like forgotten."

There was a general murmur of agreement with the suspicion, which Mrs. Naracott likely didn't miss.

"Well," she said, "I'm willing to overlook what happened this time. If everyone else is."

So support remained intact for Pierson House, but the benefit was not to be. Dessa was too relieved over having retained the trust of the donors—however shaken—to mourn the loss of whatever added funds a benefit at the Verandah might have brought in. She'd made the first payment on her loan and somehow, even without the Plumsteads' help, she would make the second and the third and every payment thereafter until the entire debt was freed.

Soon after the meeting ended, Mr. Hawkins escorted Dessa out of the church. If she wasn't mistaken about the lack of tension on his face, he was relieved to have it over as well.

"I wish to thank you for all you've done, Mr. Hawkins," she said. "Not only for showing your support here today, but arranging to have the posters removed. I am once again—or should I say more deeply—in your debt."

"It was Reverend Sempkins who made the most difference, I believe. If you'd lost his support after last night's disaster, I think today's meeting might have ended differently."

She swallowed hard at the reminder.

"Now it's I who should apologize."

She spared a quick glance. "Why?"

"For even bringing up last night. An evening best forgotten."

Dessa nodded. "Yes, I agree. I'm trying to do that myself."

At his carriage, he stopped short while the others boarded with his driver's assistance. "I wonder, Miss Caldwell," he said, so low she was sure only she could hear him, "if we might have a word. Privately."

"Yes, of course."

With both hands on his walking stick, he leaned slightly forward but looked to the side rather than directly at her face.

"I'd like to reissue the invitation to my dinner party." His gaze briefly shot to hers, then eluded her again. "Now that you have that evening free."

Warmth circled her heart, settling in comfortably. "Yes, I'd like that, Mr. Hawkins." She turned to the waiting carriage but stopped to face him again. "Thank you for everything you've done to help me. Considering . . . everything . . . I'm very appreciative."

"Everything?"

The heat of a blush rose to her cheeks. "Only that you weren't initially in favor of Pierson House. Your support now means that much more."

His gaze lingered on her, and she wondered what he was thinking. He always looked so serious that she was afraid she would never be able to guess at his thoughts. Perhaps, despite his support today, he didn't really believe in her mission. He did, after all, have a vested interest in keeping the donors happy.

But he only tipped his hat her way without another word for or against her assumption of his sympathies. He offered her assistance into his carriage; then after his driver closed them all inside, both Mr. Hawkins and the driver hopped up top to take them back to Pierson House.

27

IN THE DAYS that followed, Dessa kept herself busier than ever in a vain attempt to forget her most recent mistake. Through Mariadela, she'd arranged to provide several restaurants with a variety of pies and muffins to sell to their patrons. She also provided a steady supply of cookies to Mariadela's store, where they were becoming increasingly popular.

Unfortunately, creating baked goods she could concoct in her sleep did little to make the days pass quickly—days she was tempted to count until Mr. Hawkins's dinner party. As much as she'd tried ignoring the unbidden feelings developing for him, she knew she couldn't.

Still, she couldn't help but call herself foolish for not fighting harder to banish her thoughts of him, let alone allowing herself the hope of spending time in his company. The struggle reminded Dessa that as much as she wanted to follow in Sophie's footsteps, she did not have the same gift of undivided focus on God and the task He'd assigned her. She truly did still hope to earn a man's love someday. Not just any man's. Henry Hawkins's.

But how, if she could not be honest about her past? *Mr. Hawkins, I hope you don't think me forward, but there is something you ought to know about me. . . . Mr. Hawkins, I hope I'm not misunderstanding your intentions, but there really is something I ought to share. . . . Mr. Hawkins . . .*

Oh! Nothing sounded right. How could she admit that

although Sophie Pierson had rescued her from public ruin, that ruin was nothing less than secretly complete?

But she was the first to tell women like Remee that God had forgiven them of anything in their past. Wasn't the same true for Dessa?

And so, even while her mind still cried caution, she fought less and less those dreams of getting to know Henry Hawkins better. He'd already provided the next occasion to do so.

Mariadela supplied an answer to the one dilemma Dessa faced in having accepted his invitation. She eagerly offered the loan of a ready-made gown hanging on a mannequin at the store, a copy of a gown designed in Paris. Lacy sleeves of cream satin displayed swirls of beaded black circles, completed by delicate black striping along the bodice that cascaded down the full skirt all the way to the floor. It was a gown Dessa had noticed when Mariadela first hung it for show—never imagining she would one day alter it to fit herself.

Those alterations were nearly complete, but today she had an order for a half-dozen pies. Finishing the gown would have to wait.

"Miss Caldwell!" The sound came from the backyard, through the open door from the porch. "Miss Caldwell!"

Dessa welcomed the interruption to her thoughts. She set aside the lemon cream that she would add to the four pie shells cooling on the table and went to the back door, spotting Nadette and calling her in.

"Would you like a couple of cookies? I have two different kinds ready for delivery to the store. Gingersnap and shortbread. I can offer you some milk, too—"

"Miss Caldwell! Stop!" Nadette waved both hands in front of her frantically. "I can't think of food right now. You promised to help me, remember?" She looked over Dessa's shoulder at the empty kitchen as if to be sure they were alone. "Liling's sister, ya know? You'll still help, won't ya?"

Now it was Dessa's turn to glance nervously over her shoulder, even though she knew both Remee and Jane were in the dining room, sewing table linens.

"Yes, I remember. What I don't understand is why you want to help so much, Nadette. I thought you approved of working girls?"

"If they're paid! They don't pay Liling, and they ain't gonna pay her sister nothin' neither. It ain't fair, is all. Ya ain't changed yer mind, have ya?"

"No." Her hesitation to get involved in a culture she knew nothing about wasn't enough to stop this wrong if she could. "Just so long as you understand I'm getting involved to save her from prostitution. Not so she can branch out on her own to make money."

"*She* ought to be the one to make that choice, don't ya think? 'Stead a bein' forced?"

Dessa nodded, although if she succeeded, the girl wouldn't ever have to make such a choice. "Has she arrived?"

"They got word she's on the train comin' in today." She blew a disgusted puff of air through her thin lips. "With a escort to keep her intact, if ya know what I mean. It's like keepin' a man bound for the noose healthy enough to climb the steps to the rope. The sale of her first time is set for tomorrow. You know how much money they're gonna make offa her? And she won't see a cent, not a red cent! So Liling wants to sneak her away right off—tonight. I'll bring 'em both here, but I don't know what time. It'll be in the middle of the night, though. Ya sure no one else'll tell? I don't trust that Miss Remee no more. Nobody can know she's here, Miss Caldwell. Nobody."

"She'll be safe here, Nadette. I promise you that."

Nadette nodded. "Okay, then. Tonight." She started to turn away, but stopped. "Can ya be out here, on the porch? All night, so you can let us in? I don't wanna have to throw stones at yer window in case somebody sees us. Never know who'll be out around here while the sun's still down. Can ya be waitin' for us?"

"Yes. I'll be right here on the porch. All night, if necessary."

"Henry?"

He looked up from the papers on his desk, papers he must pretend had held his attention. He hadn't produced more than fifteen minutes of work in the entire hour since he'd arrived in his office. The fact that it was not only Miss Caldwell but a worn edition of a Bible left behind by his father that had held his attention was something he wasn't ready to share—even with Tobias, who was likely to welcome either subject.

Going to church these past couple of weeks had stirred something in Henry he hadn't felt in years. All this time he'd been convinced his business success had been undeserved. Striving to alleviate his guilt, paying back the money—none of that had worked.

But if Reverend Sempkins was right, forgiveness was as undeserved as Henry's success had been. He was just beginning to realize that was what made it a gift.

Henry sat back in his chair as Tobias entered.

"I wonder if we could talk for a few minutes?"

"If it's about the Fieldhurst inheritance case, we can't release the funds to that overeager nephew until all the paperwork has been—"

"No, no," said Tobias as he took one of the chairs opposite Henry. He was frowning even though recently the man had been as giddy as a child. Henry guessed his uncle felt quite proud of himself lately—ever since Henry's feelings for Miss Caldwell had become too obvious to miss. If going to church hadn't given him away, defending Miss Caldwell to the donors had sealed it. "It's personal. About my sister. Your mother."

He skipped a breath. "Is she well?" He'd made it clear long ago that he did not want to talk about his mother, so something must be wrong for his uncle to break that rule.

"She's fine, fine."

"And the store? She's still having that family—what was their name? Owen?—run things for her?"

"It's all fine, Henry." A hint of impatience clouded those few words.

"Then what is it?" Henry matched Tobias's curtness. He knew he was the worst sort of son—an absent one—something he didn't appreciate being reminded of.

"I've invited her to your investors' dinner." Pulling a piece of paper from his pocket, he held it up. It had been folded, like a letter. "And she's accepted."

Henry's heart thumped against his chest wall, not fast, just hard. Surprisingly, the notion of seeing his mother again produced less dread than anticipation. His absence from her wasn't for lack of love; he wanted to see her.

And yet, what would he say when he did? Would he tell her why he'd stayed away all these years? Didn't she have a right to know?

But knowing . . . that might be worse than simply having a neglectful son.

With thoughts too heavy to sort, he looked down again at his desk as if he would return to work. Though he spared a glance, he could not make his gaze meet his uncle's. "Thank you, Tobias."

Tobias's bushy brows shot up his forehead. "What's that you say?"

If Henry's spirits weren't so torn he might have laughed at Tobias's obvious shock. "I said, 'Thank you.'"

28

THE SOUND of crying woke Dessa from a fitful doze. Opening her eyes, it took her a moment to spot the source of those tears. They came from a small figure in the corner of the porch, who sniffed with shaking shoulders as if to hold back yet a deeper torrent of tears.

"Nadette?" Dessa looked around the dimly lit porch. Only half a moon reflected any light tonight, but it took no more than that to see Nadette was alone. "What's happened?"

"Got caught." She wiped at her nose with the back of her hand, but more tears followed.

Dessa stood, holding out a hand for the child. Thankfully, Nadette didn't resist. Dessa led her into the kitchen, where she turned up the gas lighting.

"Nadette!" One look at the girl and Dessa turned her to face her fully. One side of her face was bruised, and there was blood on the hand Dessa held. "What happened to you?"

"Aw, nothin'. Not to me. But to Liling . . . If they guess what we were really tryin' to do, she's done for."

Dessa eyed her closely, turning her face toward the light attached to the wall. "Don't tell me nothing happened to you. Your face is bleeding."

"So's my knee. I fell on some stones back of the China Palace."

"Let me see."

Nadette sat in one of the kitchen chairs and pulled up her

ragged skirt. It wasn't just her knee; the girl had shredded her skin from knee to ankle. Speckles of dirt dimmed the shine of the blood spattered from top to bottom of her shin.

Without a word, Dessa returned to the porch for the large metal tub she and the other residents of Pierson House used for bathing. Filling the tub in the curtained corner of the kitchen was easier than hauling up water to any one of the bedrooms since the water closet upstairs didn't have hot water.

"I don't need no bath—"

"Yes, Nadette, you do. And I'm going to throw away that dress you're wearing while you're soaking. I'll find something upstairs, and I won't take no for an answer."

Before long Dessa had enough warm water to fill the tub and pulled the curtain to provide the girl with some privacy. "Don't soak too long, though," she instructed from the other side of the curtain. "And I want you to come back tomorrow so we can give that leg a salt bath, once the skin has a chance to heal a bit. It'll help, but would hurt too much tonight. Now give me that dress."

Nadette handed over the remains of the dress, and Dessa threw it on the porch before hastening upstairs to the charity box. The dress closest to Nadette's size was a drab shade of brown, but it was a vast improvement over what she'd been wearing.

"Oh, that's a fine dress, Miss Caldwell!" Nadette called from the bath, once Dessa had draped it over the rope holding up the curtain. A few moments later Dessa heard the girl emerge from the water and dry herself. Nadette soon stepped out from behind the curtain. The gown was too large, the sleeves too long and a bit baggy, but she was modestly covered, cleaner and neater than the way she'd looked before.

"Sit down, and I'll braid your hair," Dessa said.

"I been thinkin'," Nadette said as she plopped onto a chair. "If I can find out where they took her, we can try again tomorrow."

Dessa wasn't so sure. "I admire that you want to help, Nadette. But if it's dangerous, I don't think you should do anything. Perhaps Liling is the best person to help, on her own."

Nadette turned her head so quickly Dessa dropped the girl's braid. "Ya ain't changed yer mind, have ya? 'Cause I haven't! And what's more, I think I'm gonna need *yer* help to get her away."

Dessa resumed the braiding, ignoring very real and increasing misgivings. She wanted to help; it was no less than her duty. But to get involved in sneaking the girl away . . . That was something she hadn't intended doing.

"It woulda worked tonight if I'd a had somebody to keep the guy busy who's watchin' her. They let Liling in to see her, but soon as they tried to get out, the guy nabbed her. Only good thing is they might not know Liling was going to take her away, really away, and not just back to her room like she said."

"They didn't see you, then?"

"Oh yeah, they did. The one who's guarding Mei Mei's door scared me right good with all kinds of yelling when I come by. I don't know what he said, but it weren't nothin' I'd like to know, I guess. He looked 'bout to bite me before he hit me. That's why I ran, and that's why I fell."

"Why do you think they'll move her, if they haven't guessed what Liling is up to?"

"'Cause they already moved her once, when somebody tried sneakin' into her room to get at her ahead a time, not two hours after they brought her back from the train. She's awful pretty. Enough to make them Chinamen crazy."

Dessa sighed. "If they're going to illegally import women, why don't they do it for wives instead of . . . well, instead of this? That's the trouble—there just aren't enough respectable Chinese women here. If there were, none of this would be happening."

Nadette laughed. "Ya think so? Then why are there so many

gals at places like Miss Leola's? The railroad brought plenty a white families out here from back East, but there's still men who just want a wife for a night. Them Chinamen ain't no different."

So, this child had something to teach Dessa, after all.

"If they ain't moved her, or if they done that and I find out where, will ya still help? Do more'n just takin' her in? I can't get too close, or they'll think right away somethin's up. We hafta send in somebody they don't know. Like you."

Some small voice inside told Dessa to go to the authorities, to seek help and handle this wisely. But how could a city that turned its back on the obvious ills of prostitution and opium dens, even the wide practice of gambling, possibly be of any help? She already knew there was a shameful lack of concern when it came to whatever went on in the Chinese neighborhood called Hop Alley.

But it was one thing to harbor the girl, quite another to steal her from those who must consider her their property. And yet that very thought quelled some of Dessa's fears. What was the right thing to do? Let the girl be offered up for the sake of someone's profit?

"Yes, Nadette. I'll help."

29

THE OPIUM smelled strangely sweet in Hop Alley, almost enticing in its fragrance. Dessa had never passed through this end of Market Street before. The scent stirred her heightened senses. It came from behind small, plain doorways that led, Nadette had told her, to the bowels of certain buildings known to be opium dens. City maps referred to them only as "Chinese dwellings."

It was through one such door that Nadette had instructed Dessa to go, at precisely two o'clock Saturday afternoon. The door was more a gate than an entryway—a shaft of sunlight revealed the sky up above between two close buildings. The scent was stronger here compared to out on the street, as if it were trapped despite the narrow slice of sky. Perhaps, to some, it was an enticement that even the dankness of rotted railings and old puddles along the passageway couldn't quell.

They had only a few short hours before Mei Mei's auction was to take place. For the first time in days Dessa wasn't preoccupied about Mr. Hawkins's dinner party, just a day away. She merely hoped to get through the next hour so she could attend the party at all.

Nadette surprised Dessa with a thoroughness of planning that seemed well beyond her years. Since she would be recognized by anyone standing watch over Mei Mei, she'd devised a plan that required Dessa to go inside and help with a diversion so Liling could spirit her sister away. Once outside, since Nadette wouldn't be able to meet them at the correct door in time, Dessa would have to take the lead.

Nadette made sure Dessa was prepared. She took her to the place she was to bring Liling and Mei Mei afterward, a borrowed crib only a few twists and turns outside Hop Alley. Nadette told Dessa she'd need to know the spot even if she was chased all the way there.

That thought had seemed almost funny at the time, but now, stepping into the recesses of Chinatown's most notorious quarters, Dessa couldn't summon a single lighthearted thought. In fact, the very surroundings weighed her steps.

She took the smallest of breaths, fearing if she inhaled too much of the deadly bouquet it would deaden her brain the way she'd heard opium did. Nonetheless, she followed the dark gangway. The steep downward slant felt like a descent from all society, even from its very dregs.

Was *this* where they'd hidden Mei Mei . . . or worse, had they brought her here to prepare the innocent girl for what was ahead?

Dessa became aware of curious eyes that stared out at her from the shadows and windows above. She refused to meet the glances. In fact, she hoped not to be identified at all. In that hope, she'd tied a scarf around her head, fastened beneath her chin, and over that she'd placed a brimmed hat. Over one of the oldest dresses from the charity box she'd added a shawl that was hardly necessary for the warmth of the day. Even so, what she wore seemed extravagant in comparison to a beggar she passed on his way up the ramp. He was dressed in what appeared to be tattered layers; what one stringy jacket did not cover, another beneath strove to hide.

But he did not speak or try to stop her—though the look of surprise, then warning, then pity crossing his ancient features nearly sent Dessa running back home.

Instead, she withdrew a handkerchief from her handbag and

covered her nose and mouth. Perhaps it would help protect her against the scent. That, and the steady prayer she sent up with each and every step.

Scriptures came to mind, bidden by her quivering heart. *Fear thou not; for I am with thee . . . I will strengthen thee . . . I will help thee . . .*

How she depended on those promises now!

At last Dessa came to another door, this one taller than the first. Opening it slowly, stopping at the first creak, she slipped through the wedge without pushing it any farther.

The air was somehow different here, still sweet, but lighter, cleaner. A set of lanterns—gas, not electric, and behind cloudy glass plates—hung close to the tall ceiling, revealing an obscure cloud floating above in an expansive room. Dessa thought the vaulted ceiling likely accounted for the somewhat fresher air around her. The height of the room reminded her of the style and durability of an angled—though dark—cathedral. Brick surrounded her, as if she'd been swallowed by it—it was beneath her feet, above her head, and beside her on each of the four wide walls.

And yet they weren't walls at all. They were shelves . . . no . . . they were beds, if she could judge by the mats spread out on those she could see. Some were heavily curtained, closed against prying eyes, leaving just enough of a transom at the top of the cubicle to release a steady puff of smoke that found its way to join other puffs in the vapors above.

In the very center of the room was a tall, cast-iron stove. She could see through its slats that it was lit, but the stovepipe did not extend so far up that it reached the ceiling and beyond, outside. Rather, the pipe rose just above the upper bunks at the sides, dividing in two and coiling downward like two snakes to disappear into holes embedded in opposite walls. She guessed they must be connected to the pipes at each bed.

Her pulse sped up because she knew she ought not be here, in this secret and most deadly spot of the city. She could go back—she should run before anyone knew she was here. Anyone except Nadette.

Her feet and fingers tingled, as if prepared for flight.

But how could Dessa go? How could she fail not just Nadette, but more importantly, Mei Mei? If God was with Dessa, she had nothing to fear, even if her heart said otherwise.

"You want smoke?"

Startled by the nearness of the voice, Dessa turned—only to see little more than a shadow among all the shadows of the room. The man was small, dressed in a high-collared dark silk tunic and Chinese cap, from which ran a long, dark braid hanging over one shoulder.

"No . . . that is, I'm looking for Gum Sing. Can you tell me where I can find her?"

Now the man peered up at her, and she saw through the thin veil of smoky air that he wasn't as old as she'd first thought. Although the lines along his mouth and eyes were set, they disappeared when he offered the hint of a smile.

"You want work for Gum Sing?"

She shook her head.

"That good. She no hire wide-eye like you, anyway. Come back when Gum Sing not so busy."

Nadette had warned Dessa she might not gain easy access, but not to give up. Gum Sing was not busy with a customer today, because she was preparing Mei Mei for the auction. If Nadette's sense of timing was correct, Liling was already looking for Dessa—if they'd allowed Mei Mei's sister to stay with her at all. Even now, Nadette herself waited nearby to set in place more confusion than this den of altered reality had likely ever seen.

"I have something for Gum Sing. A gift."

He looked down at her bag, then held out his hand. "You give to me. I give to her."

Dessa shook her head. "I must place it in her hands myself."

The man stared at her again, this time suspiciously. "Why you here?"

"I told you, to give Gum Sing a gift."

"From who?"

Dessa's heart continued its downward spiral. She'd been hoping whoever took her to Gum Sing wouldn't ask so many questions. "Yin Tung."

He repeated the name, slowly and with a touch of awe—just as Nadette had predicted he might. There were few names in Denver everyone listened to, on either side of the law. Until today, Dessa had heard only rumors of such names. People who dealt in payments to government officials to avoid arrest and had the power to straddle the line between legal and illegal. Yin Tung represented the Chinese in just such a position, or so it seemed from what Nadette told Dessa that morning. And it was only Yin Tung who dealt with those of Dessa's race.

God forgive her for the lie that Yin Tung had sent her.

"You come."

The little man turned and led her from the chamber.

The black wooden door opened first to a dimly lit hall—as if purposely designed to prepare the eyes for the coming difference in lighting. Soon they passed into another room, this one brightly lit and more traditionally decorated. A round rosewood table sat in the center, and off to the side were a pair of chairs boasting bentwood backs that resembled a type of hat Dessa had seen worn in Chinatown. Beyond, on the far side of the room, stood a tall cabinet lacquered in black and accented with the image of a bamboo grove. Beneath them, their steps were softened by a woven silk rug, decorated with peacocks and a symmetrical design along the edge.

This lovely, inviting room was a sharp contrast to what went on in the cavity attached to it. And to any dealings concerning an innocent young girl named Mei Mei.

Just past the room was a two-story staircase, polished and fine, brightly lit by a pair of windows, one atop the other. At the top was an open hallway showing a number of doors, each one closed.

The man led the way, going to a door not far from the top of the stairs. He tapped just once and the door opened. Dessa looked to see a young Chinese girl emerge, dressed in a long apricot robe that was meticulously embroidered with flowers and cuffed with a row of butterflies.

The man spoke sharply, but the girl—surely not Mei Mei since she seemed free to leave the room behind her, but perhaps Liling?—didn't heed what he said. She looked past him without concern, focused on Dessa. As the man left them to speak to someone still inside the room, Dessa saw the girl—standing so still on Dessa's side of the doorway—raise one small hand to beckon Dessa closer. Surely she *was* Liling.

In three small, silent steps, Dessa neared her. "You follow me," the girl whispered, so that only Dessa could hear.

With little more than a glance toward the room behind them, Dessa waited to see what Liling would do. She quietly closed the door, then tore down the corridor to the farthest room opposite. From beneath a generous sleeve, she withdrew a key and inserted it into the lock before Dessa had caught up to her.

Frantic whispering followed. A small whimper. Then Liling emerged, tugging a smaller girl behind. Dessa rushed to follow— only to stop abruptly at the sound of a shout behind them. Not from the man who'd shown her here, but from another, bolder voice at the base of the stairway.

A glance over her shoulder sent her heart skating with terror. A man three times her own width, half again taller than Dessa, yelled wildly. He held a tray, but just as he looked about to set it aside, a crash erupted behind him and the tray fell to the floor in a clatter of broken porcelain.

Something had come through one of the windows from the street. A candle that started an instant fire. And yet—not a fire. All smoke, but no flames. Then a moment later, a crash at another window, and another smoke candle spewed a cloud of gray. The man downstairs coughed and sputtered, going from one to the other, attempting to quench the bellows of fog.

For one blurry moment Dessa stood immobile, until Liling spoke into her ear.

"Follow!"

Dessa turned to join the fleeing girls as more voices erupted— that of the man who'd shown Dessa the way, along with a woman's voice. Dessa paid no heed. Liling pulled Mei Mei, who stumbled once and then again.

Liling opened yet another door, this one to a narrow, nondescript stairway. When Mei Mei tripped, Dessa grabbed for her tunic. It ripped, but the girl did not fall.

New clamor met them in what appeared to be a kitchen, but Liling neither hesitated nor answered the cries around them. She ran as if the devil himself were behind them—and Dessa was nearly convinced that he was.

Outside, the sun was blindingly bright, and Dessa could barely make out the shapes in front of her, with Liling leading the way to an alley. She heard rapid steps behind them and more yelling in a language she was glad she did not understand. With Mei Mei stumbling yet again, Dessa picked up the girl's other arm, and together she and Liling pulled Mei Mei along at a frantic pace.

Dessa knew the way and knew, too, that Liling depended on her to take the lead now that she'd gotten them out of the opium house. The wisdom of the route quickly made itself apparent: there might have been a more direct path to their destination, but taking gangways and extra turns made it easier to lose their pursuers.

Around one last corner and through one more gangway, then Dessa let go of Mei Mei long enough to throw herself at a familiarly scratched and scarred wooden door. Thankfully it opened as easily as she expected, and the three of them piled into the smallest parlor Dessa had ever seen.

Slamming the door behind them, Dessa put a finger over her mouth, willing the two girls to be quiet.

All three of them were breathing so heavily Dessa knew she couldn't have spoken if she wanted to, and she guessed the others felt the same. She looked around. She'd never been inside a crib before, not even to help with a delivery. Any girl that far along in a pregnancy would've had to give up such a place, even one as shabby as this.

The parlor held two chairs and a small table, leaving room for little else. There might have been a window once, judging from the outline of unmatched brick on the front wall. That was the only design on any of the otherwise-unadorned walls. Behind them was a plain, colorless curtain—bleached with age and wear to a sort of gray-white—that divided this room from another. It was hooked aside so Dessa could see the other room was empty but for the inevitable bed.

Dessa regained even breathing first and left the locked door without a word. She passed through the curtained partition, searching beneath the bed for the parcel Nadette said she would leave there—a parcel Dessa herself had provided from the charity box. Two petite dresses designed for Western women.

The girls received them silently, as if still too afraid to make a sound. Liling pulled off her far finer apricot robe and donned the larger of the two plain cotton garments. A moment later, Mei Mei did the same. But before letting Dessa take their Chinese robes to fold them inside the paper sack, Liling pointed to the design on Mei Mei's, saying something to her sister.

Then they both burst into tears and clung to each other.

"Can you tell me what you said?" Dessa gently inquired when the sisters parted. "If it isn't too personal?"

Liling raised a shaking hand to wipe away the tears on her smooth cheeks. "Personal? Yes. But I share with you." She pointed again to the design on the blue robe Mei Mei had worn, of expertly sewn leaves entwined in a way Dessa would enjoy replicating. "Sacrificial robe. The waterweed—seaweed—means purity. Now Mei Mei will not be sacrificed because of greed."

No matter how many moments of fear and horror Dessa had endured that afternoon, each one was worth it to see the happiness on the faces of the girls in front of her. Both of them were indeed striking. Pure creamy skin, shiny black hair, each with a long and slender neck. And their faces, though different—Liling's was softly rounder, her forehead not so high—both had brows that gently curved above eyes that were dark yet bright with an unfathomable depth.

The change of clothing for the girls helped to disguise them but was not enough. "Do you mind if we change the style of your hair?" she asked Liling.

The girl elbowed her sister to pull down her hair from its traditional bun, as she herself was doing. Without a comb, the new styles were anything but perfect, but with Dessa's help Liling fashioned her hair and her sister's into more Western fashions: Liling with a braid pinned just above her forehead and Mei Mei with two braids, each looped at the side, as befitting a girl so young.

Finally Dessa removed her hat and untied her scarf, wishing she'd thought to bring along two. She handed the scarf to Mei Mei and the hat to Liling.

"Your crib?" Liling asked as she put the hat on.

Dessa shook her head.

"How you know it empty?"

"Nadette delivers laundry here," Dessa said with a burst of unexpected admiration for the young expert who'd devised the escape. "She knows the girl and asked to use it this afternoon. She probably thinks Nadette wanted to make some money for herself. I suppose you know it was Nadette who threw in the smoke candles to help us escape. She knew she couldn't be at the windows and then reach the kitchen door in time to guide you here. That's why I came to help."

Dessa then looked at Mei Mei, who appeared so tired that Dessa wished they were already back at Pierson House. "Do you speak any English, Mei Mei?"

The girl shook her head.

"She understands," Liling answered, "but is afraid to speak."

Dessa patted Mei Mei's hand. "I hope you won't be afraid anymore. I want to make sure you're safe."

Liling studied Dessa. "You were in great danger today. Why did you do this? Two people not even of your kind?"

Dessa smiled. "What is my kind? I've never quite fit anywhere my whole life. I don't think I have a kind, but I will, in heaven."

"So you do it for your God?"

Dessa nodded.

"Then I thank you," Liling said.

"And your God," Mei Mei added.

They needed to leave the crib before sunset, when the girl who rented the two rooms was expected to return for her usual working hours. Before setting out, Dessa gave the sisters detailed directions to Pierson House should they somehow become separated, quickly adding she didn't think that likely. She assured them they didn't have far to go.

Just as the sun slipped behind the mountains, Dessa sneaked the girls into Pierson House by way of the back door, only to see Nadette with Remee in the kitchen—both of them sullen with tension over what had likely been a harsh and recent exchange of words.

Nadette was the first to her feet, a smile bursting through whatever vexation she'd felt a moment earlier. "You made it just fine!" She hugged both the girls, welcoming them as Remee looked on in disgust.

Remee appeared about to speak, her lips opened with an accompanying scowl, but Dessa aimed a censuring look her way. "Will you help me with dinner, Remee? It must be something quick; we haven't time to cook. It's been a trying day, so I want an early dinner to let the girls get some rest."

The truth was, she hoped to get them upstairs to the middle bedroom as soon as possible. It was small, private—and offered only a single, heavily curtained window overlooking the side of the house. No one would see them up there, from the front or the back, particularly if they kept the curtain drawn.

Remee told her Mr. Dunne hadn't been around since noon, that he'd said he was going to try for a new job tonight and likely wouldn't be back for dinner. Dessa took that as confirmation that she'd done the right thing; she wasn't yet sure they should trust Mr. Dunne.

No one spoke after that, not even Nadette, who was the only one to show any happiness. Remee stayed sulky, and when Jane joined them she was cautious around the newcomers, making no attempt to lift the cloud of concern that hovered. The girls themselves looked fearful, and Liling jumped when Remee dropped a plate. Liling let her sister sit close enough to hang on to her hand, both of them glancing often at the door.

Dessa wished she could convince them they were safe, but even as she drew the curtains that hung over the windows on each side of the door to the porch, she knew any promises of security would be hollow. How could she share with anyone else what she did not have?

One thing she did know for sure, and took comfort in: the hours of this night would be far different for Mei Mei than they would have been had Nadette not come forward.

But the satisfaction did not settle in Dessa's breast for long. After dinner, Nadette left, taking with her the only smile to be found. Everyone else seemed eager to go upstairs. Remee went first, and Dessa guessed Jane wished she could follow, except she'd volunteered to do the dishes since she hadn't helped with the preparation. Dessa didn't blame them for wanting to disappear. Perhaps they sought another escape, this one from that lingering cloud of fear permeating the room.

"I'll take you upstairs, girls," Dessa said to Liling and Mei Mei. "Come along."

Dessa provided sleeping gowns and filled the water basins in their room. Then she went to her own room to pray, but, feeling alone instead of comforted, her fears only multiplied.

Dessa returned downstairs. She helped Jane with the rest of the dishes, afterward watching her go up the stairs. Then Dessa walked from room to room. She made sure the doors were locked tight and all the curtains drawn. She peered out from a corner of each window just to be sure all was quiet. Finally, she took up a vigil in the dark at the parlor window. And she prayed.

30

HENRY SAT in his most comfortable chair in the privacy of his library, a room full of books that had helped him pass more than a few lonely nights. Yet he felt little comfort. This Saturday night had been like countless others; he'd eaten whatever Mrs. Gio had put before him. As usual, it pleased his senses and filled his stomach, but the passage of yet another meal alone left him wanting.

He reread a line of the book in his hand, one he'd recently begun: *Strange Case of Dr. Jekyll and Mr. Hyde*. Asked to tell of Hyde, one of the characters said: "He is not easy to describe. There is something wrong with his appearance; something displeasing, something downright detestable. I never saw a man I so disliked, and yet I scarce know why. He must be deformed somewhere; he gives a strong feeling of deformity, although I couldn't specify the point. . . ."

Henry slammed the book shut. A deformity of the spirit might be what Hyde suffered, but if so, it was precisely Henry's condition as well. Why else had he done what he'd done all those years ago and let it get the best of his entire life? Little had he known that his youthful impatience, his lack of trust in himself to work hard and earn his way honestly and slowly, would ruin him forever.

He stood, abandoning all effort to pass the time with a book, no matter how interesting. Despite the fact that tomorrow night at this time the entire house would be lit and full of polite guests, there was nothing for Henry to do tonight. The event, as always, had been placed in the capable hands of his butler, Mr. Barron, and Mrs. Gio. A dozen deliveries had been accepted that week, all in preparation for a meal that would accommodate twenty guests, the maximum number his dining room could comfortably hold. Already cloths draped various tables throughout the rooms as well as ornamental niches in the hallways, ready to accept the dozens of flower arrangements that would arrive in the morning to fill and warm Henry's cavernous home.

It was too early for Henry to go to bed. Perhaps he would take a walk. Fresh air now might help him sleep later.

But he made it no farther than the front hall before a knock at the door called his attention. Dismissing Barron of his duty—he saw the man even now hurrying from behind the butler's pantry in the nearby hall—Henry opened the door himself.

It came as no surprise to find Tobias there. Henry opened the door wide, about to welcome him in—glad for the company—when he saw that his uncle wasn't alone.

The slight shadow beside Tobias's wide and tall one was easily missed in the dim light of evening. But there she was. Henry's mother.

They stared at one another for what could have been too long a moment, or perhaps too short. Henry didn't know which, he was so lost in a rush of emotion. Two years suddenly seemed far too long, especially when preceded by years of scant contact. Knowing it had been Henry's decision, and his alone, cast a burden onto his shoulders he hadn't planned to face. Not tonight.

"I'm sorry."

How strange a greeting that might have seemed, but to his mother it appeared welcome. She raised a petite, gloved hand to her chin, and the moment he saw her tremble he stepped closer, ushering her inside with one hand around her shoulders and the other finding one of her hands.

"Come in, Mother, come in. Sit down. Are you hungry? Thirsty?"

"No, no," she said, her voice more tremulous than her fingers. Beneath his embrace he felt the quiver of her slight frame and wished—not for the first time—that he hadn't been such a fool. Especially since his father had died some eight years ago. How alone had his mother been? As alone as Henry?

"Come into the parlor, will you? Both of you? It's comfortable in there, with the windows open. The breeze is pleasant."

His mother, still holding his hand as if she were as reluctant as he to let go, looked around. To Henry's shame, she had never before seen his home. He'd never invited her. He wished the flowers had already been delivered, because she saw it now for what it was: half-decorated, void of any personal touch. Clean, orderly, but stark. Cold. The single portrait of her father looked as lonely as Henry's life.

A maid appeared—Ulla, Mrs. Gio's niece, who had been brought in for the party. She offered tea, but the moment she left to retrieve it, and just as soon as he helped his mother to a settee, Henry went to the table at the side of the room to pour himself a glass of water. The others declined, but he was glad to have the cool glass in his grip.

"I'm sorry I didn't let you know I was coming early," his mother said. "But Tobias seemed to think it would be a good idea if I stayed here tonight, and that I might be of help with the party tomorrow."

"The staff—" Henry began, but stopped himself. He smiled, taking a seat near his mother. "That would be most appreciated, Mother. Thank you." Then a warm thought struck him. "And you'll come to church with me in the morning, of course."

Her mother raised rounded eyes his way. "Church? I didn't know you . . ."

"I only recently began attending again." Then Henry smiled wider. He knew he was on the right road, and now his mother's presence allowed him hope of forgiveness. But he still had much to prove—to himself and to others. "To be honest, it's been very recent. Though you may not yet believe it, something has changed in my life, something that makes me regret very much the way I've treated you. I hope you'll forgive me, and that I can be a better son to you."

She held out a hand that still trembled, and the sparkle of a tear caught the light in her eyes. "You'll have to forgive me too, then, Son. The road between your house and mine travels both ways. I could have been more diligent in using that road myself."

"No, Mother. I was the one who pushed you away." Henry set aside the glass. He glanced nervously from his mother to his uncle, uncertain how to explain, or if an explanation was needed. Would revealing his past help her to understand, or would the knowledge of what he'd done only make her ashamed of him? Make her do the pushing away this time?

"Tell her, Henry. It's time."

Tobias's words reached Henry loud and clear, almost as if his own conscience had somehow spoken them for all to hear. Henry gazed at him, his surprise turning to confusion.

Slowly, without another word, Tobias pulled something from his pocket. That old brown handkerchief.

But no, Henry saw now that it was cut too roughly, frayed at the edges as if it had been torn and not neatly sewn. It had not been made for any gentleman. It was tattered, too, or so it seemed when Henry caught a glimpse of a hole.

Tobias took the material and held it up in both hands, revealing what Henry had guessed. It wasn't a handkerchief at all. But what he slowly suspected it to be made his head spin.

It was a mask—one Henry recognized.

"What's that you have, Uncle Tobias?" The question, entirely unnecessary, was meant to buy Henry some time. But it wasn't enough. No words, no explanation, no excuses came to mind.

"It was yours once, Henry. Do you recall? I found it the day of the robbery, when I chased after you and the wind blew it from your hand."

"I—" He didn't know what he'd been about to say, especially with such a confident start. A worthless, untrue denial? So he stopped. He nodded.

His mother rose, taking the scrap of material gently from her brother. "I've known about it for some time, Henry. This was from my sewing basket—material Tobias and I brought with us from Manchester when we were children."

He turned an astonished gaze from his mother to his uncle.

"I brought the material to her, knowing she'd recognize it just as I did. I never meant to tell her, but after so long, I thought she ought to understand why you kept yourself away."

His mother stood very near, placing a hand over Henry's clenched ones. "I took it as some comfort that you didn't flaunt what you'd done, Henry. But it's time we all faced the truth. Isn't it?"

Just then Ulla returned with the tea tray, pouring efficiently, silently. Tobias and Henry's mother accepted the cups, but the moment Ulla left they both set their tea aside.

"I've wanted to speak to you about this ever since, Henry. I'd hoped the notes I sent would remind you of God's willingness to forgive."

Henry stared at his mother, wide-eyed. "*You* sent them?"

She nodded. "I'm sorry they were so mysterious, but I was too much a coward to come to you directly. I'd hoped you would go to Tobias with them. If you'd spoken to him first, it might have been easier to come to me next."

Henry looked at his uncle. "You knew about the notes?"
Tobias nodded.

"Don't blame him if they were troublesome," his mother said, patting Henry on his jacket lapel. "I made him promise to keep my secret until I could speak to you myself."

Tobias shrugged, as if embarrassed. "We believed you would become curious enough about them to open up the entire subject for the first time. Evidently a failed plan."

"But, Henry," his mother said softly, "what's to be done . . . now?"

"After all these years? I don't know. I returned the money, if it's any consolation. Anonymously, of course."

"Yes, we knew that, too," she said. "It was in the papers, at least around Leadville. I know there is no warrant for your arrest, Henry, and I know you've tried to do the right thing. In fact, the boys back home play a game pretending to be the bandit tricking everyone with a make-believe gang behind him, just as you did." She smiled, just a little smile, then replaced it with a frown. "But I don't know why you did it in the first place, and I don't know why you haven't allowed me in your life all these years. Was it the shame of having been a thief?"

"Partly."

"And the other? Why did you steal? How did your father and I fail you so?"

"You? Fail me?" Henry shook his head and turned from her, too ashamed to face her unnecessary and groundless guilt. "It was my idea, my fault. My impatience. I saw how you struggled to grow the businesses—first that smithy, then the mercantile. I didn't want to waste that kind of time. It was me, Mother. All me." Then he sucked in a deep breath. He might as well confess it all; they knew the bulk of it anyway. "Sit down again, won't you?"

Once seated, Henry told it all. About the girl he'd fallen in love with in college, about how pleased he'd been to have already secured his successful life—built upon the lie he'd concocted about a wealthy investor giving him money. He would return home not only with enough to start his business, but with a wife, ready to start his family.

But then that same girl's brother, a lawyer, had been convicted of embezzling funds from the estates of several clients. His theft cast the entire family into shame. Henry would have married her anyway and taken her to Denver, far away from Chicago. It seemed a perfect solution, even to her and her family.

Until he realized that was precisely the kind of shame he risked putting her through again, should his own theft ever be uncovered. It was then he'd discovered he would never do such a thing, not only to her, but to any woman he might come to love. Or to his family.

As he spoke, the reminder of that shame resurrected a wall that had been crumbling lately, one Dessa Caldwell had successfully, unknowingly, chipped away. He'd thought he might risk it after so many years, after having made restitution. Even lately, he hoped he might find forgiveness from God—the very God she worshiped, who forgave all those she so desperately wanted to care for in the Fourth Ward. Surely he might find forgiveness from both God . . . and her?

But the social shame—that was something he wasn't sure he could risk. Not even for her.

"The entire family suffered for that man's mistakes, Mother." He took, then squeezed, one of her hands. "I didn't want that for you. I thought if I were ever caught, it was best if I were already out of your life. You wouldn't miss me."

"Oh, Henry!"

He moved to kneel before her, taking her into an embrace as she released her tears. "I know it wasn't worth it, Mother. It's taken me a dozen years to figure it out, but I know it now."

31

SUNDAY BREAKFAST at Pierson House consisted of eggs, corn bread, and syrup, with wild strawberries on the side when they could be had. It was the only meal Liling and Mei Mei would be able to spend at the kitchen table if they were to be a secret from Mr. Dunne—if Mr. Dunne was even still with them. He hadn't shown up at all last night, which had relieved rather than concerned Dessa. Perhaps he'd gotten the new job, and it offered another place to live.

Dessa noticed with some distress that the sisters had eaten little. She didn't dare go to a Chinese market but knew she had some rice on hand and would be able to serve that in the days ahead.

If their secret wasn't discovered.

Dessa was eager for Nadette's return. She would likely have news from Hop Alley about what was being done to find the girls.

But even with so much else demanding her attention, Dessa still anticipated the evening ahead. Knowing Mr. Hawkins's dinner party was tonight filled her with as much excitement as tension. She hated leaving the girls alone, fearing the only reason they were all safe now was because no one knew where the sisters could be found. How long could she hide them?

She guessed she wasn't the only one who still worried. Remee blatantly refused to acknowledge either of the new arrivals, and Jane continued to be uncharacteristically quiet.

Still, Dessa had no intention of turning Liling and Mei Mei

out—this was a shelter ordained by God, and she would have to trust Him for their safety.

She just needed to be wise. If it was true she'd once again been too hasty in her action, then she at least needed to go forward in a way that wouldn't endanger Pierson House or *any* of the girls.

That was why she intended to speak to Mr. Hawkins about what to do. Tonight.

Noise at the back door drew her attention from her task of cleaning up the stove. She glimpsed a feathered hat through the open edge of the curtained window.

"Quick! Upstairs!"

No sooner had she uttered the words and seen the girls flee—dishes left rattling, scuffling sounds up the stairs—than a familiar woman came uninvited through the kitchen door.

It was the older woman Dessa remembered as Belva. In an effort to create a calm facade, Dessa reclaimed the seat she'd used during the meal. Jane had disappeared with the sisters, but Remee had stayed behind.

"Got a full table, so I see from the empty places," Belva said in lieu of a greeting. "Why'd everybody scatter like I'm raidin' the place?"

Keeping her seat, Dessa reached around to collect plates and scrape remnants off the dishes while Remee took away the empty glasses.

"We're just being careful, Belva," Dessa said. "There are some . . . employers, as you well know, who would rather not lose their workforce."

Belva laughed, sitting opposite Dessa and grabbing the last piece of corn bread from a plate in the middle. She tore off a corner and popped it in her mouth. "I guess that's true enough. I told you Pierson House wouldn't work."

"Oh, but it is working," Dessa assured her with a false sense of confidence. "We're quite happy here."

Belva stopped chewing, her face turning to stone as she stared across at Dessa. "You won't be for long."

If Dessa had thought herself exhausted from her lack of rest that week, she was proven wrong when new tension reignited her energy. "That sounds like a threat."

Belva threw the half-eaten bread onto the scrap plate. She looked over Dessa's shoulder to the door the girls had disappeared behind. "I didn't come here to threaten you, but I did come to warn you. Last night there was nearly a riot in Chinatown. It seems two girls have tried quitting the business they were brought here for. The only thing that stopped the trouble was a word from a man named Yin Tung, telling everyone the girls were about to be caught and returned. You know anything about that?"

Dessa dropped the knife she'd used to clean the plates, refusing to meet Belva's accusing stare.

"There's a new rumor about a white woman being in on the escape. And a white kid, a girl."

Dessa folded her hands in her lap, one gripping the other so tightly that her fingernails dug into her skin.

"That has nothing to do with any of us," Remee said.

Belva turned her venomous gaze on Remee. "No?" She said the word slowly, drawing out the syllable twice as long as it needed to be. "You oughta know you can't quit this business. You get the boot on account of age or disease, or you die. Those are the only two ways out."

"I didn't get the boot."

"That's not what Leola says."

Remee shrugged. "Let her say what she likes."

"You'll never work again, not in this town."

"That's good news," Dessa said, winning her struggle for a steady breath. "In fact, it's exactly what anyone who comes here wants—to find a new line of work."

Belva *pffff*ed. "Has she tried? Nobody'll have her on the polite side of town." She stood, the chair behind her scraping the floor. "Believe it or not, I came as a friend." She eyed Dessa. "To you, anyway. There's trouble coming your way if you keep them girls here. You'd best send them back."

Dessa's heart pounded so hard all she could feel for a moment was the blood thumping painfully at her temples. She had no intention of following such advice, not after they'd gotten this far, but she also had no wish to argue about a subject she was supposed to have no interest in.

A knock at the front door made Dessa jump to her feet, an action that brought a snicker from Belva. "Relax. It's only that Mr. Hawkins who is so fond of you."

Dessa looked at her, confused.

"I saw his carriage coming down the other street, so I cut through the yards to get here faster. I knew where he was headed. Where else in this neighborhood but here?"

"Then if you'll excuse me—"

"Oh no," said Belva amiably. "As it turns out I got some business with Mr. Hawkins myself. So I'll stay."

Dessa lifted her brows. "You—you have business with Mr. Hawkins? Mr. Henry Hawkins, the banker?"

Belva smirked. "Not the kind of business you'd think, dear girl." Her face grew serious as she looked from Dessa to Remee. "You go and get that door, Remee. Leave me alone with Miss Caldwell here."

Although Remee rarely took instruction very quickly, this time she did so without any hesitation.

Dessa faced Belva, who didn't speak until after the last swing of the kitchen door behind Remee.

"Listen, if Turk knew I was here, he wouldn't take kindly to it. So what I have to say is just between you and me—and that Hawkins fellow, if you want to share it."

"What has Turk Foster to do with Mr. Hawkins?"

Belva's face softened, and she looked at Dessa with unabashed affection. "I know I'm crazy for thinking so well of you. My daughter wouldn't likely have been anything like you." Her brows gathered and she looked at where Remee had disappeared. "More likely she'd been another Remee. But Turk saw it in you too. That goodness. It got to him, I'm tellin' ya. Everybody thinks he didn't want this place to make a go, that he'd just as soon have the doors shut. Maybe that's so, and maybe it isn't. I do know one thing: I never saw him get so worked up over a gal as he's been about you. And I doubt he wants to lose out to the likes of Hawkins."

"What has he against Henry Hawkins?"

"You really don't know, do you?" She offered a humorless laugh. "All that Mr. Hawkins would have to do is snap his fingers and he could be the next senator of this great state. Something Turk wants for himself. And besides that, it's personal. He heard what Hawkins said about him, that the only reason Turk offered to do the benefit for this place was to spoil your connections to donors. It's not true. He liked you. But Turk knows you don't want *him*, and he's not so mean that he don't expect you to marry somebody. Just doesn't want it to be that Hawkins fellow."

Dessa squared her shoulders, taking in a deep breath. "You can tell Mr. Foster that, although this is absolutely no business of his, I have no intention of marrying anyone." Even as she heard her own bold pronouncement, she knew it wasn't true anymore. No *intention* of marriage, perhaps, because that depended as much upon Mr. Hawkins as herself. But hope?

"That's well and good, only ever since he had that dinner over here, sitting at the same table as one very interested Mr. Hawkins, he's had a private investigator trying to find out all he can so he can make Hawkins look bad—just in case he decides to snap those fingers about the Senate. And if he ends up looking bad in your eyes, too? So much the better." She winked. "Everybody's got a secret they'd rather not tell a sweetheart, don't they? Turk's trying to find one."

Dessa's eyes widened. "That's outrageous! Even if it were true of Mr. Hawkins—which I'm sure it is *not*—Mr. Foster has no right to interfere. And besides that, Mr. Hawkins and I have no personal relationship whatsoever." Much to her own regret, her words were technically true. If anyone could snap a finger to change something, she wished it could be her.

"That's so?"

"That is, indeed, so."

But those words did not come from Dessa. Instead, they came from the kitchen doorway, where Mr. Hawkins stood with an unmistakably sad expression.

Henry hadn't heard much of their conversation, only enough to know this woman—the same one he'd seen some weeks earlier walking to the Verandah—somehow thought it her business to pry into Dessa's private life. In relation to him.

And although he couldn't deny his wish otherwise, it was a fact that he and Dessa—Miss Caldwell—did not have a personal relationship. One near kiss did not mean much, and maybe it shouldn't go any further.

But what business could that possibly be of this woman's?

Before he could inquire, the woman smirked his way. "For somebody without any personal connection, you sure come round often enough."

"Are you living here now?" he asked.

Belva emitted a snort. "Not hardly." Then she turned back to Miss Caldwell. "Look, I shouldn't even be here now, but Sunday mornings aren't likely to have anybody up and about to see where I come and go. You heard everything I said?"

Miss Caldwell nodded.

The older woman grabbed Miss Caldwell's hand so swiftly she jumped, and Henry took a step closer. But the woman closed in on Miss Caldwell regardless of Henry's ready protection. "You listen to me, you hear? There's nothing in this for me; in fact, I'd lose the most powerful friend I've got if word traveled about me being here. Don't make it a waste of my time."

Although Miss Caldwell had seemed to view the other woman with some amount of reluctance at first, Henry didn't miss that her look now melted into acceptance. Trust, even, if he could believe that. She trusted this woman?

Once Miss Caldwell nodded, the older woman let her go. Then without another word she walked from the kitchen, letting the outer door to the back porch slam shut behind her.

"Would I be too inquisitive if I asked what that was all about?" Henry asked. "What did she say that made you assure her we weren't even friends?"

Miss Caldwell looked momentarily distressed, so much that her hands trembled as she tried employing them with the dirty dishes still sitting on the table. "I'm afraid I have some rather surprising—and irksome—news. It appears Mr. Turk Foster isn't quite finished interfering. Evidently it wasn't enough for him to try causing trouble for Pierson House. Now he wants to be sure no one will support you, just in case you're interested in running for a seat in the Senate."

The weight of his heart suddenly multiplied, protesting each pump with a whack against his chest. "I'm not at all interested in such a seat. But if I were, how does he imagine stopping me?"

"He's decided to hire a private investigator to search for some way of making you look unfit for the position."

The incredible words took a moment to make sense. Had he heard right?

Possible consequences charged through his mind, and Henry had all he could do not to look as nervous as Miss Caldwell did. "Has he already hired this investigator?" The words barely made it past his throat; it was constricted by his collar, which seemed to tighten by the second, and his heavy heart went even heavier.

To his horror, she nodded. "Some time ago, actually. Just after you were both here for dinner that day."

"I see."

She moved to set the dishes in the sink, but did not add water. Instead, she turned to face him, although for one irrational moment he wished she would ignore him. At least long enough to let him draw in a deep, fortifying breath. Under her gaze, he still could not move.

"I'm afraid Mr. Foster thinks he has the right to manipulate anyone around him. It's inexcusable, of course."

"Yes." Henry could bring himself to say no more, even though confessions and excuses and every sort of plea clamored inside his brain. *Don't listen to whatever he says about me! I've changed! I know what I did was wrong!*

She approached him, adding to his unease by looking at him directly. "I didn't mean to imply we weren't friends. I hope that we are, despite all our differences."

For one moment of abandon Henry dismissed all the ramifications of her disclosure. He shoved aside the old, familiar caution. Nothing had really changed even if he had—his past was still his, and what she'd just told him made matters worse. But in that single moment all he wanted to do was bask in the knowledge that she at least wanted to be his friend.

He didn't care what Foster did to prevent him from running for a Senate seat that Henry didn't even want. But he did care about what Miss Caldwell would think. Dessa—he might as well allow himself to call her that, if only in his thoughts.

The logical answer came to him. He must tell her the truth now, before Turk Foster did. It didn't matter if she returned Henry's unbidden affection; if she learned the truth about him from a stranger, there would be no hope at all that whatever friendship she now felt could develop into something more.

Only she was already turning away. "I assume you came with a generous offer to take us to church today?"

"Yes." The single word nearly choked him. He couldn't speak now. They were on their way to church. Others were waiting.

"I'll be ready in a moment."

Then she disappeared through the kitchen door, and he heard her go up the stairs.

32

DESSA TAPPED GENTLY on the door to the room she'd assigned Liling and Mei Mei, barely making a noise. Nonetheless, a moment later the door opened and Liling peered fearfully around the edge.

"Are we safe?"

Dessa nodded. "I'm going to church, and Jane will accompany me. Remee will stay downstairs to keep watch for anything unusual."

The expression on Liling's face, formerly so worried, now went hard.

"She doesn't want any trouble here, Liling. You can trust her that far."

Liling nodded once, quickly, but did not meet Dessa's eyes.

"I'll see if Mr. Dunne—that's the gentleman who lives in our carriage house—has returned. He can be of some help, even if we don't explain all that's going on."

Seeing Liling's face made Dessa want to stay behind. Liling was beyond fear; she seemed to be preparing herself for the inevitable. Dessa wished she could stay—the girls were just beginning to trust her. But what could she tell Mr. Hawkins? Make up some excuse? Or lie? That was no more acceptable than telling him the truth, at least right now when there was no time to explain.

"I'll return as quickly as I can, but I must go. I'm sorry, Liling. May God keep you safe."

As she turned away, Liling quietly closed the door.

Dessa stopped by Remee's room, and Remee agreed to do as Dessa asked: stand guard. Dessa knew the other woman acted more from survival than to protect the girls, but motive didn't matter to her so long as someone looked out for the place. Though what good Remee would be if men came forcefully after the girls, Dessa did not know. What good would any of them be?

She found Jane already downstairs, waiting for her with Mr. Hawkins at the door. Jane's face reflected the first hint of peace Dessa had seen on her since coming back with the Chinese girls last night.

"I'd like to check the carriage house for Mr. Dunne before we leave, if you don't mind, Mr. Hawkins."

Although she knew they hadn't much time if they were to avoid being late, Dessa hoped to find Mr. Dunne. If he'd returned, she must ask him to stay behind and watch over the house. She would have to save an explanation for later.

But her brisk knock at the carriage house door went unanswered, and when she called his name he didn't respond. Desperate to make sure he wasn't just sleeping, she pulled open the door. It moved far more freely than it once did, since Mr. Dunne had put it to more regular use.

It was empty. The place was darker than it used to be, with a canvas patch covering the hole in the roof and all the crooked slats nailed snugly back into place. It was also neat; a blanket was folded carefully at the foot of the cot, no litter or books to be found.

It was almost as if he'd gone entirely. Perhaps she should be relieved, yet she only found herself wondering where he could be. Another reason to worry. And to pray.

She would have stepped out and closed the door again behind her, but a noise stopped her, something falling to the ground. She waited, looking to the four corners. No little squirrel this time.

Perhaps she'd imagined the sound. Or perhaps it had come from outside the wall.

There was no time to figure out the source of the noise now. She pulled the door closed, then hurried back inside to join Jane and Mr. Hawkins, following them out the front door.

"I'd expected to have a full carriage again if I came to retrieve you," Mr. Hawkins said as his coachman opened the door and assisted first Jane, then Dessa, inside.

"Remee isn't quite ready to attend regularly," Dessa told him once he was seated opposite her and Jane. "Though I hope she will soon. And I'm afraid I cannot find Mr. Dunne."

"We're supposed to hope he has a new job, but I think he's off drinking somewhere!"

Dessa frowned at Jane's theory. She glanced at Mr. Hawkins. He, too, was frowning, but then he'd been frowning ever since Belva departed.

"He'll turn up" was all Mr. Hawkins said; then he looked out the window as the carriage moved onward. "I'm meeting someone at church this morning. Someone Tobias agreed to escort, since I'd thought there would be no room for her in here."

Dessa eyed him with surprise. *Her?*

He turned to hold her gaze. "My mother."

"Oh!" Jane sounded immediately buoyant. "How wonderful. I'll be so glad to meet her."

"And so will I," Dessa added. "I didn't know she lived in the area."

"She came in from Leadville," Mr. Hawkins explained, "and will stay for the dinner tonight."

"I wish I could go!" Jane raised a palm to cover her mouth, but her eyes were merry, free of any regret. "I suppose I shouldn't be so forward as to say such a thing."

Mr. Hawkins offered a smile, but somehow it didn't seem a

very happy one. "You'd likely be bored, Jane. A lot of stuffy investors and their polite but rather . . . selective . . . wives." His brows took on an apologetic slant as he looked at Dessa. "I should ask your pardon in advance for inviting you, with that sort of recommendation of the evening."

Dessa had trouble swallowing around a sudden lump that formed in her throat. If she didn't have so many other things on her mind, she'd be more nervous than ever about attending a party *with* Denver's high society instead of as its servant. Once, before taking on far more serious things to worry about, she might have been concerned about wearing a gown off a mannequin amid such a group.

And yet . . . how eager she was, still, to glimpse more of Mr. Hawkins's life, to be at his party, to be at his side.

She caught that thought. At his side? She was just a guest, and barely one at that.

Jane chatted most of the way to the church, which Dessa was happy to let her do. She was glad the girl was back to being herself, if only for the little while they would allow themselves to be away from Pierson House. Mr. Hawkins, too, seemed content to let Jane fill the silence. He'd taken to his familiar one-word answers, and if Jane noticed at all, she didn't seem to mind.

At the church, Mr. Hawkins set a slow pace to go inside, even though they could hear the strains of the first hymn. In the vestibule, Dessa felt his hand on her elbow.

"Miss Caldwell," he said, low, "I wonder if I might have a word with you? After the service, that is?"

"Of course. I hope you'll introduce me to your mother."

He nodded. "I'm sure she's here already. Tobias would never be late."

Dessa looked toward the arch that led into the sanctuary. "Will Mr. Ridgeway be here, then? And his wife?"

"Yes, they've opted to stay with my mother for the service, rather than attending their own church today."

Dessa's spirits brightened. She'd forgotten that Mr. Ridgeway's wife would undoubtedly be in attendance tonight as well. How could anyone married to such a wonderful man be anything but congenial?

In the sanctuary, it was easy to see Mr. Ridgeway, since he was both tall and wide. He sat toward the front, on the end of what Dessa had called Mr. Hawkins's pew since he'd first shown up at church. Perhaps Mr. Ridgeway had chosen the end in deference to those behind him—or rather, she saw as she neared, to extend his legs into the aisle, free of the confines of the seat in front of him.

For the first time since attending this church, Dessa did not sit with the White family. They were already there, squeezed together to leave room on the family pew for Dessa and Jane as well. But when Dessa filed into the sanctuary beside Mr. Hawkins, he led them to the pew behind the Whites. Mariadela smiled approvingly even as her husband, beside her, spread out in his seat, triggering the same action all the way down the line.

Beside Mr. Ridgeway were two women, both of them singing along with the hymn "Sweet Rest in Jesus." Dessa joined in, though she felt almost shy when both women simultaneously tilted their bonnets toward her. Though they smiled, she wondered if they—rightly so—blamed her for making Mr. Hawkins late.

"Oh, how happy am I,
With my Savior so nigh!
I have found sweet rest
On Jesus' dear breast."

Eventually, as she listened to the words she sang, Dessa felt the proclaimed rest.

Once again, Henry had trouble concentrating on the various parts of the service. Even as he enjoyed the extraordinary feelings of wanting to know God's grace for himself, of having a real family surrounding him, of reveling in Dessa's sweet voice beside him, he couldn't escape the ominous truth.

How long would it take Foster to figure out that Henry's initial investment hadn't come from where he'd claimed? Anyone who'd known him back then would recall that "a wealthy investor" had endowed Henry with enough capital to start his own business. He'd been foolish enough to talk about his "investor" everywhere, in Chicago and Leadville as well as here in Denver, though to a lesser extent. His gaze fell on William and Mariadela White, in front of him. Even they would remember. Perhaps that investigator had come round the Whites' innocently asking about him. What secret should they have made of knowing Henry back then?

He'd bragged about his secure future, his story so practiced he'd almost believed it himself. But it wouldn't take long to learn there had been no such investor. A made-up name. A figment of Henry's imagination.

It might not be easy to figure out where the money had come from, but spreading doubt about its source would be enough. Everyone knew banks depended upon the confidence of the public. Take that away, and they were ruined.

He would be ruined.

Henry glanced at Dessa, who was listening earnestly to whatever Reverend Sempkins had to say. It might not matter if she refused the intentions he wished to make known, once he told her the truth. He might not have anything to offer.

He raised a hand to his forehead, rubbing once. *Dear God,*

I know none of this is a surprise to You. I have no right to ask Your help in finding a way to avoid the consequences of my sin. So all I ask is that You give me the strength to suffer them. And maybe . . . give some of that strength—and a touch of Your grace—to Dessa when I speak to her.

33

DESSA GLANCED at her timepiece more than once, worrying throughout the hymns and sermon about the possibility of the girls' whereabouts being discovered while she was gone. If that happened, she had no idea what she would do—but she knew she needed to be there if it did.

More than once, she'd stolen a look at Mr. Hawkins. She felt led to talk to him about the situation, but could he help? *Would* he help? She hadn't forgotten that he'd been reluctant to extend her a loan in the first place, and although he seemed to have acquiesced in some ways, she wasn't sure how deeply involved in the care of Pierson House he wanted to be. Would he tell her she'd gone too far? Would he refuse to help—or worse, advise her to avoid trouble and send the girls back?

No, she was fairly certain he would do nothing so heartless.

In between each segment of the service, she sent up pleas for wisdom. She prayed, too, for the girls' protection because she knew there would be no hurrying home this morning. Not with Mrs. Hawkins and Mrs. Ridgeway yet for her to meet. If only she had nothing but the pleasure of their company on her mind, for she had no doubt they would indeed be pleasant.

After the service ended, the Whites joined them in the vestibule, and following a round of introductions, the women seemed to settle in for a comfortable chat.

Henry pulled out his pocket watch, glancing outside as the rest of the congregation emptied from the church and surrounding area. Perhaps under other circumstances he might have taken pleasure in such slowly passing time. This was, after all, part of what he'd missed all these years. Friends, family. Loved ones.

But, blast it all, he wanted to speak with Dessa and needed to speak with her alone. When, exactly, was he to have that chance? Certainly not now, with his mother and his aunt claiming her and paying her attention she seemed to be enjoying.

And the ride back to Pierson House was to be shared with not only Jane, but now his mother as well, since his carriage could accommodate her.

There was only one answer. He knew it would be frowned upon for Dessa to arrive at his party unescorted. And although Tobias and Etta had already volunteered to stop by to collect her, Henry had decided to ask if he might come for her himself a bit early. Early enough for him to escort her to his own party and be there in time to greet the first of his guests. Yet another hint revealing his intentions—intentions he remained unsure he should offer.

Still, it was the only way to find time alone with her. In his carriage, on the way back to his home before the party began.

Though he would have to wait, it wouldn't be for long.

During the short time she spent in the company of Mr. Hawkins's mother and Mr. Ridgeway's wife, Dessa almost gained a steady pulse and even breathing. Neither of them was anything like the wealthy women Dessa had known while working as a maid. They laughed easily, asked questions about her and others rather than talking about themselves or their own interests, and followed through with such topics as if they were interested rather than merely being polite.

But she knew she couldn't linger much longer. Mr. Hawkins, too, seemed ready to leave. "We shouldn't keep Mr. Hawkins waiting, I'm afraid, Jane," she said with a smile his way. "He must have a number of details to oversee before his dinner party tonight."

He neither admitted nor denied it, but that was enough to end the impromptu gathering inside the church vestibule. Mariadela said her farewells to Mrs. Hawkins first.

Mrs. Hawkins held Mariadela's hand in a friendly farewell. "It's been lovely to meet some of my son's friends, Mrs. White."

Being called a friend of Mr. Hawkins brought a smile to Mariadela's face, and Dessa caught the irony but said nothing. Nothing, either, when Mrs. Hawkins then expressed her hope and delight that she would see the Whites again that evening.

All eyes but his mother's innocent ones went to Mr. Hawkins.

"I hope that you will come," he said to William White. "And forgive the last-minute notice. It would be my pleasure."

Dessa took up the invitation, even if she had no right to do so. "Do come, Mariadela. I'll welcome another familiar face."

"We wouldn't want to make it awkward for your regular investors, Mr. Hawkins." William spoke tentatively but not coolly, as if only trying to discern the level of discomfort such an evening might cause.

Mr. Hawkins held out a hand to William. "This evening will be like no other I've had. If friends are there as well as my mother—neither of which many have known me to have—it's sure to amaze each and every investor."

William accepted that hand, then nodded. "All right, Hawkins. We'll be there."

Once they were inside Mr. Hawkins's carriage, his mother

patted her son's hand. "I'm sorry for my social error, Henry. I assumed everyone you knew would be coming tonight."

"It's more of a business tradition than a social gathering, but for the first time in its history, it'll be both." He took up her hand, kissed it, and let it go.

Dessa watched the exchange, marveling at the affection in his eyes, at the kindness and attentiveness he demonstrated toward his mother. Where was the Mr. Hawkins she'd first met—the cold, impersonal one who ran Hawkins National?

Perhaps . . . perhaps he might have a spot in his heart to help two innocent girls. It was worth a try—especially since she had nowhere else to turn.

So when he detained her outside her front door after Jane had already gone inside, Dessa was happy to linger.

"I wonder, Miss Caldwell, if you might allow me to escort you tonight? It would mean being ready for me to fetch you early, if you would allow me to do so."

She looked at him, his face earnest. "I would appreciate the ride, Mr. Hawkins."

He smiled. "I'll call for you at seven thirty."

He returned to his carriage, where Mrs. Hawkins waved from the window.

Dessa went inside, worries behind her that anything had happened while she'd been gone. Going to church had undeniably refreshed her, leaving her more hopeful than ever that everything would work out once she had an opportunity to speak to Mr. Hawkins and recruit his help.

But when Dessa tapped on the door to the sisters' room, all that appeared was a skinny arm: Nadette pulling Dessa into the small room, where the girl took a spot in front of the sisters sitting close together on one of the beds.

Nadette looked anything but happy. "How could ya leave 'em

alone? Don't ya know they're scared? And ya left 'em with that Remee!"

"Remee can be trusted, and no one knows about—" Dessa stopped herself. Belva knew.

"Ya think nobody knows? Talk in Chinatown is gettin' worse. Them on this side a Market Street that guess I had somethin' to do with it ain't gonna give us away—not to Chinamen, anyway. Don't think that'll last forever, though. All it'll take is for somebody who knows to get greedy. Somebody who'll tell on us just because they want a free smoke or a few drinks from a Chinaman's whiskey. Even that old sot you got livin' in the carriage house can be bought."

"Mr. Dunne doesn't know about the girls, and he hasn't even been here since they arrived."

"He's down there in the yard; I saw him myself comin' out of your kitchen. Looked like he's been dead drunk for a while, but was hungry enough to swipe some a that bread and stuff."

Dessa looked quickly at Liling and Mei Mei. "Did he see the girls?"

Nadette shook her head. "But don't think that Remee won't tell him, if it suits her purpose. Or that he won't see 'em himself before long. Ya think they're going to stay in this room forever?"

"We'll figure out what to do—I'm working on that. But don't worry about Remee. She doesn't want trouble here any more than I do. It's her home now too."

Nadette shrugged. "All I'm sayin' is you got to be careful."

"I already know that, Nadette," Dessa said tersely. How was she going to tell the girl that she wouldn't be home at all this evening? Yet having Nadette stay to take her place guarding the girls hardly seemed an answer, particularly if she was linked to their disappearance. "I think you'd better go. You can keep your ears open and do more to help if you see what's going on, instead of staying here."

Nadette plopped down on the empty bed and burst into tears. "I got noplace to go!"

Dessa stepped closer. "What do you mean? What about where you've been living, in the back of the Chinese laundry?"

Nadette picked up the bottom of her skirt to wipe her face. "They suspect I had somethin' to do with the trouble. They kicked me out."

Dessa rubbed her own face with her palms. She knew it was dangerous to keep Nadette here, but what alternative did she have?

Oh, Lord, keep us safe. Hold all of us secure in the palm of Your hand!

34

Although Mr. Dunne had shown up at the kitchen door to borrow the tin tub and buckets for a bath out in the carriage house, and though he'd combed his hair and shaved his face, he somehow managed to retain the stench of alcohol when he arrived at the kitchen table for the midday meal.

"We missed you at dinner yesterday, Mr. Dunne," said Dessa as she and Jane set out the food. "We thought you'd been busy with a new job."

"The job wasn't offered after all, miss." He looked straight ahead, tucking his napkin in the collar of his shirt in anticipation of the meal. He hadn't looked anyone in the eye since his reappearance.

That was it? No explanation?

Dessa knew Liling and Mei Mei would be down shortly, and if she planned to trust Mr. Dunne, she would have to do so now. That or have the girls restricted to their room all the time—something Dessa definitely did not want to do. It was bad enough they had to stay inside under a hot roof when the weather outside was so lovely.

"There is something we must discuss, Mr. Dunne."

Though he still didn't look her way, he raised his clean-shaven chin and stiffened his back. "If you're set upon giving me a tongue-lashing, miss, I know I've earned it. I know why they gave the job to somebody else once they saw me face. Put silk on a goat, and you still have a goat. And 'tis a goat I am."

"I'm sorry the job didn't work out, Mr. Dunne. But I was not about to scold you—though I can tell you've been drinking, and for your own good and health you ought to stop. I hardly imagine I'm telling you anything you don't already know."

"True enough."

"There is something else I want to discuss, and what I have to tell you is to be held in strict confidence. I must ask your help should we need it."

He lifted a brow, looking at her at last. "My help?"

"Yes." Dessa turned to Jane. "Go and get the girls, Jane. Tell them Mr. Dunne will be joining us for the meal."

She was gone in an instant, and Dessa spoke again. "I've taken into my care two sisters who will need special protection and complete secrecy while they're here."

"You can count on me, Miss Caldwell. I'm ever at your service."

"I hope that's true."

"So they've a nasty mac, have they? You're not to worry, miss. I wasn't a bouncer for nothin'. I aim to prove now, if you'll give me the chance, that I could easily have fulfilled the job I was just refused if they'd trusted me."

That he'd handled his rejection by drinking left considerable doubt in Dessa's mind. "I'm hoping to avoid any trouble. I just wanted to let you know that trouble may come anyway."

A moment later the kitchen door swung open. Mr. Dunne looked easily past Remee, and then Nadette and Jane, but when his gaze fell upon the Chinese sisters, the red rims of his eyes widened.

"Now, miss! I can see why you're in need of protection. Are you sure this is wise, when half of Denver don't tolerate the Oriental foreigners?"

"They're here, Mr. Dunne," Dessa said firmly. "They're no more foreign than any other immigrant—yourself included, I might add. I expect you to keep secret that we've taken them in."

Mr. Dunne scratched the top of his head, his brow furrowed. "I'm afraid nothin's a secret if 'tis known by three. And we're even more than that, aren't we now?"

Dessa had barely finished the alterations on the gown that Mariadela had lent her before it was time to dress for Mr. Hawkins to take her to his party. Remee, perhaps tired of all the tension of the past few days, volunteered to act as Dessa's lady's maid. She curled her hair, showing Jane how to do it too. Then she adjusted the bodice on Dessa's dress, making sure the black stripes on the cream silk sat just right along the curves provided by the corset, bustle, and petticoat foundation. She even lent Dessa a pair of black shoes and a handkerchief that matched the cream silk, making the ensemble shine. It may not compare to the extravagant evening gowns rich investors' wives would wear, but the style suited Dessa to perfection—and was by far the most expensive attire she'd ever worn.

It hadn't crossed Dessa's mind to hope she might someday don such rich apparel. True, the corset pinched to make the gown fit snugly, and the bustle was stiffer than she was accustomed to; all the layers beneath her gown felt heavier than anything she normally wore, and despite the delicate lace, the sleeves limited her movement. Heaven help someone who had to be useful in such trappings!

But looking at herself in the single mirror Pierson House offered, which hung outside the door to the water closet upstairs, she had to admit she looked like a lady of worldly means, a far cry from the servant she thought herself to be, even if lately that service had been to the Most High God instead of to those in mortal society. With the black stripes of the dress's design filled out by the curves of Dessa's figure, she looked like art set in motion.

Even Nadette, who'd done nothing but frown once learning Dessa would be out for the evening, lifted a brow in appreciation. And Liling and Mei Mei both exclaimed their pleasure over her appearance, speaking in fast Chinese and offering the first chuckle since they'd arrived.

Liling giggled. "You have big eyes and very white skin. True signs of beauty here or in China."

"Thank you, Liling . . . but why is that funny?"

"I remind Mei Mei about a story from our homeland from long ago. Of beautiful woman they say make fish stop swimming if she walk by water, or birds fall from sky because they catch glimpse of such woman—moon that pales and flowers too shy to bloom because their beauty is outshone. And we laugh because we like fish and birds and moon and flowers and are glad such things don't happen here."

Dessa looked from one sister to the other. "God makes everything beautiful, here and in China. But even though He creates beautiful things, outer beauty isn't what He cares about most. God sees beauty inside each one of us."

Mei Mei and her sister chatted again for a moment, and then Liling translated.

"I teach my sister beauty is not a blessing; it is curse. Women suffer for it, if they have it. Or if they do not, they suffer then, too." Liling looked away, all trace of happiness gone. "Only virtue is beautiful."

Dessa moved closer, forgetting the volume of her dress and kneeling before both girls. "No wonder you were so eager to see your sister spared. But listen to me, Liling. God can restore virtue if we ask Him, because of His great love for us. Because of Jesus."

Never before had Dessa been more earnest. She believed her

words. She did. She must. They weren't just for others; they were for her, too.

Liling's gaze took on a curious light, but she said nothing.

Dessa pulled herself back to her feet. "I'll do everything I can to keep you safe, and God will not forget us. I promise you that. I'm going to speak to someone tonight about helping us."

Nadette, standing nearby, folded her arms and eyed Dessa suspiciously. "Who?"

"Someone I trust."

Nadette didn't look convinced. "Let's hope that help ain't just more trouble—or if it's real help, that it don't get here too late."

The words mirrored Dessa's thoughts exactly.

***

Henry tapped on the door to Pierson House, and a moment later Jane greeted him with a wide and instant smile.

"Oh, Mr. Hawkins! How handsome you look in that fancy suit!"

Henry didn't want to enjoy the compliment. That would be far too childish. But he couldn't deny that he did, after all. He stepped inside, looking around for Dessa.

"She'll be right down. And won't you be pleased to see her! Just wait!"

Henry had already wondered what Dessa might wear tonight, much to his own embarrassment. Knowing her and this mission of hers, he guessed that she didn't put much emphasis on clothing—not the way other women did, at any rate. She had the kind of beauty that couldn't be hidden, not even behind humble clothing.

But tonight, knowing the wives of his biggest investors were more than likely going to judge such things, he'd wondered what they would think if Dessa wore her typical attire: clothing meant for a woman who paid little attention to what others thought. A plain dress, perhaps; definitely serviceable. Fit for a party? Probably not. But just as long as no one said anything rude over which he would have to intercede, Henry didn't care what she wore.

He heard movement on the stairs before seeing her. The swish of material he hadn't heard from her before, then . . .

Plain? Anything but. Serviceable? Hardly. Definitely captivating.

Taking a few steps closer, meeting her halfway into the room, he took both her hands, fashionably hidden in close-fitting gloves. "You're a vision, Dessa," he whispered, too late realizing he'd called her by her first name aloud.

Her smile said she didn't mind.

With a quick farewell to Jane, who handed Dessa a lace shawl and looked so proud she might have thought herself solely responsible for Dessa's loveliness, Henry escorted Dessa out to his carriage.

"I'm so glad to have this time to talk to you, Mr. Hawkins," said Dessa once they were settled and the carriage on its way.

"Exactly what I was about to say."

"Really? Then surely it was God who arranged this evening."

Henry wasn't sure about that. Yet, wasn't she right? Didn't God want him to be honest, at least with those who mattered most to him? He hoped Fallo took his time about getting them back to Henry's home, as he'd been instructed earlier. Especially if Dessa had something to say to him too. He ought to let her go first.

"I—" She started to speak, as if eager to do so, but stopped to hold his gaze intently. "What I have to say may come as a surprise to you, although perhaps not, since you've been convinced before that I can act in haste."

"Is there something you're worried about, Miss Caldwell?"

"Yes, very worried. I'm afraid I may need help with my

dilemma. It's about two new clients who need shelter at Pierson House."

"I'm glad to hear your mission is growing. Do you need more funds?"

She shook her head. "It's the new additions. The employers they've left behind aren't pleased."

He frowned, forgetting for the moment that he wanted to speed the conversation along to get to his own confession. "Have you—any of you—been threatened?"

"No. I'm hiding them. Their employer doesn't know I have them."

That news wasn't as good as she might hope it to sound. It wouldn't take long to figure out Pierson House was the only place in town that openly welcomed the kind of woman needing to flee a greedy mac.

"We can go to the authorities about it," he suggested, "but you know as well as I do that the law around Pierson House isn't exactly the same as the rest of the city. Payoffs are infamous. I admit I don't know much about such activities; I don't have many customers from this neighborhood."

She paused just long enough to let her face take on an even graver edge. Then her gaze fluttered, as if nervous uncertainty couldn't be hidden any longer. "They're Chinese, Mr. Hawkins. Sisters. From Hop Alley."

It took a moment for the meaning to absorb. What had she to do with Hop Alley? True, it was within the infamous heart of the Fourth Ward. He knew daring tourists came to Chinatown to see some of the strange sights and peek at places that promised opium; even on the street they could sniff a scent they weren't likely to find anywhere else. But those who lived in Denver never mixed with the Chinese—unless they sneaked into one of those drug dens, and that wasn't something anyone would admit. Even if they allowed their servants to take their laundry to a Chinese service, or ate in a restaurant that employed Chinese cooks, the fact remained: the only time the races mixed had been in a riot not all that long ago.

Henry didn't know what to say. She wanted his help, and he wanted to give it. He just wasn't sure how. He may not listen to those who blamed the Chinese for any and all economic woes, accusing them of taking jobs away because they agreed to work cheaply. Nor did he believe them guilty of poisoning society with their "heathen ways"—people were responsible for their own beliefs. But while Henry had heard plenty of accusations, he knew few facts about them, with such a clear line between his society and theirs. What could he do?

"This will take a little consideration," he said slowly. "The memory of rioting between white and Chinese hasn't died yet. Sometimes I think there are those who would look for a reason to start another."

"Selling an innocent girl shouldn't be condoned anywhere, in either culture."

"True. But what one side might consider no business but their own could be just the excuse to start trouble."

When the carriage came to a sudden halt, both he and Dessa looked out the window, their attention drawn by voices. Not shouting, exactly, but commands. Firm ones.

Confusion trumped Henry's pondering about the extraordinary news Dessa had just shared. They were nowhere near his home, so there was no reason to stop. In fact, they weren't yet beyond the edge of the Fourth Ward.

Had trouble already found them because of the girls Dessa hid?

Henry, taking up his walking stick, was about to simultaneously tap the ceiling and open the side door to investigate the delay. But he saw no rabble nearby, no riot about to erupt. Thank God.

Then the door was opened before he put a hand to it, by a single man dressed in a dark suit.

For one awful moment Henry was convinced this was a holdup, much the same as he'd once carried out. His only thought was of Dessa, whether she was frightened, and how he would protect her since he was unarmed but for his walking stick.

What sort of hoodlum did such a thing in the confines of a city, where even in this neighborhood reliable witnesses and even an officer could be found?

He'd barely finished the thought when the interloper commanded his attention by jumping straight into the coach. He slammed the door behind him, jarring the entire coach with an impressive jiggle as he took the seat beside Henry.

Turk Foster.

Since Dessa had moved to the Fourth Ward, she'd walked the streets on more errands than she could count. Never once had she been accosted. She'd attributed that to God's protection and her own swift gait, telling anyone who saw her that she was not only healthy but determined to get to wherever she was going.

But as soon as she saw Turk Foster's face—his smiling face—Dessa knew this was no assault. Just what it was, however, she had no idea.

Mr. Foster appeared entirely at ease, though Mr. Hawkins looked as amazed as Dessa felt over the sudden and unexpected appearance of their visitor. He was dressed nearly as fashionably as Mr. Hawkins, with a black tailored suit, a handkerchief peeking out from his pocket, a top hat in place, and gloves on his hands.

"Sorry about crowding you, Hawkins," he said amiably. "And

as nice as it would be to sit beside the charming Miss Caldwell, the view is much better from this side of the coach. Don't you agree?"

"What's this about, Foster?" Mr. Hawkins demanded. "Even you wouldn't stoop to highway robbery."

"No, that I wouldn't," he said with a laugh. "But I do intend to go to this party of yours. I'd hoped to offer Miss Caldwell a ride, but when I saw your coach pull up, I knew my plans could be accomplished more efficiently. This way I can speak to both of you here rather than demanding a private but curious moment in your home."

"And what is it that you want to speak to us about?"

Mr. Foster seemed in no hurry to answer Mr. Hawkins's inquiry. He was staring at Dessa with an easy smile lingering on his face. "And you once said you didn't have anything to wear to the opera. See how easily such challenges are overcome when you want them to be? You look beautiful, of course, as I knew you would."

Dessa did not reply; she gave him her profile by looking out the window instead, clutching tighter at her shawl.

Mr. Foster laughed again, this time softly. "She looks so innocent sitting over there, doesn't she, Hawkins? But she's got a secret that could send the whole city up in flames. And it would all be her fault. Not so innocent after all, is she?"

Dessa tried to swallow, but her throat was so dry the action sent pinpricks up and down the inside of her neck. Not only did he know; he was going to use the information to hurt her or the girls. Why did that shock her? Did she still think there was some goodness in him, despite his attempt to destroy Mr. Hawkins's reputation? Had she truly believed he'd treat her any differently— even though, as Belva said, he liked her?

"Miss Caldwell has done nothing wrong," Mr. Hawkins said, inspiring Dessa to cast a grateful glance his way. But was he sure about that? He sounded as if he were . . . yet what Mr. Foster said was likely true. She looked out the window again, knowing that only a few blocks away, Hop Alley was simmering. Because of her.

"What they planned to do to that girl is evil." Her words were quiet but no less deliberate. She would stand by those words, no matter what. She just wasn't sure everyone would agree with her. Perhaps Mr. Foster didn't.

"We can work out a peaceful conclusion," Mr. Hawkins said. "Money has a way of solving many problems."

Mr. Foster slid his gaze from Dessa to eye Mr. Hawkins sideways. "You've got trouble enough coming your way, Hawkins. Don't think you'll be any help in this."

"What is it you want, Foster?" Mr. Hawkins asked. Dessa thought he sounded almost . . . nervous.

"Now isn't that an interesting question?" Mr. Foster was clearly enjoying himself. "What do any of us want, except to live a peaceful, happy, productive life? Love, security, provisions, and a roof. Add a satisfying feeling of accomplishment, and we might as well believe we've found our own slice of heaven."

He lounged in the seat as if he were perfectly content, despite the fact that the carriage was not moving. Dessa wondered what had happened to Mr. Hawkins's driver and how long they would be detained. But mostly she wondered what Mr. Hawkins had already voiced: what did Mr. Foster want?

"Miss Caldwell is content with far less than most of the women I know," Mr. Foster said, looking at her. "And you have a mission. You've found your slice of heaven in the most unlikely of places: in Denver's—perhaps the country's—most disreputable district."

"I want to know what you plan to do with the information about the girls in my care. I promised to keep them safe, and I mean to do so."

He grinned at her. "Looks to me as if you could use my help." He suddenly sat up straighter, then leaned across the small space toward Dessa so that she received a whiff of the cherry laurel he must have used on his skin. "If you really want to make a difference in the Fourth Ward, Miss Caldwell, you're going to need me. Not him."

"Do you mean to help me, then?" she asked, though she had no real belief that he would.

He sat back again. "That depends, for one thing, on what you do when I tell you a little something about this man you're so eager to dress up for. He's got a secret too."

Such words confused Dessa; what could Mr. Hawkins possibly want kept a secret? He lived a life apparently as close to a monk's as Dessa had ever seen. He worked and went home, then rose and did it again. Having seen him in social settings, she guessed he probably wouldn't even mind taking a vow of silence.

"Look, I've got a deal for the two of you," Foster said, all business now. "Hawkins, you let me in on your little soiree tonight, pretend you believe I'm on the up and up. And, Miss Caldwell, your job is to pretend you think I'm worthy of somebody like you. If only for a limited time."

Mr. Hawkins and Dessa exchanged a glance.

"Been talking to Lionel Metcalf lately, Foster?" Mr. Hawkins continued to look at Dessa instead of Foster. "It must be true that Mr. Foster wants a place in next year's election, and he thinks he needs our help to lay the groundwork."

Mr. Foster held up a finger and thumb, cocking an imaginary gun in Mr. Hawkins's direction. "Your aim is straight, Hawkins. And who better to help me than the stiffest banker in town and the most saintly woman? With your help I'll get votes from *all* the wards, not just the Fourth. Enough to send me straight to Washington."

35

"I suppose I should expect blackmail from someone like you," Henry said. His entire body felt weighted, as if the very air around him had taken on a new heaviness that pressed into him inch by inch.

"Blackmail!" Foster repeated. "Hardly. This is what's called a business deal. Same thing you do at your bank every day of the week."

Henry wasn't sure which he hated more: feeling helpless against the power Foster obviously held over them, or the fact that Dessa was present to witness his forthcoming shame.

There was only one thing to be done: release the power Foster held, at least over Henry. He'd planned to make his confession to Dessa tonight anyway, hadn't he? If she by some miracle would have him once she knew the truth, it wouldn't matter what the rest of his investors thought. And if she wouldn't have him . . . well, even less did the censure of others matter then. He would have to start over, but he wasn't too old to do that. His own father had handed over the rigors of the smithy to start a mercantile when he was even older than Henry. Henry could do the same.

"The secret you hold over me means nothing, Foster. What does matter is your offer to help Miss Caldwell. As I said already, she's done nothing wrong. But if you can avoid trouble with the Chinese, it's no less than your duty. She owes you nothing in return for what common decency demands you do. Perhaps if you show some of that, you might honestly earn a few of those votes you're after."

"And who's going to tell the public at large if I do the right thing? You?" He shifted his gaze to Dessa. "Both of you?"

"If you can keep the girls I'm hiding safe," Dessa said, "I have no reason not to tell everyone that you helped. If it's the truth."

"It's no good," Henry said. "We just went to considerable trouble to distance Pierson House from this man. Now we're supposed to forget all that and pretend he's a friend?"

"That's why it's fortunate for me that I have reason to hope for cooperation from both of you," Foster said. "One without the other might not be enough, once you tell everyone all I've ever done was sincerely want to help Pierson House."

"If you think for one moment that Miss Caldwell is going to pretend you're worthy of her personal consideration—"

Foster still looked far too confident. He raised a hand to rest it amicably on Henry's shoulder and offered him a smile. "Henry—you'll have to grow accustomed to me calling you that, since we're about to face the world as allies in my upcoming campaign. So, *Henry,* let's first discuss how Miss Caldwell should present herself. As your love interest, or mine? Shall we leave it up to her, once she knows you're not all you claim to be? While I, on the other hand, have never claimed to be anything but what I am?"

Henry didn't want to look at Dessa's face, but couldn't help stealing another quick glance. As often as he'd mulled over telling her the truth, never once had he felt confident enough to predict how she might react.

He knew that moment was at hand—he just couldn't look at her until the truth was out.

Why did Mr. Hawkins seem so reluctant to look at her? Dessa was sure whatever Mr. Foster had to say about him couldn't impugn Mr. Hawkins's integrity. There was a reason his bank was among the most trusted in the city. He had a place in Denver's growth and development because of his honesty and competent use of the funds entrusted to him. Never had she been more sure that someone deserved such an important position.

"Mr. Hawkins?" She said his name gently, filled with all the hope she so easily felt when it came to his character. He'd defended her so boldly; now it was time he defended himself.

"Ask him where he got the seed money for his first business." Mr. Foster's voice was fairly a hiss. "That would be the mercantile he started as a foundation for his bank. Oh, he was smart, all right. He offered people goods and gave them credit so they could afford those goods. A perfect business plan, so that by the time he sold off the dry goods and turned all his attention to credit and money, he'd already earned the trust of the entire city. Only how did you manage to procure all those items for your mercantile to begin with, Henry? Not from your parents, who owned a far less successful shop of their own. A simple little place over in Leadville, providing not much more than miners' equipment. So where did you get the money, eh? From some generous benefactor, perhaps? Or was that benefactor nothing more than someone you made up to cover a crime?"

"That's very old history, Foster," said Mr. Hawkins quietly.

"But such an interesting history, Henry!" He folded his arms and grinned at Dessa again. "Did you know this gentleman was quite the campus man back at Chicago's Northwestern University? He excelled in all his subjects, was respected by his professors, admired by his peers—in fact, he had all the best friends one could hope for. He was even engaged to the prettiest girl in Chicago. Henry Hawkins had, everyone said, the very brightest of futures."

Dessa shouldn't be surprised by any of that, not even that he'd been engaged to the prettiest girl. But what had happened to her?

"He didn't go back to Leadville, though," Mr. Foster continued as if he were telling a bedtime story. "Who could blame him, when Denver was destined to be the Queen City of the West. But though he fulfilled—surpassed—those hopes for success in business, personal success seemed to have been left behind in Chicago. He's lived like a hermit all these years. Now why, I wonder? When he'd been so different in his college days?"

Dessa lifted a brow with interest, only to have Mr. Foster shake his head and go on. "You might assume he suffered a broken heart, since he returned alone from Chicago. But all accounts were that he was the one who broke off the engagement. Quite suddenly, too. Left the girl not only with *her* heart broken, but with the shame of having learned her brother was a thief."

Dessa looked at Mr. Hawkins. "Her brother . . . a thief?"

Mr. Foster spoke before Mr. Hawkins could. "An embezzler. Everyone found out he was pilfering funds from wealthy estates, money meant to go to legal heirs. A few thousand here, a few thousand there. Who would notice? Certainly not the bereaved heirs."

He now turned to Mr. Hawkins. "What I don't understand, Henry, is if that brother shared his ill-gotten goods with you, why was he the only one to go to jail? He protected you, yet you didn't marry his sister. Was it fear of getting caught? Is that why you hightailed it out of Chicago and set up your business so far away? But why didn't her brother accuse you? Why did he spare you—especially if you ran out on his sister?"

Mr. Hawkins pressed his lips together, looking somewhat

annoyed. "That's what comes of only having bits and pieces of the story, Foster. I had nothing to do with that crime."

"Then where did the money come from?"

Although Mr. Foster had asked the question, Dessa might have asked it as well. She wanted to know—even if it wasn't really any of her business. Somehow, she wanted it to be. She wanted to know everything about him, including his past.

"It doesn't matter," Mr. Hawkins said. But when he shifted his position, his eyes caught Dessa's. "I have no intention of discussing this with Mr. Foster. He's correct that I lied about the source of my investment money. Suffice it to say that if this news becomes public knowledge, my business would suffer. Bankers must be, above all else, trustworthy. One is not apt to keep the confidence of others after being branded a liar."

"But if there is some explanation?" Dessa asked hopefully.

"Not one that would satisfy the public, I'm afraid," Mr. Hawkins said stiffly.

Mr. Foster emitted something along the lines of a huff. "Must be worse than I thought. Here I believed somebody else did the dirty work, and our boy Henry here was just lucky to reap the benefit. You sure you don't want to tell us, Henry? What I'm thinking is probably worse."

"I don't care what you think."

"But you care what she thinks."

Mr. Hawkins looked at Dessa again. "That's between Miss Caldwell and me. I'm not about to discuss this in front of you, Foster."

Mr. Foster shrugged. "I guess our new friendship needs time to bud. But the fact is, if I spread this news around town, you're ruined. I can have letters sent to your investors demanding they inquire about the mysterious origin of your investment. I can take out newspaper advertisements telling the general public there is a cloud over Hawkins National, and there isn't one thing you can do about it because the truth—even sketchy—is on my side. Is that what you want? Or do you just want to get me elected instead?"

Mr. Hawkins did nothing, said nothing.

"Why do you want to go to Washington, Mr. Foster?" Dessa asked. "You have a robust business here in Denver. Isn't that enough?"

"You'd think so, wouldn't you? But no. My life here is too easy. I've grown to miss the chances, the challenges."

"But isn't there a reason you want to go to Washington? To help this nation grow?"

"Well, sure."

"What happens if society demands places like yours be shut down?"

"Maybe that's the best reason of all for me to go to Washington. To make sure the laws don't interfere with places like mine."

"You'll have to represent what the people want, Mr. Foster. Not your own interests."

He thumped his knees as if he'd never been happier. "Now that's what I like so much about you, Miss Caldwell. You think the best of everybody. Even the quacks who get elected."

"Maybe if you'd shut up," Mr. Hawkins said, "you might have been able to hope for our support. Especially if you agreed to help Miss Caldwell with her problem. But knowing you plan to work toward the kind of society found in the Fourth Ward doesn't exactly endear you to either one of us. So forget it, Foster. We're not going to be blackmailed. We'll bring in the authorities to help Dessa, and I don't care what you do about the information you have regarding my past."

Mr. Hawkins reached for the handle, twisting it to open the coach door. He didn't need to say a word for Dessa to know that Mr. Foster was being asked to leave.

"You'll regret this, Hawkins."

Just as Mr. Foster looked ready to exit, Dessa heard herself speak.

"Wait."

❦

Henry looked at Dessa with amazement. Surely she didn't plan to cave in to Foster's demands?

"How can you help the girls I'm hiding?"

Foster's smile was no less triumphant than it should have been over Dessa's simple inquiry. Even as Henry had to fight himself not to smash his fist into Foster's grimy smile, he knew she was probably right to ask. His only offer had been to go to the authorities—something she'd probably already considered doing herself. Even she must have known how fruitless that would be.

Foster settled back in his seat again. "If you've heard the name Yin Tung, then you know he's the key. I happen to have a way of reaching him, of negotiating a peaceful solution."

"I suppose that would take money," Dessa said slowly.

"To spare you, my dear Miss Caldwell, no price would be too high."

She looked neither flattered nor impressed, which gave Henry some comfort.

"If you have a way of contacting this person," Henry said, "you can leave the cost to me."

Foster grinned but shook his head. "No, Henry. I want her indebted to me, not to you. You must have guessed that much already."

"Doing the right thing shouldn't require anyone to be in debt to you, Foster."

"Given whatever it is you're hiding, I'm not sure you have the right to lecture anybody on what's right." Foster looked back at Dessa. "Are we in agreement, then? I'll have to send someone to

Yin Tung right away. We don't have any time to lose. They want the girl back, and all they know is that she's probably being hidden by a white family."

To Henry's relief, Dessa did not answer right away. She even looked at him, as if seeking his approval—or at least his opinion. How he wanted to talk her out of this. It was a deal with the devil. But what did he have to offer instead?

He looked at Foster. "What do you expect from Miss Caldwell in return?"

Foster acknowledged his question with a slow smile aimed at Dessa, one that Henry suspected was supposed to be seductive. Perhaps it was.

But no. She didn't receive it with a smile of her own, thank God. In fact, she still looked as concerned as she had a moment ago. Was she willing to sacrifice herself for the girls she wanted to protect? Why did he even consider such a question? There was no doubt that she was willing to do all she could to help them.

Foster cleared his throat and had the good sense to look momentarily embarrassed. "All I want is a chance to have people on both sides of town consider me as more than a gambler and proprietor of vice. I want them to think I'm respectable. To do that, I'm going to need somebody respectable to act like they believe in me first. Somebody people might listen to."

"Having me introduce you—even as my friend—to the polite side of the city isn't going to do any good if you don't follow it up with the right kind of behavior," Dessa said. "Are you willing to act like a gentleman?"

"I may be a gambler, but I *am* a gentleman."

"Are you?" She didn't look convinced, and Henry thanked God for that, too.

Foster emitted a throaty laugh. "What do you expect? For me to really reform, just to join a bunch of crooks in Washington?"

"Gambling is illegal, Foster," Henry said. "It may be socially acceptable in more parts of the country than society wants, but the fact is it's technically illegal. How do you expect to win a campaign when you're guilty of a crime every day of your life?"

"I've already thought of all this. Your friend Lionel has plenty of ideas, Henry. He knows I'm not guilty of anything unnatural, or he wouldn't have come to me in the first place. I'm a business-man. As far as official city records go, I've been the proprietor of nothing but a dance hall all these years. That's the worst anybody can say about me."

"And those tables in front of the stage, instead of seats?" Dessa asked. "Don't they prove what kind of business is done at the Verandah, despite whatever is 'official'?"

Foster waved away her concerns. "I've already made arrange-ments to modernize the Verandah, so to speak. I'm getting out of the gambling business, at least until I see how the election goes. I'm even going to live at the Windsor." He winked. "Everybody loves a reformed rake. I'm sure to win."

"What about all the gamblers, Foster?" Henry asked. "You think they're just going to forget what kind of place the Verandah has been all these years?"

"It won't matter. There are plenty of other places for them to take their business."

"That's going to cost you," Henry said. "You're prepared for that?"

Foster shrugged. "I'll still have the theater and the drinks."

"Which are just as bad in some voters' opinions."

"Look," Foster said with a hint of impatience, "I don't need to be a saint to get elected."

"No," Henry said, "you just need saints like Miss Caldwell to tell everyone to vote for you."

"Won't hurt."

"But, Mr. Foster," Dessa said, "I've already told you I'd be willing to express public gratitude if you help me with the girls. Perhaps telling the public I've hidden the girls is our only option, if you can prevent a riot. Is my open gratitude all you would expect of me in return for your help?"

"That's not very much for what I'd be doing for you, is it? I think the least you could do is agree to be seen around town with me a couple of times." His gaze spread to take in her gown with a confident grin. "Especially now that you've got something to wear to Tabor's?"

"Maybe . . ." She looked at Henry. "If Mr. Hawkins were to agree as well, and you were to keep whatever information you have about him a secret, we could both accompany you to the opera a few times during the course of the election season. It's bound to make the papers—perhaps you could see that it does. Would that be enough?"

Silence followed, long enough for Henry to hold her gaze. Was she trying to save him, too, or had she just made her choice between him and Foster, and chosen him? It might not have been much of a contest for a respectable woman to choose a man with a mysterious past over one with a degenerate present, but Henry still sensed a whiff of victory.

Added to that was the first hint of a new sort of freedom; he realized he honestly did not care if Foster revealed his secret. He'd held it so long that the thought of not hiding it anymore seemed a relief. It was time to acknowledge that his pursuit of atonement hadn't worked—but grace had. Grace from the same God Dessa believed in.

If he couldn't help Dessa's dilemma any other way, he could help her this way.

Foster wasn't smiling anymore, but he looked satisfied enough. "I don't care about ruining you, Hawkins. But if you agree to imply your support, I'll keep my mouth shut. Agreed?"

Henry held out a hand. "It's a good thing our ballots are secret, then, Foster. Because whatever I do in public may not match how I vote."

Foster took his hand. Then, letting go, he reached for the door, but only to lean out long enough to call for whoever it was that must have kept the carriage at a standstill.

A moment later Foster's man appeared, who was twice the size of Fallo. "Go, Thomas, and deliver that message to Yin Tung."

The man did not reply, just nodded and disappeared before Foster even shut the carriage door.

"Let's go to that little party of yours, shall we, Henry?"

Without a word, Henry tapped on the ceiling of the coach, and they started moving.

"One more thing, Mr. Foster," said Dessa. Her voice held the first trace of sweetness since the evening had begun.

Foster aimed expectantly raised brows her way.

"For your reformed look to be taken at all seriously, it would be wise if you agreed to accompany Mr. Hawkins and me to church each week. Starting next Sunday?"

Foster grinned, tipping his hat her way. "A fine idea, Miss Caldwell."

She smiled back. "Then perhaps your reform might become sincere. Whether you intend it to be or not."

Henry only wished he could laugh as easily as Foster, and hope as easily as Dessa.

36

MR. HAWKINS'S HOME just north of Fourteenth and Colfax was among the older mansions of the city, but also among the loveliest. Italian style and made of brick, complete with a cupola on the roof and a spacious carriage house in the yard. It boasted many tall windows with wide shutters on the first floor, latticed windows on the second. A pristine white porch greeted visitors at the front, underneath an arched portico where carriages could comfortably let off their patrons without thought of wind, snow, or rain.

Dessa knew wealthy families living along Fourteenth were already looking for a fresh place to live, now that so many commercial buildings were going up around them. They weren't all that far from her own neighborhood on the edge of the Fourth Ward. From Pierson House benefactors, she'd heard that Brown's Bluff was finally attracting the city's finest. Now that construction on the state capitol building had begun at last, years after Mr. Brown had donated the land, the Queen City's reputation would be ensured by the stately capitol adjacent to prestigious mansions planned for the vicinity.

As she took a step toward the tall, paneled door, Dessa wondered if Mr. Hawkins would soon be joining those who were migrating to the new height of society. It was easy to imagine him there, but even as the thought took shape, she wondered if whatever secret he held about his past would keep him from ever fully engaging in the society around him.

A footman opened the door before they'd reached the top step, and they were barely inside before a butler met them—while yet another footman divested Mr. Hawkins and Mr. Foster of their hats and walking sticks, and Dessa of her lace shawl.

"Sorry to be late to my own party, Barron," Mr. Hawkins said.

"We were about to send out a search party," the butler said, his tone light. "I'm happy to say your mother has been the perfect hostess."

Mr. Hawkins's brows rose appreciatively, as his gaze traveled past the wide foyer to the opening of what must be a parlor. He started to take a step, but stopped. Then, to Dessa's surprise, he turned to her and offered his arm.

Barely giving Mr. Foster a glance, Dessa moved to Mr. Hawkins's side, letting him lead the way into the party.

Dessa feared she would need far more concentration than she thought possible that evening: to remember names, participate in conversations, ask questions of some depth, and follow all the social graces necessary to fit in as a member of society instead of its servant. Thankfully she'd been tutored in suitable behavior, if only indirectly as a caretaker of propriety, making sure no one offended a member of one of St. Louis's best families.

"Mother," said Mr. Hawkins. He greeted her with a touch to her elbow and a kiss to her lightly powdered cheek—a greeting she seemed only too happy to receive.

"Ah, so there you are," his mother said with a twinkle in her eye as her gaze welcomed both of them. "I was just telling Mrs. White not to be too surprised at your tardiness. If you're anything like your father, I suspect you told your driver to take his time coming back once you'd fetched Miss Caldwell."

Dessa might have glanced at Mr. Hawkins—she could feel his own glance her way—but a rush of shyness overwhelmed her.

To Dessa's delight and relief, Mrs. Hawkins stood in a circle comprised of the Whites and the Ridgeways. Mariadela sent her an immediate smile, one of welcome, followed by a glance of curiosity. Dessa nodded toward her, hoping they might find a moment alone before the evening was out.

But when Mariadela—and everyone nearby apart from Mrs. Hawkins—caught the first glimpse of Turk Foster, Dessa saw more than one surprised look. William's was followed by a frown, and she was quite sure Mrs. Ridgeway gasped.

Unruffled, Mr. Hawkins made the introductions. "Turk Foster, a local businessman." As if he were just another investor!

Though Henry introduced Foster exactly the way the man would have expected if he thought his scheme a success, he wasn't the least irked. Foster would soon find out that Henry had no intention of bowing to his demands. Quite the contrary.

Now all he had to do was manage to get Dessa alone. Having entered with her on his arm as the de facto hostess or at the very least his especially escorted guest, then delivered her to a circle of friends, he felt her hand begin to slip from his arm. But he caught her fingertips gently, trapping her at his side.

"I wish to have a word with you as soon as we can get away," he whispered.

She nodded without a trace of surprise. Perhaps she expected he might wish to speak to her, at least about Foster's joint blackmail scheme. She had no idea that they would soon be free of every secret.

A friendly thump on his shoulder demanded Henry's attention. "Well, so this evening brings one surprise after another. Starting with your lovely mother." Lionel Metcalf bowed his head politely toward Mrs. Hawkins. "Though I hope it won't appear rude for me to say that after knowing you all these years, Henry, I'm rather surprised to learn you even have a mother. I thought you just appeared on earth one day, banker suit and all. But now to see you have such a family asset, I cannot for the life of me understand why it's taken you so long to introduce her to Denver society."

Henry held his mother's gaze. "Yes, Lionel, you're right. It's been a foolish mistake not to have enjoyed my mother's company all these years."

"And as if that isn't enough!" Lionel glanced past Henry, first to Dessa and then on to Foster. Henry had to credit Foster for at least looking like the fish out of water he was. "I cannot decide which has me more thunderstruck. Your inviting this ambitious fellow, or your having a lovely young lady at your side." He bowed toward Dessa, adding, "Lionel Metcalf, at your service."

Henry introduced Dessa properly, but even as he did so— seeing several others approaching to hear—his mind was already skipping ahead. He had so much to say, but he must wait for the right moment.

Dessa could barely rein in her whirling emotions. How was she to interpret Mr. Hawkins's behavior, except to assume he meant others to think of her as someone he valued . . . personally? Even among all his peers? She knew as well as he that she was nothing like those around them—wealthy, important investors. He even knew how many mistakes she'd made in the founding of Pierson House.

But he didn't know about *all* her mistakes. He had yet to know of her most personal, most embarrassing one.

Nor did he know that her father had been a poor schoolmaster who'd died an unknown, unrecognized soldier. Or that her mother had been the daughter of a tenant farmer who'd died penniless. That Dessa herself had been raised in an orphanage for the first seven years of her life, or that she'd been a servant. All that would likely matter to his guests. But would it to him?

She looked away, barely hearing the conversation around her. If he knew, perhaps he wouldn't be so willing to have her hand on his arm. She tried pulling away again, only to have him recapture her, with a smile that nearly banished all her doubts.

It was easy to see that Mr. Hawkins was eager to lead her out of the room. He tried twice but was caught each time by one couple or another, seeking to share their enthusiasm over his apparent transformation. From stodgy, isolated banker to one of them. A man with a mother and a woman at his side. They must soon expect his house to show a woman's touch.

Henry and Dessa had nearly reached the threshold of the parlor when the butler—Mr. Barron, she believed he'd been called—came to ask if he might announce dinner, since they were already late in serving. Henry looked almost surprised and pulled a watch from his vest pocket. He nodded to the butler, but turned a regretful expression her way.

"Dessa," he whispered, "I wished to speak to you before dinner, but evidently we're not to have the opportunity. There's something I must do, something I planned to tell you on the way here, in the carriage, before we were . . . sidetracked by Foster. I hope you can forgive me for not sharing with you first what I now feel compelled to share with everyone else tonight."

She held his earnest gaze. "I have no right to expect such a thing. But, Mr. Hawkins—"

"Henry."

She smiled. "Henry. Are you sure of what you want to do? I have a feeling this has to do with whatever Mr. Foster threatened you with tonight."

He secured both her hands in his, even as others began moving toward the dining room. She knew protocol as surely as he must:

rank went first. Henry, as host, and his mother, as honorary hostess, would likely go in before many of the others. They had no time for this conversation, even as hurried as it was.

"Dessa." His face was mere inches away, far closer than she expected in the presence of so many others. But he didn't seem to care, and try though she might, Dessa had no will to stop him or to step back. "I must do this, for your sake as well as my own. You must have guessed by now that I have every wish to invite you into my life. There is much you need to know about me before deciding whether or not to accept the invitation. I wanted to spare you from having to react publicly, but it appears I have no choice if I'm to take this opportunity tonight. And for your sake, perhaps it's best if you learn the truth with the others. That way you won't be seen as having already accepted me in spite of it all." His grip on her hands increased, and the look in his eye made everything—and everyone—disappear. Eagerness mixed with a hint of . . . fear? "After you hear what I have to say, I will understand if you want nothing to do with me. I pray that won't be the case, but I'll accept it if it is."

Dessa kept her voice as low as his had been, holding his hands as tightly as he held hers. "There is nothing you can say that will change my high opinion of you. Please know that."

He leaned even closer, as if he would kiss her right there, in front of guests who waited for the dinner procession to begin. Perhaps he was conscious of that, as he did nothing more than finish with a kiss to her cheek, nearly—but not quite—as chaste as the one he'd bestowed upon his mother earlier.

"Make no assurances until after you hear what I say when this meal is finished."

❧

Henry barely tasted the meal, though he imagined it to be another of Mrs. Gio's finest. The fillet of beef with mushroom sauce could as easily have been a bowlful of beans for the extent Henry savored it. Although Dessa was seated on his right-hand side and Lionel on his left—Foster's plate had been added somewhere down the crowded table—Henry could not bring himself to partake in the conversation much more than he did in the meal itself.

As was customary from past investor dinners, the women did not excuse themselves for coffee to be served separately from the men. Never having had a hostess—while tonight there were arguably two—no one, including Henry himself, expected tradition to change. Which suited his purpose just fine.

He did not bother to pretend tasting his coffee. Instead, Henry stood, calling attention to himself without saying a word.

For a moment he simply scanned one side of the table, then the other, briefly noting Foster eyeing him curiously, perhaps with a bit of alarm. That vaguely satisfied Henry, knowing the man would not be pleased with what he planned to say.

He couldn't help but take a glance at Tobias, then at his mother on the opposite end of the table. Perhaps they guessed what Henry was about to do. If so, neither appeared ready to object. Even his mother did not look worried—concerned, perhaps, but not fretful.

He ended his perusal with a lingering look at Dessa. What he was about to say might impact her, but at least it would be minimal. If she chose never to speak to him again, at least her own reputation would not suffer because of him.

"Ladies and gentlemen," Henry began, "I'd like to take this opportunity first to thank all of you for coming tonight and for supporting Hawkins National through the years as you have. I'm grateful and pleased that our various partnerships have been mutually beneficial. But tonight I am announcing that this will not only be the last of my investors' dinners, but that I will turn in my resignation from the bank on Monday morning."

An immediate rumble of voices—some whispering, some openly protesting—rippled through the room. Dessa herself wanted to speak, to object, but she held herself in check without taking her eyes from Henry.

"As all of you know, the foundation for a successful financial institution demands an intricate mix. What makes an investment secure more than the confidence placed in its stewards? Investors and depositors must have absolute trust in the integrity of the institution with which they do business. I stand here before you a fraud in the ideal of integrity."

Dessa had a fleeting thought that if she could have counted the gasps emitted since her arrival this evening, she might one day think such a number amusing. Not so tonight, not when these gasps were prompted by the possible question of Henry's character.

"I know this demands an explanation, and I'm prepared to offer one." He swung his hands behind his back, clasping them there. "I'm sure there are few men, even at this distinguished table, who survived their youth without one indiscretion or another. I am, I'm afraid, no exception. But my indiscretion has to do with what brings us all together: money itself."

He paused long enough to glance over the table again, and Dessa was eager to catch his eye so she could tell him—even silently—that she still believed in him, no matter what he had to say. If youthful indiscretions, as he called them, couldn't be forgiven, then she hadn't a hope in the world.

"I stand before all of you a thief."

Lionel Metcalf broke the stunned silence. He laughed. "Henry, my boy, I haven't the faintest idea what's gotten into you tonight, but I for one can vouch for the bank's utmost integrity. Those books have been examined throughout the years and not once has a penny—mind you, not a *penny*—ever been missing. If you're a thief, I'd like to know from where you've stolen."

"It's true I've never stolen from the bank. I've taken nothing from any of you. But my initial investment, the money I brought with me to Denver, was at the expense of others. You in particular, Lionel, might find this rather difficult to accept. A large portion of my seed money came unwillingly from Wells Fargo, where everyone knows you've been heavily invested for some twenty years."

Mr. Metcalf sputtered, "Just how did you steal from them, then?"

"It was a dozen years ago, in the area of Leadville. Three stagecoaches transporting money and gold from the mines to Denver were held up. Do you recall any of that?"

"Stagecoach robberies aren't all that rare—"

"Successful ones are. Particularly if they're carried out by one man alone."

Mr. Metcalf's face lit up as if he'd recalled something far more pleasant than a robbery. "Along the Rafferty Canyon! I heard about the investigations, how every one of the . . . what was it, three robberies? . . . was thought to have been carried out by a gang. Only after the last one, investigators found nothing more than sticks, carved to look like rifles of the so-called bandits, in the boulders above. That was *you*?"

Henry had only to nod once.

"Ha!" Mr. Metcalf looked as if he were pleased to have figured out a long-held mystery rather than aghast that he knew the perpetrator. "But wait! That stolen money was repaid some years ago, with interest."

"That doesn't excuse the way the money was taken in the first place."

"But a dozen years ago . . ." Mr. Metcalf stroked his chin. "It hardly matters now, Henry. No charges can be brought against you after this many years."

"I wasn't worried about that," Henry said. His eyes darted briefly to Dessa. "What I do know is that my bank was founded on a false assumption—an assumption that its foundational money was raised honestly. That's not true."

Several people spoke at the same time, both men and women. Dessa looked at none of them. Rather she studied Henry. How was it possible that this man of such staunch values could ever have done anything so far outside the standards he was known to hold?

Still, there was no question in Dessa's mind. She, of all people, knew one act—one mistake—did not define a person's character. Not forevermore.

She wanted to tell him so, but he was already speaking again.

"Please, there is more I'd like to say this evening."

The voices quieted—and Dessa realized just then that not all of them had been supportive. One man down the table had even stood, thrusting his napkin away, but Henry's call to attention stopped him. He took his seat again.

"I have two reasons for telling you this tonight." His gaze shifted to land on Turk Foster. "One of them is that the origin of my investment has been called into question. I thought it wise to inform all of you rather than have you read about vague or misleading theories in the newspapers. I'm sure there will be talk about the reason for my abrupt resignation. The bank will continue, no doubt with a new name, but I wanted the scandal nipped before it even has a chance to bud."

"I'd like to know who thought to investigate." This from Mr. Metcalf. "I must say, I've looked into your past myself, Henry, when I came to you about running for the Senate. I never found any of this."

Henry turned back to Mr. Foster, who returned the look stiffly from his seat.

"Evidently Turk Foster's investigation was willing to look further into the past."

The entire table looked at Mr. Foster, but he remained still. If he regretted what he'd done, there was no way to tell.

Henry held up a palm to reclaim everyone's attention. "Which might mean Foster is competent in what he sets out to do. Turk Foster revealed to me tonight that he wishes to run for the Senate in next year's election. He is here tonight with the hope of getting to know some of you—to test the waters, so to speak, about how society might receive such a man as himself for the job. I'm here to state that while I do not endorse his candidacy, neither am I against it. Our next senator will be for the people of Colorado to decide."

The table was quiet as they absorbed his words, so there was no competition for their attention when he spoke again. "I will add that Mr. Foster has shown a personal spasm of virtue—something this city has rarely even attempted in the past. Some of you are already aware that he offered to host a benefit to raise funds for Miss Caldwell. At the time, we were unsure of his motives. I now believe he was sincere in his effort, at least so far as it's common sense to do something respectable if respect is what you're after. In light of the fact that Pierson House, even now, is facing a unique challenge, and seeing Mr. Foster's willingness to help, I'm inclined to believe that even though his motives might have been self-serving, he wanted the best result for Pierson House."

He looked at Dessa, and even if no one else saw his face soften, she did. She knew she didn't imagine it.

"Miss Caldwell's reputation has proven she holds no boundaries in her willingness to help others. Recently she was tested in this attitude. Two young girls came to her seeking shelter, and she did not hesitate to take them in, just as her faith dictates." He paused, putting a gentle hand on her shoulder as he addressed the others. "Ladies and gentlemen, I'm telling you nothing that won't be reported in the newspapers if Mr. Foster knows how to run a campaign. Those two young girls are Chinese."

A moment of fear rose within Dessa, despite Henry's reference to her faith dictating her actions. How confident he must be that Mr. Foster's help would avoid any trouble! Would others agree that she'd done the right thing, as Henry obviously believed?

He waited a moment for reaction to that information, and it didn't take long. There was yet another gasp, a murmur here and there.

"Turk Foster is even now doing all he can to alleviate the tension that has risen because of the situation. This may not become a campaign slogan, but if you want to judge a man's character, do it by his actions. In this, Mr. Foster has proven himself capable of doing the right thing. Just as Miss Caldwell did from the start."

Dessa glanced at Mr. Foster, who still looked steadily at Henry. Was he grateful? At least that Henry didn't reveal his attempt to use blackmail as a means to gain their help?

"And finally, ladies and gentlemen, I offer you my apologies for introducing so many topics that might hinder peaceful digestion. I knew there would be few other opportunities to make known all I needed to say. I am, as of this moment, free to discuss whatever you would like and will understand and forgive if there are those here tonight who wish to break off their association with me. I do hope any backlash will be limited to me personally, where it belongs, and not extended to the bank itself. The bank will remain in the capable—and thoroughly honest—hands of Tobias Ridgeway."

37

HENRY HADN'T FELT so triumphant since he'd ridden safely away from his final robbery. Until this moment, he hadn't realized how heavy a burden that mistake had become. Year after year had added nothing but weight.

Most of it had lifted when he'd discovered God extended more than enough grace to cover his forgiveness, but the last of that weight had just now disappeared. No more hiding, no more secrets.

He was more eager than ever to speak to Dessa, but as his guests proceeded back into the parlor, he was detained. Person after person wanted to speak with him privately, and when his mother escorted Dessa away, Henry could think of no reason to demand that she stay at his side.

He did, however, take exorbitant reassurance in a smile she sent his way before walking off with his mother on one side and his aunt on the other. It was comforting, this feeling of family.

❧

"How did you take the news, dear?" Mrs. Hawkins asked Dessa as they went into the parlor.

"I'm surprised, of course," she admitted. "But anyone who's dealt with Mr. Hawkins knows he can be trusted."

Both women seemed pleased. "Of course you're right!" Mrs. Hawkins said.

Dessa glanced back to see that although Henry wasn't likely to be free anytime soon, Mariadela looked as if she would burst if Dessa didn't speak to her. So as Mrs. Hawkins and Mrs. Ridgeway began to chat, Dessa found a way to excuse herself.

But she made it no farther than halfway to Mariadela. A sudden tall shadow appeared at her side, followed by a steely grip around her wrist. The grim look on Turk Foster's face made her guess he was angry that things weren't going exactly as he'd planned. Yet what real harm had Henry done him? None, as far as Dessa could tell. Henry might not have endorsed him, but he'd offered respectable motives to everything Mr. Foster had done lately.

"I'm sorry, Miss Caldwell." He held up a note with his other hand. "One of the Hawkins footmen just handed this to me, from my man Thomas. If I'm going to live up to Henry's words that I'm willing to help Pierson House and everyone in it, we need to leave immediately."

"We?"

He nodded. "The girls need to be taken somewhere else for safety. They won't trust anyone but you to take them away."

"But what's happened? I thought you were going to pay off Yin Tung!"

"And so I did." Even as he spoke, he folded her arm through his and led her to the foyer, much to the chagrin of Mariadela, who stood staring at them from the side of the room. Dessa sent her a quick smile, hoping to convey that she knew what she was doing by leaving with Mr. Foster. She had no choice, but there was no sense alarming anyone else.

"I didn't think I'd need to pay off a mob from our side of the Fourth Ward too," Mr. Foster added. "But evidently I should have thought of that."

"What?"

Without even waiting for a footman to retrieve their belongings,

Mr. Foster led her from the house. A familiar carriage waited outside—one with the same impressive pair of horses Mr. Foster rarely went anywhere without.

"Thomas tells me a group of drunken whites went into one of the opium dens to make clear what they thought about the slave auction. That sort of thing isn't likely to be welcomed around here, not even a Chinese slave for a Chinese master. Not with the memory of so many men who died fighting to free slaves in this country." He eyed her, then raised his palms as if he wasn't even sure of his own words. "Or maybe they were just looking for a reason to fight. That's all I know. The fight that broke out hasn't stopped yet, and the last Thomas heard, they were headed to Pierson House. Even Yin Tung won't be able to stop this if it spreads."

The news landed like a heavy weight on Dessa's chest. But when she saw an eerie light dancing above in the direction of the Fourth Ward, she looked out the window with stark terror.

"Hurry, then, Mr. Foster!" She could barely speak the words over her shoulder. "Hurry!"

A fire burned in the ward; she was sure of that even before she could smell the smoke as the carriage raced down the street.

Not many blocks later, Dessa heard the whinny of the horses, Thomas's shouts, and the crack of a whip. She peered out the window and saw that the street ahead was filled with other carriages— all heading out of the ward. Mr. Foster's horses could barely go forward.

It was not possible to proceed with any speed. Without even looking at Mr. Foster, Dessa pushed open the door and leaped to the sidewalk. Pierson House was only a block away. She had no choice but to do all she could to keep the sisters safe—no matter what resulted from her hasty decision to take them in.

She heard footsteps behind her but did not stop to look. A moment later Mr. Foster outran her.

"We'll get the girls and take them back to the carriage—Thomas will turn the carriage and wait right here to take all of you away."

Not stopping, Dessa nodded.

She rounded the corner. Amid the cloud of smoke she heard shouts from both men and women. Her heart pounding now, from both running and her fear, Dessa stopped short at the sight.

There, lined up before a perfectly intact Pierson House, was a string of women arm in arm, shouting down a group of men fighting fist to fist. Chinese, white, black—it didn't seem to matter. Whether they were defending or assaulting, Dessa could not tell.

Frantically she searched the line for a familiar face. If Liling and Mei Mei were there, they were in grave danger.

But the only face she recognized was Remee's, right in the center and joined at each side by the girls from down the street. Though Miss Leola was not there, most if not all her girls were.

"Go around the back," Mr. Foster told her, pointing to the darkened gangway between Pierson House and the place next door. "Don't let anyone see you, or you could be in trouble. I'll meet you back at the carriage if I can, but don't wait for me. Get them out of here."

She was only too happy to follow that order. Picking up her skirts again, Dessa broke into another run. Just as she slipped into the shadows, a shot rang in the air, first startling Dessa then ringing in her ear.

She glanced over her shoulder. It had come from a gun in Mr. Foster's hand! Had he been carrying it all evening?

"Enough!" he bellowed.

Dessa resumed her escape and could see no more. She rushed around the back of Pierson House, stumbling up the stairs to the rear door. It was dark and quiet in comparison to what went on in front.

"Jane!" She was afraid to peal out a sound, even as she swung through the kitchen door to the unlit dining room and parlor. The voices outside were louder here, closer than ever on the street right out front. To her horror she saw the flicker of light—a torch. Were they going to burn Pierson House?

She stumbled again, this time on the stairs behind the parlor. She went straight to the sisters' small room, hoping they wouldn't scream and alert those outside—if anyone out there could even hear over the din of the fighting.

But though Dessa burst into the room, no one was there. It was empty.

She dashed from room to room, finding each one vacant. The girls were gone.

Had they been brave—foolish—enough to stand outside with Remee? Had Dessa missed them when she searched the line of women?

She rushed back to the room Jane used, with a window to the front yard. Peering out from the corner of a windowpane, she looked again at the extraordinary women who could have only one goal: to protect Pierson House. If Dessa hadn't seen it herself, she wouldn't have believed it. She wanted to join them but knew her face, of all others, might incite more rage than ever.

Neither Jane nor Liling nor Mei Mei were among them, so she had only one thing on her mind now.

To find them.

❧

Henry entered his parlor at last, his gaze roaming for Dessa. He'd been caught up in answering one question after another: Yes, he was sure he wanted to resign. No, he did not think for a moment the bank would fail without him at its helm. Did he have any real hope that a man like Turk Foster would be a legitimate candidate?

Perhaps. He needed to see for himself, along with the rest of Denver.

But Foster, he was intrigued to learn, was nowhere to be found. And where was Dessa?

"She's gone, Henry," Tobias whispered. "One of the footmen told me he delivered a message to Foster, and the man all but manhandled her on the way out."

Henry's pulse picked up, and he walked through the parlor past yet more of his guests who looked as if they wanted to engage in further conversation. "Why didn't you tell me?"

"I didn't know myself until a few minutes ago. Mariadela White came to me, concerned about it, so I went to speak to the staff."

"How long ago did they leave?"

"Fifteen minutes, at least."

So long! Henry ordered his carriage to the front of the house, where he paced until it arrived.

Tobias climbed in opposite Henry. "I suppose Foster wasn't able to stop the trouble in Hop Alley," he said, looking every bit as grave as Henry felt.

Henry did not speak. As much as he hoped the Fourth Ward could avoid any trouble, he also hoped that was the only reason she'd left with Foster.

⁂

The carriage house door was stuck tighter than ever. How was that possible? Having Mr. Dunne using it with regularity had loosened it long ago. Dessa called his name, but didn't dare say it very loudly for fear of attracting the attention of those on the other side of the house.

Nothing.

She moved to look along the side of the outbuilding, through the opening between Pierson House and the shop next door. The carriage house was certainly safer than the house itself—or was it? The wooden slats she'd repaired all those weeks ago would easily burn, if the mob had burning in mind.

Yet where else could the girls be hiding? Even now, standing in front of the carriage house, Dessa was afraid to be seen. If they weren't inside, Dessa herself might find refuge here, at least until Mr. Foster broke up the mob. If he could.

She gave up tugging on the latch and walked around to the back. She herself had pounded those nails to straighten the slats, but the wood in several places had been decaying. Even if she couldn't loosen the nails, she could likely crash through one of the boards.

But the wood was more solid than it appeared. All she did was bruise her elbow and catch the lace sleeve of her borrowed gown, tearing it.

To her own shame, she wanted to sit down and cry. Perhaps she wouldn't be seen if she stayed right where she was, behind the carriage house. Perhaps the police would arrive and quell the violence. But what was afire? She could still smell the smoke, but she couldn't see flames anywhere.

Why, oh why, had she allowed Mr. Foster to whisk her away without telling Henry? If he were here, she wouldn't be so afraid.

❧

The scent of smoke on the breeze wrapped itself around Henry's leaden heart, tugging it further into the pit of his stomach. What if Pierson House was burning? What if Dessa was in the midst of all the trouble?

"Let me off here," Henry shouted, pounding on the roof of the carriage with his fist. He'd left behind his walking stick. Traffic was so thick his carriage crawled far more slowly than the pace of his heart. With a hand on the door latch, he spoke to Tobias. "Tell

Fallo to take you to the nearest precinct. If the police aren't already on their way, demand that they come—and bring help."

"Right," Tobias said, but just as Henry was about to jump free of the slowing carriage, he grabbed Henry's wrist. "Careful as you go, Henry."

He nodded, but only once. Then he ran toward the ruckus.

☙

"That you? Miss Caldwell, that you?"

Dessa wiped away her tears at the sound of Nadette's voice from the other side of the wooden slat. "Yes! Are you in there? Are you with the girls?"

"Come around to the door, Miss Caldwell." Though her voice was not loud, it mirrored Dessa's urgency.

"I tried. It's stuck solid."

"That's 'cause we got it barred on the inside. Mr. Dunne fixed it up fine. You come round and I'll let you in."

Dessa trampled grass and weeds around the carriage house to get back to the front door in time for Nadette to open it barely wide enough to let her slip inside.

"Oh, Nadette!" Dessa hugged her close after the girl had barred the door again. "Where are Liling and Mei Mei?"

Nadette pulled herself away, waving for Dessa to follow. Dessa looked around. The carriage house was empty, looking as it always did—dilapidated and deserted. The only difference was that the blanket at the foot of the cot was missing.

In the center of the square structure, Nadette stopped. She reached down to the dirt-ridden floor and pulled on something. To Dessa's surprise a hatch appeared, opening to a cellar below.

"Watch that first rung on the ladder, miss," Nadette warned. "It's broke."

Dessa peered below, where the meager light of a single candle illuminated not much more than its immediate surroundings. Then a rounded shadow appeared at the foot of the ladder.

Mr. Dunne held out an arm, as if to assist her in her descent.

"Hurry on down, Miss Caldwell!" Nadette whispered. "Who knows what them men out there are gonna do next. At least some of them still want Liling and Mei Mei."

Dessa grabbed Nadette's arms, hope bursting through her gloom. "They'll never find them here!"

She made her way through the narrow opening, down a ladder that felt anything but secure.

At the bottom Mr. Dunne was fairly shoved aside as Jane rushed for Dessa with a cry and hug. Over the girl's shoulder Dessa saw Liling and Mei Mei clinging to one another in the far outreach of the candle's dim glow.

༄

None of Henry's shouts were heeded. Men grappled with each other as if in a bizarre dance, choreographed for a blood-lusting audience. Henry kept to the edge, not eager to get involved on either side—unless he found Dessa and she needed his protection.

But she was nowhere to be seen, not even among the line of women with linked arms who stood in front of Pierson House. The only face he recognized was Remee's. Much as he wanted to know where Dessa was, he was glad neither she nor Jane was out here with all these anger-crazed men.

The brawlers were precariously close to the women, so making his way through without receiving—or swinging—a punch was nearly impossible. Even those women in the line were involved in their own way, kicking away wrestling pairs with the heels of their shoes if any came too close. Over the fighters went, too caught up with the men they fought to pay heed to the women toppling them.

"Remee!"

It took three calls and a half-dozen more steps through the throng before Henry caught her attention. She said something, but he couldn't make out what.

"Where's Dessa?"

She shook her head, but whether she didn't know or hadn't heard, Henry couldn't tell. He squeezed closer.

"Dessa! I can't find her. Where is she?"

"Not here!"

"What about Foster? Turk Foster?"

Without loosening her hold on either girl at her side, Remee pointed with her chin toward the mass of men. Henry turned in time to receive a blow to his nose that sent him reeling backward. He fell against Remee and the woman next to her, who pushed him back without breaking their line. They were like the rope around a boxing ring, and he was in the melee whether he wanted to be or not.

Henry rammed through, ducking another punch, thrusting away a man with a precarious foothold as the fighter leaned back to swing in the other direction. The street was still wet from an afternoon rain; men in every direction were covered in a mix of dirt, mud, sweat, and blood.

From what Henry could see, Foster was also trying to stop the fight. Henry made his way closer while doing the same thing: grabbing lapels, shouting for the brawlers to quit, thrusting some outside the circle of rage. Henry thought he heard Foster warning about the police or the fire coming closer. Smoke continued to mingle with the nearly overwhelming scents around them, but Henry could see it was fruitless to try stopping the fight without a brigade of whistling cops behind them.

"It's no use!" Henry shouted in Foster's direction, but the man didn't see him. He yelled again, with no better result. Stumbling over a fallen man, Henry nearly collided with Foster—who grabbed him by the lapels and might have thrown him aside if he hadn't seen Henry's face.

"You! What are you doing here?"

Henry gasped for air. "Dessa! Where is she?"

Foster cocked his head toward Pierson House. "In there!"

"Let's get out of here, Foster," he shouted. "There's nothing to be done about the mob."

Another man blasted into them both, propelled by a punch. Henry heaved him off, forcing his way through the enraged cluster of men. Why hadn't he thought to check inside first? Surely the impenetrable line the women made out front would have broken for him.

When they were barely to the edge of the crowd, a flashing light gliding through the air caught Henry's attention. He stopped, arrested in horrified fascination. The arc of a torch twirled past the line of women, sweeping harmlessly over their heads—only to crash straight through the Pierson House parlor window.

The curtains—ones he was sure Dessa had sewn—went up in a quick burst of flames.

"Dessa!"

Incensed with rage and terror, Henry shoved through the tangle of men, landing a fist on anyone standing in his way. "She's in there!"

Those were the first words—or perhaps it was the stark dread on his face—that anyone paid heed to. Or perhaps it was the age-old fascination with fire. One by one, the fights around him stopped as men turned to watch the flames lick the inside walls of Pierson House.

The immovable line of women set on protecting it parted when Henry finished his scramble forward—but even as quick as he was to get there, he knew the front door was already impassable.

He shot back down the porch, darting around the side and up the steps to the back door. Once inside the kitchen, he could already see flames outlined around the swinging door.

"Dessa! *Dessa!*"

Snatching a towel from the sink, he covered his face and plunged through the door.

✳

Dessa sat on an upturned bushel basket with one arm around Jane, the other around both sisters, who pressed into her and each other. She'd seen the fright on their faces and knew only one way to attack such overwhelming emotion.

Even as the hymns she sang rose as prayers, Dessa's heart sped through a labyrinth of her own emotion. Besides the fear, the guilt, the regret, new resolve took hold with a grip so tight she knew this night—the result of her actions—was something she would never, ever forget. Every decision she'd made in haste had led to one disaster or another.

True, she couldn't imagine refusing to shelter the innocent girls she looked over now. But why had she taken this on all by herself? Because she hadn't thought it through or shared her concerns with others. Perhaps the authorities wouldn't have done anything. But the church? Surely Reverend Sempkins would have offered help, if she hadn't so hastily agreed to carry this burden on her own. And Henry—he'd been willing to help. If only she'd gone to him sooner.

Never again would she act without thinking first.

She was just leading a third soft hymn as, at last, she took a moment to look around at their surroundings.

It was—or was meant to be—a cold cellar. Even now, it was somewhat chillier down here than above. Shelves lined the dirt walls, which were haphazardly covered with wood and painted with tar in hopes of keeping at bay whatever critters might wish to take up residence among the fruits, vegetables, and preserves that had likely been stored here.

Now most of the shelves were empty—but for several jugs of what she guessed must be whiskey.

Her gaze fell upon Mr. Dunne, who gave her an abashed smile. Then he raised the volume of his voice to join in the chorus of "I'm Redeemed."

"I'm redeemed, praise the Lord!
I'm redeemed by the blood of the Lamb;
I am saved from all sin,
And I'm walking in the light.
I'm redeemed by the blood of the Lamb."

"I'm gonna go up and take another peek outside," Nadette said when they finished the song.

Dessa reached out a hand to caution her. "Are you sure you ought to, Nadette? That mob out there is dangerous!"

"I won't go farther than to crack open the door up there. Just for a peek."

Dessa was about to warn her again to wait, but Mr. Dunne spoke first.

"No, little miss, you leave it to me." He stood, though the ceiling barely accommodated him; then he burped. Though he'd sat mainly still on the old bench opposite them, Dessa wondered if he'd been drinking again.

"Are you sure you're up to it, Mr. Dunne?" she asked.

"That I am." He made for the ladder, but Nadette stepped in between, arms folded obstinately over her narrow chest.

"Yer breath alone will torch the place if we let ya go up!"

"Stand aside, little miss," said Mr. Dunne, attempting to

circumvent the very small obstacle she'd made of herself with a light brush to her shoulder. "'Tis neither the time nor the place to discuss me grooming habits."

But when the man teetered as he grabbed for the ladder, Dessa stood too.

"Perhaps you should let Nadette take that peek, Mr. Dunne. Your job is to protect the girls. If you go up and are spotted, you may fail in that duty."

"Now, now, miss, I'll be careful, that I will."

He reached again for the ladder, but it seemed to be a moving target. His hand missed the rail and he nearly fell into it.

Nadette scooted in front of him, squeezing onto the rungs. "Not as careful as I'll be. Stay put."

He accepted the decision more easily than Dessa expected, reclaiming his seat.

The door at the top must have opened easily for Nadette, sending in a new wave of air—one mingled with more smoke.

Dessa moved to the base of the ladder as Nadette's cry confirmed her worst fear.

"A fire! I can see it between the boards of the carriage house."

Dessa tried to climb the ladder, but Mr. Dunne reached for her, his ruddy face alarmed. "Stay here, miss. There's naught you can do up there, but plenty to be done down here. I may need yer help in protectin' them." He nodded toward the sisters, who were still inseparable and full of stark terror.

Nadette bent down, catching Dessa's attention. "I'll go and see if there's anythin' we can do. I'll be right back."

Dessa loosened her hand from its grip on the ladder's edge. "All right," she called after Nadette. "But if there's any hope—any at all—then call us to come up and grab a bucket."

But Nadette was already gone, the trapdoor slamming in her wake.

38

"IT'S NO USE, MAN! Come out!"

Henry refused to believe it. "Dessa! Dessa!"

Even now, the heat from the other side of the wall along the edge of the staircase scorched his palm when he reached for it to steady himself.

The smoke filled his nostrils, tore at the lining of his throat. Turk Foster still pulled at him, stopping him from going any farther up the stairs.

A crack sounded—close and fearsome. Something was caving in, though he couldn't see what. The sound put more force behind Foster's grip. He all but dragged Henry closer to him, and the two of them went flying down a half-dozen stairs to land with a thud on the hot wooden boards at the base.

The flames were closer than ever, but Henry didn't care. He would have turned back up the stairs in search of Dessa, but Foster grabbed him again. Henry tried shaking him off—only to regain his freedom not by his own strength but through the dazzling finger of flame that reached out for the hem of Foster's jacket. He cried out and Henry pushed him down to the floor, rolling him over to snuff the flames.

Then, seeing Foster go limp in a faint, Henry knew he had only one choice. Get Foster to safety.

Dragging him by what was left of his jacket, Henry slammed through the kitchen door, hauling Foster over his shoulder and out to the yard. There he collapsed onto the grass with the weight of the man, coughing and sputtering.

Henry rolled over, checking Foster's damage. The man was conscious again, coughing and mindlessly slapping at his own still-smoking jacket.

"I'm afire!"

But he wasn't. The flames were gone. Henry reached over to pull away the tattered jacket, seeing with alarm that there was nothing left of the material on the side the flame had first caressed.

"Lie still," he ordered. It was too dark to see the damage well, but Henry guessed he ought to make sure whatever remained of the man's shirt was no longer pressed to his skin.

By the growing light of the burning house before them, Henry could see the side of Foster's shirt had been singed as well. His trousers were still intact. Though Henry knew the house had indoor plumbing, he was glad to spot an outdoor pump between the back of the house and the carriage house nearby.

He coughed again when a new cloud of smoke hit them. The flames now filled the kitchen.

"Come on, Foster," Henry said, climbing to his feet first, then pulling at Foster from his uninjured side. "Come farther away from the smoke."

The towel Henry had taken from the kitchen fell from his shoulder, and he scooped it up. Once he deposited Foster against the far side of the carriage house, Henry went to the pump and soaked the towel, wringing it out with the meager hope of cleaning the material. Then he soaked it again with the tepid water.

Returning to Foster's side, he moved the man's arm out of the way to gingerly press the towel to the spot that had been burned. Foster winced but didn't protest.

The sound of wood cracking and falling called Henry from his duties. He let Foster hold the towel to himself, then stood to face the burning building.

"It's no use," Foster said dully.

He was right. Even a moment of frantic alarm over the thought of Dessa inside couldn't persuade Henry to try going in again. The entire house was engulfed.

"She wasn't in there," Foster said. "She must have found them and made it back to my carriage."

Henry nodded, wanting to believe it. Desperate to believe it. But if she'd been hiding . . . if she was hiding those girls from the mob in front—maybe inside a wardrobe upstairs or in a locked water closet—she wouldn't have known the place was afire until it was too late.

Why, *why* hadn't he thought to go right in, the moment he'd arrived out front? Why had he wasted time getting to Foster, simply because he'd been last seen with Dessa? Had she gotten out in time? Had Foster's carriage taken them away to safety?

He stared at the flames eating Pierson House, knowing there was nothing he could do. Except pray.

✢

"The house is afire! And there's two men fightin' in the yard!"

Nadette's frantic voice reached those below before she did, even as she nearly fell from the ladder in her attempt to rejoin them.

"You think the flames'll reach us here?" Nadette's voice was breathless with agitation. "Will they set the carriage house afire too?"

Jane whimpered from the corner. She hadn't spoken except to join them in song. Dessa glanced at her, seeing the girl wipe silent tears from her face. Her lips were moving, but no sound came out.

As much as Dessa wanted to join Jane in her tears, she knew she must offer courage to those around her.

"We'll be all right," she promised, nearing Jane and putting a firm hand to her shoulder. She looked at Liling and Mei Mei, who appeared as afraid as ever, then at Nadette. "Did you say there were only two men in the yard? Are you sure just two?"

"That's all I saw—but I didn't stay long to make sure, once I saw there's nothin' to be done 'bout the house."

Dessa glanced up at the trapdoor. It was made of wood, like the rest of the carriage house. If everything above them burned, would the smoke find its way down to them, obliterating the relatively clean air they had now, with no way out? She looked at the uneven wood that was nailed into the hard ground around them. Would that catch fire too?

But if they went up and made a run for it, would the mob catch them?

Dessa forced away her fears. She must do *something* if she was to keep the others safe. Staying here seemed anything but.

She pulled Liling and Mei Mei from their seats. "We have no choice. We'll have to run."

Jane popped up from her corner but pressed back into the shelves behind her. "It's not safe out there! And where will we go?"

Dessa was already directing the girls toward the ladder. "We'll make a run just a couple blocks away. If Mr. Foster's carriage driver is as loyal as I think he is, he's still waiting."

"But we might get caught!" Jane protested. "That mob is still up there!"

"We're not going that way. We'll circle around them, as far as we have to, and stay in the shadows."

"What if we get caught?"

"Jane!" Dessa caught the girl's shoulders and shook her hard. "Do you want to die of smoke down here or take your chances up there?"

"Oh, miss!" She burst into tears and flung herself into Dessa's embrace.

"Hush now, Jane; we'll be all right. I promise you." She just hoped she could keep that promise.

Nadette went up the ladder first, scurrying faster than Dessa would have thought possible considering her skirt. Jane, Liling, and Mei Mei went afterward, though Dessa told them to wait inside the carriage house until she joined them.

She looked at Mr. Dunne before going up. He seemed content to stay where he was. It might not be wise to have a tottering man along with them, but she could hardly leave him here to die if the smoke got the best of the place.

"You'd better see to yourself, Mr. Dunne. And not down here. They're not after you, so if you go up you shouldn't be in danger as long as you stay clear of us."

He lifted a careless palm. "Ah, miss, 'tis a saint you are to worry over me. But I'll take me chances right here." He grabbed one of the jugs and hugged it to his chest.

"Please don't drink any more, Mr. Dunne," she said. "You've done a noble thing, hiding the girls here tonight. I had no idea this place existed. I want to be able to say thank you in the morning— and not just to your memory."

He'd been about to lift the jug to his lips, but her words stopped him. "Did I now? Do you think it's true? That I played a part in savin' anyone tonight?"

"Indeed I do."

"Well, then," he said slowly, recapping the jug. "Well. So there you have it."

But Dessa could stay no longer. She climbed the rungs as fast as she could—relieved a moment later when Mr. Dunne followed. He'd left the whiskey below.

Even before she reached the others huddled together, the bells and whistles from a fire wagon came blessedly to her ears.

Thank You, Lord, for such clear direction!

⁂

The sound of the fire brigade whistles came as some relief to Henry, though it did nothing to lift his spirits despite his guess that the sound had dispersed the mob out front. The tarnished brick walls of Pierson House still stubbornly stood, but flames continued to devour everything inside.

Dessa wasn't in there. She couldn't have been.

He repeated the words over and again, silently, persistently. From moment to moment he went from trusting God and believing those words to waves of relentless fear.

If she wasn't in there, then where would she go? Had she made it to Foster's carriage? He only hoped she wasn't alone. Only Remee had been in that line, miraculously but ineffectively protecting Pierson House.

Some bouncer Mr. Dunne had proven himself. Or maybe he *had* done his job, at least so far as Jane and the Chinese girls went, since they were nowhere to be found.

Mr. Dunne! Turning round to the carriage house, a burst of hope lit his heart. Mr. Dunne lived in that ramshackle place. Maybe even now the old sot was proving himself worth something and hiding *all* of them.

Henry lurched toward the door, yanking on the handle—but it didn't budge. "Dessa!" His throat, still parched from the smoke, protested at the use, but he called her name again, then again, banging on the doors. He'd bust them down if he had to.

And then they fell open. A young girl stood there, her eyes wide, cautious. Maddeningly, Henry didn't recognize her. Where was Dessa? Did this girl know?

He nearly leaped at her, wanting to shake information out of her even before giving himself a chance to ask. But shadows—several of them—emerged behind her, and he grabbed the door instead, flinging it wide so he could identify those standing before him.

Two petite shadows. Another he recognized as belonging to Jane.

With a cry of relief he was surprised to hear come from his own mouth, he saw Dessa—and pulled her into his arms.

꧁

Dessa was crying before she even knew it. He was here! He'd come after her! How foolish and miraculous—and *wonderful*.

When Henry's mouth came down on hers, she didn't even care what the others thought. She received his kiss as if it were her first—and certainly it was, at least the first one that had anything to do with love. She tasted smoke and cinders but didn't care, except that it meant he'd been far too close to danger.

Pulling back, she saw something else on his face. A trail on his cheek that made its way through the soot covering him nearly everywhere. "Oh, but you're bleeding!"

He raised a hand to his face. "Am I?"

"Are you all right?"

He pulled her close again. "I wasn't until seeing you." He threw a glance toward the house. "I thought you were in there."

"You didn't . . . you didn't go in there after me, did you?"

"He certainly did," said a new voice from just beyond the carriage house. Dessa looked to see Mr. Foster's silhouette. He was somewhat crouched over, as if favoring one side, but when he stepped closer she saw he had a grin on his face—a face every bit as grimy as Henry's.

"And are you all right, Mr. Foster?"

"No thanks to the man you're holding."

Henry's quick grin revealed white teeth that were a stark contrast to his face. "It seems to me I just dragged you out of that inferno."

"And why was I in there to begin with? To fish you out."

Henry shrugged. "So we're even."

Dessa went light-headed at the news. Henry had risked his life—for her!

"Oh, Henry," she whispered, her vision blurring with new tears. If only he knew. . . . He may not think her worth such a drastic risk if he learned she was anything but the virtuous woman he believed her to be.

When his lips found hers again, gently, sweetly, she savored the lingering moment. It might very well be the last.

39

DESPITE A GOOD soap and scrub in the bath, fresh clothes, and a much-needed rest after last evening's adventures, Henry still smelled smoke. After more than one dream of facing a fire, he'd awakened in a panic—only to settle his head back on his familiar pillow in blessed relief. It was over. Dessa was safe. The mob had disbanded with a few broken ribs and noses, but despite the destruction of Pierson House and one opium den, there had been no loss of life. Thank God.

Finding a place to take Dessa and the others had been nearly as challenging as rescuing them. Dessa asked about being taken to the Whites', but Henry discouraged that until knowing whether the violence was truly quelled. She'd readily agreed, wanting to avoid any possibility of putting a private residence in danger, least of all one belonging to her dearest friends.

He would have suggested his own home but doubted that would be viewed as proper, even with his mother still there. He did, however, invite Mr. Dunne to stay with him, making a note to remind Barron to put away the wine he usually kept in the parlor.

When Foster offered the Verandah—wisely rejected for being too close to the source of trouble—Henry realized a public place was the best option. He suggested they stay at the Windsor, as his guests. It was, after all, still a plush hotel, capable of drawing wealthy tourists despite its location mere blocks away from the worst of the Fourth Ward. But the horrified look on the face of the girl called Liling had Dessa and even Jane quickly shaking their heads. Dessa whispered something to him about suicides in the main staircase, and so he pursued that avenue no further.

They had at last agreed upon the respectable—though not extravagant—Alvord House. It might not be one of the most popular hotels anymore, not with Market Street traffic spreading out, but the hotel clung to its elegance with free private baths, excellent meals, and most importantly, a secluded entrance just for ladies.

Foster had arranged for a police officer to escort them and another to concentrate his beat walk at the corner, on the lookout for any hint of trouble—a sign to Henry that the man might well be capable of the concern he claimed to have. It was hard to doubt a man who'd chased him into a burning building.

Orders for protection drew some attention from the hotel staff, but with Henry's generous tip they didn't ask questions.

After seeing that the girls were well taken care of, Henry had gone to the White home. Despite his ragged appearance, he was readily admitted by William and soon joined by a concerned and curious Mariadela. Henry explained, as briefly as possible, what had happened, but finished by telling them where Dessa, Jane, Nadette, and the Chinese sisters could be found. They were in immediate need of clothing, since theirs had been lost in the fire. Henry promised to pay for all necessary purchases, from shoes to shawls, and William pledged he would charge him 10 percent below cost.

As he dressed that morning, Henry had only one thought on his mind: seeing Dessa.

And that would happen soon. She'd agreed to meet him after lunch, out at City Park. It was only there, on a bench in the open parkland, that they would find any time alone.

Liling and Mei Mei were fully dressed in brand-new, store-bought Western gowns from White's Mercantile, as were Dessa and the others. Both sisters allowed their hair to be free of everything but simple pins at the sides, also provided by Mariadela, making them appear even younger than they were.

They'd just finished a late breakfast, which had been brought to the room. Though Henry had offered to pay for several rooms, none of them could bear to be parted so soon after their ordeal. So a bellboy had been called to drag in another mattress, and the sisters slept on that, while Jane and Dessa took the bed and Nadette grabbed nothing more than a pillow, curling up on the floor in front of the door without complaint.

It had been near dawn when they'd at last settled down from their anxious rehashing of the night's events. One by one, they'd talked out their experience with the hope of putting it behind them.

Dessa learned that Remee had run down the street to Miss Leola's at the first sign of trouble and somehow convinced the women there to help. Jane said she'd heard one of the girls say Pierson House may not be a place any of them wanted to join, but just knowing it was there had brought comfort. The girls now had a choice, if ever one wanted to leave—which this girl hastened to add she did not. But even if she never chose the Pierson House option, she wasn't going to let anybody take it away.

That had brought tears to Dessa's eyes. In spite of all her mistakes, perhaps her efforts weren't completely in vain. But the image of Pierson House left in shambles made her doubt herself anew. *God might have prevented the fire. . . .*

She caught back such thoughts, as if Sophie herself were there to scold her. *"We may question the circumstances God allows to draw us to Him or to teach us, but we must never question His love. His will is known to those who seek it, all in good time."*

Dessa drew in a deep breath. She'd learned her lesson about not taking on too much too quickly; now she must remember not to question His love, no matter what had happened last night—or what might happen today.

Standing before the only mirror in the room, which was attached to the dressing table, Dessa caught a reflection of the girls sitting behind her—Nadette and Jane, Liling and Mei Mei. Dessa had asked about Remee and been told she was last seen going off with some of her former sisters in the trade. Dessa wondered if she ought to worry about that, but somehow knew she didn't have to.

She wiped her face with a damp cloth one last time. She'd already scrubbed away any leftover tension from last night, but wanted to look her best. No one, not even Dessa herself, could doubt the depth of Henry's feelings for her after last night. He'd rushed headlong into a burning building for her!

Yet her heart fluttered every time she imagined meeting him today, with equal parts anticipation and fear.

"You look like you're goin' to a execution instead a meetin' a beau," Nadette said with a sharp eye on Dessa.

"He's not—"

"Don't you dare deny it now, Miss Caldwell," Jane said, coming up behind her to tuck a stray strand of hair into her loose chignon. "We all saw him kissing you."

"And he faced a fire for you; don't never forget that," Nadette added.

Dessa couldn't help but smile. "I won't. Believe me, I'll never forget that. It's just . . . Last night was rife with emotion. I'm not at all sure Mr. Hawkins will feel the same in the light of day." Especially after she told him what she had to say.

"He 'Mr. Hawkins' now, Miss Caldwell?" asked Liling. "No.

You greet him 'Henry' today. So he know nothing the way it was before fire."

Dessa turned from the mirror to face them all. Each one looked so hopeful, as if she represented their dreams too. She wanted to tell them the best of their futures shouldn't depend upon anyone but God and themselves, that her own future would be fulfilling with or without Mr. Henry Hawkins, because she was following the will of God.

But the truth was, the blessing of love was something she'd hoped for despite her busy life. That had never been more clear than since she had met Henry. Not all women shared that dream; Sophie had set such a wonderful example of that, an example Dessa had expected to follow. But she knew now that she shared a closer kinship with the women whose faces she stared at—and that their shared dream included marriage.

If it wasn't to be hers after all, she had no idea how difficult that would be to face.

Henry felt like a youth again. Excited, hopeful, insecure. He was ready to make plans for the future. A future he hoped would be shared with Dessa.

The bank was behind him now, but that didn't mean he couldn't start up another business. He could easily go back to selling dry goods—though he doubted the Whites would welcome his competition again.

Which led him to consider asking Dessa how she would feel about moving to Leadville so Henry could be nearer his mother. He knew her own modest dry goods store was capably run by the Owen family, and Henry had no desire to usurp them. But the store was on the meager side, and Leadville had far outgrown the simple requirements of miners. There were real families out there now, and with them came more sophisticated needs. Needs Henry was only too happy to be able to provide for. He'd be careful to avoid selling the type of equipment his mother offered so they would complement each other rather than compete for the same customers.

Yes, this could work out very well indeed. If Dessa wouldn't mind leaving Denver, at least for the foreseeable future.

She would most likely want to rebuild Pierson House; he couldn't imagine her thinking anything else. How would marriage, if he was blessed to have her agree, fit into her hopes and plans for her mission? Was whatever she felt for him enough to let them find someone else to oversee a venture that was so important to her?

Still, he knew he hadn't imagined those kisses last night. They hadn't been one-sided, and that made his heart dance between his concerns.

Henry resisted the surprising urge to twirl his walking stick as he paced before the park settee, their designated meeting spot. Fallo had left him there, then gone on to the hotel to retrieve Dessa. Henry pulled out his pocket watch for the third time. They should be here at any moment.

When he looked up, he was pleased to see his carriage approaching. She wasn't even late. It was only his eagerness that had made him impatient.

Waving away Fallo's assistance, Henry himself pulled out the step and aided Dessa from the carriage. She greeted him with a smile, but it wasn't the most dazzling smile he'd ever seen on her lovely face. Nonetheless, after a kiss to her hand, he did not let go. Folding her arm through his, he set a leisurely pace along the parkway, wishing he had something clever to say. Something they might laugh over to banish the unnecessary tension.

But she looked nearly as nervous as he felt.

❦

Dessa could barely breathe, let alone speak. What could she say? How could she tell him she wasn't all he believed her to be? How could she tell him that if it hadn't been for the goodness and generosity of Sophie Pierson, Dessa herself might have been forced into the kind of life suffered by the women she longed to help?

"Were you able to rest well after the excitement of last night?" Henry asked after they'd walked a little way from the carriage.

"The ladies and I were up far too late, talking about all of it."

Her arm was still linked with his, and he put his walking stick under his free arm to pat her hand. "You were very brave in all of this, Dessa. I admire you for that. And for so much more."

Now her blood pumped so madly through her veins that she felt light-headed. "May we sit?"

The settee wasn't far, and he led the way, allowing her to take a seat first. Dessa fussed with a button on one of her new gloves; she wished she could take them off, hold them, fiddle with them in the hope of spending some of her nervousness, though the afternoon breeze was pleasant enough to keep them on. "Henry—"

He smiled and lifted one of his hands as if he could catch on his palm the sound of his name flowing from her lips. "Pardon me, but do you know I've dreamed of hearing you say my name? Silly, isn't it? For too many years I've been 'Mr. Hawkins' to everyone but my uncle Tobias—and believe me, having him say my name brought me no thrill."

She'd been looking away for fear of giving away the depth of her feeling for him. He must know the important things first and not be distracted by her complete and utter hope that he might somehow love her. But hearing him say such things, she couldn't help herself. She raised her eyes to meet his, and the moment he recognized what she'd tried to hide, his smile grew wider.

"There, that's better," he whispered.

Dessa knew she shouldn't have given in, shouldn't even now gaze at him with every corner of her heart exposed. But she wanted to remember this moment as he looked at her with her own feelings mirrored in his eyes. "Last night made me realize I've allowed my feelings for you to grow, and yet we really know so little of one another. Of our pasts."

He frowned. "I know you must be disappointed in me. When I think back on it, I'm disappointed in myself."

Hurriedly, she shook her head. "No, Henry. It's not you I'm disappointed in. It's myself."

He remained still, waiting for her to collect her thoughts and speak. She knew he would wait as long as it took.

"There's much you should know about me before you truly invite me into your life."

"Tell me, then," he said gently. "Tell me everything you think I need to know."

"I was orphaned nearly at birth. My father was already dead, killed in the war. He never knew about me. My mother died shortly after my birth."

Henry took one of her hands—the one intent upon pulling at the stubbornly perfect glove—and held it in his.

"My brother was three years older than me, and we were sent to an orphan asylum. But there were others living there too—grown people with noplace else to go, people who were sent there because they had no one to take care of them. And unmarried girls who found themselves in trouble. Those were the ones who became my mothers; all those aunts helped me survive. I'm alive today because of them, Henry. Women just like those in the Fourth Ward right here in Denver."

She took a breath, then went on. "When my brother was ten and I was seven, we were put on a train and sent West to work.

My brother went to a farm in Kentucky, and I went to St. Louis as a maid of all work. I never saw my brother again. He died in an accident, falling from a loft."

She wiped a tear that tickled her cheek on its downward path. She hadn't even known she was crying. "I knew I was much better off, hired into the Pierson family home. I worked my way up from lowliest maid to assisting the housekeeper, because I wasn't afraid of hard work and I knew how to be discreet. In a family like the Piersons, that was a requirement."

"Discreet?" He said the word with some concern.

She nodded. "The only son, Sophie's older brother, was an embarrassment to the family. Anyone who helped quell the rumors—to the extent that we could—was appreciated. But then . . ." She was no longer crying. Now she was only afraid, afraid of what he might think. "Bennet Pierson was rich, charming . . . handsome. He had learned at a very young age that he had special appeal to girls."

Dessa went on, seeing that he still looked at her with interest and attentiveness. "He was quite a bit older than me, and by the time I caught his eye, he was already married. Marriage, of course, did not keep him from behavior he was accustomed to before." She pulled her hand from Henry's tender hold and put it to her forehead. "I don't know why I was so foolish, except that I was young. Barely seventeen. I knew—I *knew*—what he was like. He used the staff as if it were just one more service we provided. Before it was my 'turn,' I'd looked upon the others with pity and a bit of disgust, I think. And I never gave them a bit of sympathy when he was finished with them. Until . . ."

She didn't want to go on, didn't want to finish this confession. He must know what she was trying to tell him. Such a long moment went by that Henry cleared his throat, shifting in his seat. But he said nothing. Did he not care if she continued?

Dessa let her shoulders slump. If Henry thought as little of her as she'd thought of herself all these years, he might as well hear the rest. "When he paid attention to me, I thought I might be different from the others. He gave me little gifts, and I thought mine were prettier, more expensive. I thought that meant he cared for me more than he had the others. He spent so much time trying to charm me, never giving up despite my . . . resistance."

She sucked in another fortifying breath. "Sophie had been on an extended trip to Europe, or it never would have happened. When she returned, she requested me as her maid, and we became friends even with the difference in our ages and stations. Sophie would have set me straight before . . . well, before it was too late, if I'd let her know what was going on. She was so levelheaded, so wise. She didn't find out until she spotted one of the gifts her brother had given me. She knew immediately what it meant, and was horrified."

Dessa wrung her hands together, not daring to look at Henry. "By that time, I'd been with Bennet once. Sophie was determined I never take that risk again and demanded that her family let me accompany her to New York, where she planned to live for a while until starting the kind of mission we began here."

"But how do you know, if Sophie Pierson took you away before this—this romance—died, that the scoundrel didn't hold you in higher esteem than the others?"

The weight upon her rounded shoulders multiplied. "Sophie's mother didn't want to let me go, so Sophie had to tell her the truth—what her brother had done. When their mother confronted him about it, he denied it. Someone in love doesn't deny the object of their love just to escape a scolding. And that's all it would have been."

Henry was silent a long time, and she could think of nothing else to say. She'd offered him her only excuse—youthful indiscretion, he'd called it last night. But somehow this was different, because it was so much more personal.

"Did you love him?"

The question, quietly issued, held a hint of sadness.

She shook her head, still not looking at him. "I suppose that makes it worse, doesn't it? To do something out of blind love might be more easily forgiven. But I . . . I was foolish enough to think he might love *me* out of all the others. And I realized over the years that I was prideful enough to want to prove that. But I could never have loved him, not knowing the way he treated so many women before me."

Another long pause followed, and then Henry shifted again, setting his walking stick at their feet and turning so that he was facing her. He took both her hands in his, waiting until she looked at him.

"Dessa," he said softly, "your past isn't so much different from mine, you know. Pride was the culprit behind what I did too. I thought I shouldn't have to work all the years it would have taken me to accumulate my initial investment."

Dessa pursed her lips. She hadn't wanted to ask him about the other part of his past. She had no right, not with her own. But the question was there anyway, and she couldn't hold it back.

"And you, Henry? Did you love the woman in Chicago?"

His gaze never left hers. "I thought I did, at the time. But if I'd truly loved her, I wouldn't have chosen the money over her, would I? I could have confessed what I had done and returned the money, asking her to wait if I'd been arrested. Yet I chose to return home, pick up the money, and use it exactly as if I'd never met her at all.

"I can't say our pasts don't matter. But hasn't everything that happened in our lives before today made us who we are? I love the Dessa of today, and I know I'll love the Dessa of tomorrow, too." He squeezed her hands. "Your heart is what I love. Your compassion for others, your eagerness to help, no matter what's needed. Perhaps it's true that we have much to discover about each other. But we know each other for who we are today. And we can watch over what we'll become tomorrow. Together."

Dessa let go of his hands to cast herself at him, not caring what anyone around them might think or say. Out here, they were free of the law, even that of etiquette. She couldn't keep herself from him any more than she could capture the tears flowing from her eyes.

"I was so afraid to love you," she cried. "But that fight was no use. I think I've loved you since I first stepped into your office."

He caught her face between his palms. "Then will you do me the honor of marrying me?"

She laughed. "Oh, Henry! Yes!"

Then his lips claimed hers, and Dessa knew in this life she would never be happier.

EPILOGUE

Two years later

HENRY SCOOPED UP the crawling infant before the child reached the open candy jar at the opposite end of the counter. No sense risking the boy's single tooth on a hard piece of peppermint.

Dessa had left Cullen with him at the mercantile for the few minutes it would take her to run to the post office next door. They both knew Jeb, the Leadville postman, would have brought any mail by later, but for days now she'd been expecting a letter from Liling in San Francisco and was eager for whatever news it might contain.

"It's here!" She waved a sturdy envelope as she flew into the store.

"Well? Is she or isn't she?"

After scanning the content, Dessa raised merry eyes to him. "She is! Liling is getting married in two months and hopes we might make the trip out there. Oh! Wait until Jane finds out we're going to San Francisco!"

"What!"

The squeal came from the back of the store, where Henry already planned an expansion to accommodate more goods. His mercantile was the best in Leadville, if he was speaking to anyone but his mother. Her own store still thrived, keeping its focus on miners who continued to go after silver now that gold mining was a more distant memory.

Henry was even considering opening a real *department* store, but thought the only place for an ambition like that would be Denver. Even now, he was wondering how he might propose a partnership with William White for such a venture.

Jane rushed to Dessa's side. The girl was eighteen, and Henry was as proud of her as if she were his daughter. She'd just finished two years of schooling in Denver at Wolfe Hall and was as much an asset to the store as she'd once hoped to be, with her math and accounting skills.

But being a shopgirl—or even the wife of a miner—wasn't enough for his hopes for her. A trip to San Francisco would do her good, and leave behind, at least for a while, the attention of more than one poor miner. She ought to know she could find someone with bigger plans rather than settling for someone who might not be able to give her all she deserved.

"Remee will want to know as well," Dessa said to Jane, who nodded. Remee was the proprietress of the rebuilt Pierson House, and with Dessa's regular visits the mission continued to grow. Dessa remained the open-armed figure Pierson House had become known for.

Remee had built a reputation as a practical business partner. Though she continued to live under Pierson House's roof, with the help of Henry's investment she had taken over an abandoned clothing shop on the edge of the Fourth Ward. It was in a respectable-enough neighborhood to draw a wide number of clients, and under Remee's direction a dozen women created both men's and ladies' fashion. It had drawn a profit within the first year, and they were already planning to expand—offering real jobs to women who needed them. Such financial incentive, Dessa knew, was every bit as responsible for the growth and success of Pierson House as the acceptance offered to every woman in need.

Mr. Dunne had a job at Remee's clothing shop taking measurements for men as well as selling merchandise. The old carriage house had been torn down, taken away with the rest of the rubble from the house. A cottage built in its place, minus the drinking cellar, now served his needs. A steady job, friends who needed him, and a revived faith had helped him satisfy the void he'd tried filling with drink.

And the new senator from Colorado, Turk Foster, split his time between Colorado and Washington, where he often made headlines in both cities for having charmed one deal or another from nationwide taxpayers. His past was notorious, but his smile and open wit made him among the best-known politicians no matter which side of an issue he held.

As Dessa and Jane discussed all they would see and do in San Francisco, Henry picked up the rest of Liling's letter. He'd not only financed the sisters' travel expenses but provided them with a trustworthy Chinese bodyguard and enough money to open a small tea shop in San Francisco's Chinatown. It was that bodyguard whom Liling would marry in two months' time.

"What about Nadette?" Dessa's question pulled his attention from the letter. "Do you suppose we can arrange for her to come too?"

"Hmm." He held the letter outside their son's reach, and Dessa took Cullen from him.

Having Nadette travel all the way from New York might take some doing, despite the two months they had to work with. It had taken time to convince her to accept their help, but somehow Dessa had wrangled from the girl that her secret dream had been to go to a girls' school back East, one that would improve her piano playing. It seemed as unlikely a place as Henry could think of for the rough-mannered girl he'd observed, but he hadn't minded when Dessa asked if they could fund her education.

"It's a long trip across the country just for a wedding," Henry warned.

"Just for a wedding!" The words came in unison from Jane and Dessa, as if everyone except him would know how foolish his statement had been.

He shrugged. "Ask her, not me. Better send a telegram, though, so she can start making plans soon if she wants to come."

Dessa reached across the countertop to kiss him, her face as lovely as ever when she looked at him that way. "Henry, you're the most wonderful man I've ever known."

Henry smiled back. He would *never* tire of hearing her call him by name.

AUTHOR'S NOTE

Martin Luther once said, "Everything that is done in the world is done by hope." This is a sentiment I wanted to convey through Dessa, flawed though she is by her impatience. Dessa possesses something that's all too rare: a deep hope in and for the best of others. Seeing people with a touch of God's love reminds her of His grace for others and herself—a message I was reminded of as I wrote this story.

It's such a blessing to be able to write about the spiritual growth of imaginary people meant to be much like you and me, no matter the era. We might not get the job done perfectly, but as Dessa inferred, if we do get ahead of God's plans, it's more important that we're going in His direction.

It's my hope that Dessa and Henry's story will be a blessing to you and remind all of us that God is a God of love and *grace*.

Maureen Lang

ABOUT THE AUTHOR

MAUREEN LANG has always had a passion for writing, particularly stories with romance and history. She wrote her first novel longhand around the age of ten, put the pages into a notebook she had covered with soft deerskin (nothing but the best!), then passed it around the neighborhood for friends to read. It was so much fun she's been writing ever since.

Her debut inspirational novel, *Pieces of Silver*, was a 2007 Christy Award finalist, followed by *Remember Me*, *The Oak Leaves*, *On Sparrow Hill*, *My Sister Dilly*, the Great War series, and most recently, *Bees in the Butterfly Garden*, book one of the Gilded Legacy series. She has won the Romance Writers of America Golden Heart award, the Inspirational Reader's Choice Contest, the American Christian Fiction Writers Noble Theme award, and a HOLT Medallion, and has been a finalist for Romance Writers of America's RITA, the American Christian Fiction Writers Carol Award, and the Gayle Wilson Award of Excellence.

Maureen lives in the Midwest with her husband, her two sons, and their much-loved dog, Susie. She loves to hear from her readers at maureen@maureenlang.com or via the mail at:

Maureen Lang
P.O. Box 41
Libertyville, IL 60048

Visit her website at www.maureenlang.com.

DISCUSSION QUESTIONS

1. Both Henry and Dessa have made youthful mistakes and deal with them in ways that suggest they have neither forgotten nor forgiven their own pasts. If you were to counsel either one of them, what advice would you give to help them deal with their regrets?

2. Dessa's compassion for fallen women began during her years as a child in a foundling home, when unwed mothers and prostitutes took care of her, and grew when she made an unwise choice that might have cast her from polite society if it became known. Has anything in your own past made you more or less tolerant of the mistakes others make?

3. Henry's mother and his uncle Tobias both know about Henry's past, but neither confronts him with the truth until many years later. How would you face someone if you were aware they'd done something wrong? Would you keep it to yourself or confront that person? Why?

4. It's obvious Henry does not believe in the importance of what Dessa hopes to do with Pierson House, and

occasionally even Dessa doubts her efforts will be successful. Have you ever had to deal with someone who didn't believe in something you wanted to accomplish? How did you face that person? In what situations have you had to overcome your own doubts?

5. Dessa admits she is impatient, but she also states that she is almost always going in the same direction as God's leading. Have you ever found yourself getting ahead of what you believe to be God's plan for you? Or have you struggled with the slow progress of something you feel certain God is leading you to do? How did you handle that situation?

6. When Mariadela White sees Henry again, years after having been in business competition with him, her words suggest that what happened in the past isn't forgotten. How have you handled coming face-to-face with someone who wronged you, even after you've extended forgiveness or understanding?

7. Although Dessa has the full support of some in the community, not everyone in Denver supports the kind of mission she is starting. Can you think of a mission that might have difficulty garnering donations in today's culture, or have we as a society gotten beyond most taboos?

8. When Henry sees the stove Dessa bought for Pierson House, his reaction suggests that she spent the bank's money unwisely. But Dessa feels that the stove is a necessary investment that will contribute to Pierson House's success. Whom do you agree with? Have you ever had to convince someone to spend money on a cause you felt was worthwhile? How did that person react?

9. Dessa offers "beauty lessons" in order to remind women that God finds them beautiful—even women whom polite society spurns. How can you remind yourself that God loves everyone, even those society sees as unlovely? Do you ever have to remind yourself that God sees *you* as beautiful too?

10. Belva helps Dessa because Dessa reminds her of the daughter she might have had. When have you been ready to like—or dislike—someone, just because they remind you of someone else? What can be good or bad about this kind of response?

11. When Turk Foster offers to help Dessa raise money for Pierson House, most are appalled, but some, like Remee, encourage Dessa to accept the money. Do you think Dessa would have been right to accept donations from such a source? Can money be tainted, even when it's going to a cause you believe in?

12. Because of the offer's timing, Dessa initially believes that Turk Foster's benefit is an answer to her prayers for funds. What would you have believed in her situation? How do you determine whether a provision or solution is truly an answer to prayer?

13. When Nadette asks for Dessa's help to rescue Mei Mei, it's quickly clear that Dessa is in over her head. Have you ever tried to do something that you should have handed over to someone better equipped? What was the result?

14. By the end of the story, both Henry and Turk Foster have changed. What is the difference in their transformations? Do you notice any similarities?

15. Toward the end, Henry says to Dessa that if they didn't have the pasts they had, they might not have become the people they turned out to be. Is there anything in your past that you wish had been different? If you believed that event made you who you are today, would you still regret it? Why or why not?

Don't miss one thrilling moment of
The Great War Series

Look to the East

France, 1914. A village under siege.
A love under fire.

Whisper on the Wind

Belgium, 1916. She risked
everything to rescue him. But what
if he doesn't want to be saved?

Springtime of the Spirit

Germany, 1918. The consequences
of war force her to choose between
love and loyalty.